THE BEST OF TIMES

NINTH BOOK IN THE BRIGANDSHAW CHRONICLES

PETER RIMMER

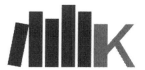

ABOUT PETER RIMMER

~

Peter Rimmer was born in London, England, and grew up in the south of the city where he went to school. After the Second World War, aged eighteen, he joined the Royal Air Force, reaching the rank of Pilot Officer before he was nineteen. At the end of his National Service, he sailed for Africa to grow tobacco in what was then Rhodesia, now Zimbabwe.

The years went by and Peter found himself in Johannesburg where he established an insurance brokering company. Over 2% of the companies listed on the Johannesburg Stock Exchange were clients of Rimmer Associates. He opened branches in the United States of America, Australia and Hong Kong and travelled extensively between them.

Having lived a reclusive life on his beloved smallholding in Knysna, South Africa, for over 25 years, Peter passed away in July 2018. He has left an enormous legacy of unpublished work for his family to release over the coming years, and not only they but also his readers from around the world will sorely miss him. Peter Rimmer was 81 years old.

ALSO BY PETER RIMMER

∾

STANDALONE NOVELS

All Our Yesterdays

Cry of the Fish Eagle

Just the Memory of Love

Vultures in the Wind

∾

NOVELLA

Second Beach

∾

THE ASIAN SAGAS

Bend with the Wind (Book 1)

Each to His Own (Book 2)

∾

THE BRIGANDSHAW CHRONICLES

(The Rise and Fall of the Anglo Saxon Empire)

Echoes from the Past (Book 1)

Elephant Walk (Book 2)

Mad Dogs and Englishmen (Book 3)

To the Manor Born (Book 4)

On the Brink of Tears (Book 5)

Treason If You Lose (Book 6)

Horns of Dilemma (Book 7)

First published in Great Britain in October 2020 by

KAMBA PUBLISHING, United Kingdom

10 9 8 7 6 5 4 3 2 1

Peter Rimmer asserts the moral right to be identified as the author of this work.

PART I

SEPTEMBER 1962

DINNER FOR THREE

1
---

*H*arry Wakefield woke to a strange room. A naked girl with a large bottom was standing in an alcove. A sash window from the ceiling halfway to the floor let the early morning light play on the girl's skin. A gas ring in the alcove was hissing.

"You want some tea? I've got to go. You'd better leave through the window into the back alley. The landlady lives in the basement in the front. Mrs Scott thinks sex before marriage a mortal sin. What's your name? My name's Elsie."

"Harry. My name's Harry."

"Harry and Elsie. Don't you have to work?"

"What's the time?"

"Half past eight. Do you usually fall asleep on the job, Harry?"

"I was drunk. I'm sorry."

"Through the window into the back garden. There's a gate into the alley. I'm going to be late."

"Put some clothes on. How'd I get here?"

"Taxi. You dropped me home. Mrs Scott's lights were out. Quite a party. Pull down the sash window from outside when you leave. We used a rubber. Not to worry."

The girl put a dress over her naked body, pulled on a pair of large white knickers, placed a cup of hot tea on the small table by the bed next to Harry, kissed him on the forehead and left, smiling back at him from the door before pulling it shut. He heard her chuckle. Harry lay back in the girl's bed and closed his eyes.

When the tea was cool enough he drank it down. His clothes were strewn on the wooden floor. Getting dressed, Harry looked out of the window. There was a small rooftop outside with chairs and a table. He could see a wooden fence and a gate in the small garden below. A head went past in the alley.

Harry climbed through the window onto the roof garden. There was a trellis down to the ground. He climbed over, turning to face the sash window. The window was still open. Testing the trellis, he went down holding the drain pipe.

Going through the gate in the fence into the alley he passed a middle-aged woman.

"Can you tell me where I am?"

The woman passed on without answering. Harry looked both ways down the alley before going right. The street at the end was unfamiliar. Harry walked on, his hangover worse in the light. At the far end of the street was a Tube station. Harry quickened his pace, smiling. For the first time that morning Harry knew where he was.

"YOU'RE LATE, Harry. There's going to be a protest march down the Strand. I want you to cover it."

"What are they screaming about today?"

"Go and find out. You look awful."

"Free love, Roland. It's everywhere. They must be protesting about something."

"Take the camera. I want photographs. Shoot the nastiest slogan."

"I'm a reporter, not a photographer."

"Then go with Sidney. Trade Unions will destroy England. And tuck your shirt in."

THE ANTI-APARTHEID MARCH came down the Strand towards Harry and Sidney two hours later. In the front rank was a black man they both recognised. Next to the man, on each side, were a priest and a girl.

Behind them came the throng carrying placards. The crowd were chanting 'release Mandela', over and over again. Sidney took photographs facing the front of the crowd. Behind Sidney were more reporters and police.

"Who's the smasher on the right of Josiah? What's South Africa got to do with Rhodesia? What's the church got to do with it for God's sake? It's politics... She's quite beautiful, Sidney. How do so many people get excited about some poor sod in jail seven thousand miles away? If it wasn't for us and the TV cameras they'd stay at home and mind their own business. They all want to be seen on the telly... You won't believe it, Sidney, but that's Elsie from last night holding a placard behind Josiah Makoni. Where are they heading?"

"Charing Cross and the Mall and up to Buckingham Palace."

"The sooner the old colonies get to run themselves and their problems, the better, according to Father."

"Did your shag know you were a reporter?"

"Probably. The party was for the media."

"What an arse on her. You ever been on a protest march? Let's get up ahead and wait for them outside the gates of the palace. Ask Josiah to introduce you to the girl and the priest and get a story. Didn't your namesake Harry Brigandshaw pay to put Josiah through school and university?"

"Josiah's father grew up on Elephant Walk in Rhodesia with Harry Brigandshaw. I first met Josiah through the Brigandshaw family. They all live in England now. Harry Brigandshaw said before he died there wasn't a future for the British farmers in Rhodesia. Too many blacks and too few British. Harry saved my father's life before the war. Dad had been abducted by the Nazis. He was a freelance journalist with William Smythe in Berlin. Harry's friend Klaus von Lieberman got Dad out of Germany. My sister Bergit was named after his wife. Do you know it's going to take three generations for us to pay back the Americans what we borrowed to fight the Germans? William says the Americans only came into the war to make sure they got back their money."

"What's Elsie's surname?"

"I have no idea."

"Why did they lock up Mandela?"

"Treason. The man wants to take over South Africa and the Boers won't let him. Much the way Josiah wants to take over Rhodesia. Dad says they're both backed by the communists. The new scramble for Africa. They're already fighting over the copper in the Katanga Province of the Congo. Tshombe seceded Katanga backed by the American CIA and murdered Lumumba, the Congolese Prime Minister. The Americans don't admit it, of course. Lumumba was a communist. The cheap way to gain control of these tin-pot countries is to find a local leader and support him with money and military training. It's not about right or wrong. It's about power."

"I just take photographs."

"That's my Sidney. You know something? This brisk walking has got rid of my hangover."

THE GATES of the palace were shut, guarded by the sentries of the Household Cavalry. Neither man blinked in the face of the protest, staring straight ahead below the peak of their hats, at ease, their rifle butts on the ground thrust in front of them. There was no flag flying from the mast over the palace. Uniformed police had taken up positions in front of the high rails that protected the forecourt.

"I want a photograph of that priest and Josiah with their arms on each other's shoulders, Sidney. Brothers in arms. Roland might get the irony. Go on. You've got to push for what you want."

"Excuse me, Mr Makoni. Can I have a shot of you and the reverend with your arms around each other's shoulders? *Daily Mirror*."

"Of course," said the priest, smiling. "The man wants a photograph for the *Mirror*, Josiah."

With the priest still smiling, Sidney took a series of photographs as quickly as possible, watched by Harry. There was no sign of the girl called Elsie. The crowd was milling around, not sure what to do. Most of the placards were resting on the ground, the marchers tired from their walk. The pretty girl who had been at the front of the march on the right of Josiah was watching Sidney take his photographs. Harry walked up to her.

"Harry Wakefield of the *Mirror*. Can I have your story? It's breaking up. The Queen isn't in residence. Come and have lunch. You must be tired after your strenuous walk. My paper sympathises, of course. Man's a prominent lawyer. Can't have the Boers locking up lawyers, can we? What's your name?"

"Petronella Maple."

"That's a start. Where are you from? That accent isn't English."

"Rhodesia. Born and bred. My mother and father own a farm."

"Aren't you protesting against their way of life?"

"Of course I am. Colonialism is immoral. I'm a member of the British Communist Party."

"Are you coming to lunch?"

"Of course not."

"How do I interview you?"

"Right here."

"Is the priest a communist? I thought communists didn't believe in God. Where does Josiah Makoni get his money from? He doesn't have a job."

"The party look after their own."

"So he's funded by the Russian Government?"

"The party, Mr Wakefield."

"Who are funded from Moscow. Why's such a beautiful girl so angry?"

"I hate injustice. You can write that down."

"May Sidney take your photograph with Josiah?"

"Excuse me… Elsie. We're going. The Queen isn't here."

"Hello, Harry. What a surprise to see you again so soon."

"I don't think so."

"Petronella and I were at Manchester University together… Josiah, it's all over. I've given the petition to a man in the Queen's household who wouldn't open the gate. That was fun. Lots of TV cameras. Should be in everyone's living rooms on the six o'clock news… Did you close the window, Harry?"

"I forgot. I was halfway down the drain pipe."

"Naughty boy. We should do it again sometime."

Perplexed, Harry watched Elsie take Petronella by the arm and lead her with Josiah and the priest to a waiting taxi. Next to Harry, Sidney was laughing.

"You should be more careful who you get into bed with, Harry. You were set up."

"Come on. It's over. Want a beer in the pub."

"Did you get anything?"

"A sad story of daughterly love."

"You won't get anywhere with that girl, Harry. Didn't you see the proprietary way she put her hand around Josiah's shoulder after they got in the taxi? Those two are lovers if you ask me."

WONDERING what Petronella Maple's parents had done to her to make the girl hate their way of life, Harry drank a pint of bitter in the Green Man and went back to the office in Fleet Street. Sidney had gone his separate way to develop his film. Harry couldn't get Petronella's face out of his mind; the look of sexuality deep in her eyes.

When the photographs came back, Roland liked the headline 'Brothers in Arms'. Under the picture of the two men arm in arm, one a priest, one a communist, the colour of their skins in deep contrast, Harry wrote his brief article about Josiah Makoni, the man determined to make Southern Rhodesia a free democracy after the looming breakup of the Central Federation of the two Rhodesias and Nyasaland. At the end, Harry asked 'Who is the priest?' By the time Harry was ready to go home, his article and Sidney's photograph had gone to press, his job done for the day.

"There's a call for you, Harry. Some girl."

With his mind thinking of Petronella, Harry went to the phone.

"This is Elsie Gilmore, Harry. We should meet."

"So you do have a surname?" said Harry, smiling. "Who was that priest? Tomorrow he'll be Thursday's mystery man. Sorry about leaving the window open. Once I was over the parapet I didn't have the strength to climb back again."

"I'm worried about Petronella and Josiah."

"You knew I knew Josiah when we met at last night's party?"

"She's a friend of mine. A mixed-up girl. What you and I did last night when the taxi dropped us off had nothing to do with it."

"Are you a member of the communist party?"

"We all get sucked into saving the world at varsity. Only Petronella took it seriously."

"What did her parents do to her to make her hate their way of life?

Do you really believe Southern Rhodesia would do better under Josiah Makoni? What does he know about running a country's economy? Running anything for that matter."

"His intentions are good... What are you doing now?"

"Getting out of the office. Buying some pork pies and eating them. Going home to my modest flat in Holland Park to have a bath. There's a pub down the road in a cul-de-sac where I'll sit and drink beer until nine. Then I shall go home and go to sleep."

"What's the name of the pub?"

"The Horse and Hounds. Why?"

"I'll be waiting. Petronella and Josiah are taking a plane to West Berlin."

"What's that to do with me?"

"The Russians aren't interested in one man one vote more than once. They want to control Africa when the colonials are kicked out. Josiah sees power. Petronella is on a crusade."

"Are they lovers?"

"Who cares?"

"I'm a newspaper reporter."

"Who wants a story. I want to stop her getting hurt."

"We're all going to get hurt one way or the other in the end. If they want to sell out to the Russians it's their business."

"It might change the attitude of the British government to the breakup of the Federation. Allow the Southern Rhodesians to get full independence from Britain."

"Who do you work for, Elsie? You're tangling me in some kind of web. You've screwed me once. Be careful."

"Enjoy your pork pies."

"And the name of the priest?"

"I'll tell you later, Harry. Have a nice bath."

"Where are you?"

"At home. With the windows shut."

NOT EXPECTING Elsie to find the pub with only the name to go by, Harry went about his day. An hour later he bought the pork pies from the corner shop down the road from the Holland Park Tube station. Eating the cupcake-sized pies as he walked down the road, Harry contemplated the luxury of soaking in his bath, the small pork pies tasting delicious. Into Anderson Street, where the big green leaves of the plane trees gave his home street a touch of the country, Harry ate the last of his pies. The street, as far down as the Horse and Hounds, was empty. The old townhouse, built in the reign of Queen Victoria, had been converted into three flats, Harry's being the one at the top where once had been an attic for the children's nursery in a time when the Victorians had themselves ten children. The flat was suitably comfortable with a fireplace for winter, a lounge that incorporated his dining room, a bedroom and study with a typewriter ready at the desk. The furniture had come from his mother and father, his flat up the steep stairs a home from home. The window in front of the desk gave him a quiet view of the rooftops and the pigeons.

The hot bath made Harry relax. It was nice to be home. Nice to be independent. Nice to be alone.

By the time he reached the Horse and Hounds all thought of Elsie had gone from his mind. All he could think of was the girl called Petronella.

"Hello, Harry. Aren't you a bit late?"

"So you found the place?"

"Of course I did. I wanted to see you. Buy me a gin and tonic. This one is my second. Nice little pub at the end of a cul-de-sac. Where's your home?"

"Up the road."

"How convenient."

Harry went up to the bar and bought the drinks, taking them back to Elsie at the small corner table where she had made herself comfortable.

"You'd better tell me what this is all about."

"I want you to expose Petronella in your paper. She's taking Josiah into East Berlin. She told me. They're meeting a man called Shostakovich."

"Any relation to the composer?" said Harry, sitting down with a smirk.

"I have no idea except she's going to get herself into deep trouble."

"You haven't said who you work for."

"Oh, it's not my job. It's friendship. I work for Sainsbury's as a marketing consultant. Working out what people want on the shelves. What moves fast. It's all about shelf time in a supermarket. Getting the right goods in and out as fast as possible... We met at Manchester University when we were both younger. She seduced me, Harry."

"By her charm?"

"We were lovers."

"As in lesbians? Wow. I've never made love to a lesbian before."

"I'm straight now. It was only Petronella. I don't want her hurt."

"So what must I do for your lady lover? It's not a crime to be a communist. Not in England. No crime to being a lesbian so far as I know. It's men making love to each other that gets them into jail. Women they don't seem to worry about... What a waste."

"I've tried to make her see sense. Why I joined the damn march. Why I went to last night's party to find a newspaper reporter who'd listen to me. Exposure in the press. All I can think of is to stop my friend getting hurt."

"Sidney thinks she's having it with Josiah."

"Oh, she's doing that. She wants a hold on him. The way she kept me under her thumb. Petronella likes to dominate."

"That bit I can imagine. Cheers, Elsie. Nice to see you again. Do you still love her?... I'm sorry. You don't have to cry."

"Will you help me, Harry? She's way out of her depth."

"I made it a double... Why is it the pretty girls get themselves into the most amount of trouble?"

"They have the power over other people. I can't get her out of my head."

Neither can I, thought Harry, smiling ironically to himself. 'Power,' he thought. 'Women like that are downright dangerous.'

THEY HAD STAYED at the Horse and Hounds until the pub closed at ten o'clock. They were the last to leave.

"Come up to the flat and I'll call you a taxi."

All he could think of was the two of them together sending his hormones into overdrive. He went ahead up the steep stairs and opened the door with his key. A small table lamp had been left on in the lounge.

"The phone's in my study. Make yourself at home."

"This is nice. A fireplace. Wow."

"They pay newspapermen better than they did in my father's day. There's a brandy decanter on the tray. Help yourself."

In his study staring at his silent typewriter, Harry listened to the number of the taxi company ring and ring. When he went back into the lounge she was standing in front of the mirror wearing nothing but her knickers, the large bottom more erotic than in the morning before he climbed out of her window. Harry took a moment to control himself.

"There's no reply. I'm going to walk up to the Bayswater Road and flag down a growler."

Before she could turn round and change his mind Harry was out the door taking the stairs down to the front door of the flats two at a time. A man needed his pride. There were no rules anymore. Without his self-esteem what would he have?

When he got back with the taxi ten minutes later, luck giving him the chance to do what his mind told him, she was waiting outside on the pavement. The light from the street lamp played up into the plane tree. She smiled at him softly.

"I can wait," she said sweetly.

"Goodnight, Elsie. I'll think through what I can do for Petronella and Josiah."

"The thought of the two of us together usually drives men crazy."

"Goodnight, Elsie. Happy dreams. I have a lot of work to do in the morning. Roland only tolerates the odd hangover. Why the pay is good."

"She'll never let you touch her."

"I'm not sure what you are talking about."

"Oh yes you do... Goodnight, Harry. Thanks for the drinks."

2

*I*n the morning, after a long, trouble-free sleep alone in his own bed, he was called into Roland's office. Roland Cartwright was the sub-editor of the *Daily Mirror*.

"You look chirpy, Harry. Got some sleep? We've tracked down your mysterious priest. His name is Harvey Pemberton. Went to Rhodesia after the war as a Catholic missionary to proselytise in the black township of Harare just outside Salisbury. He's a good man. There aren't many of them these days. Founded the Good Faith Mission where Josiah Makoni got his secondary education paid for by Harry Brigandshaw. The Mandela march was a coincidence, to give them a bigger profile. Using Mandela's plight to promote their struggle in Rhodesia. He's not the only missionary to get into politics. Garfield Todd, the previous Prime Minister of Southern Rhodesia, was a missionary sent out to Africa from New Zealand. All in the name of God. There's only a fine line between politics and religion these days. The Second, Third and our own Fourth Estate are blurring together again. Feeding off each other. Religion and politics mixed have caused most of humanity's misery. And we do the stirring."

"What's he doing over here?"

"Stirring. With our help. That caption of yours this morning,

'Brothers in Arms', may be dangerously prophetic. Pemberton believes his religion mixed with Rhodesian black politics will save the country from communism, from atheism. Give politics the heart of goodness. I want you to write an article on the good work of the Reverend Harvey Pemberton."

Harry looked around the room, a sardonic grin on his face.

"Why are you smiling, Harry?"

"All good intentions. Josiah Makoni has flown to West Berlin with that girl I interviewed yesterday. To meet a man called Shostakovich in East Berlin."

"How do you know?"

"Can you use your contacts to find out who this man Shostakovich is and why he would want to meet Josiah? I said I'd help someone."

"Politics and religion. They never mix. Does the priest know?"

"I shouldn't think so. People use each other, Roland."

AFTER LUNCH, Roland Cartwright called Harry back into the office.

"Are you sure this Pemberton is a good man, Roland? I don't see him pure as the driven snow. Before I write my piece I want to do some research."

"What's your interest in Petronella Maple? Are you after her body? Did you know her maternal grandparents are stinking rich? A friend at Scotland Yard gave me the background. They watch all the troublemakers. It's their job. Shostakovich heads up the Russians' African bureau in Moscow. Same sort of thing as our Colonial Office, that shortly will be out of business the way we are handing everyone their independence as fast as we can get out of the door. Of course he would be interested in Josiah Makoni. The Russians want control of Africa's raw materials, especially those such as chrome which are considered strategic, a weapon in the ongoing East-West cold war. As the world develops, raw materials are going to have a greater political importance. Petronella Maple is right in the pocket of the Russians. They're not so sure about Josiah. He wants Rhodesian independence under black rule. Anyone who will help is a friend. Our Josiah has been to Russia a couple of times looking for funding in his struggle. And guns.

If Rhodesia gets independence under the control of the white colonists there's going to be a guerrilla war that could go on for years. Except in Malaya, no one has ever won a war against terrorists. Our Petronella is a spoiled brat. Her mother's family started the family fortune in Jamaica more than two hundred years ago. They were sugar planters. Big plantation with hundreds of slaves. Later, they came back to England to process their own sugar. There's more money in selling packets of sugar into the shops than growing sugar cane in Jamaica. Sheckland-Hall is her mother's maiden name. Sheckland-Hall Limited is only second to Tate and Lyle in Britain and the commonwealth. The money used to buy Petronella's father's tobacco farm in Rhodesia came from the Sheckland-Hall fortune. They have a country estate in Surrey. Have done for years. Petronella has an allowance from her grandfather. Why she has never had to work."

"Does he know she's a communist?"

"Probably. Doesn't care. A small indulgence. It's said most university students start life wanting to change the world as socialists and grow up into the blue-blood Tories. Part of growing up. He probably can't imagine his granddaughter is dangerous."

"Why Manchester? Not Oxford or Cambridge? Or Edinburgh?"

"The girl wanted to make a point. All those slaves in her family history might have made her uncomfortable. The same way her father has cheap labour on the tobacco farm in Rhodesia. Ashford Park is a big tobacco estate."

"She's having an affair with Josiah."

"All part of the same feeling of guilt. She wants to save herself from the money that got her where she is. Who the hell knows what's in another person's mind, let alone a woman's."

"She'd like that comment. My conquest the night before last has turned out to be Petronella's one-time lover. She wants to save her friend from herself. Or so she says. I think its blind jealousy for being dumped."

"Maybe you're a bit too close to it for your own good, Harry."

"Petronella is the most sexually attractive woman I ever set eyes on."

"Men and women. No wonder the world's in such a mess. People either want to kill or screw each other. Maybe it's all the same thing. The same primal force. Love and hate. Who knows? When it comes to women I don't know what I'm talking about, Harry. Do you understand women?"

"They're usually after something, Roland."

"Aren't we all? How are you getting along with the piece on the reverend?"

"It'll come. The best journalism takes time."

3

The punch up began on the Friday morning with three provincial papers and the *Manchester Guardian* challenging Harry's 'Brothers in Arms'. The general indignation was much the same: 'How dare the *Daily Mirror* suggest a man of God was propagating armed conflict with the white settlers in Rhodesia?' Harry had to smile. Any good argument sold copies of the newspapers, especially when the public felt indignant. It was all there in the other newspapers: 'The Reverend Harvey Pemberton was an Englishman. A missionary doing the work of God. For the Church of England. Dedicating his life to helping others. Those less fortunate. Men and women living in poverty under the harsh rule of a colonial government that only cared about the settlers that had stolen the land from the likes of Josiah Makoni who only demanded back what was rightfully his. While the *Daily Mirror* of all newspapers, that should have known better, had the gall to suggest a man of the cloth was plotting an armed revolution.' The final 'what has the *Mirror* got to say about that' answered the prayer of every sub-editor trying to increase his paper's circulation.

Harry sat down at his typewriter in his office and began to write his rebuttal. 'Why are our friends in the Fourth Estate so up in arms? Do they know what we don't? The "Brothers in Arms" that we referred to were Josiah Makoni being schooled by the Reverend Pemberton as a boy at the Good Faith Mission.'

Satisfied there was no more he had to write on the good life of Harvey Pemberton, Harry put on his coat to go home, giving the article to Roland on his way out.

"Monday morning should be fun for circulation."

"Did your caption have an intentional double meaning?"

"You know it did, Roland. Nothing like stirring up shit. For the Tuesday edition I'm going to keep up the stirring by asking if there is ever smoke without fire."

"Has that girl come back from East Berlin with Josiah?"

"I'll find out. Elsie will know."

"Get an interview with her."

"Yes, sir."

"And this time keep it in your pants."

"Does it matter if 'Brothers in Arms' is all hot air?"

"Not if it sells newspapers. Always make it look as if you are fighting the good fight, Harry. That's the trick a newspaperman should never forget. The Fourth Estate will come out of this smelling like a rose. You watch. Champion the underdog. Always works. Makes people feel self-righteous. Less self-guilt at having more than the poverty-stricken sods in Africa dying before they're forty. It's always good to put the blame on someone else. Like Petronella Maple's parents along with the rest of those damn high-living colonials with all the house servants. They're a perfect punch bag."

"And if Josiah Makoni is planning an armed struggle?"

"That's his problem with the Russians and the white settlers. It won't affect the lives of our readers. The underdog, Harry. Always champion the underdog. The likes of this Petronella Maple may end up with a bad conscience but that's her problem. The price of trying to do good. The price of revolution. At the end of revolution a few get power and riches while the people suffer. How it works. But don't tell that to a reader indignant about British Colonialism. Maybe later we'll be ripping apart the likes of Josiah Makoni for making a mess of it. Who knows? Tell the average reader what he wants to hear... What's right one day is wrong the next. And vice versa. All we need to do is appear to be right at the time... Have a nice weekend."

. . .

ON THE MONDAY while Harry was eating his lunch, Roland Cartwright opened the glass-windowed door to his office.

"Our reverend had made a bolt for it back to Rhodesia before our friends in the press could collar him. First plane back to Salisbury after 'Brothers in Arms' hit the newspaper stands. Makes you think, doesn't it? What's in that sandwich?"

"Chicken, tomatoes, lettuce and fresh onion. I make them myself. Want one?"

"I don't mind if I do."

"Every Sunday lunch my mother or Betty Smythe roasts two chickens and give me one with the lettuce, onions and tomatoes. They think I don't eat properly. Each morning like a dutiful son I make my lunch box before leaving the flat."

"Quite delicious. You'd better concentrate on the girl and Josiah to keep up the public's interest. The personal side of any story is always the best. Life's about people. I have the address of Petronella's grandfather for you and Sidney to follow up. Get a photograph of the family mansion. Get an interview with the old man if you can. All that money in Surrey made out of hard-working slaves in Jamaica. Should make an eye-catching headline. You can take the company car and drive down when you've eaten your lunch. How's your father?"

"You know he flew to Rhodesia twice for the *Daily Mail* to interview the Federal Prime Minister, Sir Roy Welensky. Welensky says if he's given two million more white immigrants he'll turn the federation in the heart of Africa into a dominion as rich as Canada. The land, the minerals and the labour force is there, all it needs is the skills to make everyone rich. That busting up the Federation is the worst scenario for everyone, black and white. Of course we won't do what Welensky wants after Macmillan's 'wind of change' speech to the South African parliament in Cape Town, according to Dad. The British government want out of Africa. Want the firebrands to take over and get off their back. Dad says we don't give a damn what happens to the people of Africa so long as it isn't our problem anymore. Like Pontius Pilate, they want to wash their hands. William Smythe agrees with him. Every week the Wakefield and Smythe families sit down to Sunday lunch."

"Don't you get bored with all the old people?"

"Not when Ruthy is there."

"Who's Ruthy?"

"My Godfather William Smythe's daughter. She's nineteen. A real smasher. A few years ago I couldn't stand the girl. Now she's grown into a beautiful woman."

"And you can't keep your eyes off her."

"Something like that."

Shaking his head, Roland dropped the car keys on the desk and licked his fingers.

"Thanks for the sandwich."

"You're welcome."

Smiling at the thought of Ruthy, Harry watched his boss leave as Sidney came into the office.

"Any sandwiches left?"

"We're driving down into the country."

"Driving, are we?"

"He ate the last one. I should start a sandwich business. Do you know anything about architecture?"

"Not much."

"We want photographs of the Sheckland-Hall mansion. Been in the family for years. Our priest has made a run for it. You can have the last apple in my lunch box, Sidney. Why do mothers still worry about their children long after we fly the nest?"

"Could be they love them. I envy your family Sunday lunch, Harry."

"It's a tradition. Are you ready to go?"

"Why don't you buy your sandwiches from the sandwich shop?"

"My mother would kill me. I'm going to try and get into the mansion. There must be a way in through the gardens. Woodlands Court. Here's the map and the address. I drive and you navigate."

"Apples are good for you."

"That's the point, Sidney."

4

wo hours later Harry drove the company car along the lane in front of the Sheckland-Hall estate. With all the housing development, Woodlands Court was an oasis of fields and trees in the suburbs; the high, old brick wall fronting the house right on the road. There was a single wooden door made from old oak that served as a front entrance with a pull-down handle that functioned as a front door bell. Harry suspected if he yanked the old metal handle a bell would ring somewhere inside. Harry could see three storeys of back windows rising to the old chimney pots that clustered high above the roof. All the windows looked dead, as if there was no life inside them. In the tree-lined lane where Harry and Sidney stood trying to make up their minds what to do, they could hear a pheasant call from inside the walled estate, contrasting with the close-knit rows of houses behind them, most of them brand spanking new.

"England's being built over," said Sidney. "Won't be long before we'll be one big housing estate from Brighton to Manchester. Can you imagine what the land inside those high walls is worth? How big are the grounds?"

"Fifty acres, I'd say. Let's drive round to the back of the grounds again to those old oak trees. There was a back gate that's far away from the house."

"Or we can climb one of those trees and get on top of the wall for a better look. I have a good telephoto lens. The place looks so old. When it was built the countryside between here and London extended for miles upon miles. Not so much anymore."

"You're right and we're in Surrey."

"The rural land seems to be getting eaten up. You wonder where it will all end."

"Most people like living in suburbia. Makes them feel safe with neighbours close by. Someone to talk to."

"You don't want to ring that bell?"

"Only get a servant and a 'Mr Sheckland-Hall is not at home'. The perfect brush-off. Family have been doing it for a couple of centuries."

Circling the walls of the estate, Harry parked the car under the shade of a spreading oak. On the other side of the road, opposite the high wall, were houses where no one seemed to be at home.

"Kids at school. Ma and Pa up in London working in their offices. You need two incomes these days to afford the mortgage on one of those houses. In the winter, the parents never see the light of day. What a life we've come to. Moles. Burrowing away to make a living and bring up the kids. I'm never going to get married and fall into that trap."

"Sidney, no girl will marry you. You drink too much and change the girls too often."

"Safety in numbers."

"You'll fall hard one day. We all do. Why there are so many of these houses... Give me a leg up. I'm going up the tree. That thick bough goes right over the top of the wall into Woodlands Court."

"Haven't climbed a tree since I was a kid."

"When I'm up in the tree you can hand me the camera. We'll climb up onto the high wall."

"You think anyone is looking?"

"I don't give a shit."

"Give me a hand up the trunk."

Harry climbed the tree and sat on the wall, his legs hanging over into the grounds of Woodlands Court. Sidney followed and walked unsteadily along the bough of the oak and dropped down next to him on top of the wall.

"No clear view of the home from here, Harry. Can we jump down without breaking our necks? You go first. The strap is long enough to hand the camera. These oak trees are thick foliage higher up the tree. There's no one around."

Like thieves they dropped down between the wall and the rhododendron bushes. Harry gave Sidney back his camera. Through the front of the bushes they could see the old house across the fields. Two horses were grazing the lush summer grass. The pheasant called again. A long terrace in front of the house was empty of people. A round table with an umbrella through the middle was the only sign of human life. Sidney looked through the telephoto lens of his camera, searching the house.

"There's a bottle of something on that table."

"Can you see anyone?"

"Only sign of life are those two horses. I've never ridden a horse."

"Take photographs, Sidney."

"How do we get out?"

"Through the gate. There'll be a way of unlocking it from the inside."

"Aren't you two trespassing?" said a voice from Harry's right, making him turn sharply to see a man with a broken shotgun standing just inside the bushes. The old man had a smile on his face. He was dressed scruffily, his trousers and boots covered in mud. The accent floored Harry. The man was educated. "Why do you wish to photograph my house, young man? Thieves don't normally photograph the scene of their crimes. What are you up to?"

Harry relaxed. He could see the shell cases in the breech of the broken shotgun. The man was enjoying himself, almost laughing.

"We're from the *Daily Mirror*, sir. I met your granddaughter at the rally outside Buckingham Palace."

"Ah. Petronella... You'd better come up to the house for a glass of sherry. I take a glass of a summer's evening. Yesterday's rain has muddied the paths. You'd better be careful. I was after one of those pheasants. They breed so quickly. In season, of course. Would never shoot a game bird out of season. After retirement, an old man gets bored. You'll find the same if you both live long enough and don't break your necks jumping off my walls. You were lucky the ground is soft from the rain and the leaves. So sad. This place is being swallowed so to speak. Have you ever felt totally surrounded? My name is Sheckland-Hall as you so rightly guessed."

"Harry Wakefield and Sidney Cross."

"Welcome to Woodlands Court. My daughter has a farm in Rhodesia she called Ashford Park. A touch bigger place than this I should think. Never been there. After so much travelling in my business I detest aeroplanes. Florence comes over to England. Much better... This is all about Rhodesia. Such a shame. All that hard work about to go to waste. Extraordinary what a few good farmers and a lot of British capital can do for a backward country. My money of course. My son-in-law is a dear chap but he never had a bean. Anyway, you want to talk about Petronella. What's she done now?"

"Consorting with the Russians in East Berlin. With Josiah Makoni. The Russians want to make Rhodesia a puppet communist state."

They were walking one on either side of Sheckland-Hall.

"Poor Petronella. She has such good intentions. She's gullible. I give her what she wants. An old man's indulgence. They all grow out of it, trying to change the world. Sadly, when they change the world it's rarely for the better. World is a mess. I'll be glad to be out of it. Only a few more years. Where did you park your car?"

"Outside the back gate."

"Should be safe. This is England. Though even in England these days you can't be sure. So what do you think of my Petronella, young man?"

"She's very beautiful."

"Ah, that she is. That she is. The last source of hope for an old man. Her grandmother was just as beautiful. I miss her so much. Have you ever missed someone so much you want to die and join them hoping there's a heaven? The older you get, the less you are sure... Now all we need are two extra glasses and another bottle of my best dry sherry. So nice to drink in company. Will you stay to dinner? So why is the *Daily Mirror* interested in an old man? You say my granddaughter is in East Berlin so you knew she wasn't here. I gave up reading the popular newspapers when I retired from business. I only read the *Times*. Mainly the obituary column. All my friends are dead. Most of them long dead in the First World War. What were we doing in those trenches slaughtering each other? How many Beethoven symphonies did we destroy before they were written? How many Shakespeare plays? How much poorer would the world be if those two men had been killed in battle as young men. And we call ourselves civilised. I've told Florence to get out of Rhodesia before the Russians, with the help of my granddaughter, stir up a war. My housekeeper, Mrs Weatherby, bless her soul, mentioned the 'Brothers in Arms'. Priests should never be allowed into politics... So here we are. One glass and one bottle of sherry. Won't you both sit down? The view from the terrace is so peaceful. We Sheckland-Halls have been in this house a long time. Since the family came back from Jamaica. Money made from slavery paid for this house, according to my granddaughter. She's still happy to spend my money, of course. When you've never had to make money it all looks so easy when you see another man has been successful. The ones who never made money call it luck. The slaves were housed and fed. Lived a lot longer than they would have in Africa. But I'm not defending my ancestor. Or maybe I am. But without the plantation owner and his knowledge of how to grow sugar cane no one would have been fed. We're all slaves, Mr Wakefield, in one way or the other. We're all being exploited. Part of human nature. We exploit each other... So what can I tell you for your newspaper?"

"May we photograph your house?"

"'The house built on slavery.' I can see your headlines. Please carry on while I look for another bottle and two more sherry glasses. I'll tell Mrs Weatherby you are staying to dinner. On a summer's night like this I suggest we eat on the terrace. Over a glass or two you can both tell me all about yourselves. Other people's stories are far more interesting don't you think?... Petronella... Do you think she is in trouble? Playing with fire, I suppose. Trying to placate her conscience after her life of privilege. I wish she would meet a nice young man to knock some sense into her... You'll have to go down on the lawn for a good photograph. They want me to sell this place. The developers. Florence can sell it when I am dead. Shouldn't be too long. I'm seventy-two. I was twenty-four when the war started. Went right the way through without a scratch. I was a regular officer. Didn't join the family firm until after the war had ended, in 1919. I can still see their faces. My friends. My dear friends. So much waste... I'll get the glasses and put my gun back in the gun case. Fact is, I never shoot the pheasants. Like to look at them. My wife said meat should be bought from the butcher."

Harry watched Sidney walk down the stone steps from the terrace to the far side of the lawn to take his photographs. The old man had disappeared into the silent house. From the back of the house, from the road, Harry heard a car hooter. In front of him was another world of rambling flowerbeds bursting with colour, tall elm trees lush with green leaves, a fish pond floating with lilies, the sound of birds. England close to London as it used to be. A rich man's home in the country... Harry read the bottle of sherry. Spanish. When Harry bought sherry it was the cheaper South African stuff. The one small glass was exquisite cut-crystal, the sun shining through making the facets of the glass sparkle like diamonds. He sat himself down at the round table in the shade of the umbrella. The pheasant called again, a sharp, distinctive cry.

There was no sign of the old man ten minutes later when Sidney came back with his multiple photographs of the old house.

"The house looks so comfortable with itself, Harry."

"It is," said the old man carrying two glasses in one hand, the stems of the glasses through his fingers. In the other hand was a bottle of the same Spanish sherry. Sidney couldn't keep his eyes off the second bottle, wetting his lips with the tip of his tongue. "Mrs Weatherby has told me she will be serving dinner in the dining room, the proper place for guests."

Harry saw the old man had changed from his muddy boots and trousers into a grey pair of flannels. Having got up from the iron seat, he sat down again with the old man and Sidney. Sherry was poured, each of them given a glass.

"To a good life," said Sheckland-Hall, raising his sherry glass. "Enjoy it while you can... So, young man, you have your eye on my granddaughter? Only explanation."

"Of course not, sir."

"Then why are you blushing?" The old man's eyes were smiling at him, full of laughter. "Good luck to you, young Harry. First it's her looks they're after. Then it's her family money. So many of them I can't count. Petronella is twenty-five years old. In my day that was old to get married. Now they live together I'm told. End of the family... Do you like my sherry?"

"Most excellent, sir," said Harry.

"You can stay the night if you don't wish to drive. There are so many bedrooms that never get used. Mostly, I like being alone. To think back on my life. Relive the parts I enjoyed... We'll start with you, Harry. Tell me about yourself. What does your father do?"

"He's the head of the foreign and commonwealth desk at the *Daily Mail*."

"There was a man called Wakefield snatched by the Nazis in Berlin before the last war."

"My father. I was named after Harry Brigandshaw who helped my father back to England."

"I remember the story... Harry Brigandshaw. Now there was a man. I first met Harry Brigandshaw in Flanders."

"He was my godfather."

"And you, Sidney. What's your claim to fame?... Oh, please help yourself to the sherry. Why I fetched the second bottle. Newspaper men have a reputation... No. Please carry on. I have the rule I pour the first glass of the evening. Then my guests help themselves. Do either of you have wives?"

"No, sir."

"Money can corrupt a girl, you know, even one as bright as Petronella. She once said 'Grandfather, I'm going to try everything. Yes, everything.' She said unless you tried it all you did not know what you were missing. Oh, my goodness. The youth of today. Hedonism. All about pleasure."

"Aren't her politics serious?"

"Ask her, Harry. What a beautiful evening. England on a perfect summer's day. Perfection. And so horrible in winter, all those days and nights locked up in the house. Why there's an empire. If England had had a climate like today all year round there never would have been a British Empire. Why would my ancestors have gone to Jamaica? Sunny days make a man feel better... East Berlin, you say?"

"To meet a man called Shostakovich."

"A relation of the musician?"

"I have no idea."

"All that lovely martial communist-inspired music. Long after they have forgotten Lenin they will be playing Shostakovich's ninth symphony. And his tenth. Harry Brigandshaw was in the Royal Flying Corps. His brother George had been killed in the trenches. Harry said he had come over to take his revenge. At the end of the war he shot down

Herr Klaus von Lieberman in a dogfight behind the British lines. Landed his Sopwith Camel in a field next to von Lieberman's burning wreckage and pulled him out. They became friends. Both of them hated the war by then. That gesture gave your life, young Harry. The story of von Lieberman intervening with the Nazis to have your father released came out in the papers after the last war."

"My sister Bergit is named after Mrs von Lieberman."

"Is she? Help yourself to the sherry. All those strange ways we get to be sitting here. What happened to Harry?"

"He went back to Rhodesia to die. He went alone. His second wife did not like Africa."

"His first wife was likely his true love."

"He's buried next to her and their unborn baby on the farm. On the other side lies his mother. The children from his second marriage are all living in England. Except Anthony. He was shot down over Berlin in June 1944. He would have turned twenty-one the following Wednesday."

Sidney poured himself another glass of Spanish sherry. The old man had looked away. Far away. For a long while the old man was not at the table, his expression far away in the past. The shadows of the elms on the lawn lengthened. A pigeon called and was answered from a tree on the far side of the lawn.

"She mustn't do anything stupid. She and Josiah. There are so many young people who will die in a war. The generals seldom die. Always the young. A few of us are lucky. Wars achieve nothing but destruction. The Russians should know better by now. They lost more people than any of us in the last war. So stupid. All for some causes that mostly never do for humanity what we want them to do. We're our own worst enemy. I sit here a lot on my own thinking. All I do is think. Such a pity so many people like my Petronella don't think properly, they are so emotional about some damn cause. They can't see the consequence. That old road to hell paved with good intentions... We're having roast beef of old England for dinner. I hope you will stay. Fancy you being called after Harry Brigandshaw. Only that one meeting in Flanders. He came to our mess. The RFC airfield was close to our mess. We were all so young and full of ideals. Fighting for king and country. You will stay to dinner?"

"We would be delighted."

"The youth are most important. Old fogies like me have had our lives.

Found it all hollow. You still have the excitement for life. Like my Petronella. I hope he's related to the musician. So much better to compose music than orchestrate a war... The birds are singing. Can you hear them? Help yourself to the sherry."

Harry watched the old man while Sidney filled up their glasses from the bottle of sherry. There were tears in the corners of the old eyes, the long stare into the past having left them moist. Harry could see pain and sadness but not any hope, the look of a man disappointed with what he had found in his life.

"You have two sons," said Harry to cheer him up.

"They run the family business. We package sugar and sell it around the world to the retail stores, buying our raw sugar where we can find it. We even buy sugar from Rhodesia. There's a big farming company in the lowveld that has tamed the water of the Zambezi River to irrigate the sugar cane in the dry season. Some of the best sucrose content in the world. Welensky's Kariba Dam is meant to irrigate vast areas of bush on both sides of the Zambezi River. Northern and Southern Rhodesia. Kariba was to be the crowning glory of the Federation. Plentiful water to irrigate and produce hydro-electric power to power the whole country. Now who knows? With Northern Rhodesia about to come under this man Kaunda, they'll fight over water rights and who gets the power. Without white farmers they'll never irrigate the land. All those pump stations and irrigation programmes. It's complicated. Requires highly skilled brains. Nothing gets done by waving a wand. Ask my ancestor if he were around. There wasn't much in Jamaica when he arrived on the island and started the plantation... Winfred and Horace. They run Sheckland-Hall Limited well. They were both well educated. A good boarding school and then Oxford. Only Petronella chose Manchester University to make her point... I don't see much of the boys. Far too busy. Their children have their own lives. What do they want with an old grandfather? The money is coming to them anyway. We all get together here over Christmas. The whole house fills up. It's more a meeting for the whole family than visiting me. Since my wife died I get lonely. Last year Petronella came for Christmas. There was a row with Horace. She called her uncle a capitalist parasite. I had to calm them down. In my day young ladies were never rude to their elders but not anymore. This year she wants to bring Josiah to the party. Should be fun. I sit back and watch them all bickering. Why do people enjoy all this modern bickering? They all have something to say. Especially their wives. Horace and Fred's wives hate each other. You see I made Winfred the managing director. He's two years younger than his brother. Has a better grasp of business. There always has to be one man at the top. Running any business by committee is a disaster. Shouldn't have retired. By then they both wanted me out of the way. So all I have is Petronella. She comes on little visits. I look forward to them so much. My goodness. We'd better crack that second bottle of sherry. You won't have to change for dinner. Not that you brought your evening clothes with you over my wall. I hope you took good photographs. Have another glass of sherry. When I'm tipsy in the evenings I don't mind so much. Harry Brigandshaw. I'll be blowed."

It was dinner for three at a table big enough for sixty. The dining room boasted one of the biggest chandeliers Harry had seen outside of a hotel. The ceiling was high. In the centre dome of the ceiling someone had painted a stag hunt, and the evening light of the dome's ring of windows played on the eyes of the hunted stag. The animal looked frightened. Harry guessed the scene was from the Scottish Highlands. There were old paintings on the walls, most of them so dark with age the portraits were invisible.

An old maid brought in the sirloin of beef and plonked it on the table in front of Sheckland-Hall, seated at the top of the table with Harry and Sidney on either side of him. The old maid walked away very slowly. Slowly, Sheckland-Hall got up to carve the meat. The old maid came back with a dish of roast potatoes and vegetables and placed it unceremoniously on the table. She never said a word. Two bottles of red wine were also there with their corks drawn. The old man was quite tipsy, poking the beef with the point of the knife. Then he sat down. He smiled at Harry.

"You can carve the bird."

Harry took the carving knife gingerly. The three empty plates were put in front of him by the old man almost cracking the bottom plate. The old man smiled, pointing the bottles of wine out to Sidney. The old man was enjoying himself. When Harry began to carve the 'bird' the meat ran red with blood. The meat in Harry's opinion was cooked to perfection. While Sidney poured the wine, Harry put a small slice on the top plate for the old man and passed him the plate. From his limited experience with old people they didn't eat so much. Sheckland-Hall was more interested in the wine, trying to get up with his full glass to make a toast and thinking better of it, sheepishly smiling at Harry filling up Sidney's plate with slices of roast beef. Harry knew from old that Sidney would be hungry. With the second plate in front of Sidney, Harry carved for himself. Both of them piled on the roast potatoes and the vegetables. The old man put one potato on his plate alongside four green beans. He was still smiling.

"To your namesake Harry Brigandshaw." Again he tried to get up without success."

"To my godfather," said Harry Wakefield.

"Did you know Henry VIII knighted a piece of his beef with his sword? It was his favourite. Why it is now Sir Loin. He was a trencherman, Henry VIII. And a bit of a womaniser. So you fancy my Petronella, young man?"

"I've only met her once."

"That's usually enough. No idea where she gets her looks from. Flossy looked more like a horse. They say horsey women look like their horses. How's the wine, Sidney?"

"Wonderful, sir."

"Should be. Been in my cellar twenty years. Get the wine direct from a man I know in France. Never eat much. Cheers. Your most excellent health. So nice to have company. Why is it the body of wine improves so much with age but not the body of a man? My joints are clogging up. Can't complain. If you don't grow old you're dead. What do you think of Mrs Weatherby's cooking? Damn fine cook. Been cooking my food for thirty-five years. Janice served us the food. They're sisters, Mrs Weatherby and Janice. Both husbands died in the Great War."

Harry and Sidney tucked into the food. The old man watched them, drinking his wine. Harry carved them both a second helping, no longer caring about his article for the *Daily Mirror*. He was trying to imagine Petronella sitting next to him at the table. Like their host, Harry was getting himself drunk. In ancient times when the guests ate and drank too much they slept under the table or passed out in their seats. He didn't care. Sidney had juice dripping down the side of his chin, not seeming to care. They were all enjoying themselves.

"You'll have to excuse me," said the old man, pulling himself to his feet.

The old maid called Janice appeared and helped the old man out of the dining hall, the terrified stag in the dome of the ceiling looking down on them as they went. Harry and Sidney were left on their own.

"More meat, Sidney?"

"Why not? Pity to waste it. There's still a full bottle of wine... He's pissed as a newt."

"I can't drive back into London."

"We can sleep in the car."

"How do we climb back over the wall if the gate's locked?"

Sidney giggled. "Let's finish this wine and the food... With all this, why does she want to be a communist? You should ask her, Harry. What a waste. Good looks and all this. I could get used to this style of living. I thought he was going to shoot us."

When they had finished the second bottle of wine the old maid came back again.

"My compliments to the chef," said Harry, getting up from the table. "Do you by any chance have a room where we can sleep? Mr Sheckland-Hall said..."

"There are two rooms, the beds made up. Breakfast will be served at nine o'clock in the conservatory."

"Gets better and better," whispered Sidney to Harry as they followed the old maid out of the dining hall.

"We'll be late for work."

"Who cares?"

With the wine and sherry mixed nicely, Sidney blew the stag a kiss up into the high-domed ceiling.

THERE WAS no sign of the old man in the morning. The old maid walked them out of the silent house, through the elm trees and across the fields. She had an iron key six inches long which she inserted in the gate. The key had an elaborate wrought-iron handle. Outside, the car was still waiting. A small boy was standing in the front garden of the house opposite the wooden gate in the high brick wall. The small boy stuck out his tongue. When Harry looked back over his shoulder the gate was closed, the old maid gone. Their breakfast had been bacon and eggs, two pork sausages, devilled kidneys and fried tomatoes with a toaster rack full of toast. There was tea or coffee. Both Harry and Sidney had slept like logs in their respective rooms in the old house. When Harry looked back from the gate the boy was gone. The company car started first time.

The photograph of the old house brooding among the elm trees came out the following morning. Harry wrote about the family's history and their involvement with slavery. The headline was 'Sins of the Father'. Harry himself felt guilty. He had liked the old man. The story of slave money buying a farm in Rhodesia was prominent, the theme of exploited labour the same, the question 'Does life ever change?' Harry wondered if Harry Brigandshaw would have liked what he wrote. There were always two sides to a story. Harry would like to have asked 'Is it wrong to give a man a job?' but knew mixed in with the abuse of slavery his editor would have him crucified. Everyone at the *Mirror* believed the skids were under the British Crown Colony of Southern Rhodesia. And rightfully so. Harry felt like a Judas at a man's table and stabbing him later in the back. He didn't expect to hear from Sheckland-Hall again.

On the following Tuesday the old man proved him wrong.

"Come down to Woodlands Court for the weekend, dear boy. I have a surprise for you."

"Sorry about my article."

"We all have a job to do, Harry. After lunch on Saturday."

"Is she coming?"

"That's my point. I want you to talk some sense into Petronella."

"And Josiah?"

"He's gone to Moscow so I am told."

"Does she know the press will be there?"

"Not the press. You, Harry. Of course not. We can drink another bottle of sherry."

Harry told Roland Cartwright.

"Take the company car. Only sits in the garage at weekends. The 'Brothers in Arms' story has faded but there will be more to come on Rhodesia to interest the public. Gone to Moscow has he?... See what you can dig up."

"Thank you, Roland."

"You're welcome. You've been in the old man's wine cellar. Now keep out of his granddaughter's pants."

PART II

OCTOBER 1962

LOVE OR LUST

1

"The world has strange ways, young Harry. My granddaughter tells me Harry Brigandshaw educated Josiah Makoni at the Good Faith Mission and Fort Hare University in South Africa. The world so often goes round in circles. If you will excuse an old man I'm going to my bed for an afternoon nap. Six o'clock on the terrace for a glass of sherry if it isn't raining. Florence says in Rhodesia you know exactly when it is going to rain. For months in their winter, not a drop. Were it but the same in England."

They watched the old man walk away, up the steps of the terrace and into the house.

"Did you organise this?" snapped Petronella.

"Actually not. He phoned me at the office."

"Why?"

"We had had a most congenial dinner together after Sidney and I climbed over the back wall."

She was even prettier mad, thought Harry. He was enjoying himself. He had arrived through the front door two hours earlier, let in by the old maid called Janice. Harry had yanked the handle hanging outside the high front gate making the sound of a hammer hitting a brass bell inside the gate. Janice had a smile on her face.

When she led him into the lounge, Petronella was sitting with her grandfather. The girl was wearing a loose shirt and long pants. When she turned round and saw him her expression changed to annoyance, her large breasts swaying inside the shirt. Harry was sure the girl was not wearing a bra and he smiled. Involuntarily Petronella covered her front with her arms. Then she ignored him. Harry and the old man shook hands before the maid was told to show him his room.

The old maid took Harry up to the same room where he had previously slept, where he put down his overnight case, all the other women that had been in Harry's life blown out of his mind. And it wasn't the family's money either, which simply wasn't that important to Harry.

"You need to be comfortable," his father had told him soon after he left prep school. "Enough for your needs. Too much money can be a curse. Attracts all the wrong people. You can only eat one meal at a time, Harry my boy. Everything one at a time. Remember that when you grow up to become a man."

Only when the old man had left did Harry smile at her. He had gone back to the lounge where he drank a cup of tea, before the old man went for his nap.

"Why don't we go for a walk round your grandfather's estate? We're stuck with each other for the weekend."

"Are you on newspaper business?"

"What do you think, Petronella?"

"Stop looking at me like that."

"He loves you, you know. Very much. He doesn't have much."

"He has all this. All that obscene amount of money."

"And all he wants is a little love."

"He's lonely since grandma died. Mother said he was lonely before. That their great love for each other was a sham. Come on then. We'll go for a damn walk."

"How was Shostakovich?"

"How the hell did you know?"

"The British government know a lot more about Josiah's capers than you think. We haven't been running an empire this long not to keep an eye on troublemakers."

"Josiah talks about Harry Brigandshaw." They had walked across the lawn into the fields.

"So do a lot of other people. He was one of those rarities in life. A good man. Let's forget politics. Talk about ourselves. Do you love him?"

"Rhodesia is so unjust... Did you sleep with Elsie?"

"That's for her to talk about, not me. She's jealous you dumped her."

"It was just a fling."

"Not to Elsie. Be careful. You know that old saying about a woman scorned. Love, hate and politics, especially other people's politics, can be a lethal concoction that can blow up in your face."

"Who told you about Shostakovich?"

"My sub-editor. My boss. It's the job of the press to report facts. It's not about Rhodesia, Petronella. It's about communism as a tool for the Russians to create their own extended empire. Once it was the tsars wanting a Russian empire which the tsars spread across Asia. Now they call themselves communists. It's all the same. Power. The pursuit of power. The Russians want to conquer the world."

"What the hell do you know about it? What do you care? All you people ever want is a story."

"People are easily manipulated. When people want something. The Russians and the Americans want us British out of Africa. They want to trade with Africa. Gain control of the minerals for their industries, a competition that's going to get nasty. The likes of Josiah are puppets on a string. It's got nothing to do with right or wrong. Or with helping the poor people of Africa out of poverty."

"Communism is a fair distribution of wealth. It's the right way for a burgeoning world to go forward."

"Don't you believe it. It's a weapon. Like fascism. Like religion. Like all the other blindfolds ruthless men use in their pursuit of power."

"Josiah isn't ruthless. Neither was Jesus Christ. You're talking rot."

"All good men have been manipulated. Right down through history. Their good ideas are used by wicked men."

"You can't defend racism. It's evil. People look at us together as if we are doing something wrong."

"Do you love him?"

"That's not the point." They walked on again before Petronella spoke. "I went to Harry Brigandshaw's funeral at the Salisbury Cathedral. With my parents. I was thirteen years old. Josiah was there though I didn't know who he was. He had taken the bus from Fort Hare in South Africa fearful the payment of his university fees would not continue."

"I know. Harry Brigandshaw was my godfather. Uncle Harry had put a codicil in his will to protect Josiah. Josiah should remember that when he gets on the racial band wagon that's now an argument more about the American civil rights movement than the white man in Africa. In Africa, the two races need each other to prosper. My godfather told that to my father and William Smythe. We all need each other to prosper."

"That's why I have joined the Zimbabwe African National Union."

"They want to kick out all the whites. To take back the land they say the likes of your parents have stolen. Towards the end of his life, Harry Brigandshaw said there was no future for the white man in Rhodesia. After the death of his mother Elephant Walk was sold. Your friends, according to Uncle Harry, are going to destroy their country."

"Of course they won't. With black rule, Zimbabwe will prosper."

"Do you really believe you are doing the right thing?"

"Of course I do."

"Some would say that with all this," said Harry, waving his hand, "the loss of your family farm in Rhodesia doesn't matter."

"I hate money."

"You'd hate it more if you didn't have it."

"What do you want, Harry Wakefield?"

"You, Petronella. Not your money. Not your politics. Just you."

She gave him a look of surprise mingled with curiosity before walking ahead to one of the horses Harry and Sidney had first seen when they went over the wall. Harry's excitement was pumping. The look was sexual speculation sending his hormones into turmoil. The girl put her hand out to the horse, feeling the stallion's muzzle. The animal whickered.

"What's the point of riding him round fifty acres, jumping over poles? On Ashford Park in Rhodesia I used to ride all day round the farm. I love Africa so much. Did you know I speak Shona as well as I speak English? Picked it up as a child playing with the *piccanins* when we didn't understand the difference in the colour of our skins. It's so stupid. When I grew up, my friends were taught to call me Miss Petronella. To be deferential. Suddenly I didn't have any friends. An only child, I was on my own. Josiah talks about his father, Tembo, growing up on Elephant Walk with Harry Brigandshaw. Josiah told me the story of Harry's father saving a seven-year-old boy called Tatenda after his village was attacked by a Matabele impi, killing his parents. Tatenda had been in the bush with the cattle when Lobengula's impi attacked. They burned down the huts and abducted the young women, herding the Shona cattle back to the Matabeleland."

"We're all a product of rape and pillage somewhere back in our history. Or our ancestors wouldn't have been born. Survival of the fittest. We humans are not very nice. Is Tembo still alive?"

"Yes. He's very old. Back in the kraal on Elephant Walk with his fourth wife, Princess, Josiah's mother. Tembo kept four wives. As for the foreman on Elephant Walk, he was rich. The farm's now owned by Anglo-US Incorporated. Growing citrus. They respect Harry's wish to let his employees live on the farm as long as they live. One day we will all be free and live in harmony. Own our own land again."

"I hope so. Just don't be taken in by Russian money in pursuit of your goal. They are not interested in you or Rhodesia. Or whatever you want to call the country. They're interested in themselves. And your minerals. What are you going to do about Joshua Nkomo now the African Nationalist movement has split in two? He's a Matabele. Josiah should remember what they did to his grandfather. It's the Matabele tribe against the Shona tribe all over again. Nothing changes. Certainly not rape and pillage. It's the old story in life. If you have something, there is always someone who wants it. Your wife, your daughter, your cattle, your land."

"How do you know so much about Rhodesia?"

"I make it my business when I'm writing a story. To know my facts. To look at it all in perspective. It's the Cold War. We're all part of it. Russia and America fighting for hegemony. And when that's all sorted, as it will be, man will think up something else to argue about so the likes of me have something to write about... Do you want to ride that horse?"

"You are not as bad as I thought you were."

Harry smiled at her. They walked on, leaving the horse grazing the lush summer grass. Clouds were building up in the October sky behind the old house.

"We won't be drinking our sherry on the terrace. Grandad gets quite tipsy. Says it's his only vice. That what else can an old man do on his own."

"Where do you live in London?"

"Shepherd's Bush. I have a small bedsitter. Most of the money Grandfather gives me is given to the party. Donations like mine pay for Josiah and his friends to do their work."

"You're not far from me. I have a flat in Holland Park. Quite a nice one. I'm not much of an altruist. Pay my taxes. When's he coming back?"

"Not for a while."

"Undergoing military training, I suppose."

"Officers' course."

"How do they understand each other? How do they talk to each other?"

"In English."

"That's good irony. The Russians use our language to teach people how to kill us."

"He's a freedom fighter."

"One man's freedom fighter is another man's terrorist. Why does it always end in war?"

"The only way sometimes. People won't listen to reason."

"And give away what they have spent their lives building up. Like your mother and father on Ashford Park."

"They were given Crown Land by the colonial government for seven and sixpence an acre."

"Land is only worth what it produces. What was on the land before your parents turned it into a prosperous farm?"

"Are we having an argument?"

"Trying not to, Petronella. So how long is Josiah going to be away?"

"Six months. Then he's going back to Rhodesia. Into the bush to start training freedom fighters."

"Should you be telling me this? He'll be arrested if I write it in my articles quoting Miss Petronella Maple as my source."

"If they know about Shostakovich they know the rest of the story. They'll have to catch him if they want to arrest him when he goes home. No one in the villages will give him up. They're fighting for their freedom as much as Josiah. More so. They don't have education or their land."

"Could we have dinner one night? I have a favourite Greek restaurant in Soho where they play Greek music and smash plates. You can use me if you want to leak out information to the press for the party. So you're a card carrying member of the British Communist Party and the Zimbabwe African National Union?"

"Yes I am. And proud of it."

"Dinner for two next week Friday. How do I call you?"

"Let's get past this weekend. I'll put up with you for the sake of my grandfather."

"So good of you, my lady."

With a sweep of an imaginary hat in hand, Harry bowed to her low. The girl laughed. Deep inside Harry felt excitement. When a girl laughed there was always hope.

"Just please don't get your fingers burned, Petronella. People have a nasty habit of using each other."

"I'll try not to."

They walked on towards the house slowly. Neither of them was in a hurry. Harry was thinking of the implication for Petronella's parents of Josiah's training. Not wishing to get into an argument, he looked at her gently.

"Do you love your parents?"

"Of course I do. My father's a pompous old goat but I love him. He was a young man with good looks and not much else. All he had to offer was his charm. Mother was an heiress with a face that faintly resembled a horse. They gave each other what the other wanted. Mother had a husband the envy of her friends. Father was given the money to start his tobacco estate. Mother tells him what to do and everyone else on Ashford Park, riding the estate on a handsome horse waving a riding crop. The labour force are scared stiff of her. Father is a pussy."

"They could lose their farm and their lives if Josiah starts a guerrilla war against white rule."

"Then they will come back to England if they have any sense. The first whiff of a bush war and mother will be on the boat. She has all this and more to come back to. Grandfather would love to have them back at Woodlands Court. Father wouldn't mind. England with a pile of money is a wonderful place to live. He would join a London club and play out his life as a gentleman telling his cronies all about his daring days in Africa. My family have got their money through inheritance for generations. Father married it. What's the difference?"

"But you want to live in Africa. With Josiah."

"He wouldn't want a white wife. Bad for politics."

"But what would you do?"

"The party will give me a job once they gain control of the government. I have a good degree. They'll need me."

"As much as they need you now?"

"I hope so. Josiah will owe me that much."

"And the rest of the white community. How will they look at a renegade?"

"Those that don't like it and don't support the new government, those who don't want to live under black rule can come back to England."

"For third and fourth generation that may be difficult."

"Then they'll have to lump it. I'm not the only white in the party. They've oppressed the blacks for so long maybe it's their turn."

"Would your parents still love you?"

"Of course they will. I'm their daughter. In the end they will be proud of me for what I'm doing. We'd better walk quicker, Harry. It's beginning to rain. I hate the English climate."

"Do you hate England?"

"I'm an African, Harry. Born and bred. I grew up with the blacks. The only real friends I've had in my life. Come on. Run. Beat you to the steps up to the terrace."

Smiling to himself sadly, Harry let her get ahead, glad he would never present his own parents with such a dilemma.

The old man was waiting for them on the terrace holding up an umbrella. Harry and Petronella were laughing as they ran past him to get out of the rain. The old man smiled at Harry.

"Who's for a nice glass of sherry?"

"I'd like a beer. What about you, Harry? What's for dinner?"

"Roast duck with all the trimmings."

"Mrs Weatherby is such a good cook. You'll love her cooking. I'm soaked. We'd better change. Grandfather, can you wait ten minutes for your glass of sherry?"

"I'd wait all evening for the pleasure of your company."

"Such a charmer." Standing on tiptoe, she kissed the old man's grizzled cheek, making the old man beam with pleasure.

"I'll be in the lounge when you've changed."

2

*I*n his room on his own, Harry rummaged in his bag for a dry shirt. The trousers would have to stay wet. He was smiling. Petronella came out of a room just down the corridor when Harry left his. She had changed into an evening frock. Put on some make-up. She looked ravishing.

"What did you take for a degree?"

"Social science. There has to be a better way than classism or racism. My tutor said we all look exactly the same under a bus. That the only difference between us is the luck of our birth."

"You don't believe in genetics? Good breeding? Inheriting good looks from your father?"

"Is that a compliment, Harry Wakefield? You don't see any resemblance to a horse?"

"Not a trace."

"Nurture against nature. It's an old chestnut."

"You won't win the Derby by mating a race horse with a cart horse. Chances are the progeny couldn't pull a cart, let alone win a horse race."

"We all need equal opportunity."

"Isn't nurture as much the parents as the schooling? I learnt more questioning my mother and father than I did questioning my teachers. My mother is a speech therapist. Runs her practice from the ground floor of the house. Why I speak English with the correct pronunciation. From a small child she constantly corrected me and Bergit. My command of language for my writing came from my mother."

"She had the privilege of a good education. Can we stop arguing? What do you want, a beer or a sherry?"

"Of course. A glass of sherry. To be polite. This is your grandfather's house. I'm his guest."

"I'm his granddaughter and I'm going to have a beer."

"You look gorgeous."

"Stop that, Harry."

"Why?"

They walked down the long corridor to the wide stairs and descended to the hallway in silence. Outside the rain had stopped. Through the open door, they could see the white-painted iron table dripping with water on the terrace.

In the lounge, the old man was waiting. On the side table stood a bottle of sherry and a bottle of beer. The same Spanish sherry Harry had drunk with Sidney. The old man smiled gently when he saw his granddaughter had changed into a dress. The old man poured the beer into a tall glass and handed it to Petronella. He gave Harry a glass of sherry, lifting his glass to both of them in turn. They all said cheers together.

"To happy times," said Sheckland-Hall. "It's turned into a lovely evening. A little wet but the last of the sun's come out."

They sat either side of old Sheckland-Hall in the dining room, facing each other. Petronella looked even more beautiful to Harry in the light of the chandelier. By the time they had finished the bottle of sherry in the lounge the twilight had almost gone. On the table, set for three, in front of the old man sat open bottles of wine. With the soup they each took a glass of white wine. Harry was careful not to slurp. When he watched her with the spoon to his mouth, he dribbled the soup when she slowly raised her own spoon looking at him. There was only a small amount of clear soup in the soup bowl. Janice brought in the roast duck, crisped to perfection. The old man pointed to Harry. Janice smiled at Petronella as she had when she brought in the soup, placing the big bowl next to the ladle in front of Sheckland-Hall. The duck was put in front of Harry. Janice brought him the carving knife and fork with the plates. The soup bowls had gone back to the kitchen. The old man poured red wine into their second glasses standing one bigger than the other next to their place settings... He was getting tight. Petronella smiled at him. Harry carved the duck onto their plates, passing the first with three pieces of duck to the old man who put it in front of Petronella. The old maid put the bowls of vegetables and the roast potatoes on the table in front of Petronella, smiled at her again and left. Clearly, Harry thought, the girl was a favourite at Woodlands Court.

Before they ate, the old man raised his glass of red wine, having emptied his smaller glass of the white.

"To my darling grandchild."

The old man drank down half his glass of wine, and put it down gingerly in front of his plate. Harry had carved him a small piece of the breast. Petronella had helped him to one roast potato and a spoonful of greens. When Harry tucked into his plate of food, the Brussels sprouts were cooked to perfection, still hard in the middle. The old man put down his knife and fork with a clang and drank his wine. They watched him drink as they ate. When they had finished their plates the old man got up and left the table, formally shaking Harry by the hand and kissing his granddaughter. They watched Janice lead the old man away.

"He's pickled," giggled Petronella. "Woodlands Court has the best food in the world. Isn't Janice a darling?"

Harry filled up Petronella's glass with red wine.

"You want some more of this duck?"

"A girl has to watch her weight, Harry. What would a girl be without a figure? Most girls just have their bodies to attract men. Not like my mother. You have some more. Eat as much as you like."

She was playing with him. Speculating. Hanging out the hook for him to swallow. The empty chairs down the table stared back at him. He looked up at the roof, seeking out the stag with the frightened eyes. The painting of the Scottish stag hunt was dark, the chandelier throwing most of its light down on the table. The sherry and wine had made her more beautiful.

"Do you only write for the newspaper? You haven't tried anything else?" She was smiling. Exploiting every journalist's weak spot.

"I've wanted to write a book. You knew that."

"Why don't you?"

"One day. A man has to make a living. Money is what attracts the girls. Money and cars. A nice flat. Can I give you a lift back to London tomorrow? Shepherd's Bush is just around the corner."

"That would be nice."

"You don't have a return ticket on the train?"

"Of course I do. You'll save me the Tube fare from the station to Shepherd's Bush."

"My pleasure. What time do you want to go?"

"As late as possible."

"What do you do in the week?"

"Work in the ZAPU office. We're in the same building as the Anti-Apartheid movement. They've loaned us an office."

"How many of you?"

"Just a few."

"All right. And Friday for dinner?"

"We'll see, Harry. Why are men always in such a hurry?"

"Do you use up all the chairs over Christmas?"

"Most of them. My uncle's wives have a cat fight. They hate each other."

"The younger brother is managing director. I heard from your grandfather. Want some more wine? When we've finished the red we can go back to the white. Do you have music over Christmas?"

"Do you want me to sing?" She was laughing at him, Harry was sure. Not that it mattered. She was there. Getting prettier with every glass of his wine. "I like Greek restaurants. There's always music."

"So do I. It's why I go there."

"Soho?"

"Yes, it's in Soho. Wine?"

"Why not? Janice and Mrs Weatherby don't drink. Better to drink the white or the bugs might get in the bottle. Grandfather has thrown away the cork. Tell me about yourself, Harry."

"There's nothing to tell."

"What's the book going to be about?"

"I don't know. You have to be forty to write a good novel. To have experienced life."

She had big blue-green eyes and auburn hair, the light of the chandelier bringing out the colour of red. The nose was slightly turned up. The ears small and delicate. Her hand on the wine glass stem a perfect length neither small nor long. He would make her the heroine in the book when he got down to write it, his first novel too often put off. The fact she wasn't wearing a bra under the frock didn't matter anymore. It was her face. Her face was perfect.

"Do you have Celt blood in you?"

"Probably."

"It's the red in your hair and the green in your blue eyes."

"You're tight, Harry."

"Probably. Does it matter?"

"So long as you can climb the stairs."

"I can always climb stairs."

"I bet you can. Did you climb stairs to Elsie?"

"You know I did. You know where she lives."

"Did you sleep with her?"

For a moment Harry saw a flash of jealousy, the face in front of him across the table turning sour. He would remember the sudden change of mood for his novel. The moment lost, Harry carved himself a piece of the duck and ate it in his fingers, licking them afterwards.

"It's the sweet orange sauce."

Her fingers had tightened on the stem of the glass. For a split second Harry thought the delicate stem was going to break. The tension in her hand relaxed and her smile came back again. She lifted her glass.

"To the struggle."

They looked hard at each other, Harry not lifting his glass.

"Lift your glass, Harry, if you want me."

He looked at her sadly. His excitement ebbed. Like a randy dog with a bucket of cold water thrown over him.

"Why won't you drink?"

"My father told me never to drink to war, however righteous the cause. People die in wars, Petronella. Good people. On both sides. Too often war turns righteous people into thugs."

"To hell with you. I'm going to bed."

Slamming her glass down on the table breaking the stem, Petronella got up from the table and walked out of the room.

Harry sat a long time on his own drinking the wine. When both bottles were empty he got up. He was drunk, steadying himself on the corner of the table. Looking up for the stag Harry nearly fell over. He couldn't find the light switch. When he looked back from the door the old hall looked so empty. Empty of spirit.

The house was so quiet as he walked up the long stairs along the long corridor of the house, the boards creaking as he walked to his room. Her door was open down the corridor, light spilling out. He was tempted. For a long time Harry stood in the dark corridor looking at the light from her room. He turned the door knob to his room and went inside, closing the door behind him. He wanted more from her than a one-night stand.

As he stood by the bed he hiccupped. The hiccups wouldn't stop. Slowly, taking off his clothes Harry got into bed. The last thing he remembered was hiccups and the picture of her face, the blue-green eyes, the turned-up nose, the delicate ears.

3
_____

*I*n the morning, feeling terrible, Harry got up, dressed in the shirt that was now dry, packed his bag, wrote a note of thanks to Sheckland-Hall and walked out of his room.

He left the note on the half-moon table downstairs next to the front door and let himself out into the chilly morning. The sun was shining low through the trees, the birds still calling. His car was in the driveway below the terrace. Throwing his bag in the back, Harry got into the driver's seat and turned on the engine. Leaning his elbow on the car window Harry looked up at the face of the three-storied house. The morning sun was shining on the windows. She came to the window of her third-storey bedroom and looked down on him, the noise of the car engine having brought her to the window. She waved at him. One, single wave, Harry not sure what it meant. Harry waved back and put the company car into gear, letting off the brake. When he looked back from the elm trees that parted the driveway he couldn't see her room through the trees.

Feeling sad, Harry drove back to London, the traffic light in the early morning. He was still on the hook. That much he knew.

"Be careful, Harry," he said to himself. "That one's dangerous."

When he reached his flat in Holland Park an hour later he went back to bed. When he woke at lunchtime his hangover was sickening.

"Why the hell do I drink?"

Looking at his watch, Harry dressed and went out of the flat and under the plane trees to the pub at the end of the cul-de-sac for a hair of the dog. The pub was open. He was hungry. And there he was, he told himself. Stuffed.

"You look like shit, Harry."

"Thank you, Harold." They were both Harry but Harry liked to call the publican Harold. They were the only two at the bar, the others at the tables eating their Sunday lunch. He had phoned his mother the previous Friday saying he wasn't joining the Wakefield and Smythe families for Sunday lunch. He had promised to pick up his cold roast chicken for his week-day sandwich lunches when he returned from Woodlands Court.

"Was she worth it?"

"I'm in love, Harold. Please don't talk. Or I'd like to be. She's a bisexual communist who wants to start a war in Africa to spite her family. Tobacco farm in Rhodesia. Plantations two centuries ago in Jamaica with all those slaves. Girl's got a guilt complex. But oh is she pretty. What is it with some women that just pulls you?"

"You sure pick 'em, Harry."

"I sure do. Can I eat at the bar? What you got? I get the munchies on a hangover. Can you pour a glass of red wine in my beer now I've drunk half of it? Shock treatment but it works."

"Roast lamb and mint sauce. All the trimmings."

"Perfect. Bring it on."

"What's her name?"

"Petronella. Petronella Maple."

"She's in the *Sunday Times*. You can read mine if you want. Her boyfriend is in Russia, in Siberia, undergoing military training."

"How the hell did they find out?"

"You missed this one. Page three. You really want wine in your beer?"

"Please. I wasn't going to tell Roland. She said I could. Now I will. After six months Josiah Makoni is going back to Rhodesia to train terrorists in a bush camp. Petronella thinks the security forces won't be able to find him. They should be careful not to underestimate the Rhodesians. Some of those farms were given to officers who went through Burma."

"In the meantime you are going to climb into his girlfriend?"

Harold poured out a glass of wine and poured it into the beer. Harry was left on his own wondering if journalism was such a good career after all. What if he got Josiah killed by the Rhodesian security forces? Wingate and his men had chased the Japanese out of the Burmese jungle. And the Japs had known what they were doing. He'd be as bad as the rest of them, getting Josiah killed.

When the plate of roast lamb was put in front of him he had finished his beer laced with wine.

"Just a beer, Harold."

He was feeling better, his hangover dissipating. He picked out the knife and fork from inside the rolled napkin and tucked into his food. Later, after a nap, he would pick up the roast chicken in Chelsea and have a chat with his father about journalists' ethics.

"This lamb is good."

"You want to read their article? I've folded the paper."

"You're a star, Harold. Wasn't it Bertrand Russell who said 'people would rather die than think, and many of them do'?"

"Don't ask me. You're the philosopher, Harry."

"I don't think either Petronella or Josiah Makoni have thought through what they are doing. They're blinded by the passion of their cause."

"What about lust, Harry? Don't forget the lust." Harold was laughing at him as he put down the new pint of beer. Harry went on eating, enjoying every mouthful.

Half an hour later, when Harry left the Horse and Hounds after reading the *Sunday Times* page three article warning all the parties of a looming revolution in Rhodesia if everyone failed to solve their differences, the British colonial power, the Rhodesian minority white government and the African Nationalists, he had had just the right amount of food and beer to make him sleep. Harry always thought there was something nice and decadent about a nap after a good roast Sunday lunch.

WHEN HE WOKE in his flat up the road from the Horse and Hounds he no longer had a hangover. It was six o'clock by his watch. The company car was still downstairs parked in the road only due back when he went to work the following morning.

All the Sunday lunch guests had left his parents' house in Chelsea when he arrived by car in style to pick up his weekly chicken.

"You timed that well," said his father. "Just had a nap."

"So did I."

"Thought you had driven from Ashford."

"It became complicated."

"Girls are always complicated, Harry. Except your mother. Are you grabbing the chicken and making a run?"

Harry gave his father Harold's copy of the *Sunday Times* folded at page three. His father began to read the article when they sat down in the second floor lounge, his mother's practice taking up the floor below. Harry sat in silence watching his father read.

"I wonder what Harry Brigandshaw would think of this? All that effort and money put into Josiah's education. Maybe it was inevitable. Only the ignorant are easily controlled. Do you know where they got this story? There wasn't a whiff of it at the *Daily Mail* last week. Your mother's in the kitchen. Go and say hello to her. Bergit has gone off somewhere with Ruthy. William and Betty went home after lunch. We've been friends such a long time. There's nothing better than old friends, Harry. You have so much history together."

Harry went into the kitchen and kissed his mother. The basket with the chicken, tomatoes, cucumbers and lettuce was packed ready for him on the kitchen table.

"Are you rushing off?"

"No, Mother."

"You want a drink? You want supper?"

"Just you and Dad."

"Now what do you want?"

"Dad's advice, I suppose."

"How was the girl?"

"She's a bisexual communist."

"Oh, my goodness. Isn't that going too far?"

"I didn't go anywhere. Left at sunrise. She wanted me to condone a war in Rhodesia. A liberation war she called it."

"How old is she?"

"Not old enough by the look of it. She's twenty-five. Thanks for the tuck box. I'll put it in the car later."

"You got a car!"

"Company car until tomorrow morning."

"Go and talk to your dad while I do the chores. I have an early patient. Poor kid's got a cleft palate and can't get his tongue around his words. Therapy helps. Tip of the tongue. You remember."

"How could I ever forget, Mother?"

While his mother did the chores in the kitchen Harry unloaded his problem in the lounge. His father had read the page three article and was staring into space. A wood fire was burning in the grate as much for comfort as warmth. The Chelsea townhouse, pinched between neighbours, was warm and winter had yet to come.

"Your only job is to report the facts. You can't take sides to favour an event whatever your personal feelings. Or worse, suppress something you know should be in the public realm. Don't think of this man alongside your connection with Harry Brigandshaw. If he's going to lead a guerrilla army to gain his political ends, he's not concerned about who gets killed. His own people who he will laud as martyrs, or the white people he hates for stealing his land. Whether he's a good or bad person shouldn't matter to a newspaper reporter. Tell them what you know, Harry. Publish and be damned."

"She doesn't care. Doesn't think they'll find him. I'm not so sure. There's a Judas in every political pack. A lot of those whites know the bush as well as anyone. Harry Brigandshaw, and his famous father the hunter, who roamed all over the country."

"It may make the colonial office more determined to make all the parties see sense."

"Do they care or do they want to wash their hands of the colonies and for Britain to look towards Europe for our future?"

"And the girl? I sense she's your problem. She's different. Complex. Probably attractive. Those are the girls that make you unhappy. She wanted you to drink to her struggle that isn't really hers with all that family money to fall back on. She has nothing to lose."

"She wants to go back to Rhodesia."

"She sounds like a spoiled brat to me. Who wants her own way. There's a lot to be said for not being born into money. There's no challenge. No excitement to finding a man and building the comforts of home together for your family. There's no challenge. Leave her alone, Harry. Report what she said. I got into trouble with William in Berlin before the war by reporting the rise of Adolf Hitler. They wanted to kill me. If Neville Chamberlain had not gone the route of appeasement the world may not have been torn apart in a second world war. Hitler and Germany had every reason to hate the allies for the Versailles agreement that ended the Great War and bled Germany to catastrophic inflation and unemployment. The Germans needed a Hitler after that. Not that he did them any good. This time the Americans saw sense and helped build a new Germany out of the ashes. The right answer is simple. The whites should get out of Rhodesia. But they won't. So they'll all fight over it. What's new? Whether your Petronella and Josiah are morally right doesn't matter a damn. In the end some of the people will survive. Get on with their lives. Maybe Josiah wants to be a hero. Report the facts, Harry. That's what we do. That's our job."

"I'll tell Roland tomorrow."

"Who wants tea?" said his mother from the kitchen.

"Just what I need. A cup of tea."

It all sounded perfectly logical coming from his father. The trouble was he fancied her. That was the snag. The girl in the third-floor window. The wave. The date and smashing plates. Blue-green eyes that looked right into him, making him want so much, making the rest irrelevant. He had told Harold flippantly he was in love. Maybe he was. She was exotic, desirable and different. Friday at the Greek restaurant in Soho. Give her a ring. He'd find the number. The spice was in the chase. In the danger. To hell with it, he told himself. Give her a ring. See what she says. See what happens. Or the girl will haunt you. The one that got away. The one he really wanted.

With his mind in further turmoil, Harry drank his tea. His mother was watching him. Smiling. As mothers did. He smiled back at her. His father watched their exchange and smiled himself. They were happy. His parents were happy.

When his sister Bergit came back with Ruthy Smythe they were flushed with excitement.

"What you two been up to?"

"None of your business."

"How's my future lover?" asked Ruthy.

"Don't say things like that, Ruthy. Your father would have a fit."

"It's the sixties, Aunty Janet. Women's lib. We're allowed to say what we think. Johnny Masters has invited me out."

"What about me?" said Harry, trying to forget Petronella and concentrate on Ruthy.

"You'll always be around, Harry. That's why you will be my future lover. One day when both of us are in despair."

"You want some tea, Ruthy? I can make a fresh pot."

"I can make it, Mum. You sit down."

"I'll help you, Bergit."

The kitchen door closed on the lounge. Harry could hear the two girls giggling on the other side of the door. They've been smoking pot, he said to himself. Maybe she was right. One day they would be lovers. Lovers in despair. She was nineteen, a lot of years to find her happiness. They had always been friends. Since children. Old friends. His father was right. In Ruthy he would always have a friend. A friend in need. They were lucky. The Smythes and the Wakefields. Lifelong friends and neighbours. The girls were still giggling. It had to be pot. And Friday was five days down the road. Friday at the Greek restaurant. Dancing to the music. Smashing plates. With Petronella.

"Got to go, Mum. Need a booze-free sleep. Thanks for the talk, Dad. Don't know what I would do without you both."

"Don't forget the chicken and the salad."

"How could I ever forget?"

"You should have breakfast in the mornings."

"Never have time. Say goodbye to the girls."

"What are they giggling about?"

"Don't ask me."

*I*n the cold light of morning what to do wasn't so simple. There was Sheckland-Hall. Twice Harry had accepted the old man's hospitality, the second to talk some sense into the girl, the girl all the old man had to look forward to. Making the granddaughter a pariah in the eye of many people, especially the old man's friends, would be contrary to Harry's understanding of his acceptance of the second invitation.

After parking the car in the basement and returning the key to reception he went and sat down in his office and twiddled his pen. There was more to write about than Josiah Makoni and the looming gloom in Africa. There was a murderer on the loose in the south of England who had raped and strangled a girl of thirteen, the very fodder of his newspaper.

At lunchtime, his mind far from the trials and tribulations of Africa, he took out a chicken sandwich from his lunchbox and began to eat. On the brown crisp bread was real butter. The sandwich was delicious.

"Good old mum."

Through the glass of his window Sidney was grinning, pointing a finger at the sandwich. Harry shook his head. He was hungry, the leftover munchies from his weekend drinking.

He had finished all the food in the tin box when Roland Cartwright came in.

"The *Sunday Times* got the jump on us, Harry. You're losing your story. Can't have that. What did you find out? Did you put the car back in the basement? A politician in military training is hot news. The editor wants to know more. Just pulled me over the coals in his office. Don't let me down, Harry. Why I got you that salary increase at Christmas. Help me out. What's going on? What's his girlfriend up to? What does she know?"

"It was a waste of a weekend, Roland."

"Don't lie to me. I know when people lie to me. Why I was such a damn good reporter before they put me behind a big desk. What's the drop? What's she to you anyway? You've got the run of London on your salary. Girls are girls. They're all the same when you've had them. So you slept with her. That's it. No you didn't. You want to. That's worse. Don't tell me you fancy the damn girl. She's a bisexual communist. You told me yourself. Throw in a bit of miscegenation and you've got the whole box of tricks. Don't let the bitch cloud your judgement, Harry."

"She says he's not coming back to England after his military training."

"That's better. Go on. Have you got any of those chicken sandwiches left?"

"I've finished them all."

Roland stared at him in silence. Waiting.

"He's going into the bush when he gets back to Rhodesia. Not through the front door. He won't be presenting the Rhodesian government with his passport. They'd confiscate it if they didn't put him under arrest and charge him with treason. He's going to start a guerrilla army. Petronella says they won't be able to catch him in the wilds of the bush. I'm not so sure."

"See? That wasn't so difficult. Write it all down, Harry. Put it on my desk by three o'clock. Tomorrow's edition. That part's much bigger than being trained as a terrorist. We'll bury the *Sunday Times*."

"She calls him a freedom fighter."

"Put it all in. A bit about her grandfather with all that money. An exposé of the family's history of slavery. Where their damn money came from in the first place. Keep it simple. Just the gory facts. Sound bites, Harry. Good ones sell newspapers. Make her look like a hero in defiance of her family. Build her up. You say she's beautiful. Perfect. Get Sidney to take a good photograph. Make it look as though you're on her side. When are you seeing her again?"

"Meant to be Friday."

"Good boy."

"But Josiah's going to get hurt."

"That's not your problem. They're freedom fighters, don't forget. Some will get hurt. Heroes. They all want to be bloody heroes don't forget."

"What about the murder in Brighton?"

"What about the murder? There's a murder somewhere in the world every minute. Probably less. Freedom fighter heroes going into the bush to fight for their freedom are much bigger stories. Especially when they're black. And their girlfriend is white and beautiful. Where are you taking her?"

"To that place in Greek Street where they dance and smash plates."

"Perfect. She'll love it. Let Sidney stay in the background with his camera. Photographers take pictures of dancers all the time. She doesn't have to know until we have that beautiful face in the morning paper. Are you sure you are not hiding one of those homemade sandwiches?"

"No, Roland."

"Three o'clock. On my desk. The photograph of the heroine can come in a later edition."

"On the dot. I'll start right away."

Leaning across the desk, Roland opened the tin.

"It's empty."

"I said I'd finished them."

"I thought you were lying."

Harry typed fast for twenty minutes, absorbed in what he was writing. His father, a journalist all his life, still typed with two fingers. When Harry had said at the age of sixteen he wanted to follow in his father's footsteps, he had been sent to typing school in the summer holidays. He was the only boy among the girls still too shy to know his luck. Ever since, he had thanked his father for those classes.

Concentrating, Harry tweaked each sentence until he was satisfied. Rhythm, Harry, he told himself. There's a sound to language. Make it sing. Only then did he retype the article without the mistakes.

"It's all in the detail, Harry," his father had said. "If you want to succeed in life whatever you do has to be perfect. If a job's worth doing it's worth doing properly. Cliché but true. Why it's a cliché, repeated so often. Get it right. The rest will take care of itself. You won't have to bullshit your way through life."

ROLAND CARTWRIGHT WAS NOT in his office when Harry put the article on his desk. It was a quarter to three by the clock behind Roland's desk. Under the clock was another cliché: 'There's always a deadline'. Harry smiled at the clock. The catchline heading read 'Is this girl right? Judge for yourself!'

He had described her growing up on the farm. Losing her black friends. Being lonely as hell. And there it was. All of it.

He asked the girl at the reception desk to find out for him the phone number of the office of the Zimbabwe African National Union. With her other chores it took her half an hour to track it down. Roland put his head round the door as he was contemplating the number.

"You should write a book, Harry. This is good. A good story, fact or fiction. The bleeding hearts among our readers will love it. Have you made your date for Friday?"

"Not yet."

"Get on with it."

Roland was whistling as was his habit when he had got his own way. The man was a ruthless shit. Harry felt he had exposed himself as much as Petronella and Josiah. He felt physically sick. Best let her hear about that bloody article before I give her a ring. There was a bad taste in his mouth. A bitter tasting bile had come up from his stomach. She wouldn't go out with him after this. Poor old Sheckland-Hall. He had betrayed the man's hospitality. There had to be some honour among men. He tried to think of Ruthy but it didn't work. When he thought of Elsie with the big bottom he had a flash of both of them in bed together. His sexual excitement mingled with loathing. Josiah with her didn't matter so much. He was a man. A real man to put up with military training in the Siberian winter. They should have been friends. Not fighting with each other.

Switching his mind onto work, Harry finished what had come in the mail. There were letters from his readers. Some attacking him. Some praising what he had said. The luxury of his own byline. Harry replied to each one, answering their questions as best he could. Some of the more exotic letters would be printed in the *Daily Mirror*. The life of a journalist. When he had finished his stomach felt better. It was six o'clock when Sidney rapped on the glass of his door.

"Want a beer, Harry?"

"Why not? I'm going to stop drinking the whole month of February. Shortest month."

"How was your day?"

"Bloody awful."

"That girl still bugging your hormones?"

"I like her, Sidney."

"Oh, Harry. You're twenty-six. You got all the rest of your life to look forward to liking someone. Now it's all about sex. As many and often as possible."

"You're a filthy predator, Sidney. Do you ever get enough?"

"Not often. And when I do it only lasts half an hour and I'm thinking of the next one."

"One day you'll fall, Sidney."

"Not me… The receptionist is coming with us. I asked her."

"Never date a girl at work. A real bugger for both of you when you break up. I'll introduce you to Ruthy. She's smoking pot. No, better not. Ruthy deserves much more than a sex-starved journalist."

"What about your sister?"

"Don't so much as think of it. Come on, Sidney. I want you to take some photographs on Friday if I can find the courage to phone her up."

"Think of it as business."

"I can't."

Harry went home early after two beers leaving Caroline the receptionist with Sidney. Harry tried to keep the newspaper out of his private life. Not that it probably made any difference. Betty Smythe, Ruthy's mother, had been William Smythe's receptionist after he went freelance. Harry's godfather had been happily married for half his life. There had been a rumour in the family for years that William had fancied the actress Genevieve, before she was married to Harry Brigandshaw's nephew, Tinus. It was all too complicated for Harry as he took the Tube back to Holland Park. She was going to hate him after his article, of that much he was certain. No one should want their private life washed in public.

For an hour he tried to read a book, a task he set himself to improve his vocabulary. He read with a dictionary next to him. He read the words but did not hear the story. There was a phone in his study, the third room in his flat. The ZAPU office would be shut.

Saying to hell with his conscience he walked out of the flat, down to the Horse and Hounds. The pub was too close, his salary just big enough. He had never saved a penny in his life. It was Harold's night off. No one he knew was in the Horse and Hounds. On his own at the end of the bar, Harry drank whisky, the one drink that did not give him a hangover. Later he went home and went to bed, falling asleep in minutes. When he woke the birds were singing from the plane trees and it was morning. Another day. Another day at the office. Another day in the life of himself as a journalist. For some reason he wondered what had happened to Elsie. The girl called Elsie. The girl with the big bottom.

WHEN HARRY PHONED on Friday morning, letting his article have three days' distance, he was put straight through to Petronella.

"Thought you'd forgotten our date. What an article. You can write, I'll say that much for you. What's the name and address of the restaurant? I can meet you there. Most nights I work late. Paddington is nearer to Soho than Shepherd's Bush. Poor Grandfather. He thought we had had a fight."

"Hadn't we? I saw your light on when I went up to bed. The door was open."

"Oh, Harry. I'd gone to the bathroom. Those old houses have one bathroom a floor. Grandfather doesn't like the corridor lights to stay on at night. The wiring's so old. Thinks the house will burn down. Why I left the door open. You naughty boy."

Harry could hear her laughing as he gave her the address of the Greek restaurant. She was playing with him.

"What time, Harry?"

"Eight o'clock."

"I'll be there. Grandfather likes you."

"Before or after he read my article?"

"Don't be silly. A Sheckland-Hall would never read the *Daily Mirror*. Far beneath them. A tabloid! That's the nice part about it. Neither my rich uncles or their friends would dream of buying the *Daily Mirror*. Just people who sympathise with the oppressed. I'm looking forward to smashing some plates."

Roland Cartwright looked pleased. He had sat patiently while Harry made the phone call. He had a way of making sure he got what he wanted.

"She didn't give a damn."

"Women are complex, Harry."

"She'll stand me up."

"Just be there. Eight o'clock. With Sidney in the background. Don't forget to book a table."

Left on his own, Harry felt elated. She was going to meet him. The door had not closed.

SHE WAS SITTING at the table looking prettier than ever, a sweet smile on her face. The owner of the Greek restaurant was ingratiating as he led Harry to the table. His name was Dimitri.

"I'll come back for your order, Mr Wakefield."

At the time Harry made the booking he had told Dimitri to send the bill to the *Daily Mirror*. The restaurant ran an account with the paper.

"You're on time," said Harry, sitting himself into a chair. "Most girls keep a man waiting on a date."

"Is this a date, Harry? I thought it was business. You must come here often."

"So you aren't upset with my article? Making you public like that?"

"The phone hasn't stopped ringing. Donations are coming in. Free publicity in a journal is the best advertising. Elsie sends her love."

"You were after donations?"

"Of course we were. We chat up the press, Harry. That's part of our jobs."

"Elsie said she works for Sainsbury's. As a marketing consultant."

"That she does. We couldn't send Josiah to Moscow on his trips from what I get from Grandfather. We need funding. The backbone of any

NGO or political party. Raising money. Elsie helps when I ask her. She'll do pretty much what I ask."

"I'll bet she will."

"Don't be jealous, Harry. Can I have a drink? I presume your newspaper is paying for this? Something exotic. Something Greek. Ask that nice man. I'll wave to him."

"Did you ask Elsie to pick up a journalist at that party?"

"I would never do something like that. Now would I? She liked you, Harry. Next time don't fall asleep on the job."

"Elsie works for ZAPU part-time?"

"She helps us out in the office in the evenings."

"Do you pay her?"

"She thinks I will," said Petronella sweetly. "We shall see. Now, how was your week?"

"Why are people giving you money?"

"Your readers, most of them working class, dislike the idea of the white Rhodesians lording it over the blacks. It reminds them of themselves before trade unions. Before Britain began to dismantle the class system. You know some of those white Rhodesian farming families own tracts of land as big as Surrey. We can't have that in the second half of the twentieth century. It's all meant to be egalitarian. Everyone equal. The working class don't like a new breed of feudal barons sticking their noses up in their air."

"What have you got that's exotic and Greek, Dimitri? Your special lamb, of course. The lady would like a cocktail."

"I'll bring you both our speciality. And a bottle of wine?"

"Of course. Does it have a name?"

"Of course it does, Mr Wakefield. Dimitri's special. Lamb for the lady?"

The owner went off with the order to the kitchen followed by the man to be their waiter for the evening.

"He's so ingratiating. Does he tell little jokes?"

"Sometimes, Petronella. It's his job. You get the likes of me to do your promotions. He does his own."

"It's demeaning."

"Not to him. He enjoys his job. Enjoys pleasing people."

"You know the poor will always hate the rich."

"Depends what you want from life. Harry Brigandshaw said he envied the black villagers with their mud huts down beside an African river. They were all one big family. Helping each other. All the aunts and uncles. Grandparents. Siblings and cousins. All one big happy family. They fished in the river. Hunted the forest. Knew what edible food to gather from the bush. Grew a few crops. They were all in harmony under the sun. Not cooped up in some Manhattan flat with four walls to look at. Or the smog of London to breathe. They were free. Went to bed when the sun went down and got up when it rose. Teaching them our way of life will destroy all that. Make them unhappy."

"They had such short lives."

"But happy ones according to Uncle Harry, whose father saw them long before our civilisation started to corrupt them. Better to live a short, happy life than a long one that's miserable. Why they have all those shrinks in America. Can you tell me the word for depression in Shona? I didn't think so. There probably isn't one. Suburbia, Petronella. You want to give them cities with everyone living on top of each other making the party do for them what their families did in the past. Politicians want to control people. As do the priests. What Uncle Harry said. I live in suburbia. All I have ever known. A flat or a townhouse cheek by jowl with my fellow man."

The drinks came in the silence, Petronella looking at him sadly.

"You've never been poor, Harry," she sighed. "You've never been poor. Or oppressed. You and your family are part of the English elite. A life of privilege. Like your Harry Brigandshaw my mother admired so much. She didn't like his second wife. Mother said she was common. His first wife, Lucinda, the aristocrat, she liked the sound of her. My mother's a snob."

"We're arguing again."

"I think we are. Cheers, Harry. I'm going to enjoy dinner. When do we get to smash some plates?"

"I like your dress."

"Now that's better. What a nice looking bottle of wine."

The restaurant had filled up, Dimitri flitting from table to table in front of his waiters. The band tuned up and began to play. There were three of them. The instruments were like mandolins but not the same. One of the band sang while he played. Some people got up to dance.

"You want to dance, Petronella?"

"Not my style. Elsie likes to dance. Is Dimitri really a Greek name?"

"I have no idea. Just know his name is Dimitri. We don't have to jump around on the dance floor. It's too small anyway. This is probably a love song if I understood Greek."

"Are you sure he's singing in Greek?"

"I have no idea."

"We can try."

On the dance floor Harry took Petronella into his arms. She was soft, the smell of her close, so sweet, just a touch of perfume, she turned up the tip of her nose just in front of his face. He wanted to suck her ear it was so small. Pull it into his mouth.

When they got back to the table the lamb was brought to them by the waiter. They ate in silence, smiling at each other. The lamb, like the Dimitri special, was delicious.

"That was good, Harry."

"It was. Have some wine."

"Don't get me drunk. I have to go home on the Tube."

"We could take a taxi."

"I suppose we could."

"Have you heard from him?"

"Who?"

"Josiah."

"I don't expect to. For a long time. Let's not talk business. This time why don't we talk about you? Who is Harry Wakefield? Where did you come from? Where are you going?"

Harry hadn't seen Sidney come in. He was going from table to table offering to take photographs. When he came to their table he asked them if they wanted a picture. They both sat back in their chairs and let him take photographs. Harry paid him for the photographs, writing down his address. It was the way of itinerant photographers who had to develop the pictures. Sidney moved on to the next table.

"That's a hard way to make a living," said Harry. "I feel sorry for them. One rung up from begging."

"Will you get the photographs?"

"Probably not. I'll ask Dimitri. There must be some control over the chap or he wouldn't have got in the door. Here comes the next one. Selling flowers."

"It's for the poor people in India, sir."

"How much is that bunch of flowers?"

"As much as you are willing to give. All for a good cause."

"I'll bet it is," said Harry, giving the girl ten shillings.

"Thank you, sir. You are most kind."

"Have one on me."

The young girl looked at Harry and smiled. She was not very pretty.

"I will, sir."

The girl holding the bundle of flowers went on her rounds.

"There should be proper social security for someone like that," snapped Petronella.

"What about the poor people in India?" Harry was smiling. "At least she's trying to do something for herself. There you are, Petronella. A lovely bunch of flowers."

They drank the wine and talked trivia. Harry had had enough of being serious. Whatever was in the Dimitri special had gone straight to his head. Harry couldn't keep his eyes off Petronella. When they danced she came close to him.

"I don't think I want to smash plates," she said when they got back to the table.

"You want another bottle of wine?"

"Better not."

"Coffee?"

"Keeps me awake."

"Was this business or a date?"

"You tell me, Harry. I'd better go home. Thank you. I'll walk to Piccadilly Tube station."

"What about the taxi?"

"Maybe next time." She was smiling at him again. Playing with him.

"Will there be a next time?"

"You should take out Elsie. She really liked you. You owe her that much."

Before Harry could call their waiter to give him the bill, she was standing up, her small bag in her hand. He walked her to the door where Dimitri gave Petronella her coat. They parted at the door. Harry went back to their table. There was still a glass of wine in the bottle. Sidney came over to join him.

"How did it go, Harry?"

"You know, I have absolutely no idea."

"I'm in the wrong business. I got six tables to pay me for photographs. Twelve quid for an hour's work."

"You are going to develop the photographs and post them?"

"You think Roland will let me keep the money?"

"Give me back my two quid."

"Dimitri wants me to do it again."

"He's always polite to customers. She was looking so pretty."

"She'll look just as pretty in the morning newspaper."

"You want some wine, Sidney? There's only one glass left."

"Then get another bottle."

"Excuse me, are you a professional photographer?"

"As a matter of fact I am. For the *Daily Mirror*. Don't worry, you'll get your photographs."

The man walked back to his table. Everyone at the table craned their necks to look at Sidney. They were all smiling.

When Harry and Sidney left the restaurant the bunch of flowers was still on the table. The flowers were drooping. They needed water. They looked sad, lost and lonely.

PART III

JUNE TO JULY 1963

HEROES OF THE REVOLUTION

1

*J*osiah Makoni and Livingstone Sithole slipped over the Rhodesian border at the end of June. The rains had finished three months earlier. They had travelled down Lake Nyasa from the newly independent Tanganyika where they had helped set up a military camp. Josiah had met Livingstone in Siberia, both doing their military training. The crossing into Rhodesia was a kilometre up from where the Mazoe River, on its way to the Zambezi, crossed the Mozambique border. The country was wild, not a sign of another living soul. Crossing the Zambezi had been the most dangerous part of their three-week journey, the *makori*, a canoe carved from a single tree trunk, difficult to paddle across the swift-flowing river watched by the crocodiles. They were both hot, tired and hungry, neither of them used to living off the land. Through Nyasaland and Mozambique neither of them had carried a gun. To succeed they had to be invisible. Two more poor Africans on their way to find a job on one of the white-owned tobacco farms in Southern Rhodesia. They were dressed in old second hand clothes and looked what they were, dirty and hungry.

"Can we make a fire, Josiah?" said Livingstone in Shona.

"Of course we can. When the guinea fowl go up to roost I'm going to knock one out of the tree. Dad taught me the trick. Once up in the tree with the light fading they don't like to move."

"How far are we from the road that links Salisbury with Tete?"

"Twenty miles. Maybe more."

"I didn't know this part of the country was so empty of people."

"In three days I want to be home. My poor mother. She'll get the surprise of her life me turning up. What I want most in the world is a proper meal, Livingstone. My mother is the best cook in the whole of Africa. Meat and vegetables, slow cooked in an iron pot over the open fire."

"Do you think it will work?"

"Don't look so nervous, Livingstone. A white man isn't going to jump out at you from the bushes. Recruiting our people to fight for their rights shouldn't be difficult. We're going to pay them once they get to the training camp. Have faith in the course, my friend. First we are going to walk back to the Mazoe River. We'll catch some fish. I fished it as a boy from where Harry Brigandshaw built the first Mazoe dam. How's your leg?"

"Bloody awful."

"Could be worse. We're both still alive. If Petronella could see me now."

"Do you miss her?"

"I miss her body. And she's raising good money for ZAPU. Without money you can't do anything in this life."

"I'm hungry."

"Come on, Livingstone. This is just the beginning. It's probably going to get a lot worse."

By the river it was beautiful. They found mopane worms in the trees, with which they baited the hook of Livingstone's fishing line which he kept in his one good pocket. When the sun went down it began to grow cold. Livingstone caught a Zambezi bream. And another. Josiah stalked the guinea fowl roosting on the low bough of a tree, whacking one with a stick. The bird fell from its perch, Josiah picking it up and wringing its neck. They cooked the fish over the fire, the smell exciting, his mouth watering with hunger. When they ate the fish it was soft and sweet. Josiah gutted the guinea fowl and placed it in its feathers in the hot ashes of the fire. They could hear wild animals all round them. A second fire was left burning to keep off the animals. A hyena made its call from the darkened bush, sending fear through Josiah. He had eaten all his fish and was hungry, like the hyena. A wild dog barked. A lion roared from far away in the hills. He was back in Africa, pleased to be home, the only place he had ever wanted to live. He put more wood on the second fire sending firelight up into the riverine trees, some of them tall, fed by the water from the river. A pack of baboons got up in the tree above the fire and crapped all over them making them laugh. They yelled at the baboons, chasing them out of the tree.

"This tree must be their home," said Livingstone. "When's that bird going to be cooked?"

"Tomorrow morning. Give us strength for the day's walk. Later we'll walk at night. The moon will be better in three days' time. Full moon in a week. That fish was good."

"Made me more hungry. If only we had a gun. I could knock off one of those impala we saw earlier."

"It's so good to be home... My mother's name is Princess," Josiah said, smiling into the light of the fire. "My dad paid her father twenty cows. The most expensive bride in Mashonaland. She was his fourth wife, each with their own hut and children. I was my mother's only child. A girl from England painted her after she saw my mother at Harry Brigandshaw's funeral. She was so beautiful, my mother. The girl gave me the painting. I still have it, kept in England. Livy Johnston is now a famous artist, the painting of my mother worth a lot of money. I will never sell it. In exile in England it was all I had to remind me of home. Mum and Dad can't write so there were no letters. When I got my degree at Fort Hare and again at the London School of Economics they were so proud of me. I sent them messages through Kim Brigandshaw who started Photographic Safaris. Kim's a drifter. Never done anything with his life. Has a small allowance from his father's estate. Enough to live off. Last I heard he was doing bit parts on the West End stage in London."

"You talk a lot about these Brigandshaws."

"Our tribes go back generations. Harry Brigandshaw's father saved one of our tribe after a Matabele impi destroyed his father's village. Harry and my father, Tembo, grew up together on Elephant Walk. Harry paid for my education."

"And now we want to kick them back to England."

"None of the Brigandshaws live in Africa. They're English. Back where they belong. My education was part of their payment for what they took out of Africa. Harry Brigandshaw understood. He knew there was no future for the white man in Africa."

"What about Petronella?"

"We shall see."

"Are there any young girls in your father's village?"

"Probably. I'll put some more wood on the fire. Those lions are getting closer."

"Will the fire keep them off, Josiah?"

"I hope so. It's all we've got."

"The people we recruit will have to come back this way. They won't have our training."

"They're Africans. In their own country."

"Some of them will end up as dinner."

"Probably. Not everything is easy in life."

"What degree did you get in London?"

"PPE. Philosophy, politics and economics. Same as Tinus Oosthuizen, Harry Brigandshaw's nephew. Harry put him through Oxford. Tinus lives in America most of the time. His wife is the actress, Genevieve. She's famous in America."

"Never heard of her."

"She's old now. Acting serious parts on the West End stage. How Kim got his jobs. Where are your family, Livingstone?"

"I've told you a dozen times. You never listen. They live in Harare. My dad's the delivery boy for a company that makes neon signs in the industrial sites. Rides a scooter with a box on the back."

"I'm sorry. There were so many of us together in Siberia. Everyone's stories jumble in my mind. I won't forget again. I'm going to lie down and listen to my stomach rumble. Try and get some sleep. Whoever wakes up must stoke the fire."

"That last roar was closer, Josiah."

"Sleep next to the fire. It's cold at night. The fire's nice. We'll be all right. I know we will."

"I'm not so sure."

"You're twenty-three. I'm thirty-one. You get more philosophical as you get older."

"I'm not going to sleep."

"Good. You can stoke the fire. Goodnight."

Josiah lay down on the ground where he had piled some leaves and pulled a thin blanket over his shoulders. For a while he listened to the rumbles in his stomach; he was still hungry. Then he fell asleep.

When he woke it was morning. The fire had burned down to ashes. Livingstone was snoring, lying on his back.

Josiah got up and stretched. He felt good. The birds were singing. The lions had stopped roaring. At the river, down from the bank where they had camped, impala buck were drinking at the water. Two warthogs were on the other side of the river looking at him. Josiah went to the first fire and pulled his guinea fowl out of the ashes. Slowly, carefully he pulled the feathers and skin off the bird letting out a smell so good.

With his foot, he tickled Livingstone's ribs, waking him up.

"Breakfast time. Wake up. What happened to the fire last night?"

"I have no idea. God, that smells good."

"Come and eat."

THREE DAYS later Josiah arrived at the Mazoe Citrus Estate in the first light of morning having walked through the night. He was amazed. As far as the eye could see were swirling orange groves riding up and over the hills. The dam he remembered was now much bigger. At the foot of each circled tree, straight lines of them into the distance, were sophisticated drip irrigation pipes putting water directly onto the roots of the trees. Over where once had been the Brigandshaw family compound of five houses was a field of winter maize, overhead sprays watering the plants, the sun making colours in the mist of water. Everywhere he looked was lush. In the near distance, down by the river that flowed out from the sluice gates of the high concrete dam, was the old Elephant Walk native compound just as he remembered. On the other side of the dam that cut the gorge of the river was water. Lots and lots of water. He was home. Truly home.

They had cut the road to Salisbury two days earlier, getting a lift on a truck. They had sat on top of the bags of maize on the back of the truck. The driver was a white man. The man needed help unloading his maize at the grain marketing board depot when they got to Salisbury. For three hours, Josiah and Livingstone had sweated the two hundred pound bags off the farmer's truck. He paid them with a smile and a shilling. They had walked from the depot along the road to the black township of Harare where Livingstone introduced Josiah to his parents. That night and the following day he had stayed in the township where Livingstone was to look for recruits. They parted company, Josiah conscious of being alone.

Down the sides of the path to the river and his father's huts were orange trees. Some of the fruit was red. Josiah, wanting to slow the moment, picked one of the ripe oranges. He peeled the fruit, throwing the bits of peel into the trees. There was no one around. The fruit was sweet. Josiah picked and ate another orange as he idled along. A fish eagle called above the river high up in the morning sky. It was a beautiful day. The huts looked all the same. His mother was standing outside her hut on the dry hard-baked earth. When she saw him she began to cry. His father, stooped with age, came out of the hut. Josiah ran to them, folding his mother into his arms.

"Josiah, Josiah, Josiah."

"Hello, Mother. Hello, Father."

Then they were all crying.

Helping his father, they went inside.

"Are you hungry? Where have you come from? Why are you here? How long will you stay?"

"Mother. Slow down. All in good time. Just let me have a good look at you. My mother the Princess."

"You're so thin. What have you been doing with yourself, Josiah? When did you leave England?"

Not wishing to involve his parents in revolutionary politics, Josiah kept his mouth shut. Recruiting on their doorstep would be a mistake. There was a pot of cold stew on the hob which he ate with relish using a wooden spoon.

"Have you got any money, Josiah?" said his father when Josiah had finished scraping the bottom of the pot. "We get a pension. All of us. A white man comes out from Salisbury at the end of each month. We receive half what we were being paid when we were working on Elephant Walk for Harry Brigandshaw. And that continues for a man's widow. I will give you some money. How long are you staying?"

"A couple of days."

They looked at each other, his father's eyes sad.

"All that education," sighed Tembo. "There's a store on the citrus estate that sells us necessities. No more expensive than Salisbury. Owned by the company. You can go and buy what you need. A new pair of shoes... So you did not fly into Rhodesia?"

"No, Father."

"Then they don't know you are here."

The round hut had no windows. The open door let in the light. His old bed was still in the corner opposite the big bed of his parents. With four wives his father had not slept every night in the hut.

"What happened to the three other huts?"

"My children live in them when they come home. Goodson is still in the police."

Josiah got up from the small table having wiped the bottom of the pot with his fingers, licking them clean. He was still hungry.

"Is my brother here now?"

"No. He's stationed in Bindura. He looks so smart in his uniform."

"I'll bet he does. What do the others do?"

"Lovemore died. So did his sister Happiness. They were much older than you. A father should never have to bury his children. One of his boys is working on the mines in Johannesburg. We never hear from him. When children grow up they go their own way. We worry about our children and grandchildren more than they worry about us. So long as they are happy, we are happy. Are you happy, Josiah? Why don't you have a wife?"

"I have a girlfriend in England."

"Is she nice?" asked his mother, smiling. "What's her name? What does she do?"

"Petronella. She works for the party."

"She's a nice Shona girl? Who are her family?"

"She's white. They own a tobacco farm outside Macheke."

Both parents looked at him surprised.

"You will stay in England with her?"

"No, Mother. Not for always. Is my fishing line still in the drawer?"

"Have a look. I haven't moved anything. Sit down. You're still hungry. I'll cook you some food."

When the mealie pap was cooked Josiah ate his fill, the first time since leaving the ferryboat at the southern end of Lake Nyasa. He sat outside the pole and dagga hut on a wooden chair his father had salvaged when they knocked down the Brigandshaw houses to make room for the maize field, the old houses in disrepair. They avoided the subject of politics and Josiah's half-brother Goodson. He would have to be careful. Goodson's mother, the eldest of the wives who dominated the four families, had been jealous of Josiah's much younger mother. Goodson would be thirty-five, the last of her nine children.

Taking the fishing line out of the old drawer, Josiah went down to the river. In his mother's kitchen garden behind the hut he had dug up some worms. His father had gone off on village business, stooping in his old age, the old eyes running with moisture.

The river was peaceful under the trees. Where he sat was at a bend in the river. He could not see the dam. The gorge was deep. Josiah baited the hook out of habit and threw the line in the river. He was a small boy again, no longer a politician. He would like to have read a newspaper but had not dared to look for one.

Two young girls came down to the river and sat on the bank. They were looking at him and giggling. Both of the girls were pretty with firm young breasts. He had not had a girl since Petronella, before he went to Russia. Desire flooded through him. The girls had seen the look he had given them. One of them came over. The other disappeared. She sat next to him and touched his thigh. Closer she looked younger, sixteen or seventeen. They were hidden from the village by the green of the leaves on the trees.

"Hello, Josiah. You've come home. Don't you want a wife?"

The girl's voice was soft. He took her hand. She put his hand on the inside of her thigh. There was nothing under the material of her yellow dress. Nothing. She lay back and pulled him on top, helping him take off his trousers. The late morning sun dappled them through the trees. For a long time they lay on their backs holding hands looking up into the canopy of the trees. The girl had been a virgin. An hour later they made love. Again she cried out at first in pain making Josiah the more excited. Both of them fell asleep. When he woke the girl was gone. He did not know her name. For the rest of the day he could think of nothing but the girl by the river.

At home his mother was smiling. So was his father. The iron pot was over the open fire outside the hut. He was hungry again. After they ate in the early evening they all went to bed in the hut. He was back in his own bed. He was home. All night he dreamed of Petronella. Once he woke sweating with fear. His father and mother were snoring in their corner of the rondavel. Then he slept until morning, woken by the call of the frogs from the river. All day he did not leave the hut. When it was dark he said goodbye.

"Be careful," said his father.

They hugged each other. Then he hugged his mother. In the new shoes his father bought for him at the store, Josiah walked out into the night. There was a moon. He followed the path through the orange trees to the road that lead north to Concession and the new white farming block of Centenary. Looking back he could see the moon reflected on the surface of the dam. It was beautiful. He put his best foot forward and began to walk. If the girl had known his name it would not take long to get back to Goodson. He had had to go home. He had owed that much to his mother and father. He still did not know the young girl's name as he walked, whistling in the moonlight. The new shoes were pinching him, his new jacket warm in the cold of the night. Owls called to each other from the trees. He could hear the swish of the overhead irrigation watering the field of maize. He could smell the scent of the water. He ate two more oranges from the trees. It was not so bad. His mother had cried. His father had looked at him from his chair. The man was so old. Josiah knew without being told his father hated what his son was doing.

Much later when the moon went down Josiah sat under a tree. His feet were hurting. He had walked some twenty miles. In the bushes he could hear the scrabbling of animals. The owls, some far away and faint, were still calling each other.

WHEN THE LIGHT came up in the morning, followed by the sun, he was close to the fence of a white man's farm. The scrabbling had been the sound of cattle. One of them, a big bull, was looking at him, grass hanging from his mouth. The bull had stopped chewing. Josiah looked at the fence between them on the side of the strip road.

A car went by on its way to Salisbury, the white driver taking no notice of a black man sitting by the side of the road under a tree. The sun was warm on his face before Josiah got to his feet. His feet still hurt from the new shoes. Another white farmer passed down the road in a truck. The man stared at Josiah. A kilometre further up the road the strips stopped, giving way to a dirt road. When a car passed it trailed a long cloud of dust that made Josiah choke. He was eating the white man's dust.

Later, off the road, were rows of tobacco curing barns, the flues from the barns not showing any smoke.

Behind the barns on a ridge was a white man's bungalow, the garden green and lush. There were sprinklers watering the garden.

For the rest of the day Josiah walked on up the dirt road. He had learnt to turn away and cover his face when the occasional car went by. When the sun climbed high it was hot. Josiah drank from his water bottle.

At the end of the third day, Josiah came to a Tribal Trust Land and the huts of his people. He had survived hunger by picking cobs of maize from the white man's fields. On one side of the TTL was a white man's farm, the land full of long grass and trees. Far away on a high ridge he could make out a house, the land round the bungalow lush and green. On the other side the goats had eaten what was left of the grass to the roots. Most of the trees had gone, cut down for firewood. Long-legged chickens, thin, were scratching the dirt from side to side. Small children with malnourished pot bellies stared at him from outside the huts. An old woman stared at him where she sat on an old wooden chair. One of the chair's legs was missing. Josiah approached her.

"Which is the headman's hut?"

"Over there."

She didn't smile or get up. Josiah walked to the headman's hut. They would give him hospitality, a Shona custom for travellers.

When the men and women came back from the fields at the end of the day he sat down with them. Some were young men of military age. When he told them about the training camp and how much they would be paid he could see their eyes light up, their tiredness go. All of them were thin. Life on the TTL, surrounded by the white man's prosperous farms, was hard.

"We can either work for the white man for little pay or stay where we are."

"Not anymore, my friend. Now you can join the army. When we win we will give you the white man's farms."

"How do we get to Tanganyika?"

"I will explain to you. Go in small groups. Help each other. Our people will feed you on the way. Spread the good word."

That night the drums played. The people were happy. Josiah sat on the ground nursing his bare feet. The blisters were terrible. The six months in Siberia had not wiped out the soft life of London. It would be a week before he could walk without pain. Only then would he put on his shoes. With his sore feet in an old bucket of water, Josiah watched his new friends dance to the drums. The headman had brought out gourds of fermented maize beer. The young men were drinking and dancing with the girls. Josiah smiled and tried not to think of the aches and pains in his body. He would have liked to move on the next day but his feet wouldn't let him. A fire had been built near the drums throwing firelight on the dancers. Some of them were swaying in a trance from the rhythmic beat of the drums. There were two cowhide drums. When one of the drummers was too tired to continue another took over, not missing a beat. Josiah drank some of the thick white beer. After the third tin mugful he felt better. They wanted him to dance. He got up and stood on the one spot and swayed with the beat. The rhythm was intoxicating, taking his mind away from his body.

When he went to bed in the headman's hut he was tired and happy. Then he slept, his thin blanket over his body on the hard-baked floor.

When he woke in the morning the headman's wife was brushing out the evil spirits as she did every day. In her hand was a bundle of brush tied at the top to give her a grip. Each sweep was a few inches above the ground. She smiled at Josiah as she swept the brush towards the door. Josiah smiled back at her.

When he went outside on his swollen feet, the men and women had gone to the fields. From the entrance to the hut Josiah looked out over the village to the white man's fence and the faraway house on the hill. For a long time Josiah looked at the bungalow. There was woodsmoke coming from a chimney. Probably a kitchen fire making the white man's breakfast, the thought of bacon and eggs with Walls' pork sausages making him hunger for good English food with a cup of hot coffee. He could have got a job in London. The big corporations wanted men with degrees in economics. The thought brought him back to Petronella, making Josiah wonder what she was doing on a Wednesday morning. The headman had said that yesterday was a Tuesday. Josiah had had no idea. When his feet were better he would walk north to the other side of the Centenary. To the other side of the white man's farms, down to the Zambezi Valley where more of his people lived. Then he would walk through the valley and visit the tribal villages. Deliberately, Josiah stopped himself looking at the faraway house on the hill. He was home with his people. That mattered the most. They would eat at lunchtime, the one meal a day. Until then he would stay hungry with the rest of them.

Echoing over the valley came the sound of a motorcycle bringing Josiah's eyes back to the house on the ridge. He could see the house would command a view of the country all round, and to the distant blue hills towards the Zambezi Valley. He envied the man living on the hill with a family.

"That house must have the perfect view," Josiah said to himself in English.

The headman's wife looked at him queerly, the *tokolosh* brush still in her hand. They were both so different. For a moment Josiah wanted to throw it all up and go back to London. Find himself a good job. Buy a house. Settle down and have a family. Live like a white man.

"You're not going far on those feet," he again said in English. Only softly, so the headman's wife couldn't hear. He smiled at her. She smiled back and went about her work.

"You'd better stop speaking English before you piss them off. Damn those new shoes. Think, Josiah. Always think what you're doing."

2

*C*lay Barry, member-in-charge for Centenary, strode across the lawn hitting the hard black gaiter of his right leg with his swagger stick. He could see Jeremy Crookshank eating his breakfast on the *stoep*, the place wide open. He waved when Jeremy looked up.

"To what do we owe the pleasure, Clay?"

"That looks good."

"You want some breakfast? Come and sit down. I'll ring for Silas. Bacon and eggs. Colcom's best pork sausages and fried tomatoes. How does that sound? Come and sit down."

"Why aren't you in the lands?"

"The pleasures of having an assistant. Bobby Preston is watching the gang. The boys are weekly boarders. Peace and quiet. What can I do for you?"

"That chap Josiah Makoni is back in the country. Wasn't he a friend of Livy's?"

"They knew each other in London. Never met the chap myself. Did you come on a motorcycle? Thought it was Bobby back from the lands."

"When I go alone I prefer a motorcycle. Lets the air in my lungs. That really does look good."

Clay sat down at the breakfast table, making himself comfortable.

"The connection with Livy was Harry Brigandshaw. She saw Josiah's mother at Harry's funeral. Painted her later from a sketch. At an exhibition at the Nouvelle Galerie, *Princess* was on display. Josiah had heard from my brother Paul and paid a visit. Later, Livy gave Josiah the painting of his mother... Silas. Another cup. Can you cook the same again for Inspector Barry?... What's the problem, Clay?"

Clay Barry waited for Silas to go back to the kitchen before he answered the question, watching Jeremy carry on with his breakfast.

"He's been all over the papers in London this last year. Our friends over there say Josiah went to Russia for military training. His girlfriend blew the whistle to a reporter at the *Daily Mirror*."

"Charming. Who's his girlfriend?"

"A friend of yours. You worked for her father. Must be ten years ago. She's a communist."

"Petronella! Now there was a stuck-up brat. As bad as her mother. Tried not to give me my bonus at the end of the first season. Livy had a row with them at Roger Crumpshaw's wedding. Right out in the open at Meikles Hotel. Does the mother know Josiah's the boyfriend? That should be fun. She's a snob, is Flossy Maple. Snob of the first order. After the row I left my job. Later old Bertie Maple gave me my bonus from the safe where he kept the boys' wages. It was all Flossy Maple's money. She was a Sheckland-Hall. Pots of money. She was the one trying to gap me. A real bitch. Haven't seen them for years. How do you know Josiah is in Rhodesia? What's he doing here?"

"Stirring up trouble we think. His brother is a constable at Bindura."

"You mean he shopped his own brother? What has the world come to, Clay?"

"We think he's recruiting an army. Funded by the Russians. All part of the Cold War. They are only half-brothers. The member-in-charge at Bindura thinks Goodson is jealous of his younger brother."

"You know Harry Brigandshaw paid for his education? Brother Paul's married to Beth, Harry's only daughter."

"Fort Hare in the Eastern Cape is a breeding ground for African Nationalism. Mugabe was at Fort Hare. If I'm not wrong, so was Mandela. Keep your eyes and ears open, Jeremy. Let's leave it at that."

"Last night they were playing the drums all night in the TTL. Sound travels far at night."

"That's odd. They usually only party on Saturday nights."

"Thought it odd myself. Here comes your breakfast."

"Didn't know I was so hungry."

"Tuck in. When the fire's hot the food cooks quickly. Better give us a fresh pot of tea, Silas."

"So how are the boys?"

"They're fine. They still miss Livy. Still talk about her."

"Their poor mother. Shocking way to go. Eaten by lions. Sorry, Jeremy."

"I look at Livy's painting of Carmen every morning in the lounge. Her eyes follow me."

"Is Livy coming back to Africa?"

"Livy thinks we're all doomed in this part of the world. That the white man has no future in Africa."

"Has she seen Josiah recently?"

"I have no idea. How's the sausage?"

"Perfect."

"No, Livy's not coming back. We still write to each other. We own a block of flats together in Chelsea close to Livy's studio. She wants me to sell World's View and go back to live in England."

"Are you going?"

"When Africa gets in your blood you are doomed in more ways than one. World's View is my home. Just look at that view, Clay. Would you want to go and bury yourself in London under that leaden grey sky? There's space in Africa. A man has his freedom... Thank you, Silas. I'll pour the tea."

"If we don't get our independence with Britain's agreement you won't be able to get your money out of the country. The British government are threatening economic sanctions if Winston Field doesn't toe the line. The Federation comes to an end in December. If you are thinking of selling World's View and getting your money out of Southern Rhodesia you haven't much time left. That's as an old friend. Just don't quote me or they'll all get in a flap."

"You think we won't survive on our own after Welensky hands over?"

"There are two hundred and fifty thousand whites in the self-governing Crown Colony of Southern Rhodesia. You think that's enough to defy the world? I don't think so. We have our heads in the sand."

"What are you going to do?"

"My job. I was born in Rhodesia. So were my mother and father. This is my only home. We'll soldier on. Just don't think you will be able to change your mind later on and still get out your money."

"It's not that bad surely? The blacks need us to run the country. To keep law and order and run the economy."

"Tell that to Josiah Makoni. Did they teach you to use a rifle in the navy? Didn't you do your national service in the Royal Navy just after the war?"

"We all did our square bashing. Army, navy, or air force. I was a good shot. Still am. You want some more breakfast?"

"Could Silas rustle up a couple more of those sausages?"

"Of course he can. What that bell's for. You playing cricket on Sunday?"

"Not this week. This Josiah business has caused a bit of a flap. He's a dangerous bastard. The man's educated and clever."

"My father said it was all the same wherever you were in the world. If you have something of commercial value there's always someone trying to get it off you. By fair means or foul... That you, Silas? Two more sausages for Inspector Barry... Do you think Winston Field is a good prime minister?"

"Who knows? Some say Ian Smith would stand up better to the British. Now there's a real Rhodesian."

"Pass me your cup and I'll pour you some more tea."

"Do you miss Carmen very much?"

"Carmen and Livy. Both of them. Very much. Can't look at other girls. Anyway, I have my hands full bringing up the two boys... What's Sir Roy Welensky to do when he's no longer Federal Prime Minister?"

"Write a book, Jeremy. They all write a book. Brush up their image for posterity. Argue their mistakes. It's rather like a motor car accident. When you get the statements independently from the two drivers you can't believe it's the same bloody accident. Who are Centenary playing this weekend at the club?"

"Macheke. My old side. I always like playing against Roger Crumpshaw. I worked for him after I left Bertie Maple and his bitch of a wife... Josiah and Petronella. If it was all over the papers she must know. One up to Josiah."

"How was the season?

"Best ever. Best yield and best prices. Quality wasn't so good. I sold it all while prices were high. Some of the buyers are building up their stocks of tobacco."

"In case of sanctions. That'll bugger up the prices."

"Bugger up everything. My brother Paul looks after my investments in London. Sent him thirty-three thousand quid from this year's crop."

"That's a lot of money out of the country."

"You have to think ahead. I only just got all the tobacco through the curing barns before it over-ripened in the lands."

"Doesn't help a policeman. All we have to look forward to is a pension. Thanks for breakfast."

"Always my pleasure. See you in the club."

"Get some runs on Sunday."

"I'll try."

Left to his own, Jeremy stared out into the distance. He heard Clay kick-start the powerful motorcycle. He felt uneasy. Clay, the ever sanguine Clay, looked worried. It was the drums. He could still hear the drums from the night. Menacing. Something wrong. Maybe they knew. The drums talking. There was so much he didn't know about Africa.

"She's right, of course. You're living in a fool's paradise."

Jeremy sat thinking, his tea getting cold. He had no other profession except the navy and they wouldn't want him back again at the age of thirty-five. What would he do in England? A man had to work. Couldn't do a Kim Brigandshaw and bugger around for the rest of his life, however much money he got out of the country. Livy would always have her painting wherever she lived. What would he do in England? They didn't grow tobacco in England. Farming was different. Cold, dreary, soaked by the rain. A man couldn't sit on his *stoep* having breakfast in the morning and look out over the hills and beyond forever.

When he drank his last cup of tea it was lukewarm. Getting up from the breakfast table, Jeremy followed Clay's path across the lawn to the sheds where he had left his motorcycle. He would visit the stumping where Bobby was watching them clear a new land for next year's tobacco. It was his farm. Everything he saw he had dreamed about and created himself. Out of the virgin bush. All that tobacco, all that maize to feed the people. All those jobs.

"To hell with it. You only have one life. Enjoy what you have while you have it. Let tomorrow take care of itself."

Feeling better with himself, Jeremy found his two-stroke motorcycle and kick-started the motor to life.

"It's not all bad. You could have been stuck in an office in London like Paul for the rest of your life, working for your father-in-law's company. Bored out of your mind. Never creating anything worthwhile all your damn life.

Clay was right. It was good for a man to get the air down his lungs.

3

S itting on a bench outside the headman's hut, his feet out of the bucket of water, his new shoes on the ground next to him, Josiah was conscious of a second motorcycle far away in the hills of rolling country, the sound different. Then he heard the first motorcycle again, more powerful, much nearer to the TTL. The headman's wife came out of the hut where she had been working thumbing the corn off the cobs of maize into a stone mortar where she would crush them into mealie meal with a stone pestle ready to cook into mealie pap. She listened and looked frightened.

"A police motorcycle," she said. "Best you go, Josiah. Quickly."

"Where do I go?"

He was panicked, looking from his swollen bare feet to his new shoes that had done all the damage.

"Go into the bush."

The roar of the heavy motorcycle was getting closer, drowning out the distant, fading sound of the second motorcycle. Josiah got up and ran, forgetting the pain in his feet, adrenaline giving him strength to flee. He ran away from the sound of the motorcycle through the scattered huts and into a field of young potatoes, the green of the shoots, watered by buckets brought up from the river, coming up to his knees. He ran on, not looking back. The ground was now hard from lack of rain leaving no spoor as he fled through the bush. Simulation in Russia with a rifle in his hand had never felt the same. He was cornered. They knew. They were looking for him. Someone had told the police. They would shoot him on sight and ask no questions. Josiah ran on into the veld where some trees were still growing. Deep in the trees was an anthill higher than himself. It was an old anthill with a hole in one side where the aardvarks had pushed inside to feast on the termites. Josiah crawled inside, his heart pounding. He could hear the motorcycle, slower and closer, hoping the bike would go past the village. The sound of the engine stopped. Josiah cowered in the hole, feeling the white ants crawl over his bare feet. They were not biting. He looked back over his shoulder and hoped he was hidden. Then he began to pray to God through his ancestors that no one would find him. He no longer thought of his feet or his lunch. All he felt was the most powerful desire for survival.

CLAY BARRY PUT his bike up on the stand and looked around, hands on his hips. No one came anywhere near him. No one liked a policeman. There was a song they sang in the British Army about the military police. Some of the newer recruits from England were prone to sing it in the mess when they'd had a few drinks. 'All coppers are bastards' went the opening line. Taking the swagger stick from under his left arm with his right hand he began a rhythmic tapping on his hard black gaiter. He was surrounded by huts. A chicken came up and scratched the hard-baked ground in front of him. The chicken took no notice of his well-polished leather boots and scratched all round. Clay took off his peaked hat by lifting the band from under his chin. He wiped his brow with the back of his hand. Once he stopped riding the bike the sweat began to trickle down from under his hat. With the band pulled tight above the peak he put the hat back on his head and strode towards the headman's hut. All the able-bodied men and women were working the fields. The place was dry and arid. So different to Jeremy Crookshank's lush green lawns. Clay felt sorry for them. Living in the TTL was a life of hard sweat and toil. There was little reward. Around him eternal Africa. As it had been ever since man came out of the caves and down from the trees.

The old woman he knew to be the headman's wife came out of the hut and stared at him. Clay was a big man with broad shoulders, she an old stooped woman. He smiled at her, stopping the rhythmic banging with the stick on his gaiter. Her eyes said she hated him. 'All coppers are bastards,' sang in his head. It was all part of the job.

"Where's Chirow?" he asked her in Shona.

"In the fields."

"Which fields?"

"I don't know."

"I'll wait for him to come back for lunch."

The old girl looked frightened. Her eyes went to a new pair of expensive brown leather shoes. Clay bent down and picked them up.

"Nice pair of new shoes," he said to her.

The shoes smelt. Someone had been wearing them. Holding the shoes, Clay looked around. Potbellied *piccanins* had come out of the shade of the huts to look at him. They all needed proper feeding. Left to their own peasant farming the people were always hungry. They needed tractors and fertiliser. Modern farming. They were still doing what they had done a hundred years ago when there were only a few people in groups of huts scattered through the bush. Clay's grandfather, who had come up from South Africa on the Pioneer Column on the orders of Cecil Rhodes, had told him all the stories of the bush empty of men and teeming with animals. Now there were too many people – with their goats, that when desperate for food ate the roots of the grass. There were no trees in the compound. No shade. Clay waited patiently in the heat of the sun. Everything looked normal. Except for the shoes. And the drums Jeremy had heard last night. Drums on a Tuesday.

Clay waited into the day. No one came back from the fields. Someone must have gone to tell the headman. Clay again picked up the shoes and noted the make. The shoes were made in Bulawayo. They were too big for Chirow who never wore shoes, the soles of his feet as hard as nails. Clay put down the shoes in front of the old woman and smiled. She looked away from him. He'd take a bet the shoes had come from the company store on the Mazoe Citrus estate. Where Goodson reported his brother had been seen with their father. Josiah was walking. Walking with sore feet. They'd pick him up soon enough.

"Not very bright," he said to himself out loud in English. "Too much academic education, old boy. Bloody Russians are useless."

He said goodbye to the old girl in Shona. Said he would be coming back. As he left, he kicked the new pair of shoes, bringing the fear back into her eyes.

"What have you been up to here, Josiah?" The poor sods would end up as cannon fodder. Fighting for communism. For the Russians. And when it was all over they'd end up with bugger all. If they were alive. The bastards. All Russians were bastards. And all the rest of them back through history. People using other people to fight their wars.

The bike fired at the first kick. He let out the clutch and turned the bike round. She was still looking at him. With the chin-strap back in place he began to ride home, the wind in his lungs, the sweat on his brow evaporating.

"Sell your bloody farm, Jeremy. Before it's too late."

Where will it all end, he asked himself? Or was there never an end? Only the petty day-to-day squabblings of man. Then he looked all round him, throttling back the BSA motorcycle, the big engine idling smoothly. All round was the beauty of nature. Birds in the sky. Cattle in the white man's fields. It was all so beautiful.

The slow ride home to the Centenary police station calmed him down. Removed his sadness. Made him glad to be alive.

Fred Rankin was waiting for him in the charge office, his second-in-command.

"Didn't find anything," said Fred. "Everything normal."

"He's in the TTL behind World's View. Had breakfast with Jeremy. Told me last night they were playing the drums. On a bloody Tuesday. Be a good chap, give the Mazoe Citrus Estate a ring. Ask them if they stock brown shoes made by Watsons. They have a factory in Bulawayo. I'm going home for a shower. Been standing in the sun half the day. The old girl's body language reeked of fear. My guess is they're recruiting. They'll have a training camp somewhere in the bush we have to find. Find that camp, keep it watched, and we'll catch Josiah Makoni."

"How did he get in the country?"

"God knows. Chances are there are more than one of them fanned out through the country."

"Does this mean trouble?"

"Big trouble, Fred. Big fucking trouble if we don't jump on it quick. I'll be informing the army. Bloody Russians. Why can't they keep their argument with America in Europe? What's it got to do with Africa? This won't affect the Americans. Just poor sods like us. And Josiah Makoni. Why the hell did Harry Brigandshaw have to educate him? There's an old saying. 'A little knowledge is a dangerous thing.' A lot makes them conniving bastards."

"Had Jeremy met him?"

"Only his artist girlfriend. That farm is so beautiful. No wonder he called it World's View. You can see forever... Mary's cooking some fish she brought out from Salisbury. Plenty to go round. Bring Joyce. Around six o'clock in time for sundowners. A cold beer. What wouldn't I give for a cold Castle."

"Don't break the rules, Clay. Six o'clock the bar opens. All across the Centenary. We'd love to come. I'll phone the Citrus Estate right away if the exchange in Salisbury can put me through."

"Six o'clock."

"Six o'clock. On the dot. Fish, you say? Haven't had a nice piece of fish for ages. I'm sick of beef."

"Tomorrow I'll get the army to send in some choppers and stake out that TTL. He can't go far. My guess is his feet are sore. Why he left his shoes. Too late to get the army out now."

"There's so much bush around there. They all look the same to the army. One black looks like any other. If he's blended in it'll be difficult."

"Why we need to find that training camp... Anything else while I've been away?"

"Not a bloody thing."

"See you tonight. They're going to launch a war of terrorism. Like they did in Kenya. Only more sophisticated than Mau Mau. More equipment. Better training. It's going to be a right royal bugger."

"We'll cope."

"I suppose so."

4

*J*osiah walked back to the headman's hut when the sun went down, covered in red dust. He was trying to think. The motorcycle had driven away long after it had arrived, suddenly breaking into life and sending his heart racing. The termites had not bitten him. He could walk on his feet, the blisters more on the sides of his toes. When he saw the scattered brown shoes, as if someone had kicked them, he understood. More than anything, university had taught him to think.

None of the young men, his friends the night before, came out to greet him. The headman and his wife looked frightened. The policeman, wherever he was, had waited after seeing his brand new shoes.

"You've got to leave," said the headman, looking perplexed.

Josiah rubbed some of the dust from the anthill out of his hair. His feet were now hurting and he hadn't eaten all day.

"It was the member-in-charge," said the headman's wife. "He picked up your shoes and smiled. The Scorpion. He's clever. You better go before he comes back with his men and police van. He was looking for you."

"My brother, Goodson, is a policeman in Bindura. A sell out."

"You must go," said the headman.

"I can't with these feet. Think of the struggle. When we liberate our brothers you and your wife will be heroes. Heroes of the revolution. Children will know your names. Better I stay and work in the fields. They don't know what I look like. On my own in the bush they will see me. Among my new friends they won't."

"A hero of the revolution?"

"That's what I said."

"And if your brother comes?"

"I will kill him. My friends will kill him. He will be an enemy of the revolution."

"How will you kill him?"

"With my bare hands."

"They won't let you. They have guns."

"My brother can't check the face of everyone in the fields. How can he do that? If they come, everyone will keep moving around. They will see the same faces. Confuse them. I haven't seen my brother for almost thirteen years. The year I went to Fort Hare. He was jealous. Goodson was jealous. He hated me. So did his mother. She was my father's chief wife. My mother was young and beautiful. Most nights my father stayed in the hut with my mother. Goodson will not recognise his brother."

Josiah watched them smile. Neither knew his face had been more recently in the British press. The police in Rhodesia would have copies of the newspapers.

"There is nothing to worry about," said Josiah, putting his arm round the headman's shoulders, his other round his wife. "Heroes of the revolution. Both of you. What are we having to eat?"

"This morning, before the Scorpion came on his motorcycle, we killed a chicken. Slow cooked in the pot with beans and vegetables."

"Like my mother cooks."

"Heroes of the revolution," said the headman's wife.

"That's right. Tomorrow I work for my keep. You are both good people. Tomorrow my feet will be better. I will work in the fields."

He smiled at them in turn as they went inside the hut. In the middle, below the ventilation hole in the centre of the peaked roof, was a three-legged iron pot over the fire. Where three sticks joined in the fire right underneath it were small flames licking the bottom of the blackened pot. The headman's wife took the lid off the pot and smiled up at him. The smell was so good.

"When will the food be ready?"

"Soon."

"After supper I will sleep. Tomorrow's a big day."

"Heroes of the revolution," said the headman, beaming.

"That's right."

Josiah was so hungry he wanted to grab the food out of the pot. Burn his hands. It didn't matter.

The old woman took the iron pot off the fire and replaced it with another one.

"Mealie pap," she said, smiling.

"How long?"

"An hour. We are always hungry. It doesn't matter."

JOSIAH CARRIED two buckets of water up from the river, his sore feet covered in mud. The buckets were heavy, the distance from the river to the potato field over a kilometre. It was hot, the sun right overhead. They had only eaten half the chicken the previous night, saving the rest for today. Never before had Josiah been so poor. His father as bossboy of Elephant Walk had always put plenty of food on the tables in the four huts of his four wives and their children. When there was drought Harry Brigandshaw had used money saved from the good years to bring food from Salisbury to feed the gang. His father, Sebastian, had done the same before he was killed by the Great Elephant.

Josiah put down the buckets to rest his back. There had to be a better way of getting the water up from the river. He could see in his mind's eye the overhead irrigation at the Citrus Estate swishing in the sun. Soon the river would dry up. There wasn't a dam. From far away he felt the vibration of engines, his whole mind coming alert. He had felt the vibration before in Russia. Then he heard the sound of the engines and the rotor blades going round and round. Helicopters. They were helicopters. Three of them. Picking up the buckets, Josiah plodded on up the hill. He had blended in looking like the rest of them. The girl behind had a bigger bucket balanced on her head. She walked on past him, her back so straight. The girl was young and pretty. She hadn't noticed the helicopters, but if she had she didn't care. The potatoes they were growing were precious. The helicopters were definitely coming their way, the sound growing as he humped his buckets. Then he saw them over the trees. He was wrong. There were four of them. Headed for Chirow's village. 'Damn those bloody shoes,' he said to himself in English. 'How bloody stupid could I have been? Panic. Never panic. I panicked. Left them for anyone to see.' The dust from the anthill was still all over him. There wasn't enough water to wash the previous night. Now he was glad he had not swum with the children in the river. He looked dirty like the rest of them. Impoverished. Poor. He was going to be all right. He was certain. They were not going to shoot him. If Goodson was in one of the helicopters he would avoid his eyes. Bend his back like the rest of them. Look like the rest of them. One more black toiling in the midday sun, one more poor African.

His stomach churning, he went on up the hill. The helicopters were hovering over the huts throwing up clouds of dust. They didn't care what they did to the people. He hated them. One day he would have a rocket launcher in his hand and blow them out of the sky. He hated them. For the first time he really hated them. It gave him strength.

When Josiah came back with two more buckets of water, white men were walking through the field of potatoes looking at the people. He had covered his feet thoroughly with mud down at the river to hide his blisters and look like the rest. He went about his business slopping water on the potato plants. They were higgledy piggledy, one plant here, one plant there. There had been no method in the planting. Done properly in ridged rows they would be easier to water. None of the plants would miss out. They would dig twice as many potatoes from the same field with little more work. He would suggest planting in straight rows to the headman. All the time Josiah kept his head down, not looking at the soldiers. The men were all young, most of them fresh out of England. It was a way for young men to get out of England, joining the Rhodesian army or the British South Africa Police. A way out of the cold. The British had done it for centuries, sending their best young men to the colonies. Josiah felt in the wet soil around the potato plant that was struggling to grow. Deliberately he wiped the sweat from his face. All the young men and women working the field had done the same at the headman's request. The soldiers walked on through, spread out in a line. They walked on down the slope to the river where the children were playing. They didn't talk to the people. The people didn't look up from their work. Both sides were oblivious of each other. The men in the field moved around so the same soldier would not come back and see them.

Later, the helicopters took off. All four of them. All the white men had gone. Josiah smiled. So did the men who were going to the camp in Tanganyika. They were confident again. Happy again.

Josiah waited over a week but the white men did not come back again. He had swapped his new shoes with a man whose feet were the same size as his own. The man was proud of his new shoes. The old shoes were soft and pliable. They didn't hurt Josiah's feet. On the last night they brought out the maize beer and danced to the drums. It was a Saturday. All night, Josiah danced with the pretty young girl who had carried the bucket from the river balanced on a cloth ring round the top of her head. In the small of the night they made love in the bushes.

In the first light of dawn Josiah began his long walk to the Zambezi escarpment following the dirt road that led out through the white man's Centenary block. Twelve of the young men from the village had begun their journey to Tanganyika earlier in the week. Josiah had shaken the hand of the headman, giving him an African handshake which included the palm of the hand and the thumb. He had kissed the man's wife.

"Heroes of the revolution," she had said.

"Heroes of the revolution. Both of you."

Along the road a truck driven by a black man gave him a lift. There were three other blacks in the back of the open truck. His feet were no longer hurting. Later in the day he found the path at the top of the escarpment that led down into the valley. A small river tumbled over the cliff, the water turning to mist before it hit the bottom. The falling water looked like a bridal veil. Down below, some three thousand feet, was the Zambezi Valley, trees and bushes far as the eye could see. In the far distance Josiah could see the big river. There was a haze in the valley, shimmering in the heat of the day. Josiah swam in the river fifty yards back from the drop. The flow of the river had cut a rock pool out of the rocks. Over to one side his eye was caught by a bunch of flowers below a wooden cross. On the cross, above a burial mound, was an inscription. The inscription was in English. The words 'Go well, my darling' were burned into the wood. There was nothing else on the cross. There was the fresh bunch of flowers at the foot of the grave. The colour of the flowers had first caught the eye.

"I wonder who you are," said Josiah.

Then he looked up from the cross at the distant view.

What a wonderful place to be buried, he thought. Then he began his descent where the dirt road wound down the side of the escarpment. The road was steep but passable, even for a truck. Josiah began to whistle. He felt good. They hadn't found him. He hoped the twelve men arrived safely. He could feel the freedom all round him. It felt good. As he walked he thought of Petronella. 'Wait for me,' he said. 'Stay well my darling.' He was a sentimental old fool and he didn't give a damn.

5

The ball clipped the leg stump sending the bail flying, Jeremy Crookshank not concentrating on the cricket. He walked off the pitch without looking back while Roger Crumpshaw grinned at him from his fielding position at mid-on. Going in first wicket down, Jeremy had scored a duck for the first time playing for Centenary.

"It was a good ball, Jeremy. You can't win them all." Roger Crumpshaw was still grinning.

Jeremy thrashed the air with his bat in frustration. Fred Rankin passed him on the way back to the pavilion, a surprised look on his face.

"What happened?"

"Wasn't concentrating. Took my eye off the ball. We're going to lose this one if you don't score some runs."

Back in the pavilion Jeremy took off his pads and walked into the bar. The afternoon sun had been hot out in the field. There was no one else in the bar other than Noah the barman. The Centenary-Macheke game, postponed for a week, was going to end in a loss for Centenary. Roger Crumpshaw, Jeremy's old boss when he left the Maples' farm, had scored sixty-three runs hitting the Centenary bowling all over the ground. Looking back from the bar through the window to the veranda that ran the length of the pavilion he could see some of the wives. The wives were pretending to watch the cricket. The previous week one of the umpires had gone down with malaria at the last minute causing the match to be postponed. Carmen had seemingly enjoyed watching the cricket and socialising in the bar after the game. The previous morning, while Bobby Preston was watching the gang on their half day of stumping, Jeremy had driven the car to her grave, leaving her favourite flowers from the garden. Visiting the grave always made him feel lonely. Made him feel sorry for himself. Both boys had gone with him, the boys placing the flowers on their mother's grave. They stayed at the grave most of the afternoon. When they got back to World's View, all of them feeling miserable, Jeremy had opened a bottle of wine. By then it was six o'clock and time for a sundowner. Later that night, drunk on his own, the boys having been put to bed by Primrose the nanny, he had heard the drums far away in the TTL.

Playing cricket on a bad hangover, thinking of his wife, had led him to scoring a duck. By the time Clay Barry walked into the bar an hour later, Jeremy had drunk three beers.

"Why are you in uniform on a Sunday, Clay?"

"A policeman's work never ends. There's no sign of him. The man's vanished into thin air. One of the men in Chirow's village was wearing his shoes this morning. Said they were his. The man had shifty eyes."

"You want a drink?"

"Why not? Nothing more I can do today. How was your cricket?"

"Bloody awful. Scored a duck. Took the kids to see their mother's grave up on the escarpment. That waterfall is so beautiful. Last night I got drunk. What do you want to drink?"

"We were lucky to find her so far from her car. There wasn't much left by the lions."

"I don't want to talk about it."

"Sorry, old chap. I'll have a Castle. Make sure it's ice cold, Noah. The army found nothing. Not a trace of him except those damn shoes. Hope he's run for it back to England. Would Livy know if he got back?"

"I could always phone Petronella. She'd love to hear from me. When she was a kid of thirteen we thoroughly disliked each other. Little Miss Snob. Too high and mighty for the farm's lowly learner assistant. Why are people snobs? I'm being sarcastic. The last person I would wish to speak to is Petronella Maple. Has Goodson heard anything from his father?"

"Not a thing. We did confirm the company store sold him a pair of Watson's brown shoes."

"Have you chaps visited him?"

"He's very old. What can he say? Told them to leave him alone."

"There's a lot of bush out there. You can't cover everything. Where's Mary?"

"She's coming."

"Fred's batting. Doing better than me. You have to concentrate when batting. Keep your eye on the ball. Haven't heard from Livy for a while. She has an old flame in London. Works in the City. Pots of money. Wouldn't be surprised if they married."

"Wasn't she married briefly to one of the Brigandshaw boys?"

"Livy's little girl was Frank's daughter. Calls himself St Clair these days. Found out his mother had been playing around with the Honourable Barnaby St Clair. Flossy Maple said she wasn't surprised. That the woman was common. Oh, well. Cheers old boy. Another one down the hatch. Don't have much else to do these days. By now Carmen and I would have been a perfect match. Couple of drunks."

"Be careful driving home. There are cows on the road where the fence with the TTL has broken. Here comes Mary. What are you going to have, darling?"

"Isn't it a bit early, Clay?"

"It's Sunday. Had a lousy week. One big bloody frustration."

"Maybe it's all a storm in a teacup."

"I only wish it was."

"I'll have a lemonade, Noah... Why are you still in your uniform?"

"Too lazy to go home and change."

"How's the umpire? Malaria isn't good."

"We got a chap out from Salisbury. Didn't know his name. Someone said he played for Rhodesia before the war. A bit before my time."

As the beers went down Jeremy cheered up. By the time Macheke won the game he was quite happy. Clay and Mary had gone home. Clay didn't like to get drunk in the club. Said it was bad for his image. The boys came into the bar from where they had been playing around the pool. Primrose stayed just outside the door of the bar watching the children. Next to her, each held by a hand, were her own children. A boy and a girl. All the children were friends. It was time to take everyone home. And sit on his veranda. Drink on his own.

"Are you going, Jeremy?"

"Sorry, Roger. Give my love to Pamela. The boys. They need to go home. Bit of a bugger playing mother and father. Come on, Phil. Home James and don't spare the horses. Where's Randall? Take your eyes off them for two minutes and they've gone."

The bar had filled up. Jeremy shook hands with Roger Crumpshaw. They found five-year-old Randall outside on the grass. He was playing with some of the other boys. Trying to use a cricket bat the size of himself.

"Bat's too big, old boy. Come on. We're going home. Where's Primrose got to?"

"I'm here, Mr Jeremy."

"Good. Everyone in the car. We're going home."

"How many runs did you get?" asked Phillip.

"A duck, I'm afraid. Third ball. Wasn't concentrating. You've got to concentrate playing cricket. Remember that."

Jeremy ruffled the hair of five-year-old Randall. Were it not for the boys he would have done something more stupid than getting drunk in the bar. Ever since Livy had taken Donna back to England. Donna was the same age as Randall. She wasn't coming back. First Carmen driving into the bush drunk on her own and running out of petrol. Then Livy coming out from England and going home. He was no good at looking after his women.

"Did your kids have a nice day, Primrose?"

"They swam in the pool."

"I'm glad. All kids together. All good friends."

osiah reached the Zambezi River two weeks later, his feet sore, his spirits high. Through the valley he had recruited in eleven villages, most of them poorer than the village of Chirow. It was hard country for crops and domestic animals. If it wasn't the elephant getting into the scattered fields of arid maize, where half a bag of corn to the acre was a success story, it was lions killing the goats and the cows. Most of the villagers hunted for a living using traps and wires. Josiah's offer to get them into a better life fell on eager ears. He hoped many of the young men would follow him across the river into what soon would be Zambia, the independence agreement having been struck with Britain. In his pocket was the fishing line he had taken from the drawer in his father's hut. Josiah was hungry for fish. The acacia tree on the bank of the river under which he made camp for the night was forty feet high, its roots taking water direct from the river. He was once more alone. The river was wide. On both banks were animals drinking the water, a small herd of buffalo a hundred yards from his camp. With the food gathered for the night, Josiah went down to the edge of the water and threw in his line. On the hook he had tied a mopane worm with a length of cotton he had pulled from his tattered shirt. On an island in the stream he could see the crocodiles lying out of the water. They were not far away. All of them seemed to be watching him. One of the smaller crocodiles slid down into the water, only the eyes and nose visible and pointed towards him. It took less than a minute to get his first bite. The river was teeming with fish. The second bite was a big one taking out some of his line. When Josiah landed the fish it was a Chessa, all of ten pounds. Thinking of Livingstone Sithole, hoping he was safely back at the camp in Tanganyika, Josiah gutted his fish and impaled it on two sticks he cut from the acacia and placed it ready to go on the fire. The sun was going down, painting the sky a vivid red. The surface of the river reflected a pattern of clouds washed by the red from the sinking sun. It was beautiful, making him happy. Almost as happy as catching his fish. He was tired and content, enough done of his job, time to go back to the camp from where he would travel to Dar es Salaam and take a plane back to London. He was not to be training the new recruits. He was more important to the party in London where the British had given him residence. He would see Petronella and help them raise money to pay for the camp. It was always money. Always the money. The Russians provided the military training but not all the money to pay the recruits.

Before the light went, Josiah lit the fire and piled on the wood. He was high up on the river bank too steep for the hippopotamus to come up from the river. Or the crocodiles. The sky was blood-red round the edges of the clouds, duck egg blue low down on the horizon in a swathe of clear sky. The cicadas were screeching from out of the riverine trees. Most of the elephant grass had been trampled by animals going down to the river. On the opposite side, still Northern Rhodesia, a herd of elephant came down to the water from out of the trees. Josiah felt eyes watching him from all around as the shadows lengthened in the fading light, the fire catching hold and burning up bright. He was glad of the fire. As the sun sank away the temperature began to fall quickly. Midday in the valley was hot. At night it was cold. Taking some of the burning coals from his fire Josiah made a second, smaller fire and began cooking his fish, holding the sticks one in each hand. When the fish was cooked he pulled off the flesh and fed it piece by piece into his mouth. All the time he watched the colours change in the sky going darker, the colour bleeding away. When it was quite dark, the fish half eaten, he lay down by the fire. He was tired, his body aching, the mosquito and tsetse bites itching. He had been too frightened of the crocodiles to swim in the river when he went to catch his fish.

On the third day by the river a *makori* came by going slowly downriver. Josiah shouted to the man. The man turned the boat and came into the bank. Josiah gave the man a little of the money his father had given him. The man ferried Josiah across to Northern Rhodesia. He had slipped out of the country as easily as he had slipped in. The journey home was over. For the moment. Josiah waved at the other side of the river to say farewell and turned to go north. The man on the *makori* waved back.

All the way north the people were happy, no longer fearing the colonial government. Next year their hero Kenneth Kaunda would be running their government, giving the wealth from the copper mines to the people. They were all going to be rich.

All the way north to the Tanganyika border they helped him on his way. The white men who gave him lifts were no longer so arrogant. Josiah felt happy for everyone. They were soon to be free. One of the bites he had scratched had gone septic. He was just in time by the look of it, as it had become inflamed on his arm. When he walked over the border into the newly independent Tanganyika the fear left him. He had gone over the invisible border where no one was around, walking through the bush.

"I'm alive," he shouted. "I'm still alive."

Soon after he cut back to the road and flagged down a safari truck. There was a picture of a lion on the side of the truck. At the back were bench seats for the tourists.

"Where are you going?" said the driver. The man was white. "I'm picking up some American tourists at Chunya to take them hunting. The Americans like killing our animals. Do you speak English?"

"You can drop me at Chunya, if that's all right?"

"You speak perfect English. You should put something on that arm. In the cubbyhole is some antiseptic. Rub it on. You're bitten all over."

"Sleeping rough."

"You got to watch yourself in Africa. You're from the camp, aren't you?"

"What camp?" asked Josiah looking surprised.

"Where they have all those Russians. You been down south?"

"Drop me at Chunya, if that's all right."

"Have it your way. Use that antiseptic. Saw a man years ago with a festering sore like that. Lost his arm. Turned into gangrene."

"It's only just started. I scratched the bite."

"You're lucky. They have a Russian doctor at the camp. You're educated aren't you? Why do you dress like that? Next time you go in the bush take a mosquito net. Hang it from a tree."

"I'll remember."

"You'd better. Africa can kill you."

"That it can."

"You need a bath."

"That I do."

Josiah was smiling. So was the man. The man gave him dried meat to eat. The meat was salted. Josiah chewed happily, putting the ointment on his arm.

"You're very kind."

"I love Africa."

"So do I. Very much."

"It's the bloody politicians who bugger it up. You're lucky not to have got malaria. Or sleeping sickness. Some of those bites on you are tsetse. They can both kill you. I take malaria pills for the mosquitoes. Can't do much about the tsetse. I'll drop you at the camp. Not far out of my way. The Americans are flying into Chunya by light aircraft tomorrow. Costs them an arm and a leg hunting elephant. Most of the money goes to the new government. I love what I do. When you've lived in the bush most of your life you can't go and live in a city. I get my tips in US dollars. They pay those out of the country. There's always a way round. Whatever new rules they make there is always a way round. Do you understand my English?"

"Every word of it. Thank you. I've done a lot of walking recently."

"Not used to it. How long have you been living overseas?"

"Ten years."

"That's a long time. Makes you soft. America or Britain?"

"England. London to be exact."

"You can keep the big cities. Give me the bush any day."

"You're very kind."

"Pays to keep in with the new crowd. Why I gave you a lift."

The man dropped Josiah right at the gate of the camp. There was a fence around the camp and a guardhouse at the gate. Josiah had never before seen the man on the gate. The man was in camouflage uniform. There were many more people moving around the camp than when he had left with Livingstone Sithole. Everyone he could see were strangers. The white man had turned his safari truck round and hooted as he went past on his way back to Chunya and his American clients. Josiah smiled, wondering if the Americans on their light plane knew they were coming to a place so close to a terrorist training camp with communist Russian instructors.

He doubted if the man in the truck speeding away down the dirt road throwing up a trail of dust had told them that when they booked their safari. When he turned back to the guardhouse the guard looked at Josiah with suspicion. Josiah had waved to the man in the truck when he hooted.

"What do you want?" said the man in Shona.

"To come in," said Josiah politely, beginning to enjoy himself.

The ointment on his arm had stopped the festering bite from itching. His stomach was full of the safari man's biltong. Neither had asked each other their names.

"You want to join the army?"

"I am the army. I started it. Has Livingstone Sithole got back from Rhodesia?"

The man looked at him startled, not sure what to do.

"Have there been many new recruits from down south? What's your name?"

"Jackson."

"My name is Josiah Makoni. Now, will you let me in please? I've had a tiring journey."

The man's face broke into a grin. "You're alive. Comrade Sithole thought you were captured or dead. Every police station in Rhodesia has a picture of you. Asking for information. The *Rhodesia Herald* and *Bulawayo Chronicle* had your picture on their front page."

"I didn't get time to read the newspapers."

"I'm from Gwelo. Over a hundred new recruits. It's wonderful. They're still coming in."

"That's the stuff, Jackson. Now may I come in?"

"I'll telephone Comrade Sithole. He'll be here to help you. I have to abide by my orders. My goodness. Josiah Makoni. You're a hero."

"I hope not a hero of the revolution."

"A hero of the revolution."

"It hasn't started yet."

"It will, Comrade Makoni. We are getting men. Now it will start if the British don't give us our independence at the end of the year."

Josiah waited for Livingstone in the guardhouse. They were both alive. Alive and well.

Ten minutes later, when Livingstone drove up to the gate, he was smiling all over his face. They embraced each other. Josiah wanted to cry.

"You were so long getting back I thought you were dead."

"They found and lost me. They're not as good as we think. Does anyone have a cold beer in this establishment?"

"The officers' mess are going to have a party for you. I told the others when I got the call from the guardhouse."

"With the Russians?"

"The Russians keep to themselves. Except when it comes to the women. The Russians like black girls. Young black girls. They pay them."

"Every army camp attracts whores."

"I suppose it does. How were your mother and father?"

"My father doesn't approve."

"Neither does mine. He thinks I'm going to get killed. After all that sacrifice to give me an education. You're covered in bites. That arm looks terrible."

"First a cold beer. Later the doctor. How are you, friend?"

"I'm good, Josiah. I'm so glad you made it."

"So am I."

"There's mail for you. From England. I think it's Petronella."

"Good. First that beer."

"Come on. Thank you, Jackson. He's from Gwelo."

"He told me so. Lots of new recruits."

"Lots of them. They like being paid and fed three times a day."

"I'll bet they do. Hell, it's good to see you."

PART IV

SEPTEMBER 1963

A LONG WAY TO SLIDE

1

_____

They made love in Petronella's bedsitter in Shepherd's Bush the third night Josiah got back to England. The Russian doctor in the camp had patched up Josiah's arm leaving a piece of his skin red. Later it would turn black like the rest of him. He was so in need of a woman. On the camp all the girls had been with the Russians. Livingstone said the Russians had given the girls a venereal disease and best to keep away. Petronella's letters had said she wanted him. He had decided to wait.

"My own brother shopped me," he said in bed, his body satiated with sex.

"That's quite ironical. People say I shopped my parents saying they don't deserve their farm. That Ashford Park belongs to the people."

"Goodson is jealous of my education. Why are people jealous?"

"Everyone is jealous of something. Harry Wakefield is jealous of you. So is Elsie."

"Are you sleeping with her?"

"Every now and again. I like the change. Keeps her mind on the business of raising us money. That makes you jealous. Makes you horny. Do you want to do it again?"

They coupled passionately, both of them frantic. When it was over Josiah was satisfied.

"You should go away more often. Builds it up in you. My word." She was smiling at him, her head turned to him on the pillow.

"Are you having an affair with Harry Wakefield?"

"My word, you are jealous. You were away a long time. Don't tell me you didn't have sex on your journey."

"Only twice. One of the girls was seventeen."

"That sounds nice."

"For you or for me?"

"For both of us."

"Are you screwing him?"

"You don't want to know. Why do we fight after sex? Before you are always so sweet to me. Where are we going to dinner?"

"I don't have any money."

"I don't give all Grandfather's money to the party. We'll go somewhere nice. You can be nice to me. Your loving Petronella. I was told the Rhodesian police had caught you. I was so sad. Now you are home. Tell me what you did."

"I don't want to talk about it. Are those clothes on the floor all right for tonight?"

"Did you eat properly?"

"Never been so hungry in my life. Now I know what it's like to be poor. To go for days and weeks subsisting on the white man's maize cobs stolen from his fields. They have so much. Our people so little. It isn't fair."

"Life isn't fair."

"Do you believe in the struggle?"

"Of course I do, Josiah."

"Why? Why do you want to destroy your own family farm?"

"My mother's a bitch. Dad married her for her money. She's got her nose in the air. I hate her."

"I love my parents. They love me. Only Goodson hates me."

"What's the difference? Hating a brother or your mother. She always puts me down. Ever since I can remember. Come on. Put on some clothes. I'm hungry. Sex always makes me hungry."

To Josiah the girl was an enigma. She lived in the one small room, didn't drive a car but when she dressed up to take him to dinner to be paid for with the grandfather's money, she was dressed in clothes the cost of which would have fed his father and all four families for a year. He was unable to understand how anyone could hate their parents. He loved his own so much. Goodson hated him. He did not hate Goodson. He did not hate anyone except the white men for stealing his country.

When they were dressed, Josiah was wearing his only tie with his one grey suit, the tie given to him by the London School of Economics when he graduated. They took a taxi to a restaurant in Mayfair, one of the most expensive parts of London. The man who greeted them at the door seemed to know her. He gave Josiah a first look of disbelief. Then the man smiled at Petronella and led them to a table where he pulled out her chair. While she was sitting down he gave Josiah another look of disapproval. The *maître d'hôtel* was one of those white men Josiah could hate.

"My grandfather has been patronising the Berkeley for the last fifty years. My two uncles come here regularly. Especially on a Wednesday night."

"Today is Wednesday," said Josiah, looking around.

"We're early. I wanted a good table. Porter is a good sort when you get to know him. Never turned me away. Never dared."

"Does your grandfather run an account at this restaurant?"

"All I have to do is add fifteen per cent for Porter and sign the bill."

"Do you expect your uncles?"

"And their wives. Especially their wives. They come most Wednesdays. Uncle Winfred has a townhouse up the road. At the top of Piccadilly. Not far from Buckingham Palace. He's the current managing director of the family business. He was given the job after my grandfather retired. Winfred is two years younger than Horace. Their wives hate each other. It runs in the family. I've brought Elsie here once or twice. She loves the place. Harry Wakefield came with me once when I wanted a favour. He wanted me. I wanted a favour. Worked perfectly."

"Did you sleep with him?"

"Please, Josiah. Not in here. That's so common."

"Why is everyone looking at me?"

"They don't see many black people in the Berkeley. They can't afford the prices. They have a wonderful system. You'll see when Porter gives me the menus. On my menu it will show me the prices. On yours it won't. He knows I am paying the bill. It's bad form to brag to your guests the price of the food. Or the wine. We'll have a bottle of wine, won't we? To celebrate. When you've had a glass or two you can tell me what you've been up to... Thank you, Porter. Are my uncles coming tonight?"

"I believe so, Miss Maple."

"Put them at a table nice and close."

"As you wish."

"This is the celebrated Josiah Makoni. He's just back from Rhodesia. I'm sure it will be in tomorrow's press. Josiah is going to be prime minister of Zimbabwe. Where we come from. Only now they call it Rhodesia. What are you going to have, Josiah? The food is quite delicious. A bottle of your best Burgundy, Porter. This is a celebration."

"I'll ask the waiter to bring you your order. His name is Biggs tonight. Will that be all for the moment?"

"We'll order the food after a nice refreshing glass of wine."

When the *maître d'hôtel* left them Petronella giggled.

"He's such a pompous ass. If Grandfather wasn't one of his best customers he'd have thrown you out on your black arse before you got in the door. Tell you were not dressed properly or something ridiculous. All very polite of course. Look at them all gawping at us. I love it. People are all equal, Josiah. They should remember that when they stare."

"Do your uncles expect you?"

"Of course not. Spoil all the fun. Uncle Winfred lives next door to the Honourable Barnaby St Clair. His brother is the eighteenth Baron St Clair of Purbeck. Or is it the nineteenth? Very old family. The Cavalry Club is almost next door. Uncle Fred's a member of course. Went in the Royal Dragoon Guards at the start of the war. Won the Military Cross. Aunty rather likes the idea of living next door to the son of a baron. Lord St Clair. Dorset. Very old family. There's a connection there with you, Josiah. Your mentor, Harry Brigandshaw, was married first to Barnaby's sister. Don't remember her name. She died in an accident. There was a tremendous scandal according to Aunty. Funny how we're all tied up in the end."

"Livy Johnston was married to Frank St Clair. I know that scandal. The second Mrs Brigandshaw was playing around when Harry Brigandshaw went back to Africa."

"So you know Livy?"

"She painted a portrait of my mother. I've still got it. You've never visited my digs."

"Must be worth a fortune. She's famous."

"Never sell my mother."

"I'd sell mine for sixpence. Here comes the wine. Hope you like it."

Inwardly, Josiah felt annoyed. Her sex appeal made him always come back. Petronella was playing with him. Playing with ZAPU and the British Communist Party. The wine came. Biggs poured a small amount in the bottom of Josiah's wine glass.

"Taste it, Josiah. Didn't they teach you anything at the London School of Economics? Sometimes an old wine is corked. Turned to vinegar. You have to taste it first."

"It's very nice, Petronella."

"Good. Drink up. You're giving me nasty looks again."

Josiah ordered his food. It was all in French. Petronella had told him what to order. When it came, the fish was not as good as the ten-pound Chessa he had pulled from the Zambezi. The other guests had stopped looking at him to get on with their food. The restaurant had filled up with people. A table for four next to them was conspicuously vacant. Josiah had his back to the entrance to the Berkeley facing Petronella. The wine had gone to his head. He loved her again. A piece of beef the size of the palm of his hand was put in front of him. Next to the beef were three green beans. All in one neat row. On the other side of the fillet a small red carrot and a new potato. On the potato was sprinkled green parsley. There was more foliage at the top of his plate that looked inedible. Just for decoration. Petronella smiled at him and picked up her knife and fork. Josiah watched and did the same. There were so many knives and forks by the side of his plate. They ate in silence. Josiah finished his meat in four mouthfuls. He ate the three green beans and the carrot. The potato went down in one bite.

"Isn't the food lovely, Josiah?"

"Perfectly lovely."

"You're catching on." Petronella giggled. She had drunk two glasses of wine. "Here they come. Don't turn round. Aunty Barbara is in the lead. Oh, good. She's seen me. Don't turn round. Good old Porter. Not a word to them... Hello, Aunty Barbara. Uncle Horace. Aunty May. Uncle Winfred. This is my friend Josiah Makoni."

The two aunts and two uncles sat down at the vacant table next to them. Both women looked appalled. Petronella looked away from them and picked up her wine glass. Josiah had stayed in his seat, not wishing to embarrass himself. He doubted the uncles would have put out their hands. All of them were looking up at Porter waiting with the menus. Ignoring their niece, Petronella leaned across the small table towards Josiah. She was giggling.

"Isn't this fun? Aunty May is one of three sisters. April, May and June. Can you believe it? Let's have another bottle of wine. I'm enjoying myself. All I need now to make my evening perfect is my mother sitting with them at the table. Mother's the eldest of the three children. She'd have a fit. In the Berkeley!"

"You're a bitch, Petronella," Josiah whispered.

"Probably. But a nice sexy bitch, Josiah, and you can't get enough of me. Cheers again... Please, Biggs. Bring us another bottle of this wine... Are you still hungry, Josiah?"

"Of course I am."

"When we've finished our meal we'll go and sit with them."

"No we won't."

"Why ever not?"

"I'm not an idiot."

"Oh, Josiah. Do they make you feel inferior? What a pity. Poor Elsie Gilmore felt the same."

"Did they know she was a lesbian?"

"Please, Josiah. Elsie is bisexual. The new liberated women. What we've all been fighting for. Equality. Equality for the people."

Petronella giggled into her glass of wine.

"But did they know about you two?"

"Of course they did. The same way they know about you and me. I told them. You should have seen the expression on Aunty May's face. April, May and June. Isn't that a giggle? I didn't tell them about us in so many words."

Josiah finished his meal, the table next to them ignoring him. He drank down the last of his glass of wine.

"You'll have to excuse me, Petronella. I'll see you in the ZAPU office later in the week. I have important business to attend to tomorrow. As you know. It's my day to meet the press."

The woman called Aunty May had looked across at him, Josiah deliberately having raised his voice.

"Are you going?" said Petronella.

"Afraid so. Lovely dinner. Please thank your grandfather for me."

"Where are you going?"

"Back to Holland Park. The old house where I roomed. They kept my bits and pieces in the attic including Livy Johnston's painting of my mother. We should do this again sometime. Next time it will be on me. Probably a Lyons Corner House. Not as grand. Just the portions are bigger. We Africans go for quantity not quality."

Putting his napkin on the table next to his empty plate, Josiah stood up. He looked towards the next table and nodded his head.

"So nice to have met Petronella's uncles and aunts."

He walked out of the restaurant with his head held high. Porter opened the door for him.

"Goodnight, Porter. Miss Petronella is staying awhile with her aunts and uncles. I'll recommend this restaurant to my friends."

Grinning to himself outside, Josiah looked back through the still open door. Half the people in the restaurant were looking at him. The door closed and he walked on down the street to catch the Tube train back to Holland Park. When he had looked back he could see Petronella standing up staring after him.

"One to Josiah."

Feeling good with himself, Josiah began to walk to Piccadilly Circus.

INSIDE THE RESTAURANT Petronella sat back down in her chair. Porter came across to her, smiling. He was carrying the bill.

"Will that be all, madam?"

"Thank you, Porter. You added on your usual fifteen per cent?"

"Thank you, madam."

Petronella signed the bill without looking at the amount. It was bad manners to add up a bill in the Berkeley. Then she got up and turned to the next table, a smile back on her face.

"Hello, everyone. May I sit down? Josiah has important meetings tomorrow. He's just back from Africa."

"You'd better sit down," said Uncle Winfred.

"Have you written to your mother?" said Aunty Barbara.

"As a matter of fact I haven't. My parents don't approve of my politics. Porter, would you be so kind as to ask Biggs to bring across that bottle of Burgundy? You can waste food but never the wine."

"You should write to her," said Uncle Horace. "It can't hurt you."

"But what I say could hurt them. They've joined the new right wing party. The Rhodesian Front. Who want independence for the whites whatever Whitehall has to say. They talk about a unilateral declaration of independence."

"Sit down," said Uncle Winfred. "Have you seen Father?"

"Last weekend. Says I'm the only one who visits him."

"What nonsense," said Aunty May. "We all go down for Christmas. Almost a week. There's nothing to do at Woodlands Court. Except ride horses. Never did like horses, like your mother. So that was just business. You shouldn't bring him here. What will these people think of us? Lady Westford put on her glasses to have a better look at him. They'll all be talking."

"I don't care, Aunty May. One day Josiah will be prime minister of Zimbabwe. Welcome at Buckingham Palace. Seeing you live so close, Aunty, have you been invited to Buckingham Palace?"

"Of course we haven't. Winfred doesn't yet have a title. I tell him to give more money to the Tory party but he won't listen. That will be so nice when we have a title. I mean, Winfred is managing director of the company."

"They never knighted Grandfather," snapped Aunty Barbara.

"He didn't give enough to the party. Ask Petronella. She knows all about politics and giving money to the party. Are you going to live in this Zimbabwe if Josiah becomes prime minister, heaven forbid?"

"Heaven won't forbid, Aunty. God is on the side of the righteous."

"So starting a revolution is righteous."

"Of course, Aunty. If the cause is just. Africa belongs to the Africans. Not a few self-styled feudal barons on big tobacco farms."

"Aren't those farms the cornerstone of the Rhodesian economy?" said Uncle Winfred.

"They can be equally well run by the black people."

"I wonder. I think my sister and your mother might just disagree with you on that point. Now tell me. How are you? How was Father when you saw him?"

"Old and lonely. And bored."

"Yes, I suppose he is. But we all have to retire sometime. Hand over the reins. He doesn't even come up to board meetings anymore. You should ask him about that. He's making himself into a recluse. He should have found himself another wife after mother died. There are plenty of elderly widows. Not good for him sitting there drinking on his own."

"We can't keep running over there," said Aunty May. "We have our own families to look after."

"How are the boys?"

"Happily for me, at boarding school."

"Do they like it? I hated boarding at the Salisbury convent."

"They should have sent you to boarding school in England. Those religious schools put a lot of nonsense into a girl's head. When you're older you'll realise that life isn't so simple."

"I came over here to university."

"Wrong university. Manchester for goodness sake. That's as Labour as the London School of Economics. All bolshy if you ask me. Those Russians will never produce a flourishing economy under communism."

"Capitalism only makes the rich richer."

"Nonsense. Anyone who works hard can make money. Ask Porter. He's rolling in it. Asked Winfred for tips on the stock market last week. Waiters investing in the stock market. My word. What has the world come to?"

"He's an exception."

"No he isn't," said Uncle Winfred. "Not anymore. Let's not argue. Such bad form. Seemed a nice enough chap."

"Who, Uncle Winfred?"

"That chap at your table. I was going to shake his hand."

"How good of you."

"Don't be rude, Petronella," snapped Aunty Barbara.

"Not at all, Aunty. I think shaking Josiah's hand would have been very nice. Have to go. Lovely seeing you."

"Don't you want to finish your wine?"

"Not really."

As Petronella walked out of the restaurant she was lonely. All the way back to her bedsitter in Shepherd's Bush. At least Aunty May hadn't told her to get a proper job and stop living off her grandfather. That was one small mercy in her ongoing fight with her uncle's wives.

When she went to bed alone she was thinking of Josiah. Of Elsie. Of Harry Wakefield.

FEELING FLAT, Josiah let himself into his room. The uplifting effect of the red wine had worn off. He was hungry. Every time after making love Petronella obsessed him, his need even greater. When she mocked him the need increased. Made him think all the time of her eyes and her body. Calling to him. Making everything else go out of his mind. Ever since he had first made love to her he could never get enough. All the other women in his life had come and gone, the sex quickly satisfying his need for them. The need for some went quicker than others. All of them had faded in the end. Except Petronella. What her aunts and uncles thought of their relationship he didn't care. He wanted her body. Always he wanted her body. Deep in the African bush he had lain under the trees while mosquitoes feasted on him thinking of Petronella and her sexually erotic body. She never quite let him possess her. Sometimes at the end she patted his cheek. And smiled knowingly with her tongue in her cheek.

The picture of his mother on the wall came into focus when he turned on the light.

"What do I do, Mother? I can't get enough of her. I hate what she does to me but I can't get her out of my system."

The portrait looked back at him. Mute. He took out a loaf of bread from the cupboard below his two-plate cooker. There was butter on a plate. Cutting and buttering slices of bread, Josiah ate and ate, hoping the food would stop his desire.

"What a bitch. She took me there to show me up. To laugh at me. The sex before had been part of the plan."

The bread made no difference. Josiah took off his clothes and got into bed. He hated wearing a suit. He had worn his suit to impress her. The tie he threw over the back of the chair. He switched off the bedside lamp and tried to sleep. She liked making a fool of him, knowing her power. They were all so damned condescending. As if by talking to a black man they were doing him a favour. One day, with real power, he would teach them a lesson.

Much later, Josiah fell into an exhausted sleep. When he woke in the morning he was still tired. The first thing he thought of was Petronella.

"Damn you, bitch."

Making tea in the teapot, Josiah began to plan when next he would see her. What they would do.

When he went out of the room he was humming a tune. There was nothing he could do. He wanted her again so badly what she said and did to him did not matter. He had to have her. Again and again.

His first meeting of the day was with Harry Wakefield. Petronella had arranged the interview with the *Daily Mirror*. To let him tell them what would happen in Rhodesia if the British government failed to give them independence with a 'one man one vote' election. They were going to be told about the training camp in Tanganyika. A camp to train the people's army for the aftermath of a free and fair election. Josiah had all the right politically correct words. He would threaten the British by talking about the new black army. Tell the paper the whites in Rhodesia were no better than the Boers in South Africa who were locking up their black opposition. The Anti-Apartheid Movement would be on his side. If they threw him out of England he would go to Sweden. They had agreed to meet in Holland Park close to where they both lived. Under the trees. Without any witnesses. ZAPU needed the socialist press on the side of the struggle. He was feeling better with himself. For the first time since leaving the Berkeley he was not thinking of Petronella. He had to think through carefully how much he was going to tell Harry Wakefield. As he walked into the park he was thinking of Harry and Petronella.

Was she or wasn't she having an affair with him?

2

He knows, thought Harry Wakefield as he stood up from the park bench to shake Josiah Makoni by the hand. The man knows.

"Nice of you to give us an exclusive interview. These days people go to the television stations. We have a rumour you're training terrorists in Tanganyika. Is it true?"

"Not in the way you see it."

"Did Mr Shostakovich in East Berlin have anything to do with it?"

"Who is Mr Shostakovich?"

"The man at the African desk in Moscow. You and Petronella went to see him. The Reverend Harvey Pemberton ran back to his mission in Rhodesia. Just before you went to Russia for military training. Did they teach you anything?"

"Why did you bother to interview me if you think you know so much?"

"You know Petronella. She uses people, Josiah. She wanted me to come to this meeting. What could I say?"

"To succeed as Zimbabwe we require a people's army. Not those indoctrinated by the Rhodesian army. Those soldiers are against the people."

"Then so is your brother Goodson, by the sound of what's coming out of Salisbury. We have our African correspondent in Salisbury. Said your face was plastered all over the place. They called you a missing person. One of the papers offered a reward. Won't say which one."

"My brother is jealous of my education."

"I'll bet he is. Won't you sit down? Easier to take notes writing on my knee. Now you give me your side of the story."

"You won't twist what I say?"

"Why should I, Josiah? Tell you what. I'll give you my draft to read before I send it to press. There's always two sides to an argument."

"Is this an argument?"

"Not with me. You have an argument with the Colonial Office. Quite legitimate if you ask me. What happened to the Reverend Harvey Pemberton? You three cut quite a dash outside the gates of Buckingham Palace. My friend Sidney got some good photographs. Then you were striving to get Mandela out of jail. My editor is right on your side. More important to you, so are our readers. Haven't had a squeak out of the reverend since he went home. What happened to him? In London he was most eloquent."

"The Rhodesian government gagged him."

"Did they now? May I quote you?"

"That you can. There's no freedom of the press in Southern Rhodesia. Either official or voluntary. The Rhodesian press is owned by the whites."

"People are inclined to report what sells newspapers. In England we pride ourselves in being liberal. Why my newspaper wants your side of the story, Josiah."

"The army we are training is to maintain peace when Rhodesia becomes Zimbabwe."

"And when's that going to be?"

"When the Federation breaks up in December."

"That early?"

"Why should Zambia and Malawi get their independence and not Zimbabwe?"

"You're referring to Northern Rhodesia and Nyasaland."

"Why should they be any different to us?"

"Both of them are British Protectorates. Southern Rhodesia is a self-governing Crown Colony with its own police force and army. The British government has to take into account the Rhodesian government. They've been running the place for forty years."

"They stole our country."

"Or made it what it is today. That's their side of the story. That without the white man's money and skills there wouldn't be today's mining and agricultural industries. They put in the railways and the roads. And a lot more. I'm just quoting the Rhodesian government. They also give exclusive press interviews."

"Cecil Rhodes stole our country."

"Under a charter from Queen Victoria. Why the police are still called the British South Africa Police. Which has nothing to do with South Africa."

"My people will fight for their independence."

"Are they all your people, Josiah? The Matabele wouldn't agree. They are Zulu. Didn't they kill one of your ancestors? Didn't my godfather Harry Brigandshaw's father rescue a young boy of your tribe? If Sebastian Brigandshaw hadn't found that boy, perhaps your tribe wouldn't have survived. The wild animals would have got a seven-year-old boy in the bush on his own. Don't you personally owe the white man something? Don't you both need each other?"

"You're biased."

"Not really. If I was biased I wouldn't be here. Roland Cartwright, my immediate superior, wouldn't allow me. You tell me your side of the story. I'll write it down. We're not enemies."

"Aren't we?"

"Of course not. Why should we be?"

"Petronella. I was with her last night. At the Berkeley."

"This isn't personal, Josiah. Be careful. Now, where were we?"

For what seemed like a long time to Harry they glared at each other. Then Josiah began to talk and Harry wrote it down. They were both jealous of each other. It was not a good start. Some women loved setting their men at each other's throats. They liked to watch men fight over them. He would have to be careful. He was a fool to have got involved.

"Keep away from her," said Josiah. "She's mine."

"I don't think Petronella is anyone's. She's certainly not mine. However much I would like to hope otherwise. She uses men and women to amuse herself. She uses politics to amuse herself. The lady has been spoiled all her life. There's no challenge for her so she makes life difficult. For everyone around her. For you and me, Josiah. For Elsie Gilmore. For her parents. The only one she doesn't antagonise is her grandfather. He has the power to cut off her source of money. Oh she butters him up all right. Sweet as pie with Grandfather. And when he dies and leaves her money she won't have to be nice to anyone. You, me or the dog. Think about it. He should have chopped off her allowance when she left Manchester University. Made her find a husband or a job. She uses that old man like the rest of us. Which way do you live?"

"Towards Notting Hill Gate."

"I'm the other way. Do you first want to read what I write?"

"Not if you say your readers are on our side and my story will sell your newspaper."

"Are we enemies, Josiah?"

"Of course we are. We're obsessed with the same woman."

"Life's a bugger and then you get married. We have no control over her. Remember that. Be careful, Josiah. She's dangerous. She'll switch sides quicker than your brother Goodson."

"You don't know what you are talking about."

"Sadly I do. For both of us. I'm going back to the quiet of my flat to write up my notes. This will be in tomorrow's newspaper. Look after yourself. I mean it. There are some nasty people out there. There'll be more people than you in your party imagining themselves as president. Africa is a nasty place to play politics. To train armies. The Russians couldn't care less about you and your ZAPU party. They want control of the world. Like the Americans. One day your people in Africa will look back on Colonial rule with nostalgia. Today's prosperity and law and order. Peace and quiet. The arrogance of the likes of Petronella's mother won't look so bad in retrospect."

"You don't know what you are talking about. Colonialism is evil. No people should be oppressed by another race."

"Just by a few of their own people?"

"The whole world abhors colonialism."

"The modern world. The Americans and the Russians. Who have their own ways to conquer the world. America with money and capitalism. Free trade which suits the Americans. They want world markets for their industry, not colonialism. The Russians want to dominate the world with an ideology. Be careful what you wish for, for these people of yours."

"Are we arguing?"

"Probably. Look after yourself, Josiah. I really do mean it. And may the best man win Petronella. My guess is she'll screw both of us. In more ways than one."

Harry watched Josiah walk away, his shoulders hunched. Harry sat back on the wooden bench with his notebook by his side. An old lady with a small dog on a long lead walked by down the path. The trees kept the dog and the old lady in shadow. The dog bared its teeth at Harry sitting on his bench in the sunshine.

"Don't do that, Benjie." The dog snarled at Harry.

"That's all right, I love dogs."

"The question is do dogs love you, young man? They can sense aggression."

"I was not being aggressive towards your dog."

"Benjie thinks you were. Come here, Benjie."

The woman pulled hard on the leash, half throttling the dog by its fancy collar. The leash pulled the dog away from Harry, jerking it off its small feet. Up ahead Josiah was walking down the side path that led out of the park. For some reason Harry had wanted to kick the dog. Taking his frustration out on a defenceless animal. He had never before wanted to kick an animal. The old girl was right. Dogs could sense aggression. Like the aggression he had felt from Josiah Makoni. Petronella had them both at each other's throats. Why couldn't he fall in love with Ruthy, he asked himself. Ruthy was a better person than Petronella. Beautiful. Kind. And they were friends. A life with Ruthy Smythe would be without complications. They would live in harmony. Both of their families would be happy. The children of best friends marrying each other. What could be better? Instead there was Petronella eating away at his insides. Using him as a plaything. Making him come when she called.

For half an hour Harry sat on the bench and stewed. The article on Josiah was mostly written. The rest was in his head.

He got up and went home to his flat and the typewriter in his study. For half an hour he typed and corrected until he had what he wanted. He was late for work. On the Tube train there were only three people. The rest of them had gone to work.

In the office he gave the article to Roland Cartwright.

"Thought you had taken the day off."

"Wasn't sure he'd pitch up. Josiah Makoni exclusive. In the park. We both live down the road from each other."

"So he's back."

"For the moment."

"Does your Petronella know he's back?"

"She slept with him last night."

"Harry. Watch yourself. They have diseases in Africa. Why the African population never took off without the white man's medicine. Is this any good?"

"I think so. The man's a revolutionary. Thinks he's going to be king."

"Don't they have chiefs in Africa? Good work. Nothing like a righteous revolution to stir the sympathy of our readers. He is righteous, I presume?"

"He thinks so. We all think what we want. We all think we are right."

"The self-righteous have been around a long time. Did your girl set up the appointment? My word. She does like playing around."

"And then there was Elsie."

"Who's Elsie?"

"Her girlfriend. Her lover. She fucks all of us, Roland."

"What has the world come to?"

"Everyone does what they want. The new age of freedom. Everyone has the freedom to do what they like."

"Dump her, Harry. Find another girlfriend."

"Not so easy."

"She's got you by the balls. No offence, Harry."

AT FIVE O'CLOCK, when the condensed article on Josiah Makoni went to press under the headline 'Will this man save his people?' Caroline put the call through to Harry sitting at his desk. Outside his office, sitting on the front of Caroline's desk dangling his feet, Sidney Cross waved at him through the glass window of his closed door. Sidney was smiling.

"Hello, darling, it's me. Did Josiah keep the appointment?"

"He said you went out with him last night."

"Of course I did, darling. To make sure he kept your appointment. It's not easy fundraising for the party. We need publicity. Are you all right to go to Woodlands Court on Saturday? Grandfather so enjoys your company. Thinks you're a good influence. Which you are."

"He says you did more than take him to dinner at the Berkeley."

"Did he now?"

"Not in so many words."

"Don't be silly, darling. Josiah is business. That affair was over when he went to Russia. Why are you men so jealous? We're having a lovely time you and I. It's a pity you don't have a car. Can't you borrow the company car for the weekend?"

"No I can't."

"You don't have to be rude. What's the matter with you? Are you coming?"

"I'm coming."

"That's lovely. I saw the uncles and aunts last night. They were quite rude to poor Josiah. Just because he has a black skin. Uncle Winfred says Grandfather isn't attending board meetings. I've been told to have a word with Grandfather. I'll come to your flat when I leave the ZAPU office on Friday evening. We can have a lovely weekend together. Got to run. We can visit that lovely pub of yours down the road from your flat."

"Why don't you take Josiah?"

"Don't be silly. Grandfather would have a fit."

The phone went dead. She never said goodbye. She just put the phone down. One of her habits that annoyed the hell out of Harry.

Sidney came into his office with Caroline. Everyone on the morning shift was going home, the new staff arriving.

"Why are you so glum? You usually cheer up when she phones. Have you two had a row? We're going to have a drink. Want to come?"

"She's seeing Josiah again. He's only been back in England four days."

"In the biblical sense?"

"I think so."

"Dump the bitch," said Caroline, her arm tucked neatly into the crook of Sidney's arm. Sidney was patting her hand possessively. The two of them looked so damn comfortable to Harry.

"I wish I could."

"Is it the money?"

"Of course not."

"Men. I'll never understand men," said Caroline, contradicting herself by smiling up at Sidney.

"I'll never understand Petronella Maple."

"Propose to the girl."

"She might accept."

"Isn't that what you want, Harry?"

"I'm not sure, Caroline. I'm just not sure if I should want her. I never know where I am with the girl."

PETRONELLA SAT STARING at the phone. The desk was a cheap second-hand one with ink spills all over it from the days when people wrote with fountain pens. Her chair was uncomfortable. There were no carpets on the floor of the small ZAPU office.

Neither of them satisfied her. They were both too quick. The only person who could bring her to climax was Elsie. Elsie had patience. Elsie knew what she was doing to a girl.

"Elsie, darling, shall we go for a drink? It's time to get out of this office. There isn't even a picture on the wall."

"Don't you want me to work?"

Petronella smiled at Elsie Gilmore making Elsie blush. Petronella felt better. The weekend was going to be boring. All Harry Wakefield did was stare at her. The man was besotted.

"So you're sleeping with Josiah again?"

"Why is everyone so jealous? I don't pry into your lives. When I'm not around you can do what you like. No one belongs to one person. We belong to ourselves, sweet Elsie."

"Why don't you take me to Woodlands Court?"

"Can't do that now, darling. I've just asked Harry. Anyway, if Grandfather found out what we are doing to each other he'd have a fit. And we can't have that now can we?"

"He goes to bed drunk. We can have adjoining rooms. People from his era can't imagine us in bed. Let alone making love. They don't even know it exists."

"Woodlands Court's so boring."

"Not if we are together."

"Tempting, darling. Let's go and have a little drinkie. Josiah's going to be in the limelight again tomorrow. The phone will start ringing. I've told Harry to pass on anyone who wants to help us. All those people who contribute to the Anti-Apartheid Movement will understand our cause. ZAPU has to be seen as a liberator. People love liberating other people. Especially when an article like Harry's makes them feel indignant. Did you ever do it with him again?"

"No I didn't."

"What a pity. Maybe a threesome."

"Don't be disgusting."

"Keep your shirt on, Elsie. I was only joking."

"I never know with you."

Petronella giggled. She stood up and walked to the hat stand in the corner, put on her small hat just at the right angle, looking as she did so in the small mirror behind the stand, then picked up her pink umbrella and turned to Elsie.

"Do you like my hat? It's a warm September evening in London. We don't need our coats. Cheer up. I'm paying. How was work at Sainsbury's today?"

"We're launching a new in-house brand of tinned goods."

"Isn't that nice? Come on. I'm thirsty. Men drive me to drink."

Outside in the street Petronella looked up at the old Victorian building where ZAPU had their office at the back of the third floor next to a branch of the Anti-Apartheid Movement, surrounded by small offices of NGOs, all claiming their funding, all doing their good works. To Petronella, some of them were quite ridiculous. The Anti-Vivisection League. Another one was all for saving whales. Another wanted to ban fox hunting. They all had an axe to grind. They all sought funding. All registered as charities with some of the managers driving home in fancy cars paid for by all the fundraising. Petronella smiled. It was another form of business. Just another way to make a living, the righteous indignation of most of the individuals mostly for show.

"They'll knock that building down sooner or later, Elsie. Some property developer is going to make a fortune. Paddington's going to have another of its every hundred year renaissances. We'll end up in Cheapside. At least around here a girl can walk into a pub on her own with all the feminist rights movements demanding girls get treated the same."

"Do you really care about ZAPU?"

"Of course I do. We're going to liberate the black oppressed. We all believe in the cause. What they taught us at Manchester University. That life wasn't all about making money. You have to think of other people."

To make her point, Petronella kissed Elsie on the lips, sticking her tongue down Elsie's throat and making a man walking by from the other direction look at them. In the man's look Petronella could see his rush of excitement. It made her feel good. She took Elsie's hand and led her down the road and out of Sutherland Avenue. There was something about a girl with a big bottom that turned her on.

"Taxi! Taxi... Thank you, driver. The Savoy."

"We're going to the Savoy!"

"I've had enough of slumming for one day. Life's a game Elsie. You've got to live life before it's too late. Did I lock the door to the office?"

"I did."

"Good girl. You're so clever. Whatever would I do without you?"

*J*osiah Makoni read the article the next morning surprised that Harry Wakefield had not been vindictive. There were many ways to damn a man with faint praise.

He had cooked himself bacon and eggs with three pork sausages on the two-plate stove in his room. Eaten it with buttered toast on the small table in front of the window pouring tomato ketchup on the sausages. After two cups of tea he had gone downstairs into the street and walked up to the nearest newspaper vendor where he bought the early edition of the *Daily Mirror*. He was on the fourth page with a photograph they had taken of him before he went to Russia. Next to his picture was a photograph of Petronella. A photograph she had posed for in a restaurant. The man with her was not in the picture. She was described as the Rhodesian activist raising money to fight for the rights of the underprivileged black people in her country who did not have the vote. There was no mention of Josiah's military training in Russia. The camp in Tanganyika was referred to as a refugee camp for displaced Rhodesian blacks who were going to fight for their rights against the British government handing power to the whites when the federation was dissolved at the end of December. He was portrayed as a mouthpiece for the oppressed black people of his country. The article raised all the right questions. Did Britain want apartheid in Rhodesia? Was a white man better than a black man? The article was careful not to mention an armed struggle, instead calling for people who believed in human rights to help the party fighting for those rights with financial contributions. The article was better than Josiah could have hoped for and wondered how much of it was due to the influence Petronella had over Harry Wakefield. The final appeal – *Do the right thing, Britain. Let them have the same unqualified independence as the other two members of the fracturing federation* – was a kind of rallying cry to the socialist left in Britain, the *Daily Mirror*'s main readership.

"The man's good," said Josiah, standing on the pavement next to the vendor after finishing Harry Wakefield's article. Communism, Russia, armed conflict were kept to the side. In the quotations Josiah was speaking the moral right. There was no offence given. No worry he would be forced to flee to Sweden where the government was outwardly in favour of 'one man one vote' for Rhodesia.

When Josiah arrived an hour later at the ZAPU offices in Paddington he was greeted with handshakes and smiles. Petronella was looking pleased with herself. Among the people milling around the small office was the Labour Member of Parliament for Paddington. The branch secretary of the Anti-Apartheid Movement was standing next to the Member of Parliament. The other faces were new. They began clapping him as he shook the MP's hand. The photographer from the *Daily Mirror* and three other newspapers took flash photographs of them shaking hands. Josiah felt elated. He felt good with himself. Then she kissed him with her mouth open in front of the newspapers who took their picture, everyone in the small crowded room smiling.

"The phone hasn't stopped ringing with pledges, Josiah. I'm so excited. Look at all these wonderful people. It's all going to turn out all right. We'll get our independence. How can the British government not agree with our demands? One man, one vote. ZAPU will win the election in a landslide. It's over, Josiah."

"I hope so."

"We'll be going home. Both of us. Together. Isn't it just wonderful?"

Petronella was beaming at the photographers.

.   .   .

"You'll want to see this, Harry," said Sidney Cross, coming into Harry Wakefield's office after lunch.

"You can't say that's a peck on the cheek."

"Let me see," said Roland Cartwright, taking the photograph of Petronella kissing Josiah on the mouth. "My goodness, Harry, you really are in the middle of this. This can go on tomorrow's front page," he said, turning back to Sidney as Harry took a look at the photograph.

"She's coming round to the flat after work. We're spending the weekend at her grandfather's place."

"Right on the front page. You got just the right tone this morning, Harry. Not quite disloyal to our kith and kin in Rhodesia. Englishmen don't like seeing Englishmen run down. All that human rights and the morally right thing to do was perfect. The powers-that-be phoned to congratulate me on your article. Better to sort it out before the blacks and whites go to war is the paper's official opinion. Not afterwards. Can't fault the paper on that one. The pressure is now on the British government to put pressure on the white Rhodesians for a compromise. A period of power-sharing was brought up by my boss. We're running that one tomorrow. Time's running out. We don't want someone to do something stupid. The deputy prime minister in the new Rhodesian Front Cabinet, a chap called Smith, is shooting his mouth off, saying the black people don't have the experience to run a country with a modern economy. Says Rhodesia is the breadbasket of central Africa. That the white farmers will go if the blacks take power. Then there'll be nothing left. He's a farmer. The other farmers are listening to him, according to our chap in Salisbury. Smith says the blacks don't have the skills to run the country. Simple as that. That the entire economy will go belly-up. I'm not a farmer or a politician. If we don't help make everyone see sense there's going to be big trouble for everyone in Rhodesia if you ask me. The bloody government here keeps flip-flopping depending on who they spoke to last. No one is listening to the other side. She really is a beautiful girl, Harry. The whole weekend together. Wouldn't mind that myself if I was thirty years younger. Our readers are going to eat her up. Intelligent and good-looking. And on the right moral side in the argument. What a lucky boy you are, Harry. You don't mind us publishing this do you?" said Roland Cartwright, again looking at Sidney's photograph. "That's some kiss."

"Of course not. Why should I?"

"Thought she was your girlfriend. That's a wet one, Harry. If you ask me she's got her tongue stuck down his throat. Just look at that expression on our Josiah's face. Pure lust if you ask me."

"She does it for publicity."

"Works for me. Is he coming with you to visit Grandad?"

"No, he isn't."

"That's something. How you youngsters get your love lives into such tangles I'll never understand. In my day you had to marry a girl before she would go to bed with you. Before she'd kiss you like that. My wife was a virgin. So she tells me. Oh, dear. Everything does change. Have a nice weekend. Good photograph, Sidney. Caught that one just at the right moment."

"Thank you, Mr Cartwright."

"Since when was I Mr Cartwright, Sidney? You kids have a nice weekend. Are you still going out with Caroline? Lucky you. There used to be a rule that we didn't date the staff. Everything flew out the window after the war."

"The First World War or the Second?"

"Don't be rude to an old man, Sidney. You'll be saying the same to your grandchildren. If some girl doesn't castrate you first."

AT SIX O'CLOCK in his Holland Park flat waiting for Petronella Harry Wakefield poured himself a stiff drink, Sidney's picture of Petronella and Josiah driving his jealousy to the point of hysteria. He had thought of coming home late hoping she had gone until that idea seemed worse. All afternoon he had tried without success to concentrate on his work. Writing with his mind in a turmoil had proved impossible. He sat at his desk and stewed, leaving at five o'clock on the dot and walking fast to the Tube station. He would have run down the street except for the commuters going home and getting in his way. It was the rush hour. The trains were full. He thought of taking a taxi but couldn't find one before being swallowed up with the rest of them walking down the steps to the Underground.

When she came she was smiling. Cool as a cucumber. Pretty as paint. The most beautiful girl he had ever seen.

"You answered the door quickly. Is that a drink? Naughty Harry starting without me. What a day. Your colleagues in the press have been all over us. Do you like my hat? You've made Josiah quite a hero."

"When's he going back to Rhodesia?"

"Not for a while unless the British government change their mind. Can I have a drink? That office is too small for a crowd. We had the Member of Parliament for Paddington all over Josiah."

"I saw the photograph."

"Of the two of them shaking hands. That looked nice for the newspapers."

"The picture of you and Josiah. Sidney took the photograph."

"Dear old Sidney. He's always creeping up on me with a camera."

"You were halfway down his throat."

"Never do anything in half measures is my motto. Where are we going tonight? I told Grandfather we'd be at Woodlands Court for lunch. He's so looking forward to it. Poor old man. So lonely in that great big house all on his own. Ten families could live in that great big place and still not be on top of each other. Josiah's becoming quite a celebrity."

"Do you really think he can run Rhodesia?"

"Of course he can't. He's never run anything in his life. Everything he ever had has been given to him. Harry Brigandshaw paid for him to go to school and Fort Hare University. The Fabian Society put him through the London School of Economics. He's never had a job in his life where he had to show a profit. The party pay him. I and the rest of us raise the money with the help of people like you, darling. That article of yours has been so good for fundraising. People are tripping over themselves to make pledges."

"Why do you do it?"

"To spite my mother, of course. Don't let's argue, darling. Let's have a nice drinkie together. Are you taking me somewhere nice? You haven't said you like my hat."

"It makes you look more beautiful."

"That's much better. What a lovely evening. September in England can be so beautiful. I usually hate the English weather. Are we going to be in your newspaper? I hope it was a really nice photograph."

"Roland's putting you and Josiah on the front page."

"I'll have to thank Roland personally. You know, I rather think he likes the look of me. Dirty old man. And Sidney for taking the photograph. Exposure. That's what it's all about. Can I open the window? It's so stuffy. Why didn't you open the window?"

"I had other things on my mind."

She turned and looked at him, her head on one side, a finger to her cheek. It was infuriating to Harry. Then she laughed at him her eyes full of inward humour, a private joke all to herself.

"Do you want to screw me now or later?"

Harry couldn't open his vocal cords to get out a reply.

"Silly darling. I want a drink. All day talking and running after other people getting them to sign their pledges. A girl needs a drink. Relaxation. A nice meal in a charming restaurant. Charming conversation. I love being wined and dined."

"So it's all about getting back at your mother."

"Don't be ridiculous. I was just joking about Mother. It's about the cause. Being right. Doing the right thing for the people. Not being selfish. What's the matter with you, Harry? You look all upset."

"But if he can't run anything how's he going to cope?"

"They'll get someone else, of course."

"And you'll come back to England?"

"You'd like that, Harry. Oh, my poor Harry. We'll see. Everything in good time."

"So you want to be with him?"

"Shut up, Harry. You're beginning to bore me. Pour that drink or I'm going home. Why do men think they are so important? All Josiah wants to talk about is you and what I'm doing with you. Enjoy yourself, Harry. Life's too short. Nothing ever lasts. Me. You. The empire. Probably communism. You have to enjoy what's happening at the time. Now be a good boy and pour me a bloody drink before I walk back out the door."

Then she was smiling at him. He watched her walk slowly across the floor. Stand on tiptoe. Kiss him, her tongue pushing open his mouth. Harry stood stiffly controlling himself.

"Now what's the matter, darling?"

"I'll pour you that drink."

"Make it a stiff one while I open the window. There's a pigeon on the roof cooing away. There are so many pigeons in London. There. That's better. A little fresh air. My word. What a lovely evening. The plane trees look so green. Are we friends again?"

"Of course we are," he said, getting himself back under control.

"We're going to have so much fun at Woodlands Court. We'll be given two bedrooms of course but we'll only sleep in one. How does that sound?"

"Here's your drink."

"Cheers, Harry. You should relax more. You're all tense. Take it easy greasy, you've got a long way to slide. We had a learner assistant on the farm when I was a girl. That was what he used to say. Said people put too much meaning into life. Quite a philosopher. His name was Jeremy. Jeremy Crookshank. Had a row in public with Mother about not getting his end of season bonus. My mother really is a bitch. All that damn money. She likes to control people. Put people down. Always putting me down. Father didn't care. Had what he wanted. Had her money. Mother had me and then couldn't have any more children. Something wrong with her tubes. I'm lucky to be alive."

"Do you always use people, Petronella?"

"What are you saying?"

"You used Elsie to get at me to get at the paper. You play people off against each other. I'm not going down to Woodlands Court tomorrow."

"Why ever not? What's got into you, Harry?"

"You. I'm going to save myself. You'll have to find another newspaper reporter to manipulate."

"Have it as you will, Harry. Suits me. You'll come crawling back, of course. They all do. That's why you're all so boring. Thanks for the drink. I'm going to walk home to Shepherd's Bush. I'll take Elsie down to Woodlands Court. She'll love it. Poor old Harry. You really can be a twerp."

Harry watched as she put down her drink and walked to the door. She was giggling to herself, a smile on her face, shaking her head. She turned to him as she opened the door.

"Take it easy, Harry. Don't forget. I'll be seeing you."

As Harry stood staring out through the open window he hoped he was going to be all right. He felt hollow. Drained of emotion. A little lost. Like mother like daughter, the girl was a bitch.

"Pull yourself towards yourself, Harry. Get her out of your system.

Find a new woman. That one can destroy you. She's got your balls in a twist."

Through the window down in the street he could see her walk away. She turned and looked up at him at where he was standing in the window. She waved. Harry forced his hands to stay by his sides. The sound of the girl's giggle came up to him on the soft summer air passing through the foliage of the plane trees. She had got so far under his skin it physically hurt.

Sometime after Petronella was lost to his view Harry closed the window and sat down to his drink, the half-drunk glass of Petronella's sitting on a coaster next to his own. On the glass was a faint smudge of her lipstick. Harry picked up her glass and drank from the side with the smudge.

"Damn you," he said when he'd finished her drink. "Now I really am miserable."

A long while later, Harry stood up. There was always the Horse and Hounds at the cul-de-sac at the end of his road. And Harold the landlord. He'd go and talk to Harold. And get himself drunk.

4

*T*he two families gathered by one o'clock on the Sunday, the Smythes and the Wakefields. Ruthy Smythe had brought a boyfriend for the first time. Ruthy had turned twenty the previous May. She was a shorthand typist for a firm of solicitors in the Temple. The boyfriend was doing his articles. An hour earlier Harry had arrived first, surprising his mother.

"Where is she, Harry?"

"Gone to hell where she should be. What are we having for lunch?"

"Two roast shoulders of lamb. You'll have to do with cold lamb in your sandwiches unless your father and William eat the lot. Mint sauce, the mint fresh from the back garden. Roast potatoes and roast swedes. Brussels sprouts and runner beans from yesterday's Portobello market. Gin and tonics for cocktails. Red wine at the table. Do you think we drink too much, Harry?"

"Probably. Where's my sister?"

"Bergit hasn't arrived yet."

"Are Ruthy and Bergit still smoking pot with Sammy Bell?"

"He's gone to Australia on the £10 assisted passage."

"What's he going to do in Australia?"

"Get a job, I suppose. What's happened to Petronella? You were meant to be visiting her grandfather."

"Josiah Makoni's back from raising an army. She's back with him. Their picture will be on the front page of the *Mirror* today. Kissing. I can't stand it, Mother."

"Get yourself another girlfriend. They say the only way to get over an affair is to start another one. Just don't start an affair with Ruthy. William would have your guts for garters. Anyway, she's bringing a boyfriend to lunch according to Betty. Where are they all? I'll just put the meat in the oven and come into the lounge. Your father is still reading the Sunday papers. You'll get over it. You're not married to the girl, thank God."

"You don't like her?"

"Not particularly. But that's not the point. I don't have to live with her. She's got too much money and not enough sense if you ask me. Does she know anything about politics? A university degree is one thing. Knowing how to use your brain quite another."

"How's your business?"

"I prefer calling it a speech therapy practice. They're all still stuttering their words. Some not as bad as they used to. Go and talk to your father. You look terrible, Harry. Have you been drinking?"

"All weekend. We had a row on Friday night. We're not seeing each other anymore."

"I've heard that one from you before about mistress Petronella. You'll run back to her again when she clicks her fingers. Can't see what there is in the girl. What all you men see in her."

"You're a woman, Mum."

"Yes, I suppose I am. Sounds like your sister letting herself in the front door. I need to concentrate. It's like feeding an army, the Smythes and the Wakefields. Give me a kiss on the cheek and go talk to your father."

"Why are you red in the face?"

"Hot flushes. Change of life."

"Oh, my goodness. Don't they call it hot flashes in America?"

"My face flushes not flashes. The Americans always get their English wrong, according to your father. Give me a few moments and I'll be fine. They come and go. Who did she take to Woodlands Court instead?"

"Her girlfriend. Elsie Gilmore. And I mean girlfriend."

"I have no idea what you are talking about. Or wish to know. Can't Roland Cartwright give you an overseas assignment? Hong Kong or

Tokyo? You'll soon forget her in the East. My poor son. All part of life. Your father said your article was good. Never get time to read. Now get out of my kitchen."

"I THINK YOU'RE WRONG, HARRY," said his father, taking off his reading glasses and putting down the paper. "Giving these African colonies independence is going to be a mess. A few at the top will get rich at the expense of the rest of them."

"But then it's their problem and not Britain's. How are you, Dad?"

"As you see me. The newspaper business never changes. You been over-drinking again, Harry? That's a big problem for a newspaper man. Everyone meets to talk shop in a pub. You should watch it. Drink three pints of water before you go to bed. Flush out the system. Make friends with the barman so when you're included in the round he pours water in your glass from his special gin bottle. Works for me. Give you problems later on in life, alcohol. All fun when you are young and depressing as you get old. Find yourself a nice girl like I found your mother and settle down. Roast lamb for lunch. You need a woman to look after you, that's the trick. So she dumped you?"

"I dumped her."

"Tell me another one. Go and answer the front door. That will be William and Betty with young Patrick. When your godfather and I first met as cub reporters on the *Mail* before he went to the *Manchester Guardian* there were just two of us to lunch. Now there are two families and a total of eight."

"Do you miss being single?"

"Not one minute. And I mean it, Harry. Pour yourself a drink. Hair of the dog. You really do look terrible, son. We're going to Devonshire for a week's holiday. Just me and your mother. You'll have to buy your lunch like everyone else for that week. There won't be a family Sunday lunch next weekend."

"Where are you going?"

"Hope Cove. Peace and quiet. Your mother needs to get away from all that stuttering."

"Why don't you go somewhere exotic?"

"Had enough of foreigners in my time. Hope Cove will be perfect.

Walk the beach. Put my feet in the water. I'm going to finish the newspaper."

"Don't worry about me."

"Dumped you did she? That's a real bitch."

"Dad, it's not funny."

"Oh yes it is. From here it's hilarious."

THEY HAD BEEN SITTING at the same long mahogany table for as long as he could remember. It was Harry's job on Sundays to unwind the top of the table and fit in the extra leaf. During the week there was the one family and a shorter table: on alternate Sundays the families visited each other for lunch. Ruthy had been a small girl, sitting on a cushion. Patrick her brother had sat in a high chair. Now she was a beautiful woman with a boyfriend. They were now friends. Best friends. More of a friend to Harry than any other person he could remember. All the years of his life his parents had lived in the same three-storey house with his mother's practice on the ground floor, the dining room and living rooms on the first floor. The bedrooms were on the top floor each with its own dormer window. There was a small garden out the back, the front of the house opening up close to the street and the line of trees, leafy in the summer, bare in the long winters when everyone kept inside. The German Luftwaffe had missed their house in Chelsea right through the war. For Harry, the house was a place of permanence, a place of security, a real home that would never go away. He had forgotten how important a part the Sunday lunch played in his life during the months he had spent with Petronella.

"I don't like family lunch on Sunday, Harry. You can go on your own. It doesn't matter if I don't see you. Please yourself. I was going to come round and visit you on Sunday. Never mind."

"But why don't you come with me?"

"All those people bore me."

"William Smythe bores you? He's one of the most celebrated radio and print journalists in London. I can listen to his stories all night."

"Then you listen to them. I'm not coming."

"Don't you like my parents?"

"They don't like me."

"They'll get used to you."

"I don't think so. All your mother talks about are silly people with stutters. When I bring up socialism or African politics your Mr Smythe clams up. Literally. I can see the muscles in his jaws grind together he clams up so tight. And as for that Ruthy she glares at me. As if I've stolen something that belongs to her. Patrick is just a boy. I don't like boys, Harry. They bore me. You run along to your family. Don't worry about me."

"I won't go then."

"Of course you won't. Why didn't you say that in the first place?"

Thinking of Petronella, his mind far away, he had not heard a word of the table's conversation. Ruthy was staring at him. Bergit dug him in the ribs.

"Come back, Harry. You're miles away," said his sister. "It's Sunday. You're not in your own flat. If you don't want those roast potatoes put them on my plate."

"You've eaten too much already."

"Of course I have. That's the whole point. It's Sunday lunch. We'll all fall asleep in the lounge in our chairs. What's the matter, Harry? Or is it that a silly question? Either marry her or forget the bitch."

"Don't do that," said Ruthy, staring at Harry.

For a moment there was silence. His mother brought out the sweet. He still had enough room for the trifle laced with half a bottle of sherry. As he ate the trifle spoon by spoon the smell of the sherry reminded him of what he was missing.

"He's gone again," said Patrick.

"I'm sorry. Bad hangover. What were you all saying?"

"That Africa's in a mess," said his father.

"Yes, I suppose it is. So is most of the world. Always has been. It's the people. People never change however much they try and learn."

"Quite the philosopher today, Harry," said William Smythe. "I've asked Josiah Makoni to come on the BBC talk show I do on Wednesdays."

"Has he accepted?"

"Not yet."

"He won't go. Won't want to be interviewed live. You can always ask Petronella."

"Ah, Petronella. How is she, Harry?"

"We've split up."

"That woman's a bitch. She's not good enough for you."

"What was that all about?" said Harry as Ruthy burst into tears and ran out of the room.

"You're an idiot," said Bergit. "I'll go and talk to her. Is it permanent this time, Harry?"

"I hope so. I really hope so. What's the matter with Ruthy?"

"Why don't you go and ask her, Harry?"

Harry looked at the articled clerk on the opposite side of the table.

"Don't look at me. We just work together. I don't have any family. Ruthy thought a family Sunday lunch would be good for me."

"I thought you were her boyfriend?"

"Ruthy and me? She wouldn't look at me."

"How's your trifle, Max?"

"It's perfect, Mrs Wakefield. I haven't had a good lunch like this for as long as I can remember."

"What happened to your parents? Ruthy did say you were on your own."

"A bomb. Direct hit at night when Mum and Dad were sleeping. I had been evacuated out of London to Cornwall in the Blitz."

"No uncles or aunts?"

"Uncle Steve was killed in Burma. He'd never married. Mother was an only child."

"I'm so sorry. I shouldn't pry."

"I was five years old. There was a little money from the house. War damages. Paid by the government. Put me through boarding school. My godfather became my legal guardian. He had been through the end of the First War with my father. Bonded in the trenches. Uncle Walter is a bachelor. Never quite knew what to do with me. Some people say he is gay. Probably why he kept me at such a distance. Go after her, Harry. You're her best friend."

"But why did she cry?"

"Why is my brother such an idiot?" said Bergit, coming back into the dining room. "Go and talk to her, Harry. She's in my room. Men! Why are they all so stupid?"

"Did she ask you to send me up?"

"Of course not."

"Then don't jump to conclusions. Sit down and finish your trifle."

When they all went into the lounge to sit in comfortable chairs the conversation died out. The man called Max had made his excuses when they left the dining room, profuse in his praise of the lunch. On his way out he looked up the stairs. To Max, it seemed to Harry, the lunch to meet her family had been a date. The man was confused.

In his chair with his mind switched off other people's problems Harry began to nod off to sleep. Those awake around him had their own private thoughts. What people thought and said was so often different. Ruthy had not come down.

When Harry woke it was five o'clock. He was the only one still in his chair. The hangover had gone. He felt better. In the kitchen his mother and sister were doing the dishes. Harry got up and joined them.

"Can I help? Where is everyone?"

"Did you enjoy your sleep?" asked his mother. "Get a tea towel and do some drying up. You know where to put everything. They've all gone home."

"Tonight I am spending on my own without one drop of booze."

"You can take what's left of the lamb. I've filled the box with lettuce, cucumber and tomatoes. You were right to leave her alone. Just a thought, Harry. Why don't you take Ruthy to the jazz club one day next week? Just the two of you. The one in Oxford Street."

Harry smiled at his mother as he dried the dishes.

"Don't you find her attractive?"

"Not when Petronella is around."

IN THE MORNING when Harry went to work there she was again. On the front page of the newspaper. The two of them kissing.

"Your girlfriend phoned," said Caroline at reception. "Says our man on today's front page is giving a live interview on BBC this Wednesday."

THEY MADE LOVE the next day making Harry oh so happy. All the dark clouds lifted. She had knocked on his door unannounced just before nine in the evening.

"What are you doing here, Petronella?"

"Don't be silly, darling. What do you think I'm doing here? Why the thunderous looks?"

She had stood on tiptoe as was her habit. She kissed slowly until Harry responded. The door of Harry's flat was kicked shut with the heel of her shoe. He had carried her into the bedroom.

"Is that better, darling?"

"Much better, thank you." Harry was smiling, his hands folded behind his head. Even the ceiling looked beautiful.

"Did you have a nice weekend, Harry?"

"Lunch with the family. You should have come."

"Much better to come this way, darling. Don't you think? Much more fun."

"Did she go with you?"

"Of course she did. Don't start that one again. I wanted to thank you properly for getting your godfather, that nice William Smythe, to interview Josiah on the BBC tomorrow. All that publicity is so good for our cause."

"He didn't want to be interviewed live."

"He told me so. I had to persuade him. Men are so easily persuaded. So are girls, come to think of it. I've got to go now, darling. You'll be all right now. Give me a little kiss."

When Harry picked up Ruthy Smythe the next day to take her to the Wednesday jazz evening at 101 Oxford Street, he was betwixt and between. He had phoned her and made the arrangement the previous morning. Before the evening knock on his door.

"Oh, Harry. She's back again."

"How can you tell?"

"Your eyes are shining. Yesterday your voice on the phone was flat as a pancake. Whose idea was this? Yours or your mother's?"

"Why did you cry on Sunday?"

"Girls are allowed to cry whenever they want. Come in, Harry. The place is a mess. The girls aren't home yet. Do you want to go out? You can sit and tell me what's going on with Petronella if you prefer?"

"I'm besotted by the girl. Can't think straight. Never been like this before."

"Maybe it's love, Harry. I hope not for your sake. Everyone knows she's bad news. Even her parents."

"It's worse than that. Love can be mutual. Calm and peaceful. This is lust. Pure bloody lust. Never properly satiated. I can't get enough."

"Poor Harry."

"Let's go to the jazz club. I can't talk about it. Chris Barber is playing. You like Chris Barber. We can have some food afterwards."

"One day this will be all over," said Ruthy quietly.

"That articled clerk fancies you."

"But I don't fancy him. Isn't life full of irony? I was hoping you would come round looking miserable."

"She uses me. Uses all of us. Doesn't give a damn about anyone. But I can't get away."

"You can always come and cry on my shoulder."

"I know that. You weren't crying about me on Sunday, were you? My sister gets her wires crossed."

"Would it matter if I was, Harry? You're in her grip. Nothing Ruthy can do about that... Come on. We can have fun. Like the old days."

She took his arm and they walked side by side from the flat in Knightsbridge into Kensington Road. Harry hailed a cab. Opened the door for Ruthy. Got into the back of the taxi and sat down next to her.

"Where to, governor?"

"101 Oxford Street."

He was going to try and enjoy himself. She was smiling at him.

"We've known each other all our lives, Ruthy."

"I know we have. Isn't this fun? Just the two of us in the back of a taxi. Going out to have fun. Cheer up, Harry. Women like that eventually self-destruct. They're so unhappy in themselves they want everyone around them to suffer. When their sex appeal goes they find themselves all on their own. No one wants to know them. Most take to the bottle. A few, the brave ones, kill themselves."

"Not Petronella. She's far too much in control."

"Mark my words."

"Are they your words or your mother's?"

"Does it matter, Harry? One day you and I will be laughing at mistress Petronella. By then, what she does with herself won't matter. Didn't Beth's husband play along at the jazz club? A clarinet. What's his name?"

"Paul Crookshank. Funny how so many of our lives are tied up with Beth's father."

"My father says Harry Brigandshaw will live forever, the legend growing with the years."

"He was my godfather. Now there was a man. I wonder what Uncle Harry would have thought of Petronella?"

"Not very much, I shouldn't think. Mother says he was a good judge of character. I've never been to Africa. I always wanted to go."

"Roland Cartwright wants me to go. Take over from Johnny Masters as our man in Salisbury."

"Are you going?"

"If they send me. Quite a leg up."

"Can I come and visit?"

"Why not, Ruthy?"

"I'd be so excited if I was going to Africa... She's not going home? Is that why you are going?"

"She says she'll only go home when the blacks are in power."

"She's going to have to wait a while from what I hear from Father. He's interviewing Josiah Makoni tonight. Live. Next Wednesday he's interviewing the Rhodesian High Commissioner. He doesn't expect a happy end. Says everyone involved is talking past each other. Foreign correspondent, Harry. That's wonderful. A great boost for your career. So much better than a shorthand typist. Girls get all the boring jobs. Do you want to have children, Harry?"

"One day."

"So do I. One day. Where are you taking me to supper? The Lyons Corner House will do. I'm not expensive."

"We'll go into Soho. Chinese. You like Chinese?"

"I love Chinese. This is so much fun."

"Everything will turn out fine for you, Ruthy."

THE CHINESE RESTAURANT was owned by a Chinaman from Hong Kong who had spent the war years in a Japanese prisoner of war camp. There were plastic tablecloths on the square tables. Small Chinese lanterns in the centre. The ceiling was low. The Chinaman had a big smile and big teeth. On a previous evening he had chatted to Harry while Harry was waiting for a guest he had been assigned to interview.

"He was in a Japanese prison camp during the war," Harry told Ruthy.

"So was my cousin Joe. He was in Changi on Singapore island. The Burma railway line. He survived. Married to a Chinese girl called Cherry Blossom. Never comes back to England. Never met my half-Chinese cousins. They say Joe is rich. Exports palm oil. No idea what they do with it. I'll bet his food is good. Instead of spending money on fancy décor he spends it on the food... I'm glad we left the jazz club early. Too many people on the dance floor. Couldn't hear yourself think. We were having to shout at each other. When you come back from Africa you can write a book. As a kid I went tobogganing with Dorian Brigandshaw on Headley Heath one afternoon when we were staying with the Brigandshaws for Christmas. I must have been five or six. He's made a lot of money out of his novels. With a big African novel you could go and live in the country and write to your heart's content. You always said you wanted to be a novelist. That journalism was just a means to an end. We used to talk about it a lot, Harry. Never lose your dreams. Without dreams life gets boring."

"Do you get bored?"

"Of course not. I have my dreams."

"What are they, Ruthy?"

"I'm not telling you."

"What you want to eat, missy?"

"Oh I'm sorry. Whatever you recommend. Do I have to use chopsticks?"

"You can use a spoon, missy."

The Chinaman was smiling at her. He was short. Shorter than her when she wore flat shoes. Harry told him to bring them different bowls of food, reading the names off the menu.

"I'm not drinking alcohol tonight, Ruthy. Do you mind drinking Chinese tea?"

"That will be nice. Me and the girls have a rule not to drink during the week... Are any of the Brigandshaws left in Africa?"

"Beth's brother-in-law has a farm in Rhodesia. A tobacco farm. I'll ask her to give me a letter of introduction. His name is Jeremy. Jeremy Crookshank."

"Isn't that a bit old-fashioned?"

"Probably. Anthony, the eldest of the Brigandshaw sons, was killed flying a Lancaster bomber over Berlin. The rest of Uncle Harry's children are in England. I always called my godfather Uncle Harry. He touched so many lives. Your father's. My father's. Without him I wouldn't be sitting here. He's buried in Rhodesia. Alongside his first wife and their unborn child."

"What happened to her?"

"She was shot by Uncle Harry's CO from the RFC. The Royal Flying Corps. The man was obsessed Uncle Harry had been after his fiancée because the girl wouldn't marry him. Mad as a hatter. Shot dead by Tembo, Josiah Makoni's father, after Mervyn Braithwaite killed Barend Oosthuizen, Uncle Harry's brother-in-law, on the platform of Salisbury Station. That day he was trying to shoot Tina, Harry's second wife and mother of Beth. They had let him out of the lunatic asylum. During the First World War Braithwaite was a hero. Fighter pilot. The world is always going round in circles. Tonight, round about now I should think, your dad is interviewing Tembo's son on the BBC. We all seem to be linked, Ruthy."

"Why can't we go through life just being friends with each other?"

"Life doesn't work that way I'm afraid... Just look at all this food."

"What is it?"

"I have absolutely no idea. I just read it off the menu and hope for the best."

"Spring roll, missy. Shrimp. Chinese rice. Very good. You enjoy, missy. Lots more to come."

She smiled after the little man as he hurried away.

"He's so small for a man. Are they all small?"

"Not all of them. Some of the northern tribes I believe. We know so little about China in the West. Oldest civilisation in the world. Enjoy the food."

PART V

SEPTEMBER TO DECEMBER 1963

HOW WELL WE RATIONALISE

1
---

*W*hen the interview was over, William Smythe thanking his guest Josiah Makoni, Jeremy Crookshank turned off his shortwave radio. All three of them sat back in silence. The radio mast outside Jeremy's study window shone in the pale moonlight, the mast rising high above the house on the ridge. A soft, hot wind came through the open window, through the fine wire mesh of the mosquito gauze. There was one small gas lamp burning on the table behind the elaborate radio.

"He sounded so bloody confident," said Clay Barry, the member-in-charge for the Centenary police station. "They must have a lot more Russian backing than we know about. And Chinese. There's a rumour the communist Chinese are getting into the act."

"Can we really stop Harold Macmillan's 'wind of change'?" said Jeremy.

"If we don't we might as well bugger off now," said Fred Rankin, Clay Barry's second in command.

"Anyone want a drink?" said Jeremy, getting up from the wooden chair he had been sitting on while he fiddled with the radio.

"Why not? After that diatribe I need a drink. The man's given me the shivers. How many more are there like our friend Josiah? He as much as admitted to Smythe he's training a guerrilla army... Where'd you learn how to work one of these fancy radios, Jeremy?"

"In the Royal Navy. Doing my National Service just after the war. Three years if you wanted to go in the navy. Two in the army or air force. I was the radio officer on HMS *Lynx*... Tonight was a good night for reception. Next month when the clouds build up for the rains it won't be so easy. Must be quarter past nine in London. We're an hour ahead of Greenwich meantime."

"Is it that late? Better go. If I don't get a good night's sleep I can't think straight in the mornings. I'll have to write a report on that broadcast. No one else around here has a fancy shortwave radio. Maybe it's all bluff. Talk. Like every other politician. There's no way the blacks could run this country. The place would dissolve into physical and economic chaos."

"Josiah doesn't think so."

"Wish we'd caught the bugger."

"What would you have done? Thrown him in jail. Made a hero out of him in the eyes of the rest of the world."

"Told you, you should have sold this place."

"It'll come right in the end."

"You're an eternal optimist, Jeremy. Thanks for supper. My poor wife. She never sees me these days. And when I get home I'm dog-tired and all I want to do is sleep. Poor Mary. It's a lonely life being married to a policeman."

"Joyce says the same. Goodnight, Jeremy. How's the farm?"

"The seed beds go in tomorrow. The cycle starts again. Just hope the rains are good. It's all about rain, farming in Africa. I'll see you both out. There's nothing I can do except hope. Rhodesia is such a wonderful country. We've done so much with the place."

"That's the trouble, old boy. Now it's worth something. When all this was bush no one gave a damn. Bit like the Transvaal. When they found diamonds and gold, what happened? The Boer War. Something of value. Everyone wants to get their hands on something of value. Like your tobacco with the price so bloody high. You tobacco farmers are making a fortune."

"All this politics pushed up the price of good Virginia leaf. The cigarette companies have been stockpiling in case we go down the tubes.

Supply and demand. What they like to call the free market system. Makes you laugh when Josiah wants to kick me off my farm."

"Funny old world. Made you a pile of money last season. Us poor policemen can look forward to a pension. If we are lucky. See you at the club over the weekend. There's no cricket. Tennis and drinking. Tough life in Africa... What a beautiful night. Three layers of stars. You can see all the way to heaven. The Southern Cross is real bright tonight. South over there. When I rode horses on patrol we followed that star. Goodnight. How are the kids by the way?"

"Fast asleep in their school dormitory, I hope."

"You should get married again."

"There isn't exactly a surplus of eligible girls in Rhodesia. I'm getting too old. Thirty-six next year. Soon I'll be forty. Too old for another family."

"Do you ever hear from Livy?"

"Not anymore. She's going to marry her boyfriend so I hear from Paul. He's some bigwig in the City. Commodities or something. The chap's loaded. Been after her for years. His money and her fame. Not a bad way to go. She certainly didn't want to live on this farm with all its political problems. Certainly not now. Certainly not after that interview we just heard. Underneath it all he was threatening us with a bush war if we don't hand over the country at the end of the year when the Federation breaks up. Livy's a practical girl. She has to think of Donna. In the end it's money that counts. Security. Love is the cherry on top."

"I suppose so. Goodnight, old boy. Just don't go back inside and get drunk on your own."

"I'll try not to."

Standing in the colourless glow from the sickle moon, Jeremy watched the police van drive away down through the avenue of gum trees. When the lights of the truck had gone, to reappear briefly down in the valley below his house on its height up on the ridge, Jeremy went back inside the house and into the lounge. Everything was deathly quiet, except for the high-pitched screech of the crickets.

"Are they cicadas or crickets?" he asked himself. "No one ever gives me a straight answer."

Silas had left the ice-bucket on the bar, next to a clean empty glass. Jeremy filled the cut crystal glass up with ice and poured over the whisky, squirting soda water on top from the syphon. Then he turned to Livy's portrait of his wife on the wall.

"Cheers, old girl."

For a long time he stood looking at Carmen. Her eyes followed him back to the bar. The stiff drink had gone down in one long swallow. Jeremy poured himself another one. Turned down the gas light in the lounge. Went outside to stand on the lawn and enjoy the night. The moon reflected the water in the swimming pool. A buck barked, one short bark, from somewhere far behind the tobacco barns. The compound was quiet. There never was a sound from the native compound on a Wednesday night. Jeremy sipped his drink, the ice clinking the side of the glass. The whisky tasted good.

"It's not all bad," he said to the night. "Not all bad."

An hour later, Jeremy went to bed and slept through the night, the birds waking him up in the light of the morning. He got out of bed and walked out down to the pool. He was wearing his bathing costume. Jeremy dived into the cool water of his pool and swam backwards and forwards for thirty brisk short lengths. When he walked back into the house he was dry. Breakfast was laid on the table, the smell of freshly made coffee making him smile. Silas came in with the toast and the bacon and eggs. They smiled at each other. Jeremy had drunk just enough whisky the previous night not to give himself a hangover. He was happy. A new day on the farm.

"Thank you, Silas. That all looks good."

THREE WEEKS later the phone rang while Jeremy was eating his dinner. Three longs and two shorts, his call sign on the party line that he shared with twenty-three of his fellow farmers. Puzzled as to who would call him out of business hours, he got up from the dining room table. During the day there were occasional calls from farm suppliers in Salisbury that he took in his office next to the workshop and barns. Bobby Preston, his twenty-year-old assistant, was on leave in England; his first trip back to his family in two years. No one else phoned the World's View number at night.

"Hello."

"Who's that? I'm trying to contact Jeremy Crookshank."

"Speaking."

"I'm a family friend of your sister-in-law, Beth. Harry Wakefield. The Harry is after her late father. She gave me your phone number. I've been posted to Rhodesia by my newspaper. Thought we might meet."

"You want to come out to the farm?"

"That would be nice. Don't know anyone here. The chap I've replaced went home yesterday. I'm at Meikles Hotel until I find a furnished flat to rent. We have some friends in common."

"Who?"

"Livy Johnston, for one. She's staying with her maiden name. She's always signed her paintings Livy Johnston."

"She's getting married?"

"She married Claud Gainsborough last week. I was at the wedding."

"Good for you."

"Are you all right?"

"Surprised at a phone call. I don't get many at night."

"I'm sorry. Is it too late? It's only eight o'clock. Donna said to send your boys her love. She says she misses them. And the swimming pool. Donna is Livy's daughter."

"I know who she is."

"You don't like newspaper reporters?"

"Not from England. They're all biased. Which paper are you with?"

"The *Daily Mirror*."

"Oh, my God! Your paper would throw every white person out of Rhodesia."

"Not quite that bad. I try to be unbiased. My godfather, William Smythe, taught me some ethics."

"I heard him interview Josiah Makoni. I have a shortwave radio."

"Then it really is a small world. Sorry to have bothered you."

"I'm sorry. You caught me on the hop. I'm coming into town tomorrow. Do the buying for next season. Wrapping paper. Hessian. That sort of thing. We bale the cured tobacco. Once the seedlings go in the ground I don't like to leave the farm. I usually stay the night at Meikles. How was Livy?"

"She talked about you. Not in front of her husband, of course."

"Did she? She was a close friend of my late wife. They roomed together in Salisbury. After Carmen died, Livy and I became close. We own a block of flats together in London. She didn't want to live in Rhodesia with Donna. I'll get the desk to page you if you are not in your room. What was your name again?"

"Harry Wakefield. I'll look forward to it."

"Should be fun. You can tell me all about Livy's wedding. You're not a communist by any chance?"

"Newspaper men never admit their politics. But no, I'm not. With my mother, father and sister I voted Conservative in the last election. My sister's coming out to visit me with Ruthy Smythe. We all grew up together in Chelsea. Maybe you'd like to meet my sister?"

"What about Ruthy?"

"Ruthy and I are best friends."

"Is she pretty? Your sister."

"Stunning. Now, don't forget to look for me tomorrow, Jeremy. You can fill me in from the farmers' point of view. We get a warped view of things from London. Is it always as hot and sticky in Rhodesia?"

"October is suicide month. The build-up to the rains."

"I'll try not to kill myself. See you tomorrow."

Jeremy stayed standing after he replaced the phone receiver on its hook. He was smiling. Not that a good-looking English girl who voted Conservative would look at him. The talk about Livy had disturbed him. Reminded him of what he had missed. Missed forever now she was married again.

"Good luck to you, Claud. Just look after her."

With his peace of mind disturbed, Jeremy walked across to his cocktail cabinet. It was always the same when he felt sad. He drank. There was still ice in the ice bucket from the sundowners he had taken before his supper. He filled up the crystal glass with ice, having thrown the dregs of water in the bottom of the glass into the ice bucket. There was always melting ice in the glass when he had finished a drink. He took the new drink across to Livy's portrait of his wife and lifted his glass.

"She's married. So that's it. Alone for the rest of my life. Cheers, old girl. It's always better when the kids are home for the weekend. You and I would have made the perfect pair in our old age. A couple of drunks."

"Anything more you want, *baas*?"

"No thanks, Silas. Goodnight. Tell Primrose she doesn't have to come up from the compound tomorrow. I'm going into Salisbury. I'm bringing back the boys from school on Friday on my way back to the farm. Miss Livy got married in London. You remember Miss Livy? Thank you, Silas."

When Silas had left, Jeremy wondered what he had been thinking. His expression was always inscrutable. Silas had worked for him as cook houseboy ever since Jeremy had built the house. Jeremy was more friendly with Primrose, the boys' nanny. He was always the *baas*. Silas always Silas. It was a pity. Neither of them knew very much about each other except as master and servant.

Jeremy took his drink out onto the lawn. It would take five minutes for the mosquitoes to find him. The cicadas were screeching in a higher pitch with the rising heat. Far away behind the hills towards the Zambezi escarpment he thought he heard thunder. The moon was full. He thought of going down to the pool. He was lonely, more lonely than he had been for a long time. When she was still unmarried there had always been hope. Women changed their minds. Now there was none. No hope. The boys would grow up and go their separate ways. There was no hope. All this great big farm and no one to share it. There was a price to pay for everything but was it worth it? Standing alone on his lawn in the moonlight, Jeremy was no longer sure.

When the first mosquito bit he went inside. And poured himself another drink. All he had to do the next day was drive and pick up the stores.

When Jeremy went to bed he was drunk, staggering down the corridor to the bedroom he had shared with Carmen bouncing from the walls.

"You're drunk, old boy. Tomorrow you shall have a hangover. What a lovely bloody world."

JEREMY LEFT World's View with the dawn for the more than two-hour drive into Salisbury. He felt terrible. It was hot, the air through the open side window of the truck making no difference to his discomfort.

"Why the hell do I drink?" he said to himself. "At the time I think I am enjoying myself but I'm not."

The dust streamed out behind the car covering the few black people walking down the road obscuring them in Jeremy's rear-view mirror.

"Poor sods walking in this heat. Then I cover them in dust."

With his mind on Livy, Jeremy quickly forgot the dust cloud thrown up by the truck. At Concession the dirt road became strips making Jeremy less irritable. Later, at Mazoe, the road became full tar. The orange trees were in blossom, the smell sweet in the car. Some of the trees had fruit on them from the previous season. The straight rows of trees went on and on right up to the foothills. The road climbed up into the hills, the water from the Mazoe dam clearly visible. Jeremy stopped by the side of the road looking down on the water. There were two sailing boats out on the lake. One of the boats had red sails. Egyptian geese flew in threes over the water, two males chasing the same female. It was a pretty sight. He poured himself coffee from the flask Silas had put in the car. His mouth was dry from the previous night's drinking. In the plastic box for his breakfast he found two hard-boiled eggs and three cold sausages. He was hungry from his hangover. The thought of Livy married to Claud Gainsborough brought tears to his eyes.

"You had your chance, you idiot. Now it's too late. With the country about to fall apart no one in their right mind would buy the farm. So that's that. No point in crying over spilt milk."

Feeling sorry for himself, Jeremy drove the rest of the way into Salisbury, straight to the Farmers Co-op where he did his business. Two black men carried his supplies out to the truck where they loaded them into the back. When Jeremy drove to the centre of town it was one o'clock. Parking the truck in the hotel yard at the back of the building Jeremy walked inside and through the bar. He had time to drive home to the farm had he wanted, which meant driving halfway back to Umvukwes to pick up the boys from school. The bar was full of farmers dressed like himself in khaki shorts and shirts, bush hats on the bar counter. There was no one he knew in the bar. Most of them were youngsters.

"Give me an ice-cold Castle, Henry."

"Coming up, sir. There's a man down the bar asking for you."

"What's his name? Which one, Henry?"

Henry, the barman, pointed to a young man at the end of the bar.

"Bring my beer down the bar. I'm going to talk to him... Excuse me. Are you Harry Wakefield?"

"You must be Jeremy Crookshank. I saw the barman pointing me out to you. What are you drinking?"

"It's coming. So you were at Livy's wedding?"

"Yes, I was. Funny how small the world is. From London to here. Seven thousand miles away. I'm sorry to phone you so late last night. Are you booked into the hotel?"

"Not yet. I've done the shopping. Maybe some lunch."

"That would be nice. Did you know Harry Brigandshaw?"

"He flew a flying boat with my father. Dad was killed in the war. Harry suggested I came to Rhodesia when he was on a visit of condolence to my mother in the Isle of Wight after the war. How I got here I suppose."

"He affected so many people's lives. He was always helping people."

"So what's going to happen to Rhodesia?" asked Jeremy.

"You tell me. I've just arrived. Wet behind the ears. That sort of thing. Did you ever know a girl called Petronella Maple? She's my girlfriend."

"You poor sod. I worked for her father. Or more exactly, for her mother. I just saw them in the lobby. Going in to lunch. You want to go and meet them? The old man's all right. It's his wife I can't stand. One of those women with her nose permanently stuck up in the air, as if everyone else is beneath her."

"Petronella didn't think you'd remember her. She was thirteen last time she saw you."

"As stuck up as her mother. No offence. The rich farmer's daughter. Too high and mighty for a lowly learner assistant just out from England."

"And now she's a communist. You chaps might call her a traitor."

"Let's not get into politics in a bar. Cheers. Nice to meet you. So you're living in the hotel?"

"Room 203. At the back. Cheapest room. My paper doesn't pander to its journalists. Were you going to look me up?"

"Quite frankly, I'd forgotten," lied Jeremy. "Well, not quite. I didn't want to confront Livy getting married to Claud Gainsborough."

"I know the feeling. Petronella also shags Josiah Makoni."

"Good God! Does her mother know?"

"She doesn't care."

"Do you? You said she was your girlfriend."

"We all share Petronella when it suits her."

"Let me get you a drink."

"Thank you, Jeremy. You don't mind me calling you Jeremy?"

"Of course not. What a dreadful scenario."

"The other party in the trio is a girl."

"I don't understand."

"The young girl you told to 'take it easy greasy, you've got a long way to slide', is bisexual. She sleeps with men and women. Trouble is, I can't get her out of my system. Why I'm here, I suppose. What's that you are drinking?"

"Cold Castle. You get a Lion or a Castle in Rhodesia. Take your pick."

"I've been drinking Castle."

"So how was Livy?"

WHEN THEY WENT in to lunch Harry Wakefield looked around the big dining room. He was sweating like the rest of them, the punkahs going slowly round in the ceiling making no impact on the heavy air. It was all so colonial, making Harry smile at such an anachronism. More like the 1920s than the 1960s; not a black face sitting at the tables, the women all in print frocks not wearing hats. Most of the older men wore military moustaches. Many were red-faced from the sun and drink. It was the first time he had eaten in the hotel other than at breakfast. He wanted to laugh. Two tables away was an elderly man and a woman, the woman's face much like a horse. Something in the look of the woman reminded Harry of Petronella. When the man turned and looked at him staring, Harry was sure.

"That's Mr and Mrs Maple two tables away?"

"Yes, that's them. If you want to go over you're on your own. She's always rude to me."

"I didn't know this kind of place still existed."

"What do you mean?"

"All the *bwana* and *memsahib* business."

"You're mixing your continents. *Bwana* is Swahili. Kenya. *Memsahib* is more India."

"My generation is postcolonial. Can this really go on in the second half of the twentieth century?"

"Harry Brigandshaw didn't think so. What put Livy off wanting to stay in Rhodesia. She wanted me to sell World's View and take the money back to England while I still could."

"Why didn't you?"

"We're all eternal optimists when we've got something and don't wish to change. World's View is my home. I've built the farm up from scratch. All I will ever do, most probably, that will be important in my life. It's not just money. A farm of your own is so tangible. You can see what you've done. All the planning and hard work is visible."

"But have you got it?"

"It was too late to change. Too late to build something in England even if I had the slightest idea of what to build. Just having money in the bank to spend isn't enough to satisfy me after making World's View what it is. And there's still lots to do. More dams. More irrigation. Different crops so as not to rely on the fickle price of tobacco. Seeing a kilometre or two of flourishing crops is as much reward a man can ever get. It's primal. What's in our make-up from all our ancestors' struggle to survive through history. A farm has everything. A home. Food. Animals. Tranquillity. And no one telling you what to do."

"Josiah wants to tell you what to do. He wants to tell you all to go to hell. So does Petronella. How can she want to destroy her parents? They gave her life."

"Sounds as if you don't like your girlfriend, Harry."

"I don't. I just can't live without her or with her I suppose. What happened to your wife?"

"She was eaten by lions. Got drunk and went for a drive in the bush. The one long road that leads out into the Zambezi escarpment and then down into the valley. Ran out of petrol. Walked down the road looking for water."

"I'm so sorry."

"I'm going the same way. Drinking too much. Livy is far better off with Claud Gainsborough."

"We all drink when we're lonely. I'd better go and say hello."

"Did Petronella ask you to?"

"No, her grandfather asked me to say hello. How I met Petronella, looking for her story. Now I can't get away from the girl."

"Just don't say I sent you over. I can't stand scenes. Why are some people so damn disagreeable?"

"Maybe it's in their genes. I've got plenty of time to meet the Maples. Better another time… When's it going to rain? This heat's oppressive."

"Soon, we hope. Always the same in October. You said you wanted somewhere to stay in Salisbury. Why not Mrs Wade in Baker Avenue? She lets out rooms in her house to young people. As much for the company as the money. You get a room and she feeds you. Livy came out to see me some fourteen years ago and stayed with Mrs Wade. I found her the room. Carmen was in one of Mrs Wade's rooms. How we met. When Livy went back to England we went out together. Livy had married Frank St Clair, the father of Donna. Mrs Wade is a dear old soul. I can take you to the house after we've had lunch. I quite often visit Mrs Wade. She loves a natter. I like talking about Livy and Carmen. Did Livy look happy at her wedding? You ever been on your own, Harry? I mean really on your own? Afterwards I could show you a bit of Salisbury. Have a drink at Bretts. Introduce you to some of the fellows from town. Later you could come out to the farm and meet my boys. Weekly boarders. I'll pick them up in Umvukwes tomorrow on my way back to the farm. I'm much happier with the boys at home. I like all the noise." Jeremy knew he was jabbering. A symptom of too many hours alone on the farm with no one to talk to. All his thoughts were coming out in a jumble.

"How old are they?"

"Phillip is eight. Randall is turning six in December."

"Isn't that a bit young to be away from their mother?"

Jeremy looked at him, bewildered. "They don't have a mother. They have to go to primary school. The place at Umvukwes is the best I can do."

"Of course. I wasn't thinking. I have such a close family. You'll meet Bergit. She's coming out over Christmas for a holiday. Only time they can get away from work. Ruthy's a shorthand typist. So is Bergit. Not much else a girl can do before she gets married."

"You've missed your chance. The Maples are leaving. The old man smiled at me. Flossy looked right over my head as though she hadn't seen me."

"Do you want to give me an insight as to what's going to happen in Rhodesia from a farmer's point of view?"

"I don't get myself involved with politics. My biggest problem every year is the amount of rain. Drought is a far bigger problem to a farmer than the politicians."

"Not if they take away your farm."

"It's not the ownership of land that's important. It's the crops that are produced on the land. Any fool can own a tract of bush. The trick is turning it into productive farmland. Then you have to maintain the land with careful conservation. Crops on the same piece of soil every four years in Africa. You have to know what you're doing or the yields keep going down to nothing and the land is worthless. What happens with African peasant farming. Why it doesn't sustain itself. In the old days of half a million people in Rhodesia they could move on once they had exhausted the land. Not now with the two million people and growing fast. Some estimates say the population of Southern Rhodesia will top fifteen million by the end of the twentieth century. God help them if we don't farm properly. Or they'll starve. It's what you produce that counts. Not who owns the land. You can quote me on that if you want."

"Can't they take over your farm and run it properly?"

"Time will tell. They look at my farm now and want it. When it was bush they didn't give a damn. You need knowledge, capital and skills to run a modern farm. You can't get a mechanic out on the farm from Salisbury at the drop of a hat. Far too expensive. You have to fix the mechanical problem yourself. You have to run the accounts. Add up the figures. Know what you are spending money on. Balance the books. Commercial farming is big business. It's not raising a couple of cows and chickens, growing a bit of maize for your family. That's why the African farmers are so poor. They live hand to mouth. One year of drought and they starve. Literally."

"Can't you teach them to farm properly?"

"We're trying. With the Purchase Farms. Black farmers owning their own three hundred acres with the next door commercial farmer mentoring."

"Is it working?"

"Not very well. They want you to do everything. You show them a way round a problem and next year they make the same mistake. Their idea of farming is a herd of cattle looked after by their kids. Six- and seven-year-olds, herding a few cows in the bush. And a patch of maize looked after by their wives. Why they have more than one wife and all the children. It's a vicious circle. Now, shall we go and see Mrs Wade? Nothing is ever simple, Harry. Never black and white, if you'll excuse the pun. In my limited experience it's a few people at the top who do the thinking and get things done. In business or in farming. Or in life. The rest like to shout about it and that includes all the politicians. Black, white and khaki. The talkers. How I hate the talkers."

Harry was left at Mrs Wade's while Jeremy did the rest of his shopping in the town. The room and Mrs Wade would suit him just fine, he told himself. The room overlooked a small garden at the back of Mrs Wade's bungalow. The other two rooms were let to young men. He would meet them later when they returned from work. He went for a walk up the tree-lined avenue, happy with himself. The seven thousand-mile distance from Petronella was helping. He was glad he had not spoken to the Maples. An article on the future of Rhodesia was going round in his mind as he walked along under the jacaranda trees, a blaze of blue flowers matching the African sky. Far away he could hear the thunder growling, a sound of menace unlike thunder in England. He was sweating profusely as he walked. Johnny Masters had said the heat would be less oppressive when the rains broke. Like Jeremy Crookshank, he had asked Johnny Masters what was going to happen.

"You want my opinion as the African correspondent of the *Daily Mirror* with an eye on our readership or as a man, Harry? I've lived here three years. Cheap booze and cigarettes. Sunshine. Except for the month of October a perfect climate. Swimming pools in all your friends' houses. Steaks the size of your dinner plate. Servants at your beck and call. It's a white man's paradise. But like that thunder building up from the north there's going to be a storm. One big motherfucker of a storm. Life here is too good to be true. Enjoy it while you're here, Harry my boy. Put it in your memory bank. If there were more girls I wouldn't have asked for a job back in London. But you can't have everything. Just almost everything in Rhodesia. If you're lucky enough to be invited to one of the farms, take the opportunity with both hands. The culture on the farms is positively feudal. Not the methods of farming: they're as modern as big farming in America. Some of the larger farms are half the size of an English county. All they don't have here is a title. They just imagine themselves as lords of the manor. Hundreds of them. Will it last? Of course it won't. There's as much jealousy in our readers back home as there is in the Africans out here. It's ridiculous disparity in wealth. The blacks walk everywhere. The whites drive in their Land Rovers and Mercedes in the comfort of air conditioning. Oh, they made the wealth for themselves, don't make any mistake. No black farmer would have done it. Cut the farms out of the bush. Constructed an entire industry to supply the British with Virginia tobacco we can pay for with sterling instead of dollars. But the glaring wealth divide will destroy them. Jealousy, Harry. That's what will destroy them. And Britain won't help a quarter of a million whites, mostly British, stuck in the middle of Africa. Britain's gone socialist. These whites are the epitome of the wealthy class. They've had their fun. With the breakup of the Federation they're going to be on their own. I tell my friends to get out. While the going's good. Why I'm leaving before I grow too accustomed to the white man's way of life. No one ever had it this good before. A lifestyle never to be repeated and, if you've lived it, never to be forgotten. I'm going back to an expensive pint of beer and bangers and mash. Won't be able to afford to smoke cigarettes. Filthy habit anyway. Cough my lungs up every morning. Were it not for the tax revenue from cigarettes there are some in the Labour Party who would ban smoking. If you are lucky enough to find yourself a girl you'll have the perfect life up here in the Rhodesian highveld. Do you know there are four young men for every young girl? In the old days in India when we still had the Raj, the young girls without prospects in England were sent out on the boats. They called them the fishing fleet. Fishing for husbands. If they married well they travelled home in a cabin on the starboard side of the ship where the sun didn't come in. Port out, starboard home. POSH. Get it? The posh days are over. The empire's finished. So are the whites in Africa but they won't admit it. Often in life it doesn't pay to succeed. You become too obvious. You need just enough money to go through life, if you ask my opinion. Too much and you flash it around. People pretend they admire a successful person. Inside they're bitter with envy. Never look conspicuous, Harry. Doesn't pay. Human nature is a lot more simple than people make it out to be. A whole lot more basic. I'm going back to England by boat, did I tell you? The boat fare's the same as the plane. Going up the east coast of Africa from Beira. Through the Suez Canal the Egyptians so kindly let us now travel through after our brief war with them in '56. They took back the canal. We tried to fight them. Didn't work. Neither will Rhodesia. I'm going to ride a camel. Look at the Pyramids. Enjoy the last of the sun that's setting on the British Empire. I'm going to be one of the last POSH to travel home in style. Pink gins on deck. A cabin with a porthole all to myself. Do it in style. Won't happen again. Three weeks. Marvellous. When I get back to Fleet Street I'll again behave like a nice little socialist. But inside there will always be the memory of the last true outpost of the British Empire. Rhodesia."

"When's it going to blow, Johnny?"

"Months rather than years. You might even make yourself famous as a journalist. Reporting the last imperial wave of the hand. Anything else you want to know?"

"Not really."

2

The Tannoy woke Ruthy Smythe from her dreams.

"You've been asleep the best part of three hours," said Bergit Wakefield. "You've got to fasten your seatbelt. We started our descent into Salisbury ten minutes ago."

"Did you get any sleep?"

"I dozed. Never could sleep on an aeroplane."

"I've never been out of England."

"Flew to America with my father and mother. Harry had left home by then. Dad was on an assignment to some connection in New York. Swapped his first-class ticket for three in the tourist class. Before I got my present job. You were still at school."

"I hope Harry's remembered to meet the plane."

"Of course he has. I'd wring his neck if he'd forgotten his sister was visiting."

"I'm so excited. Do you think it will be hot?"

"In the eighties or nineties according to Harry."

"How weird. You get on a plane in sub-zero London wearing an overcoat and get off fifteen hours later in someone else's summer. How long were we stopped at Nairobi?"

"About an hour."

"I was dozing. Look, you can see houses down below. I thought it would just be bush. Look at all those swimming pools. Oh, Bergit, isn't this fun... Do you think he's forgotten the bitch by now?"

"You want a facecloth, madam?"

"Thank you... Oh, that feels so cool."

"We're landing at Salisbury airport in ten minutes."

Ruthy watched the air hostess go to the front of the plane and pull down a seat next to the galley and belt herself in. The Comet floated down to earth, kissing the ground gently with its wheels rolling down the runway, the only aircraft in sight, the jet engines screaming in reverse. At the end of the runway the plane turned, heading to the airport building.

"Welcome to Rhodesia, everyone."

"Was that the pilot?"

"Or the co-pilot. We're here Ruthy. Two weeks of sunshine."

"Where are we staying?"

"I have no idea. Takes twenty minutes to pick up our luggage and go through immigration and customs. Then the holiday begins. Do you know there are four men for every girl in Rhodesia?"

"You have mentioned it a couple of times." Ruthy was smiling.

"Let the games begin, Ruthy. We've arrived."

"It's going to be so strange spending Christmas away from Mum and Dad. Without my brother. Sitting round one of those swimming pools instead of a roaring log fire. Patrick's a pain in the arse sometimes but I'll miss him for Christmas."

"I'm sure we'll get used to a swimming pool. Come on. We've stopped. Grab your hand baggage. The seatbelt light's gone out. It's party time."

"There he is," said Bergit Wakefield, waving to her brother Harry. "He's seen us. Who's the man next to him with the perfect suntan?"

"He's a bit old."

"Not for my taste."

"Slow down, Bergit. There are four single men for every girl."

"Hello, Harry. Wow, it's hot. You want to push the luggage cart?"

"All this for two weeks? How are you, sis? This is Jeremy Crookshank, our host for Christmas. We're going out into the bush. To Jeremy's farm. He's Paul's brother. Hello, Ruthy. Give me that case. We're all in the one car. Jeremy brought the Chev Impala and not the truck. We're lucky. The main rains were late so they're not yet reaping the tobacco."

"Have you got a swimming pool?" asked Bergit, flirting with Jeremy. "How far is it?"

"Just around the corner. A two-hour drive with the top down." Jeremy was smiling.

"I've taken a week's leave," said Harry.

The car was parked outside the airport building, waiting. Jeremy put their luggage in the boot of the car.

"You know they call that the trunk in America?" said Bergit. "My last trip was to New York. Are you a bachelor, Jeremy?"

"Widower. My wife was killed. I have two young boys waiting for us on the farm."

"Oh... I am sorry... What do you call your farm? How big is it?"

"Six thousand acres. A lot of the farm is still bush. Takes many years to develop. World's View. I called the farm World's View."

"Strange name for a farm."

"You'll see why. I built the house on a ridge with a view of the world all the way round. From every window. Will you sit in the front with me? Let Ruthy and Harry sit in the back so they can talk. Welcome to Africa. The most exciting place in the world. When you've been here a while the bug bites you and you can't go back to England. Everyone thinks I should."

"What happened to your wife, if you don't mind me asking?"

"She was killed by lions."

"How awful. Did you kill the lions?"

"I wasn't there... Ruthy, you sit in the back with Harry. You two can catch up on the way out to the farm."

"Have you heard from Petronella, Harry?" asked Bergit.

"Not a word. Jeremy pointed out her parents in Meikles. Didn't speak to them. Why are you grinning, Ruthy?"

"No reason. So we're spending Christmas in the African bush. You've got a lovely suntan, Harry. I must look so pale."

"You look wonderful, Ruthy. Just wonderful."

FOUR LARGE DOGS greeted the car on World's View. All had their front paws up on the side of the open car. The one nearest to Jeremy was slobbering.

"Yes, my boy. Was I away too long? Now get off the bloody paintwork. Dogs! They get so excited. Stretch your legs. After fifteen hours in an aeroplane and more than two in my car you both need a good swim. Then we'll have a cocktail. I'm going to make each of us a big tall glass of Pimm's. Here come the kids. They get as excited as the dogs when I have visitors. Bobby Preston's been looking after the farm for a couple of days while I was in town. He's my assistant. All that Christmas shopping. Your brother took me to Bretts. Ashamed to say we both got drunk. Has a dance floor and the best band in Africa. I'm inclined to let my hair down when I go into town. Silas, please take our guests' luggage to their bedrooms. Silas had been looking after the house ever since I built the place. I'm going to make a Pimm's, Silas. Can you bring everything I need to the pool?"

"This place is so beautiful."

"Thank you, Bergit. That one's Phillip, he's the oldest. That's Randall. Randall turned six last week."

"Who looks after them when you're away?" asked Bergit.

"Primrose. She's been their nanny since the boys were born. She has a boy and a girl the same age as my kids. They all play together. Boys, say hello to Aunty Bergit and Aunty Ruthy. They are friends of your Uncle Paul. They've flown all the way from England to see you. Come on. Let's show you where you are sleeping. You can change into your bathing costumes in your bedrooms."

"What's that tall tower?"

"A radio mast. Shortwave radio. I can pick up London. I was in the Royal Navy for three years. Radio officer. They've stopped National Service in England now."

"I got deferred," said Harry. "When I was eligible at eighteen National Service was winding down."

"Takes a big chunk out of a young man's life. Didn't feel like studying when I came out of the navy. Why I chose tobacco farming in Rhodesia. Not much else for a twenty-one-year-old without a tertiary education."

"The newspaper got me deferred. Said I was an apprentice. The other way was to flunk the medical. The war was over. I hate wars. So does our dad."

"Which suitcase is which, Ruthy? You're in the last room down the corridor on the right. Just push those dogs out the way. Shumba, you're a bloody menace. They're all Alsatians from the same litter. Chap in Salisbury who breeds dogs sold them to me. Pedigree as long as your arm. They have the habit of getting in the way of visitors."

"Are they being aggressive or friendly?" asked Bergit.

"A bit of both until they get to know you. We all have packs of dogs on the farms. Shumba leads his brother and sisters into the bush hunting. Shumba the lion. The cats ignore them. Once Shumba had a go at Ingwe, the mother cat. Mother and six kittens from the same litter all grown into big cats. Ingwe gave that dog such a swipe with her paw he never went near her again. He was only a pup. Found the cat in Port St Johns on the Transkei Coast. She's feral. Half Cape wild cat. Didn't know she was pregnant until I got her back to the farm in a large wicker basket. We were fishing for musselcrackers. Caught one of nearly eight pounds. Made a fire on the beach and made a *braai*... Silas, that case goes in there, the other next door. Will you girls be all right?"

"Looks perfect."

"The bathroom and loo are across the corridor."

"I'll go get the Pimm's."

"Thank you, Silas."

"*Baas.*"

"Where's my brother Harry?"

"Down by the pool. He's been here before. Knows his way around. The boys dragged him off. Anything you want, just ask. We serve supper at seven o'clock on the veranda. We call it the *stoep*. If you want something to eat before supper Silas will make you a sandwich. We bake our own bread on the farm. A side of venison with a side of red currant jelly tonight. The jelly comes out from England. My mother served lamb that way. Lots of things we do here goes back to England. Friend of mine in the police shot the buck and gave me a hind quarter. We play cricket together at the club. You'll meet Clay Barry. See you girls down at the pool."

When Jeremy walked away down the corridor followed by his dogs they were left alone in the end room, both of them going into a fit of the giggles.

"Have you ever seen anything like this, Ruthy? This kind of life is just perfect. Pimm's by the pool. Servants carrying the bags. Venison for supper. My word, I could get used to this."

"He's got two small sons."

"They've got a nanny. Just look at the view from your bedroom, Ruthy. You can see forever. Purple mountains in the far distance. All those lovely exotic birds calling. Look at that one. Bright red and blue. No wonder the whites don't want to hand over Rhodesia. How did it feel in the back of the car with my brother?"

"I'm working on it. What do you think of my bikini?"

"You're naked!"

"That's the whole idea. Go and change, Bergit. My goodness, that does have a nice ring to it. None of this will last, of course."

"Don't be a spoilsport. Nothing ever lasts in life. Just enjoy it while you can. Do you really have to walk to the pool in those high heels?"

"Makes my bum wiggle. I'm going to marry him, Bergit. Made up my mind when I was ten. It's just that bitch who is the trouble. What has that woman got that I don't?"

"It could be the fact you are still a virgin. Men want sex, Ruthy."

"How do you know?"

"Don't ask questions."

THEY WALKED out together onto the lawn and across through trees towards the pool where they could see the kids splashing in the water. Two of the children were black. There were flowerbeds around the base of the trunks giving colour under the green leaves of the trees. Beyond the trees was the view far out to the purple mountains. Pigeons and doves were calling all round them. The dogs were chasing each other round the trees and through the flowerbeds causing havoc. Ruthy could smell the newly cut lawn. To the right was a rose bed in full bloom, red and yellow flowers, each one perfect. Flowering creepers ran up into the canopy of the trees sending her the heady scent of perfume as she passed. She wished she had put on flat shoes as her heels sank into the soft watered grass. Down by the tall fence that surrounded the acres of garden, overhead sprays were swishing water on the grass and the flowers, a rhythmic sound that was comforting. Ruthy took off her shoes and carried them. The dogs took no notice as they passed by. One of the cats was high up a tree looking down at the dogs. Both Harry and Jeremy were standing next to a table by the pool in their bathing costumes. Both were richly tanned without an ounce of fat on their bodies. At the gate of the pool, Ruthy put on her shoes. She could see the fruit and tall slices of cucumber in the glasses of Pimm's, the floating ice shining at the top of the drinks.

"Pimm's No. 1. Gin base. I splash in an extra bit of straight Booth's gin to give it a bit more kick. Fresh fruit, cucumber and mint. Best summer drink in the world. Have a swim and come enjoy the drinks. That's Happiness and Moley in the pool with the boys. Primrose over there is their mother. Say hello to Primrose. Without her I don't know how I would have coped with my boys after their mother died. The girl's real name is a Shona word that means happiness. We're inclined to Anglicise everything I'm afraid. I called him Moley after my favourite character in *The Wind and the Willows*. He was so round and cuddly as a toddler trying to walk. Now they all call him Moley. You can dive in if you want. It's deep at the top end."

"What was that big bird all blue with a flash of red?"

"A purple-crested lourie. The grey lourie is more common in these parts. We call the grey lourie the 'go away bird'. When it calls it sounds like 'go away' in a falling fade-away sound. You'll hear them. Now I've told you, you'll recognise their call. There are so many birds on World's View. Some of the very tiny ones are even prettier. They're all sunbirds."

"This place is all so beautiful, Jeremy."

"Thank you, Bergit. I think so. I love Africa with a deep passion. Like the rest of us. The place gets hold of you. Africa. Jump in before too much of the ice melts in your drinks. Are you hungry?"

"Not yet. We're going to wait for the venison."

"I find snacks ruin my supper."

"The air is so warm."

"So is the water. Don't stay too long in the sun the first few days or you'll burn. I've brought you both some suntan oil that works in the tropics. Put it on when you come out of the water."

"Will you put some on my back, Jeremy?" Ruthy was smiling at him. Bergit walked over to the edge of the pool and jumped in, holding her knees up to her chest as she splashed into the water.

Ruthy ran ten paces and dived in.

"It's lovely," called Ruthy. "Come in, Harry."

"All right."

She watched him dive right under her, brushing her thighs as he swam past, the touch very sensual.

"You touched me, Harry!"

"I'm sorry."

"Don't be sorry. I loved it. I'm so glad we came."

"So am I," said Bergit. "Come on, Jeremy. Your turn to dive. When does the sun go down?"

"In about half an hour. Sundowner time."

When Jeremy came up from under the water he was next to Bergit, holding onto the side of the pool. She kissed him on his wet open mouth.

"Thank you for having us, Jeremy. This is so much fun. Do you have a nice red wine to go with the venison?"

"Of course. The cork's been out of three bottles since you went to change. A good French red has to breathe a couple of hours before it's drunk. Or so they tell me. You want to swim a couple of lengths?"

"Come on."

RUTHY FELT a flood of wellbeing flow through her mind and body. She was standing on the side of the pool. Small birds with long hooked beaks were drawing nectar from the flowers. Butterflies with kite tails were flitting from flower to flower. The butterflies were the size of the palm of her hand, yellow with rich black patterns on their wings. Through the trees the last of the sun was playing on the thatched roof of the bungalow high up on its ridge. The tall radio mast with its wires stood out against the sky. The clouds were tinged with red.

"The flowers smell so sweet in the evening, Harry." He had come up beside her, a glass held in his hands. Condensation was trickling down the side of the glass.

"That's the size of a small bucket."

"It's all yours. Cheers, Ruthy. Good to see you. We're a long way from home."

"It's so peaceful."

"On the surface."

"Always the journalist. I'm dry already... My word this does taste good. Cheers, Jeremy. I'd raise my glass to you but I need both hands to hold it."

The light faded while Ruthy sipped down her drink. When she had finished there were small pieces of ice in the bottom of her glass with the fruit and cucumber. The light had faded in half an hour. It was still hot. Over behind the distant mountains, now shadows in the dark, thunder was rolling. A faraway menace. They swam again in the pool before walking across the sloping lawns up to the veranda of the house. Gauze meshing now closed in the long open-sided veranda that ran the length of the side of the house. A kerosene lamp was burning, making a fizzing sound. The table was laid for supper. At the top and bottom of the table were open bottles of wine. The Pimm's had gone to Ruthy's, head making their voices seem distant. Around a low table, comfortable chairs faced the last glow of red in the sky. Crickets were screeching outside the protection of the fine mesh gauze. Another sound, deeper, Ruthy had not heard before. The crickets were like English crickets only much louder. The light from the kerosene lamp took up some of the dark: as far as the dining table and the comfortable chairs. They all sat looking out at the African night. Their world had shrunk. Ruthy was still in her bikini, the towel loosely held over her knees. Perspiration trickled down the sides of her face.

When the girls went to change for dinner, Silas had lit a small paraffin lamp that attached to the side of the corridor halfway down. Ruthy could smell the paraffin burning. In her room another lamp was burning. Slowly, happily, still feeling Jeremy's copious adding of gin, she changed into a summer frock. The frock was a bright red and matched the high heels she had carried back from the pool. Next door she could hear Bergit changing in her room. The men had also gone off to change. Ruthy could hear the children laughing from somewhere deep inside the darkened house. The thunder was still rumbling but further away. She walked back into the corridor leaving the room lamp burning, not sure what to do.

"You ready, Bergit? Do we turn out the lamps?"

"Probably. Keep the bugs out. That looks nice. I'm starving. The light will stay on in the corridor."

"Don't they have electricity in Rhodesia?"

"Generators. Turn them on when they want. Romantic evenings don't want a lot of light. Have you ever eaten venison before?"

"I don't think so. The thunder's going away."

When they passed through the lounge a light was burning next to the portrait of a young girl. As they went towards the door to the veranda and the windows along the lounge the girl's eyes followed Ruthy, making her stop.

"Whoever painted this knew what she was doing. I say, it's a Livy Johnston. You can see the signature in the bottom right-hand corner."

"It's my dead wife," said Jeremy. He was standing in the doorway onto the veranda, a drink in his hand. "I knew Livy before I knew Carmen. They roomed at Mrs Wade's in town. Where Harry is staying. When Livy left me and went back to England to marry Frank St Clair, who went by the name of Frank Brigandshaw earlier on in his life, I married Carmen. There were three of them at Mrs Wade's. Livy, Carmen and Candy. They were all best friends."

"Wherever we go, Harry Brigandshaw somehow comes into it."

"Certainly in Africa. He's what ties us all together. Me, Harry, you Ruthy and Bergit."

"Isn't that strange?"

"Not really. There always has to be a connection to bring people together. You both look beautiful."

"So does your wife."

"I like to keep her light on when I'm alone... You want to come and have another drink?"

"I'm still feeling that Pimm's," said Ruthy. "I'll have a glass of red wine with my supper."

"Harry's having a gin and tonic with lots of ice."

"All right then... You know Livy is famous in London?"

"We own a block of flats together in Chelsea. My insurance against the likes of Petronella Maple and Josiah Makoni. Oh, I'm sorry. Did I say something wrong?"

"She has her claws into Harry," said Ruthy.

"Not at the moment. Come and have a drink."

The kerosene pressure light had been pumped up, giving more light to the room. The cocktail cabinet was behind the dining table where Jeremy mixed them a drink. The two boys came in dressed in their pyjamas to say goodnight. The boys shook Ruthy's hand making her want to pick them up and give them a hug. Outside it was now pitch dark. Bugs were battering against the outside of the gauze mesh that ran along the top of the low wall, trying to get into the light made by the kerosene lamp. Primrose took the boys off to bed.

"Where are her kids?"

"Back in the native compound. On Christmas Eve you'll hear the drums. Christmas Eve and Saturday nights they play the drums in the compound all night. They make a homemade beer from sorghum and dance round the fire."

"Have you ever been?"

"Never been invited. Before I go down to the compound I ask permission from my bossboy."

"But it's your farm."

"Not their village. Slowly we're building them brick houses. Gave them running water two years ago. There, my bossboy is the chief. He sorts out any nonsense. Here's your drink. How does that look?"

It was a night Ruthy knew she was always going to remember. It was all so different. She sipped at the gin Harry had given her. They were all getting tipsy, Ruthy intoxicated by the African night as much as the drink.

"I know the sound the crickets make but what's the other sound, Jeremy? The contented sound."

"Those are the frogs. It's the mating season. With the water we spray on the grass and the water in the pool we have lots of frogs. That's the sound of the males calling to the females, or so I was told."

"I like the sound. Do wild animals come out onto the lawn?"

"Why we have the high wire fence round the house and the garden. Before the fence, wild pigs dug up my flowerbeds."

"So they get as far as the fence?"

"Probably. Lion. Leopard. Hyena. I've seen them all on the farm. Or more correctly, I've seen their spoor the next morning. Leopards hunt at night. Once I heard a leopard get into a troop of baboons. Terrible noise of screaming as the monkeys fought for their lives. They sounded so human. Not a sound from the leopard."

"How did you know it was a leopard and not a lion?"

"They make a coughing sound. I'd heard two of them earlier in the night. Woke me up. Any sound from the bush that is unusual wakes me up. My subconscious mind must be tuned to any sound of danger."

"I don't want to hear dying monkeys. Will we see some monkeys?"

"Probably. If you like, tomorrow I'll take you around the farm. Most of my six thousand acres are still wild. Bush as we call it. We can go down to the river. There's a spot where I always see kudu. A big antelope with tall antlers on the males. They are very beautiful."

"I'd like that," said Ruthy. "Where's the assistant I was hearing about? Don't you have a drink together of an evening? The only two Englishmen on the farm."

"What about my boys?"

"They don't drink yet I hope."

"Bobby and I like to keep our private lives apart. We see so much of each other during the day. Would you like to drink every night in London with your boss?"

"No way. What does he do this time in the evening after he's finished work?"

"He has a wind-up gramophone in his cottage on the far side of the ridge. You'll meet Bobby Preston tomorrow. He's about your age, Ruthy. Plays Frank Sinatra records. I know the words by heart. He went to a musical in London when he went home on leave. Brought back the long-playing record. I know the words to that one too."

"Which musical?"

"*Half a Sixpence*. Tommy Steele. There's a big production number all about taking a group photograph. Reminds him of his trip back to England."

"He must be lonely."

"He hoped to bring back a wife. No luck I'm afraid. The young girls he met wanted to stay in London. Not live in the wilds of Africa. Would you like to live in Africa, Ruthy?"

"Not me. I'm a town girl. I find the constant sound of traffic comforting. How about you, Bergit?"

"I'd miss my mother."

"How sweet."

They all stopped talking as the food was put on the table.

"Thank you, Silas. That haunch of venison smells good. Come on. Time to eat. You all must be starving. I'll carve the meat, Harry. Why don't you pour out the wine?"

"Can I go outside and look at the stars for a minute?" said Ruthy. She was feeling romantic. "Harry, come and show me the stars. While our host is carving the meat. I want to capture this moment forever. The frogs. The smell of that lovely roast meat. I want to savour everything. Just for a minute. You can hold my hand in case one of those wild animals has got through the fence. Or Primrose left the gate open."

Outside, looking up at the layers of stars, holding Harry's hand so gently, it was all just perfect for Ruthy.

"Won't you kiss me, Harry? Properly. You've never kissed me properly. It's so dark out here no one can see us. Africa is so romantic."

When they went back inside, Jeremy had carved up the haunch of venison. Bergit was standing up next to him drinking a glass of red wine. She was smirking at Ruthy. Ruthy could still feel the one soft kiss. Instinctively she put her hand up to her lips. It was their first kiss that had not felt like brother and sister.

"I poured the wine," said Bergit.

They all sat down at the table. Jeremy passed each of them a plate of meat. The vegetables were in the middle of the table where Silas had left them. The serving dishes had lids on them to keep the vegetables hot. They all helped themselves.

"The red currant jelly is still in the jar, I'm afraid," said Jeremy. "Were the stars still in the heavens?"

Then they began to eat.

Half way through the meal, no one talking as they enjoyed the food, Ruthy heard Bobby Preston's gramophone. It sounded so lonely. Far away and lonely. Jeremy got up and filled their glasses, his hand with the bottle brushing Bergit's shoulder. Under the table, Ruthy was rubbing her toe against Harry's foot having pushed off one of her high-heeled shoes. She could feel his bare skin. They were all so happy.

"I'm not a pudding man," said Jeremy. "Help yourselves to more meat. Silas has gone back to the compound."

"Does he have a wife?" asked Bergit.

"Two of them."

"Don't they fight?"

"Never asked him."

"Are we all going to get drunk?"

"Probably. It's a tradition in Rhodesia. All us whites drink too much."

"Why?" asked Ruthy.

"The loneliness of exile."

"Why don't you come home? You said you've got part of a block of flats in Chelsea."

"Oh, it's not that easy. Africa is a drug. Gets into your blood. A drug so powerful you can't live without it. A few have tried. They all came back to Africa."

"Doesn't make sense."

"Nothing in my life has ever made sense," said Jeremy. "I give you a toast. To good company. Lovely to have you all on World's View. Happy Christmas to all of you."

"The music has stopped."

"Bobby's gone to bed. Us farmers get up before the sun. Go to bed early. I find after I've eaten, my eyelids begin to droop. There's nothing better than going to bed really tired. You sleep better."

"Is that why you don't have pudding?"

"Been a long day. Six hours on the road. Good food makes me drowsy. Will you all excuse me when we've finished supper? Silas or Primrose will bring you all a cup of tea to your rooms in the morning."

"Why don't you use the generator at night?"

"Makes too much noise. And then I have to go down to the barns to turn it off... There's another open bottle of wine if you want one."

"The meat was divine."

"Thank you, Bergit. Maybe your mother would like to come and live in Africa."

Jeremy was smiling as he filled up her glass full of wine.

THE MOON WAS PLAYING on Ruthy's pillow when she went to her room, making her go across to draw the curtain. Far away she could hear the noise of wild animals: strange, exciting sounds in the dark of the night. Harry had seen her to the door of her bedroom. He had not kissed her good night.

"You don't want to come in?" she had whispered.

"Please, Ruthy. My sister is next door."

"She's still in your head, isn't she?"

"Good night, Ruthy. It's lovely to see you."

"You're a fool, Harry."

"Probably."

"Are you getting over her?"

"They say time and distance heal all wounds of the heart."

"Are you sure it's your heart and not something a lot more basic? Good night, Harry. Thanks for the kiss under the stars... He's so lonely. Poor Jeremy."

"First he wanted Livy and then she went back to England. So he married Carmen and Carmen died. Livy came back again but wouldn't stay. Yes, I'd say he was lonely. Wouldn't you be?"

"Those poor boys... You want to have kids, Harry?"

"Of course I do."

"That's something. More than anything else I want a family of my own."

"Comes from growing up in a happy family. We've been lucky. Both of us. You take it for granted when you have happy people around you. Only miss it when you don't. Oh, yes. The Wakefields and the Smythes. We were the lucky ones."

"She'd make you a bitch of a wife."

"You don't have to tell me."

"Then why do you keep trying?"

"It's an obsession. A deep, terrible, life-threatening obsession. I want to possess her, Ruthy. I want to possess every part of the woman."

"But she won't let you."

"Ah, now you're understanding. Mostly, when we get everything we want from a person we don't want them after all. We've satisfied ourselves and want to move on. Why so many of us are discontented. You have a good sleep. See you in the morning."

With the curtains drawn against the light of the moon, Ruthy lay down on the bed, her red dress on the chair, the paraffin light doused for the night. It was swelteringly hot in the room with the curtains drawn. She got up and pulled them back, bathing herself in the light of the moon. There was a gentle breeze coming in through the fine mesh of the screen over her open windows. She had come to the ends of the earth for him. What more could she do? Softly, Ruthy began to cry. She was feeling sorry for herself. It was so stupid. Naked, she went back to lie on the bed.

When the moonlight left her pillow, Ruthy fell into a dreamless sleep.

When she woke in the morning Primrose was bringing her a pot of tea. The two girls smiled at each other.

"Thank you, Primrose. I thought you only had to look after the children."

After she poured herself a cup of tea, she banged on the wall to the next door room and called.

"You awake, Bergit?"

"I could get used to this. Sleep well?"

"Eventually."

"Finish your tea and we'll go get ourselves a lovely early morning swim."

Ruthy heard the gurgling sound of a suppressed giggle.

"Are you alone?"

"Of course I am. Drink your tea."

From next door came the bark of a dog.

"What's going on?" said Ruthy.

"First the cats. Now the dogs. I left my door open."

"Naughty girl."

"Not at all. Makes the air circulate better. When I woke up there were seven cats sleeping on my bed."

THEY TOOK the truck round the farm after breakfast, Ruthy and Harry sitting on a mattress in the back with the children. A full English breakfast with steak and chips. They had all been hungry. It was Saturday afternoon and half day on the farm, the gang having gone back to the compound at the end of work. Primrose, with the two girls to look after the boys, had gone home for the weekend. Ruthy had suggested it.

For five minutes they drove along a farm road. When they stopped it was next to a land of tobacco. Ruthy worked her way out of the back of the truck sliding on her bottom, the canopy on the back of the truck not letting her stand up. The tobacco plants were taller than the top of her head, the middle leaves the length of her arm and half as wide. The top of the plants had been broken off where Ruthy thought there would have been flowers. She remembered the sweet tobacco from her father's garden and the smell of the flower. All the plants were in dead-straight lines, the earth ridged up, paths down the middle of the line of plants. It was all so green. A great field of lush green in the middle of the dry African bush.

"This is the early planting," said Jeremy. "We'll be doing the first reaping just after Christmas. Then we work from sunup to sundown filling the curing barns. You have to get the leaves into the barns before they over-ripen. The plant ripens from the bottom leaves upwards over several weeks."

"How did you make all this green in the wilderness?" asked Bergit.

"First you stump out the msasa trees, roots and all. Plough the land deep. Take samples of the soil before planting and send them to the government research station for analysis. They tell us the right amount of nitrogen fertiliser and whether we need to add any trace elements to the soil. Too much fertiliser and you waste your money. Fertiliser is expensive. Too little and you don't get the right size of crop and your yield goes down. You want me to go on?... When you plant out the seedlings in the lands from the seedbeds we go back replanting again and again until every plant has taken in the soil. The plants are ridged like you see in England in a field of potatoes. Yield times good quality Virginia leaf, less expenses, equals your profit. Simple really."

"What's the snag?" asked Harry.

"Rain. Too much or too little. In a few years with irrigation pipes that cover the farm we'll be able to water the plants when it doesn't rain. Expensive. Needs electricity. We hope to get power from the hydroelectric generators at Kariba Dam in a couple of years. We've surveyed the farm from the air. Chap I knew in Salisbury who helped find my wife's car and remains. Aerial photography. Mapped out my whole farm. Everything takes a lot of capital. With all this political instability in Africa I hesitate committing everything I make. Frustrating. If we didn't have those problems we'd turn Rhodesia into the Garden of Eden in twenty years. I want to weir the Mutwa River that borders the farm. Build holding dams across five *spruits* and top them up from the weirs when the rains are flooding the bigger river. Keep surplus water on the farm where we want it instead of it ending up down the Zambezi in Beira and out into the Indian Ocean. We could grow a second winter crop of wheat and make the country self-sufficient in flour. You got to think to succeed. Can you imagine the rest of the farm looking like this? These days it's all scientific, good water engineering and planning."

"Is this a good crop?" asked Harry.

"Best I've ever grown. Come on. We're boring the girls. I'll show you what we are doing down by the river to build the weirs. This country can be so rich it boggles the mind. If everyone would stop arguing with each other."

"You're not boring me," said Bergit sweetly. "I could drive around this beautiful farm all day."

"What are you doing, Harry?" asked Ruthy, her mind having wandered to look up at two big birds circling high in the sky, intermittently calling.

"I'm taking notes. I'm a journalist. First lesson of good journalism is to know what you are talking about."

"What are they, Jeremy?"

"Fish eagles. They ride up on the thermals so high you can sometimes barely see them. Just hear their cry."

"They are so beautiful. I've never seen a bird that big."

"Back into the truck. All of you. Boys, where the hell are you? Take your eyes off them for a minute and they're gone. Get out of my tobacco!"

"Are we going to the club?" called one of the boys.

"When we get back to the house."

"I want a hamburger and a lemonade."

"Small boys," said Jeremy. "They never change. Always thinking of their stomachs. Here they come. Now get in the back of the truck. We'll take the Chev to the club. There's no cricket today. Too close to the reaping season. Some of my neighbours are reaping already."

"They're going higher and higher," said Ruthy, craning her neck to look up into the sky. "It's not so hot anymore."

"The rain's coming tonight with a bit of luck."

3

The women were wearing white tennis dresses, the young and the not so young. Ruthy could see their white legs up to their knees. There were six tennis courts all being used when she got out of the open Chev. All the windows of the car had been down leaving only the windscreen. Ruthy had been in the back of the big car with Harry and Jeremy's boys. Most of the way the boys had fought with each other. They were full of energy.

"Hello, Jeremy," called a middle-aged woman. "I'm going to the pool. You want me to look after the boys?"

"Would you, Martha? They want hamburgers and chips with a cool drink. Tell Noah to put them on my tab."

"Come along, Phillip and Randall. Aunty Martha is going to get you a hamburger."

"Why aren't you playing tennis, Martha?"

"Got knocked out of the singles and both doubles in the first round. Walter wasn't concentrating."

"Where is he?"

"In the bar I should think."

"You're a star, Martha."

"I know I am. Why aren't you playing?"

"Friends of the family from England. This is Harry, Ruthy and Bergit. Mrs Hargreaves. They farm next to me."

Ruthy smiled and waved a small hand. There were so many strangers to meet. Bergit had her arm through Jeremy's as Mrs Hargreaves took away the children. Neither of the boys looked back. Randall was asking when he could have his hamburger. The boys were happy.

"Do you think they miss their mother?" she quietly asked Harry walking next to her behind Bergit and Jeremy as they walked away from the tennis courts where Jeremy had parked the car. He had put the hood of the car up in case it rained, the whole system automatic. Ruthy had never before seen an electronic roof come up on its own.

"They were very young. Life goes on. From generation to generation."

"Quite the poet today, aren't we?"

"You want a drink?" asked Jeremy turning back to them.

"Why not?" said Harry.

"You either play golf, tennis or squash today. Or you drink."

It was three in the afternoon as they reached the long bar in the clubhouse. The bar and the area away from the bar was full. At the tables looking out over the cricket field people were sitting. The men were all in shorts and open shirts. The women who were not dressed for tennis were dressed in frocks. The men playing tennis were in whites with white tennis shoes and white socks. There were tennis rackets on the low tables among the drinks. Everyone to Ruthy seemed to be smoking. Everyone knew Jeremy.

"Wally, Martha's taken my kids to the pool."

"I can drink in peace. Blames me for getting us knocked out of the mixed doubles."

"Friends of the family from England."

Everyone waved. Ruthy was getting used to it. The first strange looks from people at the tables had turned to smiles. They were accepted. They were friends of the family. The right sort of people.

"They'd cut us dead if we weren't friends of the family," she whispered to Harry. "It's all like something out of an old book set in India. Did you ever read the book *A Passage to India*?"

"Did they ever make a film?"

"I don't think so."

"What's everyone drinking?" called Jeremy. "Hello, Clay. This is the chap you can all thank for last night's venison. Clay Barry. He's the member-in-charge of the local police."

"Was it all right?"

"Wonderful," said Bergit.

They passed on down to the end of the bar where four stools were vacant. The policeman had gone back to talking to his friends.

"This is Noah. He'll give you what you want. You can't buy a drink, Harry. Rule of the club. Have to be a member to buy a drink."

"There are so many people," said Ruthy. "Suddenly, in the middle of nowhere there are so many people."

"Saturday afternoon just before Christmas. Some are visitors like yourselves."

"Everyone knows you, Jeremy."

"Should do. Been here long enough. We all know each other in the block. This is the sum of our social life."

"It's wonderful," said Bergit.

Ruthy gave her a look. Harry gave her a smile. The drinks came.

"Cheers, everyone."

"Cheers," said Ruthy. "It's all a bit overwhelming."

"You'll get used to it."

Sipping her drink, Ruthy looked around. There was a lot of noise and laughter at the other end of the bar. At the centre of the noise was the policeman. The man was in uniform. Next to him at the bar was another policeman in uniform. In the corner behind them in a room separated by a low partition two young men were playing ping pong. Neither of them was very good. There were more young men in clusters at the tables. The older, more prosperous-looking men kept away from them. There was some kind of social segregation. One of the young men smiled at Jeremy when he saw him and waved. Jeremy made a sign for the young man to come over.

"You want a drink, Bobby? These are my guests I was talking about from England. Bobby's my assistant. Most of the young lads in the club are assistants. Looks like we'll be reaping on Boxing Day if it doesn't rain. Ruthy, Harry and Bergit, meet Bobby Preston. The boys are at the pool with Mrs Hargreaves. What are you drinking? What's Clay Barry looking so pleased about?"

"He's right behind you, Mr Crookshank."

"We caught him, Jeremy."

"Who did you catch?"

"Josiah Makoni. We were tipped off by his half-brother Goodson who's a constable at the police station in Bindura. Their father died. Josiah came back to bury his father. They were close. Must have flown into Beira and caught the train to the Mozambique border and walked round the border post. We were waiting for him. Charged him with sedition. He'll be tried for treason like Mandela in South Africa. Got him in Salisbury Central. He won't be offered bail. We also arrested the man who picked him up on our side of the border outside Umtali and drove him to Mazoe. Our old friend the Reverend Harvey Pemberton. Had to let him go but we're watching him."

"Won't you make a hero out of Josiah?"

"Who are you?"

"He's staying with me, Clay. Harry Wakefield. Harry Brigandshaw was his godfather. He's the Africa correspondent for the London *Daily Mirror*... His sister Bergit... Bergit's friend Ruthy. They all grew up together."

"The man was recruiting locals to go to Tanganyika to train in a bush camp as terrorists. To come back and kill our people. Can't have that, Wakefield."

"Call me Harry."

"I'd rather not. We're a bit allergic to left wing British newspaper reporters in Rhodesia."

"I'm sorry. Just doing my job. So Tembo's dead?"

"How do you know his name was Tembo?"

"He grew up with my godfather. My godfather paid for Josiah's education."

"Didn't repay him with any thanks... Oh, well. What can you expect?... The Federation has come to an end. He'll be given a fair trial in what is now Rhodesia. No Southern Rhodesia anymore. We're on our own. Smith's going to be the new prime minister. Can't have chaps like Josiah inciting their fellow citizens to kill people now can we?"

"They want their land back, Mr Barry."

"Inspector Barry. They want power, Mr Wakefield. All they want is power."

"Don't let's argue," said Jeremy. "Have a drink with us, Clay. And please call my friend Harry. Get to know him, you'll find he's as much on our side as he is on Josiah's. Probably for a better reason than politics. They share the same girlfriend."

"That's one I'd like to get my hands on. Miss Petronella Maple."

"So would a lot of people," said Harry, trying to force a smile.

"Will you excuse me, Jeremy? Back to the chaps at the other end of the bar. Nice to have met you, Harry. We'll be seeing each other again. The trial will be in Salisbury. Open to the press and the public. It's a free country. Enjoy your trip. How long are you staying with us in Rhodesia?"

"Quite a while I should think."

"Are you really a boyfriend of Miss Petronella?"

"I try to think so. You can't win them all. Nice to have met you, Clay."

"*Daily Mirror*?"

"*Daily Mirror*. We'll be seeing each other."

For a long moment, while Clay Barry walked back down the length of the bar, the five of them were silent.

"Being a policeman isn't easy," said Jeremy.

"Neither's being a newspaperman," said Harry.

"Wow," said Ruthy. "That was ugly."

"Uncomfortable," said Bergit. "Who's Tembo?"

"Harry Brigandshaw's bossboy on Elephant Walk. And his friend. Tembo would have died for Harry. And almost did. The Makonis and the Brigandshaws are joined at the hip."

"What a strange country."

"Not really. Just people. They're the same all over the world. I'll cable the Brigandshaw family in England. Tell them the news. Beth, my sister-in-law, will want to know."

"Isn't it history?" said Harry.

"Probably. Yes, you're right. Better to leave it in history. Poor Josiah. They'll lock him up and throw away the key."

"I don't think so. Not for what he stands for. They'll do more harm than good to themselves. Like the South African government. Political prisoners. One man's terrorist is another man's freedom fighter. Seventy years ago it was their land. Different perspectives. The world's a mess. Sorry about that, Jeremy. I almost lost my temper."

"But you didn't. Have another drink. Water under the bridge."

"You know, those two blokes are terrible at ping pong."

"Just do me a favour, Harry," said Jeremy. "Don't let them see you make notes in the club. So Smith's going to be PM. He's the one who wants to declare us independent despite what they agree to in London. What a bloody mess. You sometimes wonder what you should do in life. What's right and what's wrong. There's always a problem hanging over your head. Probably made a mistake making my life in Rhodesia. The only snag was the alternative. Living in the suburbs. Catching the eight-ten to Waterloo for the rest of my life. Working just to pay off a mortgage. Anyway, who knows what's going to happen to England? Happen to anyone for that matter. It's better to go through one day at a time or you make yourself miserable. People who have no imagination are far better off. Get on with just what's in front of them. Wish I could do it."

Ruthy watched Harry go silent, his mind far away from his argument with the policeman. She was sure he was thinking of Petronella, the sad look and pain in his eyes telling her everything. Harry wasn't even looking at the policeman down the bar. Was he thinking that with Josiah out of the way he would get her to himself? Ever since the policeman had mentioned Miss Petronella, Ruthy's day had gone sour. In her humble opinion not only were people's politics in a perpetual mess, so were people... Bobby Preston was looking at her in a way Harry would have looked at Petronella. The boy wanted her. She gave him a weak smile not even noticed by Harry still deep in his thoughts. More than anything in her life she wanted Harry to look at her with the same look she was getting from Bobby Preston... The party down the bar grew more raucous. She had never seen policemen in uniform drink in a bar before. Maybe the rules for a club were different to a public bar. She hadn't liked Inspector Clay Barry, the arrogance of the man grating. The man had power over people which she didn't like and, by the way he had talked to Harry, was prepared to use it. There were always ways for the police to make life difficult. Her father had once likened them to small men in too-big boots. She was glad she had enjoyed the venison, not knowing the man who had brought the food.

"Penny for your thoughts, Harry?"

"You don't want to know them."

"Didn't think so. Are you going to write a piece about Josiah?"

"Of course. And interview the Reverend Harvey Pemberton. He was with Josiah and Petronella outside Buckingham Palace protesting the arrest of Nelson Mandela."

"There's that woman again."

"I can't get away from her. I should go back to Salisbury right now. Would go if I'd brought the car."

"By the sound of it, Josiah won't be going anywhere soon. Neither will the reverend. Let's enjoy Christmas and forget work. I came all the way to see you, Harry."

"I'm sorry. Yes, you're probably right. The other papers will have had first dibs at it anyway. With luck they don't know about Pemberton. From my research he's a genuine do-gooder. There aren't many of them. Most of it's for show. To further their careers in the church. The missionary returned from darkest Africa after so much good work to become a bishop."

"You're a cynic sometimes, Harry."

"More a sceptic, Ruthy. Most people never do anything in life without a personal reason. Money, career or popularity. Look at him. The popular man of the moment. Everyone crowded round him, listening to his every word. Makes you sick. They won't let me get to Josiah, you can be sure of that. Petronella will be having a field day in London. 'Man goes home to bury his beloved father and the Rhodesian government arrest him.' New funds will pour into the coffers of ZANU."

"I thought it was called ZAPU?"

"There's been a bit of a shake-up and all the people we know have chosen to join this new splinter party, ZANU, who are more on the side of the rural workers rather than the townies. But they've all made a hero out of Josiah Makoni. And that bastard keeps staring at me."

"Barry? You think he can get you thrown out of the country?"

"Who knows, Ruthy? Who knows? You want to take a walk and have a look at their golf course?"

"I'd love to. I can check on the boys... Do you mind, Jeremy?"

"He doesn't mind at all," said Bergit. "You two run along."

"It's my turn to play ping pong," said Bobby.

"See you at the house," Ruthy said to him.

"I hope so."

At the swimming pool the boys were eating hamburgers, happy with Martha Hargreaves. They walked on past to the first fairway and the shadow of the trees, too hot to talk in the sun. No one was playing the first three holes. In the distance, Ruthy could see a foursome.

"How do they play in this heat?"

"They get used to it, Ruthy. You get used to anything in the end. Or so I tell myself."

"So what was here seventy years ago?"

"A few villages of mud huts on the banks of the rivers. They were nomadic cattle herders. Hundreds of years before, there was a civilisation of sorts. No one's quite sure of its extent. Built the settlement they now call Great Zimbabwe in the Iron Age. They cut and dressed stone blocks and piled them on top of each other to make fortifications. People come to Rhodesia to see them, even now they've fallen into ruin. There were a few *rongwas* in these parts. Small fortifications. Nobody is certain of the origin of the ruins. Some say it was Arab. Others a great African civilisation in the heart of Africa. The kingdom of Monomotapa. Some civilisations come and go leaving very little trace."

"Did they have roads?"

"Not when the British got here."

"How did they get around?"

"Walked, I suppose. The early pioneers got here by horse and ox wagon. The Arabs came on horses."

"What were the Arabs doing here?"

"Trading in gold. Later in people. Rounding up the young men and women and sending them to the New World as slaves."

"How terrible. How could they do that to another human being?"

"To the Arabs and early whites the blacks were primitives. They lived in grass huts, their only weapons were stabbing spears much like the Roman short sword. They had learnt to forge iron. They had no form of written language. Apart from the cattle and patches of maize, they were still hunters. Easy prey for the Arabs. More important, there was money in it. People rationalise with themselves when there's money to be made. Man is cruel, Ruthy, especially to his fellow man. Cecil Rhodes came to Rhodesia after gold, not farmland. He was a Rand Baron. Diamonds in Kimberley. Gold on the Witwatersrand. He thought there was more gold to be found than in the Witwatersrand. As it turned out he was wrong. There were small pockets of gold scattered across the country but nothing like South Africa. The only gold is in Jeremy's tobacco, the light sandveld here is ideal for growing good quality tobacco, as good as in Virginia in America at a tenth of the cost. Most of the blacks in Jeremy's compound are not even from Rhodesia there is such a shortage of local labour. They bring them down from Nyasaland."

"Isn't that slavery?"

"They came of their own free will this time. To them, plentiful guaranteed food is better than starving at home... Just look out there, Ruthy. As far as those distant mountains there's nothing. The odd bit of green tobacco. If the likes of Jeremy are finally successful in turning this wilderness into a garden of Eden, there'll be all hell let loose. Like the gold and the slaves, people only want something when it has value. Oh, Josiah is on the right track all right. It's the land of his people. And now he wants it back."

"Will they be able to farm like Jeremy?"

"Who knows?"

"It's all so weird. In the middle of nowhere, this small community. People playing golf. Playing tennis. A swimming pool big enough for the Olympics."

"A quarter of a million of them who think they can survive on their own without the support of the home government."

"Can they survive and prosper?"

"Who knows, Ruthy?. I'm just a journalist. When I'm finished here I go back to London. And if Inspector Barry had his way it will be sooner rather than later."

"I hope so, Harry. I miss you at our family Sunday lunches. I miss you a lot."

"Don't get sentimental on me, Ruthy. I think it's too hot to walk and neither of us have a hat. I rather fancy one of those bush hats. Big white hunter. That sort of thing."

"You don't even kill flies."

"And why should I? They only get one life on earth like the rest of us. We can have a swim with the kids and not go back to the bar. That policeman gives me the creeps. I never did like policemen. You bring your costume?"

"In the back of the car. Have you ever played golf?"

"Never could afford the clubs."

"I think your sister likes Jeremy."

"Nothing against Jeremy but if that's the case then the sooner you get her back to England the better. They're all living with their heads in the sand. Can't see the wood for the trees. Playing King Canute only this time they're trying to hold back the tide of history. Easy for me to talk. I don't own a farm. All that hard work. He's lost his wife and likely in the end to lose his farm, his home and his livelihood. Doesn't get much worse than that. Better a house in the suburbs and pay off a mortgage. Commute to work. A lot safer. When something seems too good to be true it usually is. When you get a chance you tell my sister."

"Why don't you tell her?"

"She never listens to me. No one ever listens to me."

"It's easier to give advice than take it."

"You can say that again. A bit like me. I can run away from England but I can't run away from myself."

"Or that damn woman."

"Something like that. Come on. Let's get ourselves out of the burning sun into the nice cool water of a swimming pool."

"You don't see it, do you?"

"What, Ruthy?"

"Never mind."

Feeling frustrated in more ways than one, Ruthy went to Jeremy's car and picked up her swimming costume.

"And what about you?"

"Under my trousers. Never took it off after my morning swim. In this heat you don't need a towel. The sun dries the body and the bathing costume. You can change in the ladies' loo."

Her small bikini was the first problem Ruthy found when she came out of the clubhouse to walk round to the pool with Harry. They were stared at. No one smiled. The looks were all 'and who are you?'

"They must know we are with Jeremy," said Ruthy, waving to the boys. Both boys had finished their hamburgers. Phillip was punching Randall none too gently, while Mrs Hargreaves lay on her back in the shade of an umbrella with her eyes closed against the glare of the sun. When Ruthy walked closer she saw that the woman was asleep.

"What are you up to, boys?"

"Randall swiped the last of my chips when I went for a swim."

"Naughty, Randall. You don't have to hit him."

"Are you allowed in here without my daddy?"

"I don't know. Am I?" Ruthy looked around, expecting someone to say they were welcome. No one said a word. Without Jeremy Crookshank they were no longer 'family', or so it seemed by the looks.

"They know who I am," said Harry. "*Daily Mirror*. Newspaper reporter."

"You think we should swim?"

"Why the hell not? Wish I'd brought my car. They really do think they own the place. Do you think it's got round I'm a friend of Josiah and Petronella? The old bag in the corner is looking daggers at me."

"Let's forget it, Harry. We'll have to go back to the bar." Standing on the lawn at the edge of the pool, Ruthy pulled on her dress. Mrs Hargreaves was either asleep or pretending. Her right hand was twitching. Ruthy took Harry by the hand and led him from the pool.

"I feel uncomfortable."

"So do I."

"There's your policeman getting into a car, Harry."

The man was looking at them, his look unwelcoming like the looks of the rest of the people around the pool. Then Clay Barry pointed at Harry with a malicious smile on his face, not saying a word. Harry stopped in his tracks.

"If looks could kill," said Ruthy. "I was enjoying our trip before we came to the club."

"I'm the enemy. The visible threat to their future. They hate me. People hate the messenger. If only I had my damn car I'd drive us straight back to Salisbury. Mrs Wade has a vacant room for the both of you. One of the boarders has gone to Cape Town for his Christmas holiday and said you can use his room. Mrs Wade's moved in an extra bed."

Inside, Jeremy was waiting for them.

"We'd better go. I'm sorry. Clay had had a few too many and was going on about you, Harry."

"I was thinking the same."

"I'm sorry. People are nervous right now with the breakup of the Federation. I know how they feel. But what can we all do? We can't take all this with us. This is our livelihood. What we made ourselves. We don't think we have done anything wrong creating wealth out of nothing, not to mention half a million jobs. No one has ever gone hungry on World's View. Or any of the farms. Without the members of this club there would be nothing. Now it's all our fault. We're the rich whites exploiting the blacks. You just can't win in life. This is uncomfortable. We'll make a *braai* round the pool at home. How are my boys, Ruthy?"

"Fighting. Over potato chips."

"We learn to fight each other so early in life. I'll go and get them. Meet you at the car. Bergit's gone to powder her nose. One of the women was quite rude to her. Clay knows who your father is, Ruthy. We'd listened to him interview Josiah on my shortwave radio. The whole club now knows. I tried to explain your family's connection to Harry Brigandshaw but no one was listening. They think the British press is out to destroy us."

"Can you drive us back to Salisbury tomorrow?"

"If that's what you want. We'll all feel more comfortable on World's View."

"Not if someone comes over to World's View for an argument."

"Sorry, Harry."

"So am I. Anyway, with Josiah arrested I have work to do."

"Yes, I suppose you do. You did come for Christmas. We're all a bit scared of the future. It's the season of good cheer. I was looking forward to spending Christmas with friends. So were the boys. They'll be disappointed. Christmas can be the most lonely time of the year. Maybe after a couple of drinks we'll feel better. Life's too short for arguments. Let's have some fun. Here she comes. What do you think, Bergit? Your brother is feeling uncomfortable and wants me to drive you all back to Salisbury."

"Whatever for? Different opinions are the spice of life. You and I were just getting to know each other. Some people get disagreeable when they've had too much to drink. Sober, I'm sure Clay is a pussy cat. He's probably under pressure. A policeman's life is never an easy one. Anyway, he has gone home to his wife."

Bergit took Jeremy by the arm and walked him to the car.

"I'll get the boys," said Jeremy. "Wait for me here. It was all going so well."

Silently, Harry, Bergit and Ruthy waited in the car, the car parked in the shade of a tree.

The boys had stopped fighting when they came back and got in the car. There was no sign of Mrs Hargreaves. As they drove from the club, Ruthy looked back at the clubhouse. Somehow it looked different to when they had arrived.

Ten minutes later they arrived back at World's View. Silas had laid wood in the *braai* built at the back of the pool. The drinks table was covered with a fresh white cloth. The glasses were waiting for them. The boys ran into the house as Ruthy took off her dress and climbed down the steps into the pool, gently swimming into the middle.

"Come in, Harry. It's so beautiful. Smile for goodness sake. What can he do to you? You're a reporter. Part of the job. Dad always says you can't please everyone. Don't take it to heart."

"Anyone for a Pimm's?," called Jeremy.

"Why ever not?" said Harry. "Sorry. He got under my skin."

"Clay can be a good friend when you need one. Clay put out every resource he could find when Carmen went missing. Like you, Harry, he's just doing his job. We've got steaks, lamb chops and a chicken to put on the *braai*. Let's enjoy ourselves. Tomorrow's another day."

"You're right. Do you mind if I use your telephone to send a telegram to my London office?"

"Be my guest. I'll show you how to ring the Salisbury exchange on our party line."

"Can the other farmers listen to what I am sending in my cable?"

"No one here behaves like that, Harry. When you pick up your phone and hear someone talking on the line you put your phone down. Politeness."

"Are the police on your party line?"

"They have their own separate line. If we were all listening to the wives prattling to each other life in the block would be unbearable. Can you just imagine? It's as much to protect ourselves. You'd likely hear things about yourself or your wife you don't want to hear. You want to send the cable about Josiah now don't you? Come on up to the house. While you're talking to Salisbury I'll get Silas to cut the fruit and cucumber for the Pimm's."

"Do you want me to tell you what I am going to say?"

"That's your business, Harry. Give them Mrs Wade's address and they'll post you a copy of your cable for your records. Poor Josiah. He's not going to have a pleasant Christmas in Salisbury Central. If he's convicted they'll send him to the bush camp where they keep the rest of the political prisoners."

"That's a bit silly. Keeping them all together with nothing to do but build hatred for the English."

"What else can they do?... Bergit, can you keep an eye on my boys?"

"So we're staying for Christmas?"

When her brother and Jeremy walked away up the lawn towards the house, Bergit had a satisfied smile on her face.

"Life's too short to run away, Ruthy. Much too short. You know, I really like him."

"Harry said it's not worth getting yourself involved with a Rhodesian farmer."

"He's a fine one to talk. A lady with a predilection for both sexes who dabbles in revolutionary politics isn't exactly a life with a future."

"She's so far under his skin he can't think of anything else."

"I could get used to this kind of life however short a time the whites still have in Africa. Live for the day. That's my motto. Tomorrow may never come. Do you really want three kids in the suburbs and have to worry about every penny?"

"With Harry that would be just lovely... Are you or aren't you coming in the pool? Boys, look out. Here come the dogs. Harry left the gate to the pool open."

In squealing and barking chaos, four dogs and two boys chased each other round the pool. One after the other they jumped in the water. Bergit took off her dress, her bathing costume underneath, and jumped in the pool.

"This is just so much fun, Ruthy. Give it time. Harry will come round... Come on. Let's splash the boys."

PART VI

DECEMBER 1963

THE LAST STRAW

_W_hile Roland Cartwright was reading Harry Wakefield's telegram in his Fleet Street office, eighteen miles away the mother of all family arguments was taking place at Woodlands Court. All the family had gathered except Petronella who was due to arrive with her friend the next day. Arnold Sheckland-Hall, weary of his daughter's tantrum, wanted his six o'clock glass of sherry in the lounge. His two sons and their wives were watching Florence Maple with smug expressions. The changing of the old man's will in favour of Petronella, effectively leaving Petronella one third of the family business along with the house, was not their problem. In the previous will, the third of Sheckland-Hall Limited and all the house went to Florence, Petronella's mother.

"My dear, please calm down. You and Bertie have that wonderful estate in Rhodesia which, I might remind you, I paid for. From what you have been telling me the farm is flourishing. I'm seventy-three. Can't be long to go now. None of us, including you, Florence, are getting any younger. Death duty in Britain is prohibitive. To pay the estate duty when I die the boys will have to borrow against their shares in the company as will now Petronella. God forbid but if anything should happen to you, my dear, soon after I leave this world there would be a second tax wallop most likely forcing the company out of the family's hands. She's your daughter. Your only child. I've just skipped a generation. From where I sit I can't see the problem. You live on your farm far away in Africa. What would you do with this house? No one in the family would be living here. Can't allow that, can we?"

"You could leave the house to Horace or Winfred."

"They like their own homes. As do their children. Petronella loves this estate. She lives in one room in Shepherd's Bush for God's sake. No wonder she has never found a suitable husband. With her third of the company she'll be able to maintain the old house properly. Keep the family continuity. Two centuries of tradition."

"She'll sell it and give the money to the party. Or some other ridiculous cause. The girl's unstable."

"The house is entailed. Has to stay in the family. Can't be sold. Been in the will of every Sheckland-Hall since we built the place."

"She's wheedled her way into your life."

"She comes and visits me... Regularly. More than I can say for the rest of you."

"Did you know she's having an affair with a black man?"

"Really, Florence. I abhor racism. He's a very nice boy by all accounts."

"He's a terrorist. If he set foot in Rhodesia we'd arrest him."

"Then you'd be very foolish."

"If Josiah Makoni gets his way he'll be prime minister of a country they want to call Zimbabwe. Then Petronella will go back to Africa. What will happen to the precious family house?"

"She says she won't marry him. That a white wife for Josiah would be bad politics."

"That's racism in reverse. You have a guilty conscience, Father. The family fortune was founded on slavery. You want to atone for the sins of your ancestors. No one's a slave in Rhodesia."

"But they still have no rights. Frankly, I can't see the difference."

"It's disgusting having sex with a black man."

"He's a man, Florence. A well-educated man. What possibly can be the difference in this second half of the twentieth century? We put away all that nonsense. You should remember in Rhodesia that all men are born equal. Now, may I go and have my glass of sherry?"

"Does Petronella know?"

"As a matter of fact she does. I wanted to wait and tell you my decision face to face. Boys, you'd better go and find your children. This family meeting is closed. Now, let's all of us have a lovely Christmas together."

"Who is my daughter bringing this time?"

"Her friend Elsie. They have been friends since university. Elsie helps in the evenings at the ZANU offices in Paddington. Charming girl. Why are you smiling like that, Florence?"

FLORENCE MAPLE WISHED she had not lost her temper the moment she lost it. Throughout her life, arguing with her father had been a pointless exercise. Her mind was in a turmoil at the news of her disinheritance, at not having an alternative life if everything went wrong in Rhodesia. Being defiant was one thing, being right in what they were doing quite another, however much they bragged at Rhodesian Front meetings. She hated the very idea that her daughter, with all her communist twaddle, was going to be proved right. That in the end the likes of Josiah Makoni would be dictating to her whether she could stay on her own damn farm. Hoping Bertie would be able to earn himself a living if they came back to England was as hopeless an idea as a black government letting her stay on the farm. All that family money and her hard-fought effort was going to go down the drain. She was no longer young. No longer able to start a new life without money. People back in England would ignore her. She would have no social standing. Bertie's charm and good looks had been an asset over the years in Rhodesia. A social charmer at dinner parties and in the club. And it was all his fault letting Petronella get her way and go to Manchester University where all those people without any breeding had filled her daughter's head with nonsense. Petronella had always been able to twist men round her little finger and now she had done it again. Her daughter would be mistress of Woodlands Court, herself out on the street, unless she used her brain and did something about it. Ever since Petronella had joined the British Communist Party at university the two of them had been unable to have a civil conversation. The girl goaded her. Ridiculed her mother's inherited wealth and position. Petronella said that if she was going to get anywhere in life she was going to do it herself by helping other people. The fact that communism, like African nationalism, would do the man in the street no damn good because it didn't work was beyond Florence's debating ability to convince her daughter, who always had a glib answer. Petronella would get all that family money and give it away to spite her mother. She wished she had never had the child, a thought that made her sick to the core of her being.

The daylight in her father's study was going, the night drawing in, the flickering from the coal fire in the grate becoming more dominant. With a forced smile on her face and the glimmer of an idea, she left the room with her immediate family, her father, her two brothers and their wives and Bertie. Outside the window she could see it was beginning to snow. Deep inside, Florence was in a state of panic. For the first time in her life she would be without money. It was better not to suggest her idea to Bertie. She would have to do what she had to do by herself. Sometimes in life you had to be cruel to be kind.

"What's made you cheer up so quickly? I know you, Florence. You're up to something."

"Don't be silly, Horace," she said to her older brother as they passed down the corridor towards the lounge. It's Christmas. Dad wants his drink."

"Don't be upset about it all, Florence. He's just missed a generation. If something goes wrong in Rhodesia you'll still be able to live your life in the old family home. Nothing will change. Petronella isn't a fool, I'll say that for her. Ideas I don't agree with but not a fool. She'll soon work out which side her bread is buttered. When we are young we all have the grand ideas to save mankind from himself. They won't be able to run your farm without you and Bertie any more than a communist government in England could run the business without Winfred and me. Anyone can take over a running business. It's keeping it running that's a whole lot more difficult. Let's all of us join Dad in the lounge for a glass of sherry."

"Where's Barbara gone off to?"

"I have no idea. Putting on her war paint most likely."

"Where's May, Winfred?"

"I have no idea and don't much care."

"You need a mistress."

"Coming from you, Florence, that's classical."

"Oh, I'm not so righteous. I like to look righteous."

"We'll all look after you."

"I doubt it. There's one thing I've learnt in life. The only person who can look after you is yourself."

They all trooped into the lounge, Florence following her brothers with a smile on her face.

"Hello, Dad. I'll have one of those sherries."

"You're not mad at me, Florence?"

"Of course not. Why would I stay mad with my own father? Sorry to lose my temper in there. It was the thought of Petronella possibly controlling my life. There are two sides to my daughter. You only know one of them. The one she wants you to see. I know. I brought her up. In the end you'll all say it was my fault."

"What other side, Florence?"

"One day you'll see. Maybe sooner than you think. It's your decision what you do with our family money, Father. I have always admired you for your principles."

"Rhodesia will be fine."

"I hope so... Thank you... Cheers to everyone. Happy Christmas."

AT HALF PAST ten the next morning, after a congenial family breakfast in the conservatory, Florence drove her father's pre-war Bentley 3 Litre to Ashford Station. She was early for the train as was her habit. Nothing annoyed Florence more than people who were late. With ten minutes to spare before the arrival from London of her daughter's train she walked into the small newsagent behind the station. Intentionally, she had come on her own, letting Bertie take the dogs for a walk round the Woodlands Court estate. Unless her husband had his regular constitutional he was irritable. Especially after drinking the way they had drunk at dinner in the old dining hall the previous night. By the time they went to bed her father was as tight as a tick, Janice, the old family maid, having to guide him out of the hall to his bed. Not once at the dinner table had anyone mentioned her disinheritance. Bertie, in his usual way, had left the question of money to her. It was not his problem. It was hers. Idly looking at the headlines, the face of Josiah Makoni, her daughter's lover in miscegenation, jumped out at her from the front page of the *Daily*

Mirror. The headline above the picture of the man's face roared 'How can they do it?' in big black capitals. Florence found a threepenny piece in her purse and gave it to the newsagent, never imagining before in her life she would be the purchaser of a rag such as the *Daily Mirror*. Then she hooted with delight.

"They've arrested him."

"Who, madam?"

"That bloody terrorist, Josiah Makoni."

"Do you know the man?"

"Not personally. I'm from Rhodesia."

"He'd gone to bury his father."

"What's the difference? We've got him. Oh, my goodness."

Ten minutes later, when Petronella's train pulled into the station, Florence was still smiling, the copy of the *Daily Mirror* shoved in the rubbish bin where it belonged. When Petronella stepped out of the train to see her mother's smiling face on the platform she looked surprised.

"Grandfather hasn't told you."

"Of course he has, darling. Isn't it wonderful? One day you are going to be mistress of Woodlands Court and a very rich lady. Your father and I are so happy for you."

"This is my friend Elsie Gilmore. Elsie, this is my mother."

"I've heard so much about you, Elsie."

"I hope it's all good, Mrs Maple?"

"What else could it be, Elsie? Come along. I have the Bentley. The porter will bring your luggage to the car."

"Where's Daddy?"

"Walking the dogs. You know your father and his exercise. So what have you been up to, darling?"

"They've arrested Josiah."

"Josiah? Do I know a Josiah?"

"I think you do, Mother."

"Oh, that Josiah. Oh dear, have they? What has he done?"

"The BSAP grabbed him at his father's funeral in Mazoe. He was very fond of his father. Elsie and I think it's disgusting."

"No politics, darling. Don't you remember our rule? It's Christmas on Wednesday. A time for harmony and joy."

"Are they all there?"

"Every one of them. Come along. Barbara is still arguing with May."

"What's new?"

"She doesn't like my younger brother being managing director of Sheckland-Hall. Do you realise, one day you'll be on the board? You'll have to watch out for Barbara. When she wants something she's quite charming. You see, with you voting your shares with Horace's you can change the managing director to Horace by outvoting Winfred."

"Grandfather is still alive, Mother."

"Of course he is. I was just warning you. She'll butter you up. So, what do you think about becoming a capitalist?"

"No politics, Mother. It's Christmas."

"Of course it is."

"Who stuck today's copy of the *Mirror* in the bin?"

"I have no idea."

"Did you buy the paper, Mother?"

"The *Daily Mirror*? Don't be ridiculous... Thank you, porter. You can strap those two suitcases on the back. Do you know this car is pre-war? My father drove it himself for thirty-five years. They didn't have proper boots in cars in those days."

Florence, again digging in her bag, gave the man a sixpence.

"You'll have to sit in the back, Elsie. Come along both of you. This afternoon, Petronella, I thought you and I would ride Grandfather's horses sedately round the estate. You haven't forgotten how to ride? Not quite like a canter in Rhodesia, of course. Never mind. Come along. Everyone's expecting you."

PETRONELLA, not used to her mother's charm, sat quietly in the front passenger seat of the old Bentley as her mother drove down the street. The previous night's flurry of snow had turned to sleet. There was dirty snow on the trodden pavements but not on the road. The news of Josiah's arrest had reached her a few days before in the ZANU office in Paddington in a phone call from the Reverend Harvey Pemberton. The office staff had stayed mostly silent for the rest of the day. The idea had been for Josiah to make a quick in-and-out trip to his father's funeral. As head of the London office of ZANU, appointed by the exiled party politburo in Tanganyika, Josiah had left the office without a boss.

Petronella, who worked for nothing while her grandfather's allowance went to pay for the running of the office, had no official position. She was the fundraiser.

"They'll send someone over from the Chunya camp, Elsie."

"How will they get him a permit to live in London?"

"The Rhodesian blacks have a lot of sympathy in Whitehall. More after this arrest at a family funeral. We must play up that side to the newspapers. Are you looking forward to spending Christmas with me?"

"Of course. Will we have bedrooms next to each other?"

"I arranged it with Mrs Weatherby on my last visit to Grandfather. I can't wait to see my mother's face after she learns I'm inheriting her share of the family money. She'll spit blood."

"What are you going to do with all that money?"

"Grandfather is only seventy-three. He'll live another twenty years."

"If the booze doesn't get him... Poor Josiah. Do you think they'll kill him?"

"Probably not. Assassinating political prisoners isn't British. They'll stick him somewhere out in the bush where he can't cause trouble. Lots of books. They may let him study. They just want him out of the way so he can't cause trouble."

"He'll still be a prisoner."

"Good for his political career."

With her mind far away, Petronella wasn't even listening to her mother's prattle. Both Josiah and Harry were now in Africa, the thought giving her a brief twinge of regret. She turned and smiled at Elsie in the back of the Bentley. Their eyes met. The car swerved.

"Look out, Mother!"

"Oh dear. I took my eye off the road. Not used to a Bentley on English country roads. Lucky the slush has cleared off the road. Did you have breakfast, darling?"

"What's all this 'darling', Mother?"

"I'm pleased to see my only child. Can't a mother enjoy her daughter?"

"You are more inclined to say what is wrong with me."

"Whatever the difference in our politics, you are still my daughter. The child of my womb."

"Mother, please."

"Well it's a fact."

"How's the Rhodesian Front? What a strange name to give a political party."

"The ruling party is flourishing. If the British government don't give us independence without any strings attached we are going to declare UDI."

"UDI?"

"Unilateral declaration of independence. They'll never send a British army to fight their own people. The army wouldn't let the politicians pit Englishmen against Englishmen."

"They'll apply economic sanctions. Stop Commonwealth preference on the tobacco."

"We still have South Africa, darling."

"Grandfather hasn't told you, has he?"

"As a matter of fact he has. I think it's wonderful for you. What would your father and I do with that old house and all that money? You can only sleep in one bed and eat one meal at a time. The farm is doing very well. The price of tobacco sky high. Commonwealth preference. We'll certify our tobacco was grown in Zambia or Malawi to the buyers. Oh, we don't need any more money. What on earth would we do with it? Can you imagine us wanting to live in this dreadful climate after all our wonderful years in Africa? The magic is in Africa. Not in England. The beautiful farm, our friends, the club. To get a horse ride at Woodlands Court you have to ride round and round. I know. I did it yesterday in the snow. No fun whatsoever. You can't sell the old house, you know that?"

"Why can't I, Mother?"

"It's entailed. From the first Sheckland-Hall at Woodlands Court. Has to stay in the family. In the bloodline. You'll be lady of the manor. Not bad for a communist."

Petronella smiled at her mother, feeling more comfortable. Her mother gave a short laugh, the laugh hollow. 'What the hell's she up to?' thought Petronella.

"Now you sound more like my mother."

"Oh, darling, you always take everything the wrong way... How are you in the back there, Elsie?"

"I'm fine, Mrs Maple."

"These old cars don't come with heaters. Father drives around in an overcoat and a blanket over his knees most of the year round. No, once you've lived in Africa you can't live in England. What a terrible thought."

Watching her mother maintain her smile, Petronella noticed the clenched teeth and movement in the jaws. Under all the top surface chatter her mother was in a blind fury. When Petronella turned to smile at Elsie her mother again took her eyes off the road, catching their brief interchange of intimacy.

"Mother, would you like me to drive?"

"I'm quite capable. At the next turn you can see the chimney pots of the old house. So many childhood memories."

"Are they good?"

"Not all of them. If we are honest with ourselves some memories are bad... Here we are. Your grandfather is so looking forward to seeing you. Best we don't talk about the inheritance. May thinks the old house should have gone to Winfred as managing director of Sheckland-Hall. April, May and June. The names her mother gave to her three daughters. Can you imagine?"

"Isn't Father looking forward to seeing me?"

"Of course he is, Petronella. Just don't talk politics. Your father's been elected chairman of the local branch of the Rhodesian Front. He's quite the politician. He's so proud. Your father the charmer. Never falls out with anyone. Why they elected him. There's talk of nominating him in the next election as the Rhodesian Front candidate for Marandellas and Macheke. Who knows, he may be made a junior minister."

FLORENCE MAPLE, pleased with her performance, drove the Bentley past the front of the house and through to the stables. All but two of the old stables had been converted to garages. She parked the car and led the way through the back of the stables into the formal gardens of Woodlands Court. The two looks between the girls had been unmistakable: they were still lovers.

"I hope you don't mind, Petronella. I asked Mrs Weatherby to give me the bedroom next to yours. We see so little of each other, you being in London and me and your father in Africa. Do you ride, Elsie?"

"No, Mrs Maple."

"Well, then, my daughter and I will go for a ride together later. I'm sure my two brothers will keep you entertained. So will their wives. They don't like each other. It's quite entertaining to watch them being bitchy with each other. You see, Winfred is the younger of the two. The managing director. I rather think Barbara is jealous. All their children are perfectly awful if you want my opinion. Spoiled brats. May has two boys. Barbara has two girls. You see, May's sons will go into the business. Such fun. When you have lots of money the only thing left to have is social standing. Why so many rich people in England buy themselves titles. Winfred is trying to buy himself a knighthood, or better still an hereditary knighthood. A baronetcy. So his eldest son Conrad can inherit the title as well as be managing director of Sheckland-Hall. Winfred wants to leave his own legacy... Come along. Here come the dogs. Run and say hello to your father. Bonner, the old head gardener, will bring in your suitcases. Before the advent of cars he was the groom."

"Petronella! Lovely to see you."

"Hello, Father. Happy Christmas."

BERTIE MAPLE PUT out his arms to his daughter, both palms turned outwards. It was more a formal double handshake. They hadn't hugged since she ran into his arms as a child. How she could be his daughter or Flossy's was beyond his comprehension. She was beautiful in the way of a seductress, unlike her lesbian friend who was big and luscious. When the big girl bent down to pat the dogs while he was greeting Petronella he noticed her large bottom. On most girls the large bottom would have been unattractive. On Elsie Gilmore it wasn't. The two girls had met some years ago at Manchester University. Communism and lesbianism: what an education!

"How's my girl? Hello, Elsie. Mind those dogs, they'll slobber all over you. Mrs Weatherby is serving elevenses in the conservatory. The sun's been on the glass roof since breakfast. Bonner has the heating on, of course. December in good old England. The boiler keeps the conservatory warm all winter giving your grandfather fresh flowers in the house throughout the year. Lovely idea. I rather think it's Mrs Weatherby's. Every few days Mrs Weatherby arranges flowers throughout the Court. Quite the flower arranger, Mrs Weatherby. Did you know she was a friend of Constance Spry, the famous author on flower arranging? Come and have a cup of tea."

Not sure if his daughter was pleased to see him, the look she gave him as they grasped hands both quizzical and enigmatic, he led the way into the house. For some years he had pondered the possibility of not being Petronella's father, the girl was so completely different to himself and everyone else he had ever known in his family. That some revolutionary pervert with a penchant for hurting people had somehow seduced his wife. Except that as far back as he could remember no other man had ever looked at his wife with a sexual thought in their minds. Flossy was horsey, there was no doubt about it. Probably why they had only the one child, the product of their honeymoon on a tropical island off Mozambique. Flossy had been one of the 'fishing fleet' who had come out to Rhodesia before the war looking for a husband. He had quickly married the rich man's daughter more in desperation than anything else, giving him a wife and the money to buy his own farm. He had hoped that under the cold, sexless exterior of Florence Sheckland-Hall he would find a girl of passion. That what she looked like wouldn't matter with the lights out. He had been desperate. There just weren't any single women in Rhodesia prepared to live in the bush. Some things worked out better than others in life if you took your chances. And now the chances of Rhodesia lasting his lifetime weren't exactly great and his wife had been disinherited. It just wasn't fair. He smiled to himself as he led his wife and daughter into the conservatory. Or was it? You never knew with life. Changes, bad ones, were often the spice of life. Every tub had to stand on its own bottom, is how he looked at it. He wondered idly what his wife would be like without her financial bottom.

The old grandfather was beaming at his granddaughter. With all his money and past life in the family business the man was a fool if he couldn't see through Petronella. They were hugging each other, the look of rage on Flossy's face enough to make Bertie laugh. Elsie was watching the two of them hug with a look of satisfied indulgence on her face. As if sharing her lover with a rich old man was going to be to her advantage. And he should know. He had married for money. Money lasted and love, or whatever they called it, didn't. When a man hadn't had sex for a couple of years there was a build-up of lust fit to burst, even for a girl with a face that looked like a horse. At least he had stayed faithful to his marriage vows. He believed in honour, duty, loyalty, trust and God. Before God he had taken Florence Sheckland-Hall for better or for worse. And there was worse to come. Which was life. In the end you died and all the petty detail of life was unimportant. He was getting old, he told himself. The whole game of life just wasn't so important. Whatever they wanted he went along with. He had been doing it all his life. If they were kicked out of Rhodesia without a penny, something would come along. Something always did. For better or for worse.

"Elsie, come along and let me pour you that cup of tea."

He was his old charming self. It was what counted. With his arm round the shoulder of his daughter's lover, he walked her to the table with the tea among the hothouse flowers of his father-in-law's conservatory.

Having done his job as the father of the 'groom', Bertie stood back from the others. The conservatory was a big greenhouse built against the side of the house with twelve-inch steam pipes from a boiler ringing the room. When Bertie put his hand to the pipe it was warm. The room was humid and tropical. At the end grew two small palm trees surrounded by flowers on high benches that filled most of the conservatory. There was a path down the middle of the foliage. At the top of the gravel path was an open area with a breakfast table big enough for family and guests. May and Barbara were sitting at the table. By the look of them they had just had a row. Bertie didn't like either of the women but kept that to himself. He had found in life it was better to say nice things about people whatever he thought. He liked to think of it more as diplomacy. Like now with his daughter, Bertie avoided a fight. May and Barbara had been fighting ever since Winfred, the younger brother, had been made managing director of the family firm when his father retired. It had got neither of them anywhere. All they had done was make everyone else around them uncomfortable.

"Why is it so humid in here?" asked Elsie.

"Bonner lets steam into the hothouse in the morning. Makes the plants think they're growing in the tropics. Those flowers over there are African orchids. I should know. Brought them across to England from my farm where they grow wild down by the river. Provided there is sunlight coming through the glass the plants thrive. Most plants need sunlight to grow. Not those ferns. They grow under trees away from the sun in Rhodesia in deep shade."

"There's such a lovely scent of flowers."

"How's your tea?"

"A little too hot for the moment. Petronella can drink tea scalding hot. You must have a lovely life in Rhodesia."

"Which you enjoy while you still can," Bertie was smiling.

"I wasn't going to say that."

"The trick of life is to enjoy what you have. You want to meet all these people?"

"Not yet. Your police have arrested Josiah Makoni at his father's funeral."

"I didn't know that. I met Tembo, Josiah's father, at Harry Brigandshaw's funeral. Harry and Tembo had grown up together on Elephant Walk. Josiah was Tembo's last child from his fourth wife. A black man takes more than one wife if he can afford them. How sad to be arrested at your own father's funeral. Rhodesia's in a bit of a pickle at the moment. Always happens in the world when the balance of power changes. The rise and fall of Rome. The rise and fall of the British Empire. The sun's setting, I'm afraid. If you live as long as Tembo you'll see more great changes in the world. He was a very old man."

"The whole world will be communist."

"You never know, Elsie. People have a habit of changing their minds when they personally don't get what they want. Churchill said democracy was a lousy way to govern but he couldn't think of a better one. All part of a man's evolution. Who knows what this crazy world of ours will look like in fifty years' time? By then I'll be dead and buried thankfully. We all think we have the solution but none of them really work. We just muddle along, some of us surviving."

"You don't hate the communists?"

"I don't hate anyone. I've found it to be a pointless waste of time. Let me show you my favourite orchid. It's so delicate. So beautiful. It will make your heart sing."

"You are so different to Petronella's mother."

"Maybe that is why we have lived together in harmony for so many years."

2

*A*rnold Sheckland-Hall, the patriarch of the family, watched Bertie show the big girl his flowers. Petronella was watching them, not sure what was going on. It was so wonderful to have his whole family under his roof even if his daughters-in-law were fighting each other as usual. It was why he had changed his will, hoping Petronella would balance the two women. Inheriting a family business, and with it a fortune, had obligations to his forebears. Ever since his father had died, the year after he survived the war in the trenches, and left him the company, his job had been custodian of a long family tradition. As a regular army officer he had been trained to command people, to look after them, to keep them to the best of his ability out of harm's way. In France that most often had not been possible. All through the subsequent years of running Sheckland-Hall Limited, he had two objects in mind: to grow the business, and hand down to the next generation no less than what he had inherited. Now his last job was to make sure Barbara and May didn't destroy the company with jealousy. Flossy, far away in Rhodesia, would have been unable to influence the company. The distance, lack of knowledge and Bertie would have seen to that. Petronella understood politics. As a working member of the revolutionary party in Rhodesia the tobacco farm of her mother and father would be safe. If the girl used more of the family income in her pursuit of politics while she grew up to understand reality it was none of his business. The girl had a good brain. A good degree. She was young. She would learn. She would burn her fingers. But most of all she would maintain the balance of power in Sheckland-Hall Limited between her two uncles, a job far beyond her mother's capability. Arnold had heard more than once in his life an old saying: 'It's easier in life to make money than hold onto it.' What he wanted from his socialist-leaning firebrand of a sometime misguided granddaughter was to hold on to the family business. To prevent the shareholders from self-destructing. If in the process he alienated his only daughter, so be it. Why those two damn women couldn't have been satisfied with what they had was beyond his comprehension. Why did they permanently have to fight with each other in the way they were now doing at his breakfast table? Why couldn't they be civil? What was the matter with them? With the exception of his own wife, whom he missed dearly, he had never once in his life been able to understand women.

"When are you coming to a board meeting, Dad?"

"When your two wives learn to be civil to each other."

"Barbara's jealous."

"Then tell Horace to knock some sense into her head... How is business?"

"Never been better. Profits this year are forty per cent up on last year's figures. We're bringing down the company debt. Next year we will increase the dividend."

"Then what do you need me for?"

Smiling at his youngest son, Arnold turned to his granddaughter.

"Is your mother all right with our arrangement, Petronella?"

"Frankly, I'm not sure. Mother's being nice to me."

"Maybe she misses you too."

"Oh God, here come the cousins."

The two granddaughters from Horace fluttered into the conservatory and settled round their mother. Not only did they flutter like birds, they twittered. Arnold had never heard either of them utter an intelligent word in their lives. Calling them Tinkerbell and Hyacinth should have been a warning. They were just like their mother. What Horace, who had come through the war with a bar to his Military Cross, had seen in Barbara was beyond his comprehension. Not only was Barbara a bitch, she was stupid, the worst, in Arnold's opinion, of all the human faults. He had once overheard two of Horace's fellow officers talking at a party about the girl with the velvet pussy, to find out later the velvet pussy they were referring to belonged to his daughter-in-law. By the sound of what he overheard, his daughter-in-law was unfaithful. The girl had to have had something. His eldest son was besotted, poor boy. Looking at his twittering granddaughters, Arnold felt sorry for any poor fool of a man who got involved with them.

"You can't imagine one of them is eighteen and the other sixteen."

"They are going to be debutantes, Petronella, and curtsy to the Queen. You missed that privilege."

"You're laughing inside, Grandfather?"

"It's their lives. What can an old man do? They are both pretty. Has to count for something."

"You should love all your grandchildren unconditionally."

"Oh, but I do. You are all that's left of my flesh and blood when I leave this world for eternity. Won't be long. Feel it in my bones."

"Don't be silly. You are going to live forever."

"Why are you always nice to me?"

"Because I love you."

"Better go and rescue Elsie from your father."

"They've arrested Josiah."

"I heard on the radio this morning. Silly boy, going back."

"It was his father."

"Yes, I suppose it was... Where are Conrad and Damian?"

"I have no idea. Am I my cousins' keeper?"

"Get out of here!"

With a deep feeling his life had been fulfilled, Arnold watched his favourite grandchild walk away. Halfway down the path between the tall flowers she turned back to him and waved. No, he thought, there were two women I understood. My wife and Petronella.

WATCHING her father-in-law's exchange with Petronella, Barbara, married to Arnold's eldest son Horace, tried not to listen to her daughters' prattle, the words going in one ear and straight out the other. Across the table her sister-in-law May was glaring at her. Today's argument had centred around May's youngest son Damian. The boy was a dunce at school having just failed his Common Entrance to Charterhouse Public School, giving Barbara the chance to gloat.

"There are special schools for backward children, May."

"He's not backward. He's dyslexic. He can't spell. Every time he makes a spelling mistake they take off a mark. No matter the subject. English. History. Scripture knowledge."

"Tinkerbell and Hyacinth are good spellers, aren't you, darlings? The trouble with Damian is he doesn't concentrate. Some third-rate boarding school will take him. How old is he now?"

"He's just turned thirteen."

"How's his reading?"

"Not as good as it should be."

"There you are. The boy's backward."

"He prefers kicking a football."

"Won't get on in life kicking footballs. I'm just glad he isn't my son."

"He wants to be a writer."

"Now I'm going to laugh. The boy can't read properly at thirteen and he can't get into a good school and now he wants to be a writer."

"He has a vivid imagination. Always telling stories."

"Tall stories if you ask me."

"Barbara, you're a bitch."

"Probably, darling. But it won't help your Damian, poor boy. Look at him at the end of the table. Is he sulking?"

"He only heard the news this morning."

Complacent with her verbal victory over May, Barbara smiled across at Petronella talking to her father. In Petronella was Barbara's salvation. Not only was Barbara pleased with how crushed Florence had looked at the news, she was still gloating at the prospect of her husband Horace, the eldest son, getting even with Winfred. They had received the news of his father's change in the will at their home the previous week.

"She'll want to sell her shares in Sheckland-Hall Limited when she inherits, Barbara. Give all that family money to the cause. My niece has a fixation about slavery. Guilt, I suppose. Her forebears were slave owners. Can't change that. In terms of the company's articles of association she'll have to offer her shares to me and Winfred. If we don't buy they'll go on the market I suppose. We're a public company listed on the London stock exchange, so offloading her inheritance won't be difficult."

"You must buy her shares and outvote Winfred. Make yourself managing director, the job that was rightfully yours."

"Don't let's go through that again," said Horace. "Fred's much better at the PR than me. Talking to the press. He comes over well on television. I hate public speaking. Get all tongue-tied. No, he's much better as MD. Anyway, we discuss any major decisions before he announces them."

"But he gets all the publicity."

"Of course he does. That's the point. He's better at it than me. I'm more the backroom boy who does the thinking."

"He makes more than you."

"Don't we have enough, Barbara?"

"What would happen if both of you bought out Petronella? You'd both end up with equal voting shares. Who would then decide who would be the managing director?"

"I'd get the casting vote, matter of fact. There's a clause in the voting rights to the Class A shares that gives me, as eldest son, the casting vote. But that doesn't matter. I'd vote for Fred."

"Not if I had something to say about it... How would you both find money to buy Petronella's shares?"

"I don't like this conversation. Dad's still alive and healthy."

"But how would you raise the money? You wouldn't want some outsider sitting on the board."

"You're right. We wouldn't. We could leverage our shares and Petronella's."

"What does that mean?"

"The banks would lend us the money using our shares and Petronella's as collateral. Provided the company stays at the same level of profit."

"What will she do with Woodlands Court?"

"It's entailed in Dad's will but that can be challenged in the courts these days. If Father really wanted to protect the old house from going out of the family he'd have to put it in a trust."

"But if she sells we could buy the house."

"Not likely. The developers would offer Petronella a small fortune. The court is now fifty acres surrounded by dense urbanisation. Ashford village is largely part of a greater London. Anyway, we wouldn't want to live at Woodlands Court. It's neither one thing nor the other. Too far out to go to the theatre for the evening. Too near to be in the country."

"You could buy that knighthood May is after and be living in the manor. You could even buy a peerage. I'd be Lady Barbara. We ought to be someone, Horace."

"But we are. We're you and me. We have a beautiful home overlooking Green Park that's close to everything. All your socialite friends."

"But they look down on me."

"That's their fault not mine. I enjoy my life in the heart of London. What more can I give you?"

"A title, a country estate, and the prestige of being head of your company."

"Why are women never satisfied? May's the same. She wants Fred to buy himself a knighthood. What on earth difference does it make?"

"People look up to you."

"Then it's their stupidity. If you have to be Lady Muck to get respect it doesn't say much for you either, Barbara."

"Don't be rude."

"I'm sorry. Let's forget the whole damn thing. Why don't we take the kids to the Christmas pantomime?"

"Tinkerbell is far too old for the pantomime."

"Yes. I suppose she is. The kids grow up so fast."

"You won't go back on your promise of having her presented to the Queen?"

"Of course not."

"There's a musical at Drury Lane."

"Wonderful. I'll buy some scalped tickets. Take my whole family to the theatre."

The conservatory was getting stuffy, the pollen from the flowers giving Barbara the first sign of hay fever. Taking a handkerchief from her handbag she blew her nose. The men had gone. Petronella was talking to Elsie. Damian and his brother Conrad had gone outside where the winter sun was still shining.

"Where have all the men gone, May?"

"How should I know? Do you have to blow your nose so loud? It's so vulgar. Tinkerbell, please go and find Janice and tell her to bring us a fresh pot of tea. This one has gone cold."

The two young girls went out leaving the two women glaring at each other across the table.

"Do you have to order my children around?"

"Someone has to."

"I'm going to talk to Petronella and Elsie."

"Good riddance."

"When are you going to grow up? You know, you really are a bitch."

"Now who's calling the kettle black? When it comes to first-class bitches you, Barbara, take the cake."

HORACE and his brother Winfred had escaped from the conservatory with Bertie. His father had given him the wink.

"I think Dad's breaking the rules."

"I need a drink after listening to those two bickering with each other. Why did we ever marry, Horace?"

"To have a family and lovely children. Or, more likely, something a lot more basic. Mine took me right to the crucial point and stopped. Every time. Said she was a good girl and needed a ring on her finger."

"So did mine... And you, Bertie?"

"I won't fall into the trap of discussing your sister. Enough to say there was a shortage of single girls in Rhodesia before the war."

"Your marriage all right, old boy?"

"Absolutely wonderful. I've learnt to always agree with Florence. About everything. Lends itself to a peaceful life."

"And Petronella?"

"What they argue about is their business. When I'm alone with Petronella I agree with Petronella. With Florence it's the same. Complete contradiction but I don't much mind. There's a bit of right in both their points of view. I don't want to fall out with either of them. Don't you think we'd better knock on your father's door?"

"Of course."

Horace knocked twice with his knuckle on the study door.

"Come in, boys... Good. You escaped. Why do sisters-in-law always bitch at each other? You want a glass of sherry? Bit early in the day but it is Christmas."

"Have you got a scotch in that cabinet, Dad?"

"No water or soda I'm afraid. You'll have to drink it neat like a Scotsman. Ten-year-old single malt. You know the Scots think it's sacrilege watering down whisky. Sit you all down. We can relax. The boys have gone horse riding and all the girls are in the conservatory drinking tea. Perfect. So. What's been happening at the old firm? You can fill me in with my slippers on in front of a roaring log fire with a glass of sherry in my hand. You know Winston always had a balloon glass of brandy on the table at cabinet meetings. They say he drank twenty-three Imperial tots a day. Didn't do him any harm. We won the war. Cheers. Why don't you all help yourselves from my cocktail cabinet? Bertie, sit down next to me when you have your drink. I have my reasons for bypassing Florence in my will. Doesn't mean I don't love her the same as my boys."

"I have no complaints. We have a wonderful life in Rhodesia."

"Long may it carry on. Never came out. Always said I would. Running the firm I was too busy. Afterwards I hated aeroplanes. So, Winfred and Horace, what's been going on?"

"I haven't told Winfred yet. Was waiting to tell you and Fred at the same time. Our chemists have developed a sweetener that doesn't contain sugar."

"Isn't that counterproductive to a sugar company?"

"We have a patent on the content of the product. 'Slimsweet' is our registered trademark. The sweeteners are small pills in a plastic box. Pop one in your coffee and it tastes like three spoons of sugar. All the women these days are trying to lose weight. We're going to have a massive advertising campaign if Winfred agrees."

"Will it make any money?"

"Our mark-up is ridiculous. Good advertising with no competitors. Sugar margins have always been razor-thin. Oh, we'll make money."

"My goodness. What next... Everyone. Raise your glasses. Happy Christmas."

They all sat down in leather chairs round the comfort of the fire, no one talking. Horace watched the small flames dance on the coals. He felt comfortable. Enjoying himself. Throughout his life his best friend had always been his brother. They understood each other. Bertie looked on edge sipping his glass of neat whisky. Horace had poured him a stiff one. It was always difficult to know what a man was thinking inside his head. Horace's father looked comfortable in his slippers by the fire. There was only one window in the study, the sun not coming into the room. A standard lamp was on in the corner. Books lined the walls. Old books. Many of them bought by the Sheckland-Hall who had built the Court at the end of the eighteenth century, when the only entertainment on a winter's day was reading a good book. No radio. No television. Just a book. A book and the conversation of friends and relatives. A peaceful world Horace regarded with envy.

His father had watched him look round the room, at once familiar to Horace and strange. All those unmet ancestors pulling books from the shelves. Men drinking and talking together away from their women and children. He could feel their presence in the silence of the room. In its history.

"Have you read them all, Dad?"

"Most of them. There's not much else to do for an old man living on his own. I find television too trivial. Too contrived. Not enough meat to it. You don't have to think... What's going to happen to Damian, Winfred? He looks upset, poor lad. As though he's let you down."

"He'll take the exam again next term but not for Charterhouse. That's why he's so upset. Charterhouse play football. The rest of the public schools play rugby. He's not big enough for rugby. Or fast enough. He's been living for football since he was nine years old. Plays centre half. Tells me that if he isn't up with the forwards they don't score a goal. That if he isn't back with the backs the other side will score. A bit like running a business, I suppose. You have to be everywhere to know what's going on. Like your sweetener, Horace. That must be our chemists' worst kept secret. I've done a projection of sales against advertising. We'll have to spend a lot of money to change people's habits."

"Are we going with it?"

"You've got to keep ahead in this world. Take chances. We'll get our heads together after Christmas and make a decision."

"On the surface?"

"Looks good."

Horace watched Bertie smile at the new innovation as Bertie turned to Winfred.

"I'm going to grow cigar wrapper leaf on the farm, Fred. For the same reason. There's a bigger profit margin in cigars. Give the Cubans a run now the Americans won't buy from them. It's always politics. You won't believe it but the Rhodesian Front want me to stand for parliament in a by-election."

"Was that Flossy's idea?" asked Horace.

"Not this time. Frankly, I think we're all walking into a mess."

"Have you told Petronella?"

"What difference would it make? She's on one side, I'm on the other. Take it one step at a time. That's my motto."

"Some say there will be a bush war in Rhodesia."

"Then we'll have to fight."

"You'll lose, Bertie. There aren't enough of you."

"Probably. But what else can we do? Most of the whites in Rhodesia don't have anywhere else to go even if they wanted. You can't start a life all over again in middle age. Anyway, what does a tobacco farmer do back in England?"

"If you've run a farm you could run a business."

"To be successful you have to know what you are doing. Anyway, life goes on. Wherever you are there are problems. Ask Josiah Makoni. Why do we all want to fight with each other?"

"Human nature. Evolution. Progress. Competition. Call it what you want. People are never satisfied."

The silence came back, each of them thinking his thoughts. Horace was not sure whether to feel sorry for Bertie or envy him. All that wide open space. All that sunshine. No smog. No living most of the time indoors... All lives came to an end. The trick was to enjoy them. Rhodesia sounded so beautiful. It was all a matter of choice. With Petronella involved with Josiah Makoni, who knew where the Sheckland-Hall bloodline would finish. Someone had said to Horace in the City Carlton Club that everyone was related to everyone on the planet. The man had written papers on evolution. The Bible talked of Adam and Eve... His mind wandering, Horace sipped his whisky, quite content.

"There must be something in the family if Damian can't spell. Right through my life I've had the problem. Genetic. Got to be genetic.

"If he's going to write, the boy had better start reading my library. His maths is good, I suppose?"

"Top of the class, Dad," said Winfred.

"Same with me. Mental arithmetic to me was always simple. From a small boy. Like Damian, don't ask me to spell. I can see when I write the wrong spelling but often can't find the word in the dictionary. Someone will invent a way of spelling for us. You talk into a machine and the machine prints out the words. He'll just have to play rugby. Send him to Cranleigh. That's an arts school I've heard. Not a snob school but he'll get an education. They're not so fussy about his marks in the Common Entrance exam. I would love to have written books. Never got round to it."

"Are we having another drink?"

"Why not? One more and then we'll go and find some lunch. What a lovely day with my family. I miss your mother so much. Bertie, would you care to do the honours? My glass just up to the pretty. Can't have Janice helping me to bed for my afternoon nap. Horace, put some more coal on the fire. Bertie must be freezing. You know, if England had had a good climate we would never have founded the colonies. Let's drink to sunshine. And happiness."

LUNCHEON WAS SERVED in the dining room, the stag hunt up in the dome roof fascinating Elsie Gilmore. The last of the day's sun was shining on the stag through the ring of small windows below the dome, accentuating the male's big antlers. She was so happy. She had Petronella all to herself for a week, her love for the girl sitting next to her overflowing. With Harry Wakefield on assignment in Rhodesia and Josiah Makoni in the Salisbury Central jail there was no competition. With a connecting door between their bedrooms, carefully planned by Petronella, they would make love every night and wake up in the mornings wrapped in each other's arms... Mrs Weatherby was serving a fish risotto made with herbs from the garden and wild mushrooms she had picked earlier in the year. It was delicious. The argument about the inheritance between Petronella and her mother had not materialised. Her lover was one day going to be rich and living in this beautiful house. Elsie looked around with better appreciation. It seemed the stag was looking at her and smiling. With conversation flowing fast across the table, Elsie turned to whisper to Petronella.

"Why don't you move out of that awful room in Shepherd's Bush and live in my flat?"

"Are you asking me to move in with you, darling?" whispered Petronella right in her ear, making Elsie's sexual need flush hot through her body.

"Why not?"

"I'll think about it."

"What are you two whispering about?" asked the old man from the top of the table, smiling at them both and looking well pleased with himself.

"Nothing, Grandfather. Just girls' talk."

Elsie watched the relaxed interchange, her life never better. At that moment she decided to give up her affairs with men permanently. She was in love. No doubt of it. At peace with the world. Even the mother was smiling at her with the same look of quiet pleasure Elsie had seen in the grandfather. Where she had expected animosity, there was nothing. Elsie wondered if the mother and father knew about Petronella's bisexuality. Not that it really mattered. The day after Christmas the parents were flying back to Rhodesia. Something to do with the start of the reaping season on the tobacco farm.

"Are you still riding the horses after lunch, Petronella?"

"Of course, Mother."

"Amazingly the sun is still shining. Twice round the estate. How does that sound?"

"Perfect to me. Grandfather serves sherry round the fire in the lounge at six. It's dark by four. Plenty of time to change for dinner."

Elsie listened complacently as she tucked into her food. When Mrs Weatherby brought in an apple pie with a rich brown crust her happiness overflowed. After her passion for Petronella came her passion for food. Lots of it. Good, homemade food just like the food served by Mrs Weatherby. Life, she decided, couldn't get any better. Under the table she put her hand on Petronella's thigh and stroked, the silk of the dress moving up with her fingers. Up and down, up and down, getting higher up the girl's thigh all the time, smiling round the table while she forked the apple pie into her mouth. Feeling the girl's body shudder she smiled at Petronella, taking her hand away.

"Is that better, darling?" she whispered close to Petronella's ear.

"I'll get you tonight."

"I hope so. Oh, I hope so."

They were going to be a family. Just the two of them. The good life had just begun.

IT TOOK Petronella and her mother ten minutes to catch and saddle the horses. The last of the pale wintry sun was filtering through the leafless trees that bordered the property. The horses were pleased to be ridden, happy like Petronella and her mother for the exercise. Taking the circular path on the perimeter, they cantered the horses. The air was cold, frost on its way. Only the old fir trees were a dull green in the fading sun. Expecting her mother's usual venom now they were alone, Petronella waited. Nothing came. Not a word. Of Rhodesia or the inheritance. Not a gloating mention of Josiah Makoni locked up in a police cell... They rode round once and stopped under the biggest horse chestnut tree south of the Thames. They stood under the tree in silence, the horses impatient. Petronella was thinking of Elsie and smiling, knowing she had no intention of moving from her room in Shepherd's Bush. She liked to keep her lovers always short of what they wanted, that way maintaining her control. She knew never to give any of them full satisfaction. To always leave them wanting more. Domestic bliss turned into bickering and lack of control. Poor Elsie. She would learn. Like the rest of them. There was a man in the record business with a fast-growing fortune she was going to tap for the party. To raise money for the Zimbabwe African National Union. She had him almost grovelling. The more she said 'no', the more he wanted her. It was always the same. You had to keep them short. Before and afterwards. Like Elsie. Except for tonight. Tonight they would play.

"That reporter's in Rhodesia. Did you know, Petronella?"

Here it comes, she thought.

"Which one, Mother?"

"Harry Wakefield. He's very liberal. But you would know that. *Daily*

Mirror. Dreadful rag... The horses are getting impatient. This time we'll make it a race."

"Haven't ridden for ages. I'll be stiff in the morning. Come on, Mother. Race you round the fields. Is there a prize?"

"Who knows? Your father's sleeping. The men were drinking in father's study before lunch. I hope you're enjoying yourself."

Petronella looked at her mother.

"What's the matter?"

"Nothing at all. Why should there be?"

"The way you said 'enjoying yourself'."

As they cantered round the field, Petronella wondered what her mother was up to. By the time they circled and came back to the house, Petronella was well in the lead.

"You won that one."

"I did. I'll wipe down the horses and hand them to Bonner for stabling. You go and change. I enjoyed myself. So nice to see you again, Mother."

3

$\mathcal{C}$ontent with his life, Arnold changed for dinner in the same bedroom he had shared with Isabella for forty years. All her knick-knacks were still on her dressing table. No photographs. He wanted to remember her as she was in his mind, not in a photograph. He touched her silver-backed hairbrush, some of her hairs still entwined in the brush. It had been Isabella's tradition to change for dinner when the family assembled. The dinner jacket was the same one he had worn for twenty years. How long was it now, he asked himself, the years muddling by since her death all merging into one. Contented years but somehow pointless. The kids had their own lives. No one to talk to. Sometimes Petronella, the image of Isabella. Poor Florence. Her mother's good looks had missed a generation... Fumbling his old fingers, he tied his black bowtie. Before, she had tied it for him. She had liked to help. To be close to him. To touch him out of love, long past the lust and youthful passion. They had grown into one person. Why, alone, he was lost, living with her memory of all the good times. He never remembered the bad. His mind was good at that. Selecting the good. Only the good. Which was better.

His afternoon nap had left him fresh and happy to be alive with his memories. He hoped the children could be so lucky with their lives. To live content. In harmony with people. At peace with the accoutrements of an old home he had lived in for most of his life, surrounded by memories of his ancestors, their portraits on the walls. He had watched Florence and Petronella galloping the horses from the window, the sound waking him from his dreams. Afternoon dreams were always the best. The most vivid. Often his dreams were more vivid than his life. A comfort and company. A place he most often enjoyed. Arnold rarely had bad dreams.

He brushed his white hair, surprised at how little he had lost over the years. None of the boys were losing their hair. It was in the family. The thought of a nice glass of his best sherry was comforting. He would get tiddly, he always did. Janice would help him to bed. Leaving the family most likely to argue. When he was at the dinner table they were not allowed to argue. Another of Isabella's rules.

"Oh, well. That was my life. Not a bad one. Can't complain. If I did it wouldn't do any good. Hope I did the right thing with Florence and Petronella."

Thinking of his granddaughter, who looked so much like his dead wife when he had met her before the war, Arnold smiled.

"Sherry time, you old goat."

With a little skip halfway, he walked to the door of their bedroom and the long corridor with the bedrooms on one side and the circular staircase that would take him down to the hall and the lounge with his family and his waiting glass of sherry. It was Christmas. He was always happy at Christmas. From when he was a small boy with all the Christmas presents under the Christmas tree. The whole family smiling. It was the time for family celebration.

ELSIE GILMORE WATCHED Janice the old maid wheel in the trolley. On top was a silver salver with a silver domed top. The old girl picked the salver up with difficulty and put it on the table in front of Horace, the eldest of the old man's two sons. Bertie, the tobacco farmer from Rhodesia, got up to help. Winfred was to carve the meat, the old man having drunk too much of his own sherry in the lounge: Petronella's grandfather was sitting at the top of his table, beaming at everyone. Janice went back to the kitchen. Bertie took the top off the salver with a flourish. They had all been drinking a little too much. The room was warm from the coal fire and the central heating despite the high dome in the ceiling right above the big, oak table which was black with age and use. On the tray was a sirloin of beef. Janice came back with a tray of Yorkshire pudding cut into small pieces. The crust of the pudding round the edge of the tray was a rich brown. Roast beef and Yorkshire pudding: Elsie's favourite. Elsie watched Petronella's uncle carve the meat, her mouth watering. The meat was underdone just enough: pink in the middle, crisp on the outside. She was seated next to Petronella, who was dressed in a beautiful evening gown that must have cost a fortune. She looked radiant and beautiful. Everyone except the two boys and the two girls were in evening dress. Janice had put the Yorkshire pudding in the middle of the table next to a tray of roast potatoes. The potatoes looked delicious. She was hungry even without having had a ride on a horse. The whole room was so grand, the lifestyle so perfect, the two women bickering not even spoiling her mood. Elsie ignored them. The men seemed happy enough. Barbara, the real bitch of the two and married to Horace, was baiting young Damian, the poor boy who had failed his exam, suggesting a spelling-bee round the table while her husband was carving. The old man at the top of the table was no longer beaming.

"Leave my grandson alone if you please."

The boy looked at his grandfather thankfully. When the plate came down from Horace covered in slices of delicious-looking meat she helped herself from the big dishes of vegetables. She took two pieces of Yorkshire pudding and a heap of potatoes, the potatoes dripping in fat.

"Are you hungry, Elsie?"

"What do you think, Petronella?"

"Looks like it."

"Have a glass of red wine to wash it down."

"What a lovely idea for a lovely evening."

Bertie was worried about his tobacco back in Rhodesia, his mind far away from the table. All the costs had gone into the crop: the ploughing, fertilising, planting. Everything rested on selling a good crop. Before the crop came out of the curing barns was the time to worry. Tobacco farming was difficult. If the crop was over-ripe it cured too dark. Under-ripe, the stems turned green. For a too-dark bale on the auction floors or a bale with green in the stems, the American and British buyers cut their price in half. All they had was in the farm. The assistant was good but it wasn't his tobacco. Bertie's wife was watching Petronella and Elsie from across the table. Not a look of friendliness or love. She was still stewing on her disinheritance. Bertie sipped his wine, sitting back from his food for a moment. He wished he was home, back on the farm, making sure there was nothing going wrong with his tobacco. One year at Christmas time it had hailed stones the size of pigeon eggs, ripping his early plantings to shreds. Another year caterpillars had chewed through half his late crop.

"What's the matter, Bertie?"

She had seen him looking at her.

"Nothing, Florence. Lovely evening. Food's delicious."

"Anyone for more meat? Pass your plates. Elsie, you look as though you enjoyed that. Nothing better than a pretty girl with an appetite."

"I don't mind if I do."

"Good girl. Just leave enough room for Mrs Weatherby's rhubarb batter."

Horace was enjoying himself having learnt to ignore his wife's arguments with May. The boy was a fine young lad. Fred was proud of him. So the boy couldn't spell. Who cares? He was healthy, full of energy. What else did they want? He'd find his own niche in life. Everyone always did. It was him being second to Fred that caused the wives all the trouble.

"Tinkerbell. You want some more?"

"I'm on a diet."

"Whatever for? You're as thin as a rake."

"I don't want to be fat like some people."

"Have it your own way."

His eldest daughter took after his wife. It was a pity. She'd make some man miserable. He just hoped Hyacinth didn't turn out the same. He hated both their names, the ideas of Barbara. There had been no point in arguing once she had made up her mind. He preferred names like Elsie. Familiar names. That made people comfortable.

"How many slices, Elsie?"

"I'll leave that to you."

. . .

MAY WAS BOILING with animosity and trying not to show it. When Barbara saw she was annoyed, her sister-in-law gloated. It was not the boy's fault. It was genetic. The Sheckland-Halls were renowned for not being able to spell. Why a few spelling mistakes had kept her son out of Charterhouse was beyond her comprehension. At least the old man had squashed the spelling-bee. Barbara was a bitch to taunt the boy. It was Charterhouse's loss, not theirs. A brilliant football player was Damian, who would have played for the school and made them proud. Lost for a few spelling mistakes in a thirteen-year-old's exam. It wasn't fair. Now he would have to go to another school where they played rugby. And the boy wasn't big enough. May sipped her wine and tried to forget about it but it wouldn't go away. To take her mind off the taunting she looked round the table.

"What's the matter, Bertie? You seem far away?"

"A farmer doesn't like to leave a growing crop. Now is high season on the farm."

"Why'd you come over?"

"Florence had heard rumours. About the will... It's the beginning of the reaping season. Evan Trollip is a nice lad but he hasn't seen as many tobacco seasons as me. Evan's my assistant. Been out of England three years. Doesn't have the experience. Experience, that's what counts."

"Don't you have black men on the farm who know what to do? Been with you for years?"

"They all know their own jobs. How to drive a tractor, which tobacco to reap, how to use a hoe, bring the tobacco to the curing barns. They don't understand the big picture. If there's a problem, Wellington, my bossboy, comes to me. They don't like making decisions. They only see what's right in front of them. Horace says the same in business. So does Fred. Employees don't like making decisions. They want to be told what to do. So if something goes wrong it isn't their fault and they don't get the blame. Truman said the buck stopped on his desk. I understand what he was talking about. Success in business or farming comes back to the boss. On the farm I'm the boss with all the responsibility."

"You want to fly home?"

"As soon as possible."

"I'm sorry. It hasn't been a good trip for either of you. Florence has looked pensive all evening."

BARBARA WAS BOILING INSIDE WORSE than usual, frustrated at not being able to get a rise out of May, hard as she tried. The boy had started to cry but that wasn't what she wanted. Now Petronella had given Tinkerbell a look of disdain at her jibe about fat people. The girl called Elsie was fat, no doubt about it, stuffing her face with more and more food. Tinkerbell was right, the girl was disgusting. Women with wallowing breasts and large bottoms deserved their disdain.

"Hyacinth, you've had quite enough."

"I'm still hungry. Dad says I can have some more."

"You should always leave the table not quite replete. Do you want to be fat?"

"I don't mind."

"But I do. You may have some pudding. Put your plate down."

"Let the girl have some more if she wants. It's Christmas."

"All right. Just this once. But just remember, Hyacinth, I don't want you getting fat."

She was looking straight at the girl called Elsie as she spoke, the girl still stuffing her face. Lazily, the girl's eyes rose from her food to look into her eyes and smile, making Barbara boil up over again. May had seen the interchange and was smiling with Elsie. She wanted to throw something. To hurt someone. Inside her it was screaming again: 'Why the hell wasn't her husband, the eldest son, managing director of Sheckland-Hall Limited with the chance of buying them a knighthood?'

"Why are you looking at me like that, Horace?"

"Nothing, darling. My mind was far away."

She glared at her husband briefly before looking round the table. Damian, the boy who couldn't spell, had stopped crying. On his face was forming the trace of a smile.

WINFRED HAD HIS OWN PROBLEMS, in particular the high price of sugar. The higher the price of raw sugar, the less he made in profit.

"You ever thought of growing sugar cane, Bertie?"

"Not enough water. Lusito Sugar have a sugar estate at Chirundu on the Zambezi River. Plenty of water to irrigate. Water. That's Africa's problem. How to stop the water in the rivers during the rainy season and use it for irrigation when it stops raining for six months. Solve all our problems. The whole idea of the Kariba Dam, apart from hydroelectric power, was to irrigate crops round the perimeter of the lake. Takes a lot of money. Engineering. People who know what they're doing. I have enough trouble growing a summer crop of tobacco plus maize to feed my people. The farm's pretty self-sufficient but you have to watch it. I grow enough maize to produce a surplus. Just in case. Sell the surplus to the Grain Marketing Board to feed the blacks in town. Everyone has to have food."

"If the politics in Africa were better I'd look at a sugar estate for Sheckland-Hall... What you think, Dad?"

"Not my business anymore. We once grew sugar, remember? In Jamaica. Have some more wine."

"You think Rhodesia will stabilise, Bertie?"

"Not in my lifetime. Too many Russians, Chinese and Americans stirring up trouble. Giving people ideas."

"What's going to happen?"

"Who knows?"

"Have some more wine."

Winfred smiled. His father was on a roll with the wine... When Janice put the rhubarb batter on the table, Damian helped himself.

"Can I pass you some, Elsie?"

"Thank you, Damian. Looks delicious."

"Mrs Weatherby covers it in brown sugar before putting it in the oven. Tastes like crunchy treacle. Rhubarb batter. My favourite."

"Mine too. I can't spell either."

"Can't you really? They say I'm dyslexic."

"So was Einstein. And look what happened to him."

"I'll give you a big helping... Aunty Barbara, can you pass Elsie the plate?"

WATCHING his family from the head of his table gave Arnold a deep feeling of pleasure. That all the pain of going through life had come to fulfilment. He filled up his glass, a French red he had kept in his wine cellar for ten years to mature, and drank knowing Janice was on the alert to guide him to his bed. Drinking a little too much was the last of Arnold's physical pleasures. Too much good food gave him indigestion. Horse riding was no longer possible. And women, beautiful women, were just a memory of pleasure gone by... They all seemed happy now Damian was smiling. Maybe not Barbara and Florence. They had their own problems. Both had glanced at him when they thought he wasn't looking. Yes, he was the cause of both their problems, but he was right. Horace was far happier being the backroom boy away from the limelight. After his boys, Petronella would take the family business safely into the next generation. With the responsibility of inheritance she would come to her political senses, if the world of communism hadn't collapsed by then to prove his point. She had a good brain which he counted on. He looked from one to the other, smiling to himself, all of them so different. He was enjoying his last glass of wine for the evening. He would sleep well, that was always good. There was a bottle of Napoleon brandy on the side table with balloon glasses for the boys and Bertie after the children went up to bed. He would have liked to join them but knew he couldn't. He was too old. Drinking the last of the wine in his glass, he looked round for Janice.

"There you are, Janice. Time for my bed. Can you help an old man up the stairs? Goodnight, everyone. Enjoy yourselves. Happy Christmas."

4

*P*etronella was tired, exhausted by a day that expected an argument. She watched her grandfather go off to bed and wanted to follow. Elsie was already on her second plate of Mrs Weatherby's rhubarb batter.

"Why don't you have some, Petronella?"

"My stomach's full and I want to go to bed. It's been a long day."

"Why don't you go up? I'll follow," she whispered. "I'll let them get to sleep before I join you. I'll wake you up... Why is your mother watching us?"

"I have no idea. Grandfather's pickled. Dad and my uncles are going to get stuck into the brandy... Maybe tomorrow."

"You can't be that tired."

"More mentally exhausted keeping one jump ahead of Mother. She's been charming. What worries me. And Dad wants to go back to Rhodesia. I think he wants to get out before there's a fight."

"What can she do about it? Your grandfather won't change his mind. Can you just imagine living in this house?"

"Would you like to live in a place like this?"

"I'd love to. So much history. It's all so lovely."

"Part of another era, Elsie. That will die with Grandfather. He looked so happy tonight. There goes Damian with Conrad off to bed... Goodnight, boys! Sleep tight. Don't let the bed bugs bite."

They watched the boys go off.

"Was Tinkerbell referring to me?"

"Probably. Takes after her mother... Goodnight, Hyacinth. Goodnight, Tinkerbell. See you all in the morning. My word, it really is nearly Christmas. That old horse of Grandfather's can still go like the wind. If the weather's good enough I'm going to ride before breakfast if I'm not too stiff in the morning."

"Have a last glass of wine and we'll go up together. I'm so enjoying myself. Twist your arm. Make you sleep better. You think your grandfather knows?"

They were whispering.

"In my grandfather's world it doesn't exist. We have to be careful. I don't want to upset him. He means too much to me."

"You're getting soft on your principles."

"One more glass of wine and then to bed. That fire is so nice. There will be fires in both our bedrooms that will slowly burn all night. When Janice puts grandfather to bed, she goes round the rooms that are going to be slept in lighting the fires. Old family tradition in winter. Cheers, Elsie. Happy Christmas."

FLORENCE WENT up to bed soon after her daughter. The fire in the bedroom made the room welcoming. Bertie had stayed down in the dining room with her brothers. They would drink brandy halfway through the night. Florence never knew what they had to talk about for so long. She undressed, got into bed and turned out the light having no intention of going to sleep. The fire in the grate made comfortable murmuring sounds. Next door was quiet. She listened carefully. The thick curtains had been drawn across the windows by Janice when she put a match to the fire. Florence remembered Janice when she was a middle-aged chambermaid. Her husband had been killed in the Great War before they had children. Maybe Janice had been lucky. Outside in the night it was quiet. Not a sound of the owls she remembered calling in the depths of the summer nights when she lay awake as a child. Her bedroom had been the one next door. The one with the connecting door where the nursemaid slept. The nursemaid was paid to look after her, her parents sleeping down the end of the corridor away from the children's bedrooms. Amelia, the nurse, was more a mother to Florence than her own mother. When Amelia left to get married, Florence had cried herself to sleep for a week, no one in the family understanding why.

When Bertie came up to bed and turned on the light she pretended to be asleep. With her eyes closed she heard him empty coal on the fire from the scuttle. Heavily, he got into bed. He was soon asleep leaving Florence to lie awake and listen. She knew every sound in the night. Every nuance of the old house. Thankfully, Bertie never snored. Not even when he was drunk. She had no idea what time it was. Fighting sleep, she continued to listen. Then it came. The creak of the door. The door through which Amelia had come to her so many nights to check she was all right, Florence happily pretending she was asleep. It was the iron hinges. The old hinges that no one had ever oiled. Then she heard them. She was certain. A whisper and sounds that made her blood boil. Right next to her! Thrusting back the sheet and blankets, Florence put on her thick dressing gown. The one she had left in England when she took the boat out to Africa to find herself a husband. So many of the young men had died in the Great War leaving so many older women as competition. She was thirty when she got on the boat and sailed from London to Beira. She put her bare feet into her slippers, took a deep sigh and turned on the light. Bertie was still fast asleep. She walked across the room. The fire was still glowing a dull red, the coals covered in white ash. She opened the door to the corridor. Took another deep breath and opened the door to her old bedroom, feeling for the light and turning on the switch. They were both in the same single bed. Wrapped around each other. When she pulled off the sheets they were naked.

"Bertie!" she screamed. "Come in here immediately. Bertie! I want you now."

She was screaming at the top of her voice. The big girl pulled up the sheets to hide them. She looked terrified.

"What the hell's the matter?"

"Look at them. Get my father. Now! Now, I tell you. And don't you two dare move. Disgusting. Utterly disgusting. My own daughter. My own flesh and blood."

With all the noises in the dead of the night the whole house came awake. Bertie went off, refusing to look at his daughter in bed with a naked girl.

"What's all this noise about, Florence? I'm an old man. I don't sleep well. Now you've woken me up and I won't be able to get back to sleep. What's the matter with you?"

"Look at them!"

"What on earth are you two girls doing in the same bed?"

Florence pulled back the sheets Elsie had pulled to her chin.

"They're naked, Father. They've had sex with each other. I heard them from my bedroom next door."

"Get out of my house!" screamed the old man, completely losing control. "Both of you. When I come down to breakfast I want you gone. Petronella. How can you have done this to me? In my own home. With my grandchildren asleep down the corridor. Get out. And never come back. Florence, we'll talk about this in the morning. You too, Bertie. It's an abomination. In my own house. My granddaughter. Oh, God, what have you done to me? What have I done to deserve this?"

"Are you all right, Father?"

"No, of course I'm not. Get out of my way. All of you."

UNCLE HORACE DROVE them to the railway station in the morning not saying very much. It was all over, Petronella had no doubt about it. She was going to lose her inheritance, that was for sure. And most likely her allowance. At that moment when they humped their suitcases up into the railway compartment she knew she did not have any money. There would not be next month's rent for the room in Shepherd's Bush. What hurt most was her father and grandfather not being able to look at her as they walked out of the house. She was on her own. For the first time in her life. All the bravado of communism and African nationalism knocked out of her in one fell swoop.

She could still hear clearly the controlled fury in her grandfather's voice as they waited for Uncle Horace and the car in the hall.

"You get not a penny. Not a penny, you understand?"

Only then had Petronella looked at her mother standing at the bottom of the stairs. Her mother was smiling. She had got what she wanted. She had known the weak spot of her grandfather's indulgences. Her affair with Josiah had antagonised her mother. Not her grandfather with his guilt of slavery, the source of his inherited wealth. Now she knew why her mother had insisted to Janice she wanted the bedroom next to the bedroom she had slept in as a child. Her mother had finally got even. The heavy door slammed shut. They were the only two in the carriage.

"What are you going to do, Petronella?"

"You don't want me in your flat now, I suppose?" There was no answer. "I'll ask ZANU for a salary. They owe me that much."

"They won't give it to you."

"How do you know?"

"They were using you. As much as you were using them."

"Where's my lovely smiling girlfriend this morning, Elsie?"

"I've never been so humiliated."

"You! What about me? That was my family back there. You wanted to go to sleep in my room instead of going back to your own."

"I suppose you're going to blame me."

"Are we having a fight? That's all I need."

"You think it will get in the papers? Oh, my God. My parents will kill me."

"Mine just have."

"She did it deliberately."

"Probably. She always wants to be in control. Money gives her control."

"You can always go back to Rhodesia and Harry Wakefield. He'll take you whatever anyone says. The man's besotted with you."

"They'd likely arrest me if I stepped back in Rhodesia. You're wrong. The party will help me. When we win power it will all be worth it. I'll be a senior member of the party."

"And me?"

"It's not about you. You have a perfectly good, well-paying job."

"Not if last night gets in the papers."

"They won't go that far. The name, darling. The name. The great slave-trading name of Sheckland-Hall. When's Livingstone Sithole due from Tanganyika to take over from Josiah?"

"Didn't know he was coming. Who is he?"

"He and Josiah started the training camp at Chunya. They started the recruitment programme in Rhodesia together. We had a cable in the office after the news of Josiah's arrest."

"How should I know? You run the office... You mind if I read a book? It will keep my mind off not having had breakfast."

"You eat too much."

"Don't be catty. Where are you going to spend Christmas?"

"How do I know?"

"I'm going home to my parents."

"Bully for you."

"You could get a proper job."

"What as?"

"How should I know? You've got a degree. For some you have the right politics. The right credentials. Now, I'm going to read."

"Don't worry about me, Elsie. I'm a big girl."

Then she sighed. A deep, long sigh as she looked out of the carriage window. All she could hear was the rhythmic clang of the train wheels on the metal rails. All she could see was the pain deep back in the eyes of her grandfather, his last solace in life shattered and gone.

"Grandad, I'm so sorry to hurt you," she whispered.

Quietly, Petronella began to cry.

HORACE DROVE HOME SLOWLY, brooding. All the rules. All the dogma. All the years of man's religious and political indoctrination to make people behave themselves. Who knew what was truly right? Was our duty to always procreate like dutiful citizens to ensure the next generation to look after everyone? The Roman army, far from home, had condoned homosexuality. Maybe then it suited them. Made the troops, fighting side by side, more brave. There was always a reason. And often not the one most apparent. Everyone had their secrets. Poor Petronella. Now what was she going to do without any money? Yes, they all had their secrets. The trick in life, he told himself, was not being found out.

Horace had been ten years old when old man Stringer caught him with nine-year-old Christine behind the raspberry bushes. They both had their trousers down looking at the strange difference between their legs: 'Come on, let me look at yours, Horace.' It hadn't been the first time.

Horace had been best friends with Stringer's daughter since they were five, the two of them most often alone together exploring the Woodlands estate. Winter and summer they got out of their houses and met in the stables. Bonner had first introduced them, Christine living in one of the new houses across the road from Woodlands Court. All the kids went to talk to Bonner and the horses. Her father was in printing in the City. Did business with Horace's father, printing labels for Sheckland-Hall. Horace's mother considered Mrs Stringer common. Christine's mother had been a hairdresser before she married Stringer, a self-made man with a successful business that sent his boys and Christine to expensive private schools. Horace's mother had frowned on his friendship which was why they always met away from the main house at Woodlands Court. The raspberry bushes had been down the small Stringer garden. From the ground they had not been visible. From the top window of Stringer's house the raspberry bushes were not tall enough to hide them.

"What are you two doing?" The father had sneaked up on them when they were absorbed with each other. "Get out, Horace. Never again will you speak to my daughter. You hear me? Never."

"Please don't tell my father."

"Pull up your trousers and get off my property. If I see you two together again I'll make a formal complaint to your father. Disgusting. What are you, an animal? Disgusting. Now, get out. I never want to set eyes on you again." The man had been in a shaking fury as Horace ran away.

Thirty-five years later the fear was still with him. The fear of being exposed. Disinherited. His own father disgusted. His mother appalled. How his life would have been if they hadn't been caught often came back to Horace. For fear of reprisal they had never spoken again. Seen each other in the street and smiled but never spoken. And Christine, later in life, a successful actress on the London stage, beautiful, sought-after, a little famous, had become a lesbian. How different their lives might have been. There would not have been Barbara. Likely, he too would have gone into the arts... Was he being disloyal to his children? Probably. Was he lucky Stringer had kept his word? He was never sure, looking back, whether the Sheckland-Hall printing account was more important to Stringer than his daughter's chastity. Friends as children, they would certainly have become lovers. Maybe husband and wife. How different his life. None of the bickering. Normal, unstuck-up children not poisoned by their bitchy mother. If he had the guts he'd divorce her. She'd be right now gloating over Petronella. He wouldn't hear the end of it for weeks. Poor Petronella. What had just happened was going to change her life forever.

"I just hope it's for the better. What is this life we have all about?"

He was miserable. For Petronella and for himself.

When he drove into the yard, there was Bonner with the horses. As Horace did so often, he wondered how she was. What their lives would have been if her father hadn't caught them behind the raspberry bushes with their trousers round their ankles. When he was ten years old with no idea what they were doing was wrong. For both, it was curiosity. Old man Stringer had carried on as if they had done something disgusting. There was no sex in their looking.

In the conservatory the breakfast things had been cleared away. Horace went down to the kitchen and made himself some toast. There was no sign of Mrs Weatherby or Janice. Likely there was a pot of tea in the lounge. Standing in front of the kitchen stove with the coal fire in its belly, he munched on his toast and marmalade, dripping butter on Mrs Weatherby's floor. Like the small boy he had once been, he wiped the butter from the stone floor with the floor cloth. As a boy he had been more frightened of Mrs Weatherby than his mother. Old habits die hard. He ate three pieces of toast and felt better.

Upstairs in the lounge, when Horace opened the door the wives were still banging on at each other. His father was sitting in front of the fire with his eyes closed, his hands clutching the arms of his chair. Horace was sure his father was awake, the knuckles on his hands were white. Janice had left a tray of tea on the sideboard. Taking off the cosy that kept the tea hot he took off the lid and looked into the pot. The teapot was full. Putting the cosy back, Horace poured himself a cup of tea. The children were nowhere to be seen.

"There are some things in a family that are better not known."

The women stopped talking. His father opened his eyes. They were all looking at him. No one said a word. It must have been something in the tone of his voice. He was thinking of Christine and not of Petronella. Then they went back to arguing with each other. His father closed his eyes. Horace drank his tea. It was going to be a long Christmas away from the office. He looked at Barbara having her usual go at May and wondered, not for the first time, why on earth he had married her. When they finally did have sex after they were married it wasn't very good anyway. Not being able to get it had driven him to marriage. When the kids grew up he was going to leave her. Find himself a mistress. Use some of the money to enjoy himself. What men did for sex when they were young and innocent made him want to laugh. There was no fool like a virgin. It was how she had caught him. No sex without marriage. What on earth had he seen in her? What a fool he had been. Idly, he wondered if Florence would now get the house and the money. He didn't care. Money, for Horace, had proved more of a burden. All Barbara had wanted was his family money. His inheritance. His position as she saw it in society.

"Well sit down, Horace. You can't stand up all day."

He looked at her and said nothing. Outside it was beginning to rain. He put down his empty teacup and began to walk from the room. The rain outside was not so bad. He would put on his raincoat and go for a tramp in the rain.

"Where are you going, Horace?"

"I'm not sure, Fred. I'm really not sure."

"Did she get on the train?"

"Yes she did, Bertie."

"I should have taken her."

"Yes you should."

"No you shouldn't," snapped Florence.

Women! They all had an agenda. He was quite sure the hiatus caused by his sister had been done on purpose. She wanted her money. Money. They all wanted money and status.

"I'm flying back to Rhodesia tonight. I've got a farm to run."

"You're staying for Christmas."

"No, I'm not."

"Of course you are."

Quietly, Horace closed the door to the lounge, found his raincoat on the hat stand in the hall, put his hat on his head, picked up his black umbrella and walked out the house. It was cold, wet and miserable. Much like himself. Poor old Bertie. Maybe Fred did better with May. He hoped so. Counting the days to when he would be back in the office,

Horace walked down the street. For some reason he had come out of the front door where across the road were the houses. One of them he passed had been Christine's. Old man Stringer had died some years ago. He hoped somewhere she was happy.

BERTIE HAD FOLLOWED Horace out of the door soon after. The women were still arguing. He had phoned his travel agent in London when Horace took his daughter to the railway station. He had not told Florence. He couldn't stand the house anymore. His wife had deliberately exposed their daughter to change her father's mind about leaving the house and the money to Petronella. Why she had so carefully chosen the adjacent bedroom. Florence was more furious with their daughter for having an affair with a black man than a woman, that much Bertie was sure of. It was the downright cunning of the woman to know her father would be unable to stomach his granddaughter's aberration that had got to Bertie. Horace had been right. There were some things best not known about one's family.

"Where the hell are you going?"

"You don't have to follow me, Florence. I'm going back to the farm. Now it's all we have I want to look after it properly. I always despised 'stoep' farmers. The type that runs his farm drinking beer on the veranda."

"The inheritance will now revert to me."

"Don't be too sure. That old man in there isn't a fool. You caught him unawares. Half asleep with the start of a hangover. He'll work it out you did that performance last night on purpose."

"Of course I didn't. I woke up and heard them going for each other. Disgusting."

"They always shoot the messenger, Flossy. He'll hate you for what you did. Petronella was all he had left. Your brothers' wives won't let them come down here except for Christmas. The old man's lonely. Our daughter was the only person who took any notice of him. You've shattered more than our daughter's life. I've booked one flight on the plane. You can fly back when you want. You won't, but when this has died down a little you should go and see Petronella. He's not only cut her out of the will, he's cut off her allowance. She's still your daughter. Whatever she's done."

"Those damn communists can look after her."

"I hope so. Enjoy the rest of your Christmas if you can. I'm going up to pack. The flight leaves Gatwick Airport at three forty-five. I'll be back on the farm tomorrow. Evan is cabled by the travel agent to meet me at Salisbury Airport. The girl on the Salisbury telephone exchange will phone it through to him on the farm."

"You'll not leave me here on my own."

"Oh yes I will."

"That farm's mine, not yours."

"It's in my name, Flossy. That's what counts. I'd better make sure we have a good crop. All we've got, or rather, it's all I've got. She is our daughter, for God's sake. What the hell were you thinking?"

Upstairs in the room next to where last night's fiasco had taken place, Bertie sat on the bed to gather his thoughts. He was going home. He was getting excited. He'd go to the club for Christmas lunch. Among his friends, without those two women permanently arguing with each other. Then he smiled. It could be worse. He could be married to Barbara.

"My poor daughter."

He'd phone her when he got home.

PART VII

DECEMBER 1963 TO OCTOBER 1964

THE POWER OF ATTRACTION

1

By Christmas day, having worked out her finances, Petronella was in a panic. There was just enough money to pay Mrs Peters her rent for January. Food and everything else was going to be a problem. She sat alone in the cold room and smiled. One minute you had it all and then you had nothing. In some ways it was a relief. A challenge. For the first time in her entire life she would have to fend for herself. She rather liked the idea. Sitting in the single bed in the corner of her room, the bed that served with its old fitted cover as a couch during the days, her overcoat on to save the shilling in the gas meter, she played through her options. Harry, who would have come to her rescue at her first beckoning call, was too far away. Anyway, phoning Rhodesia from a pay phone was too expensive if not impossible. Elsie had run off to her parents like a startled rabbit, the thought of a scandal giving her kittens. Silly girl. What the girl most disliked was her girlfriend losing her money. Petronella had watched the lady preen herself at the thought of living a life of luxury at Woodlands Court. So Elsie was off the list. Josiah was in jail in Salisbury Central or wherever they had taken him. And Elsie had been right. ZANU wanted her money more than herself.

She got up from the bed and put on the kettle, thinking of the rest of her family enjoying Mrs Weatherby's Christmas lunch. The thought made her hungry. All she had in her room was a big, old crust of dry brown bread. After making a pot of tea, she looked for the bread. Took it out of the tin. It was surprisingly good. Then she smiled. That sweet smile she gave so many men that made them all come running. She knew where he was. They were having a Christmas party. She would go round uninvited and turn on the charm. Whoever heard of a good-looking single lady being thrown from a party? He wanted her. She had kept him at bay.

"I'm going to make your Christmas, darling."

She would go on the Tube to his townhouse in Chelsea. Dressed for the kill. She still had all her expensive clothes. She would say she had come by taxi on the spur of the moment. That she had had another fight with her mother, which was perfectly true. On Monday, she would go to the ZANU office and try her luck by asking for a salary. Options. She needed her options... Thumbing through her phone book, she lost her feeling of panic. There were so many men. Each morning she would go to the phone booth at the end of the street, give one of them a ring and suggest he take her to dinner. She would fill up her diary for the week. Eat once a day. What a silly girl to panic with a phone book full of hungry young men. There were even a couple of women she could play. Life was all about give and take. If she missed a day's food it would be good for her figure. Richard Maguire had said it was a lunchtime party. For half the record industry, was the way he had said it. If Richard didn't take the bait it didn't matter. Men, stupid, sex-obsessed men. She was a good-looking woman. What else did she need?

After taking a long, hot bath in the communal bathroom on the second floor, Petronella went back to her room. With care and bubbling amusement she got herself ready. She was going to a party. The next round in her life was about to begin.

She had been there before, so finding the townhouse wasn't difficult. The walk from the Tube station was more of a pain, her small red umbrella keeping off most of the rain. When she got into Richard's street she could hear the music.

"The man is a record producer. What do you expect?"

Petronella walked up the steps and rang the bell. Rang it again and again. Nothing happened. When she opened the front door the music flooded over her. People were everywhere in the hall and stairway. All had a drink in their hand. She walked on through. It wasn't a record. In the lounge with its extended dining room a six-piece band was playing the music.

"Petronella! What a lovely surprise. We weren't expecting you. Weren't your parents out from Rhodesia? Have a drink. Sorry to shout. Everyone! This is Petronella."

Smiling, she gave him a kiss on the lips. A soft, wet kiss. She pulled back and smiled at him. He had taken her hand. The band had stopped playing.

"Let me get you a drink. What happened?"

"A real big row with my mother. Doesn't approve of my lifestyle. What a lovely party. I was lonely for you, Richard. I hope you don't mind."

"We're about to serve a fork lunch. Too many people to sit down. What did you think of the band? My new acquisition. Dylan Flower's the singer. Isn't he terrific? All we need now is good publicity. A good publicist who knows all the newspapers. You, of course, would be perfect... You want a glass of wine or a gin?"

"Gin will do."

"The record industry is all in the marketing. Creating a brand. A recognisable image. Often, the music comes second. If you tell them enough to like someone they buy the record. Publicity. Publicity. Publicity. Straight advertising doesn't work. The band has to do something to catch the public eye. Be the champion of a cause. Oh, you'd be perfect for Dylan... Dylan! Come over here and meet Petronella. If you want an advocate for your struggle in Rhodesia, Dylan's your man. He writes his own songs... How about a song for the black man's struggle, Dylan? That would catch the eye of the press. Get you on television... Is that enough gin?"

"Perfect."

"You could combine your passion for saving your people, Petronella. Terrible about Josiah. Colonialism is repugnant. Oppressing the people. We have it in Northern Ireland. A song for Josiah. Would you help us with that, Petronella? We'd pay you a fat commission. Tell the public that buying Dylan's record is all for the cause. Would you do that for us? We'd see lots of each other."

He was smiling, hoping, lust in the back of his eyes.

"Cheers, Richard."

"Will you help?"

"I'll have to think about it. Josiah's name is now even more important to our cause of black liberation."

"That's my girl. Are you hungry? Here come the caterers and the lunch. What luck you dropping in on us. After the party we can go out to dinner. Talk some more. You look wonderful, Petronella. What was the fight about?"

"My sex life. Josiah. The usual."

"Of course. Your parents are bigots I suppose. They don't approve of Josiah. Those white Rhodesians will get their comeuppance one of these days."

"Something like that. My word, that food does look good. Happy Christmas, everyone. A very merry Christmas. I'd love to go to dinner with you, Richard. You'd have to pay us a fee up front to use Josiah's celebrity."

"Of course we would. You name the fee. Dylan, you're in luck. The famous activist is going to act as your publicist. Don't you want to say something, Dylan?"

"I just write the songs and sing them. What you do with the rest is your business. Why I have a record producer."

"Good for you... Someone put on a record... My word, that went down quickly, Petronella. You want another one?"

"I don't mind if I do."

She was smiling at him. Promising. Men were so easy. He wanted her more than the publicity. Gently, she rubbed her hand down his arm, took his hand and squeezed.

"I hope you don't mind my coming without an invitation, Richard."

"Of course I don't. This is just wonderful."

Deliberately, Petronella looked down at his trousers, then slowly back to his eyes, a half-smile crossing her face. The poor boy was blushing. She could relax. With a bit of luck the first option was going to work.

"Life is so much fun, Richard. We're going to have lots of fun. All three of us... Do you have a girlfriend, Dylan?"

"Not at the moment."

"We'll have to find you one. What type of girl do you like, Dylan?" she said, smiling into his eyes.

Options. For the moment it was all about options. When one door closed you had to make sure another one opened. Everyone feeding off everyone else.

One after the other, Richard introduced her to his friends, everyone gushing. The rest of the band were packing up their gear. The noise of the music from the hi-fi was now loud enough for people to talk. They were gravitating to the free lunch being set out on the long dining-room table. Petronella took a plate and helped herself. The food looked expensive befitting a successful record producer. Imported lobster and oysters. The party was more business than pleasure. For everyone. They were all after something. All the girls were showing off their tits or their bums, not an unattractive or old woman in sight. Pop music was all about image.

"What do you call your band, Dylan?"

"Dylan Flower and the boys."

"Too bland. Too ordinary. Doesn't catch the eye. Are you and the band leaving?"

"Lunch with my mum and dad."

"We'll be seeing each other."

"I hope so."

"Mango."

"What's that?"

"My favourite fruit in Rhodesia and your new name. Or we could call you Jesus. Your hair is long enough."

"I would never use Christ's name to promote my music. Can we go out sometime?"

"Mango Boys. The name of the band... I'd love to, Dylan. How about tomorrow night? You can take me somewhere nice to dinner. I'll warn you. I'm expensive. Have a lovely Christmas with your family."

"Where do you live?"

"Shepherd's Bush. All part of my image as the champion of a good cause. The freedom from oppression of the blacks in Rhodesia. You can't look rich when the people you are supporting are all so poor. Have you heard of Sheckland-Hall, the sugar people?"

"Who hasn't?"

"My mother's family."

"Blimey."

"I'll write down my address. Seven o'clock. You won't be late?" She gave him her most enticing look, her eyes smiling.

"Not likely."

"Then we have a date, Dylan."

"Mango Boys. I like it."

"So do I. And I like you Dylan. Now off you go. Doesn't do to be late for your mother's Christmas Lunch."

"You really are hungry. How's your lunch?"

"Good. Very good. I burn up a lot of energy. Why I'm always hungry. You do have enough money for dinner?"

"Richard looks after me."

"Don't tell him about tomorrow. Keep it our little secret until we know each other better. You can keep a little secret, Mango?"

She watched him go with the band, turning back from the door to look for her. She waved. She was enjoying herself. It was all so simple. Men! Give them the hope of getting into your bed and they did what you told them. Only when they'd had enough of you did it all turn different. Which was Petronella's best-kept secret. Never give them enough. Always leave them wanting to come back for more. Unless you married them. But that didn't work so well anymore with the church losing its power over people to keep them from getting divorced. Divorce was now easy. No stigma. It just cost money if the girl was clever. How did a good girl ever get by?

With Dylan Flower on the hook, Petronella turned back to look for Richard. She had eaten enough lunch if he didn't take her out to dinner. A girl with no money had to be careful. She was having fun. Slowly, carefully, she began to work the room on her way to find Richard. To the men she liked she dropped her workplace at ZANU, saying sweetly the number was in the phonebook. By the time she reached Richard there was little chance of going hungry in the coming week.

"Dylan's gone to his mummy. He's so sweet. A big, expensive party like this and he leaves to be with mummy."

"He's only twenty-two."

"Goodness. I thought he was older. I've changed his name to Mango. Mango Boys. Has a ring to it. We want a song called 'The Struggle'. About winning one's freedom from oppression. A song that will echo with everyone who cares. Another: 'Oh, Josiah, what have they done to you?' You think I should write the lyrics?"

"You can always try. Why don't we stay here for dinner? Just you and me."

ON THE TUESDAY of the week after Christmas Petronella met Livingstone Sithole for the first time and told him the bad news. That Grandfather had stopped her allowance. That she had no money. From a smiling man he turned sour right in front of her. She had met black men like him before. They hated the whites. They hated people with more than themselves.

"I was hoping I could ask ZANU to pay me a salary. I work here full time as you know."

"The money you give to the ZANU will stop?"

"I'm afraid so."

"We rely on that money to pay our staff."

"So you won't be paying me a salary?"

"Of course not. Out of the question. Your father owns one of our big tobacco farms. On land he stole from the people. Ask him for money, not a poor exile like me."

"Josiah would have helped me."

"Oh no he wouldn't. The party decides. Not an individual."

"Do you want me to go on working here? Raising money for the party?"

"Choose for yourself... These offices are far too cramped. We need something bigger. The Anti-Apartheid movement have far better offices. I like an office to myself."

"I'll see what I can do."

"So you have no money?"

"Not a penny, as a matter of fact. Everything given to me by my grandfather went to the party."

"Why did he stop your allowance?"

"Family quarrel with my mother. She's now back on the farm with my father."

"Well, that's your problem I'm afraid."

"When are they trying Josiah?"

"They'll never let him out now they've got him. We'll have to liberate him. There's going to be a war against you whites."

"I'm on your side, Livingstone. I'm a member of the party."

"Call me comrade if you please. Have some respect."

"Am I also a comrade?"

"Only if you get us money."

"Have the British given you the right of residence in England?"

"I'm applying for political asylum. I flew here on a temporary Tanganyika passport. Why are you smiling?"

"It's so nice to meet you, Comrade Sithole. Josiah spoke about you often. So you are now the boss?"

"We are all equal in the party."

"But some are more equal than others." She smiled at him sweetly, keeping her temper under control. "Better go and look for some money. For bigger offices. Will you excuse me?"

Realising she had been tolerated for her money, Petronella put on her coat and left the office. Was Josiah the same? Mutual lust had been the foundation of their physical relationship. And a way of getting back at her mother. Were they using her? Probably. She had been so much part of the ideal, of a free, everyone-the-same Rhodesia, she had lost sight of the motives of some of the individuals. Having no money made her look at life differently. From the perspective of a hunted animal that was on its own and had to live on its wits.

"Well, isn't that just nice?"

Walking to Paddington station, her mind was alert. She felt good.

"They can take your money away, darling, but they can't take away your brains. You've got to think, Petronella."

"Are you talking to me?"

"I'm so sorry, talking out loud. What a lovely day for January."

The man had looked hopeful rather than indignant.

Tonight's the night, Richard. I need the money. A publicist. I'm going to set myself up as a publicist. Give as little to ZANU as possible. Enough to keep them interested.

Looking around the railway station, her world did look different. She stopped at the newsstand to buy the morning paper and got on the Tube. Josiah was on page three of the *Daily Mirror*. Under Harry Wakefield's byline. The new Rhodesian Front government of Ian Smith was going to try him for high treason. The trial was expected to last for months.

In the office of Downtown Music, she showed the article to Richard.

"You've got yourself a publicist for Dylan Flower. ZANU are moving into bigger offices and need the extra money. I can get our boy Mango an interview tomorrow with the *Daily Mirror* to talk about his new song supporting Josiah. William Smythe will put Mango on his BBC programme. When are you going to record *Josiah*? Now, I'll need an office with a telephone. Keep the publicity away from ZANU. The fact we are using them and the cause. Within six months, Mango Boys will be a household name. When do I get that up-front retainer?"

"We are in a hurry today."

"And dinner tonight. You can bring the cheque. This is going to be fun making a boy like Dylan famous. In the end it won't matter what kind of music he turns out. People will listen. Fame and a name. Mango Boys. Seven o'clock at that nice little restaurant off Bond Street you promised me. Café Monet. Got to celebrate in style... Now, where's that office I'm going to be occupying? By the way, happy new year.

2

*A*t the end of the summer, with her media contacts stretched to the limit, Petronella moved from Mrs Peters' room in Shepherd's Bush to a smart new flat in South Kensington. A publicist, like her rock stars, needed to look after her image.

"Where do you live, Petronella?"

"Oh, a little place in Central London."

"Mayfair? Where exactly?"

"I never invite people home."

"A good address in business is so important."

She'd had too many similar conversations not to do something about it.

The new flat, furnished lavishly with nine months' income from successfully publicising four new musicians for Downtown Music, was just off Kensington High Street. She had been given an assistant and five per cent of the record sales of her new artists to keep her motivated. By the time Harry Wakefield knocked on her door she had not visited the ZANU offices for months. She still gave Livingstone Sithole a small donation which she sent by mail. Josiah, found guilty of treason, had been sent to a prison camp deep in the bush and far from the prying eyes of the media. Petronella had not heard from him. Her father had written twice from the farm in Rhodesia, having phoned her at the ZANU office without success. Uncle Horace had appeared one Sunday afternoon at the end of January to ask if she was financially all right. He had looked round the bare room in Shepherd's Bush, appalled. She had not asked him to sit down.

"How is Grandfather?"

"He hurt himself more than you."

"We do that sometimes, Uncle Horace. Thank you for coming round. You can let yourself out downstairs. Mrs Peters won't mind. You won't be the first to come and go."

"Have you got any money?"

"Oh, don't worry about me."

"This room is terrible."

"What's wrong with it? There's a bed. A coin-operated gas heater. A kettle. A two-ring gas cooker. Even a view of the houses if you stand on a chair."

"I don't understand you."

"How's Aunty Barbara?"

"I don't understand her either"

"That's my point. No one really understands anyone else. We're too busy judging others by ourselves. How we see life. I have a degree, Uncle Horace. I worked hard at Manchester University. It is all I need. A good education teaches you to think. Especially in an emergency. When your whole world falls round your neck. Tell Grandfather I miss him. That I'm sorry. But I'm not going down to Woodlands Court to apologise. What Elsie and I did together was between the two of us. Nothing to do with anyone else. Thank you for coming. It was appreciated. I'm surviving. In the end, that's all that matters. Has been since man and beast came on this earth."

"Have you heard from your parents?"

"We live on different planets. I don't expect to. Neither do they. I am the biological product of their mating. Like all the other animals. Sorry, sad, but true."

"I'll see myself out."

"Yes, we all do that too, Uncle Horace."

She had only felt sad for a moment.

.   .   .

"Harry! What a nice surprise. Just look at that suntan. Come in. I was down at the *Daily Mirror* seeing Roland Cartwright only the other day. He said you were coming over. Something about your sister's wedding. Isn't she marrying Jeremy Crookshank? You know he first worked for my father when Jeremy went out to Rhodesia. There was a falling-out with my mother. What's new? Why haven't you written these last months? You should have phoned. Petronella's a busy girl these days."

"I phoned the ZANU office. They said you haven't been around for a while. Made a time to interview Livingstone Sithole while I was on the phone. I've been trying to interview Josiah for months but the Rhodesian government won't let me anywhere near him. You look different. More businesslike. Is it the new glasses or is it your hair?"

"Twenty-seven years old on Thursday. Are you taking me out on my birthday?"

"I was hoping tonight."

"Not tonight. Tomorrow's going to be a bitch. How do you like my new flat?"

"Did your grandfather leave you some of his fortune?"

"Grandfather is still alive. We don't see each other."

"Where did this all come from? This looks so expensive. Nothing like you. Last time we saw each other you were giving away all your money and living in that bare room in Shepherd's Bush."

"You'll have a drink?"

"I'll have a drink."

"Isn't Jeremy a bit old for your sister?"

"Bergit fell in love with Africa. All that space. All that sun. I tried to talk her out of it. She and Ruthy came out to see me for Christmas. Spent a week with Jeremy on World's View. Bergit loves the farm. Loves the two boys. She's happy. The wedding is on Saturday. Are you coming? Jeremy would love to have you."

"The little bitch of a communist! Member of ZANU! I doubt it."

"He remembers you better when you were thirteen. So, how come all this?"

"How's Ruthy?"

"Ruthy's fine."

"You know she wants to marry you... All this? Hard work. I'm a publicist for four rock bands. Have you heard of the Mango Boys?"

"Who hasn't?"

"I work as a consultant for Richard Maguire at Downtown Music. My grandfather disinherited me. My mother found me in bed with your old flame, Elsie Gilmore. I suspect Mother did it on purpose. Grandfather had changed his will leaving Mother's share to me. Amazing what people will do for money... What are you having? Come and sit down. Lovely to see you."

"So you went into business? Joined the capitalist system. Well I'll be blowed."

"Something like that. A girl has to look after herself. So how've you been? Have you got a girlfriend? When are you getting married? Is it Ruthy?"

"There's a shortage of single girls in Rhodesia. The ones that are, get a bit above themselves. They want a rich farmer to marry, not a newspaper reporter."

"How long are you staying?"

"Three weeks. Took my annual leave. I'll have a Scotch. With ice if you have it. In Africa you get used to drinking your whisky with ice."

"This place has everything. Sit down."

"The music must be playing sweetly for you."

"Five per cent of record sales."

"Including Mango Boys!"

"I made them what they are. 'Josiah' was a great hit. So was 'The Struggle'. You have to have something that appeals to the moment. The British public. The man in the street. The average Joe. They've turned against colonialism in the way Wilberforce turned against slavery. Mango Boys sing about what the people want to hear. Buying Mango Boys records makes them feel they are doing something about it. Doing their bit. I actually wrote some of the lyrics for Mango. His real name is Dylan Flower. Such a sweet boy. A bit young for me... How does that look, Harry? Bell's with lots of ice. Lots of ice and lots of Bell's. Cheers. Good to see you. So, are you taking me out on my birthday?"

"Are you coming to the wedding?"

"Should be fun. Is there anyone else coming to the wedding from Rhodesia?"

"Only Phillip and Randall, I think. Jeremy's two boys. His first wife was killed by lions."

They stood looking at each other for a moment.

"How's Rhodesia, Harry?"

"Wonderful. That's the trouble. The question is, will it last?"

"What do you think?"

"I don't know. Probably not. Maybe in some other form."

"And the whites?"

"Why are you asking? You know more than me. How many terrorists are ZANU training in those camps in what they are now calling Tanzania and Zambia?"

"They're not terrorists, Harry. We call them freedom fighters."

"What's the difference? They are being trained to kill people. Will they attack the whites?"

"If Smith declares his threatened unilateral independence. I don't have that much to do with ZANU anymore. Too busy promoting my rock bands. And you? How long are you staying in Rhodesia?"

"I do what I'm told. If I ask, they'll send a replacement."

"You want a sandwich? It really is nice to see you."

"And how is Elsie?"

"After the debacle at Woodlands Court we haven't spoken to each other. Haven't spoken to any of them except Uncle Horace."

"You really are different, Petronella."

"For better or worse?"

"I don't know. Only time will tell me. Thursday. Where shall we go?"

"Café Monet. My favourite little restaurant off Bond Street. You'll have to book. One of those arty places that people like to go."

"I like your flat. Who's the black lady in the painting?"

"Princess. Josiah's mother. Painted by Livy Johnston after she saw Princess at Harry Brigandshaw's funeral. She was then with your friend Jeremy Crookshank. Jeremy wanted to marry her. They both had kids from an earlier marriage. Livy's famous. She gave the painting to Josiah. I'm keeping it for him. It was hanging in the ZANU office. Worth a lot of money. One day it may be all Josiah's got if he doesn't succeed with his revolution. The one next to Princess is also a Livy Johnston. It's on loan. Couldn't afford to buy her paintings just yet. She married again to a chap called Gainsborough. Can you believe it? She's now Mrs Gainsborough with an artist's name more famous than her own. She wants to borrow *Princess* for a retrospective she's doing at the Nouvelle Galerie. Very upmarket. The deal was to lend me her latest painting in exchange for *Princess*. That's the Lake District with their house by the lake. The mother died and left them the family house where she paints. Gives a nice tone to my flat... Josiah's father worked for Harry Brigandshaw. Isn't it strange? We're all linked to each other somewhere down the line. I'm hoping to become Livy's publicist when she dumps her ex-husband. And there's the link again. The first husband grew up thinking his father was Harry Brigandshaw... Tembo was the name of Josiah's father. Bossboy on Elephant Walk. How Josiah got caught by the Rhodesian police, going to his funeral."

"He was my godfather. I was named after Harry Brigandshaw."

"I know you were."

"Do you own this flat?"

"Not yet. I've only been in business nine months."

Petronella watched Harry study the paintings while sipping his drink. For the first time the hunger was not in his eyes; the desperate need to take her to bed. It was happening more frequently. Men were not looking at her quite the same way. She had asked one of her new friends why her world was changing.

"The power of the silent pull isn't the same as you get older. You're lucky, Petronella. My complete power over men stopped a lot younger. When I was twenty-five. It's biological. It's deep in men's instinct to want to impregnate young girls. Better chance of survival for the child when most women died in their thirties. Why the primitive tribes in Africa marry such young girls. Or just take them. Successful men like the chief keep on taking young girls. You'll get over it, Petronella. You have to dress better to get their attention. Fancy make-up. Expensive perfume. Or you make a lot of money and take up young men. That's where I'm going. Being a slave to a man and children isn't for me. Don't want to be stuck barefoot and pregnant in a kitchen. Your biological clock ticks in more ways than one. You're going off, my girl. Losing your pull. We all go through it. One of the stages of women. Provided you've got enough money you'll always get what you want. How are your artists selling? That's what you worry about. Not nailing down some man you'll be bored with by the time you're thirty. Some say the whole attraction bit lasts no more than a couple of years. Why most marriages end on the rocks. I'm glad to be out of mine. Lucky not to have had kids. Have you been married?"

"Not yet."

"Lucky you. Keep it that way. You'll be happier. Didn't you have your eye on Richard?"

"Not really."

"His affairs last a month. I know."

"So do I... You want to go to lunch?"

"What a lovely idea."

Watching Harry Wakefield had brought back the conversation vividly. Gillian was right. She was losing her power.

"Do you want to book for Thursday or shall I, Harry?"

"You can book. You know the number. I'll pick you up here in a taxi at seven o'clock. Just like old times."

He was smiling at her, the old look back in his eyes.

"Yes. Just like old times. When did you get in from Rhodesia?"

"A couple of days ago."

"Have you seen Ruthy?"

"Not yet. Maybe I'll go round to her parents' house tonight. It's so nice to be back in England... I prefer Livy's painting of Princess to her landscape. There's something about the dark eyes. They're so happy."

"She was Tembo's last wife. Josiah his last child. The four families lived together in the same compound. Goodson, now in the Rhodesian police, shopped Josiah at their father's funeral. He was a son from the number one wife. Jealousy, I suppose. People hate other people to have more than themselves. Goodson was just a constable in the police. No education paid for by Harry Brigandshaw like Josiah, the favourite son with his university degrees. The favourite son."

"How old are you on Thursday?"

"I already told you, Harry. Twenty-seven. I'll be twenty-seven years old."

"Goodness. Time does fly... So what are you doing tonight?"

"Having supper and going to bed early. You can join me if you like?"

"Changed your mind then? For supper or for bed?"

"For both. We can't have you running off to Ruthy. How long's it been, Harry?"

"A damn long time."

"Have another Bell's."

"What's for supper?"

"Lamb chops. You can help me cook."

"I can't spend the night, Petronella. I'm staying with my parents. They're from the old school. Still think pre-marital sex is a mortal sin."

"Most people these days don't want to get married. Too busy enjoying themselves. Are we going to enjoy ourselves, Harry?"

"I hope so. I really like this flat. It's a whole new Petronella."

"Sadly the world isn't quite the potential utopia I thought it was at university. People say they are going to do things for other people. Make a better world. Most of the time they're only thinking of themselves. Making themselves appear better in the eyes of other people. And it's always easier to give away other people's money. I should know. Poor Grandfather. He must be so lonely. All on his own in that great big house."

"We could go down and visit him. If I go with you it might help break the ice. By the sound of it your mother was more at fault than you. I like your grandfather. Is he still drinking his sherry? That day Sidney and I climbed over his wall was a classic."

"Would you come with me? We could surprise him. You could tell him about this flat and my business. I hate blowing my own trumpet. Am I getting old, Harry?"

"We think we know the truth when we're young and excited. What changed your mind about Rhodesia?"

"Livingstone Sithole. He's only interested in himself. He's using the struggle to further his personal ends. I don't think underneath all the bullshit he gives a damn about the people. The first thing he did when they sent him from Tanzania to replace Josiah was to demand an office for himself. He wanted a car. Smart clothes and smart haircuts. That sort of thing. He's a politician, not a revolutionary. When I was flat broke after Grandfather cut me off, he wouldn't raise a finger. He rather enjoyed it. Seeing a white with nothing. Told me to ask my parents. That they were exploiting his people. Why are you laughing, Harry?"

"It's easier to laugh than cry. Poor Africa. All those poverty-stricken people. They're going to get nothing whatever the likes of ZANU say to the country. Chase out the white skills and they'll have an empty shell. A few blacks will get rich. How it works. Then the Russians and Chinese will take over. And they're not as benign as the British. There are going to be hard times in Africa. For everyone. Black and white. The irony is the whites will have somewhere to go. England, South Africa. Australia and New Zealand are only too happy to take in skilled farmers. The blacks will have nothing. Minerals still in the ground have no value. Uncultivated land is worthless. Well, maybe the animals won't think that until they get hunted. It's becoming a global industrialised world as the populations explode from Africa to China. Chasing out all the skills will only take them back to peasant farming. Hunting and gathering. What Livingstone Sithole and Josiah Makoni are promising won't happen. The people will be poor, not rich. Terribly poor."

"You sound like a white Rhodesian farmer."

"Maybe I do. It gets to you. From a distance, freedom from colonial rule looks more appetising. You've got to be practical. Who's going to run the place like a modern state with roads and railways, electricity, communications, education? A few terrorists who come out of the bush brandishing AK-47s? I don't think so. I did think so before I got to Rhodesia. You found that out with Sithole. He didn't want to give you anything. He wanted to take. It's going to be a mess. A big, horrible mess for the average black man in Africa."

"You've changed."

"We all change. Everything changes. And very often not for the better. Are we going to have another drink or start the cooking? Next time I come round I'll bring a case of Scotch. Oh, Petronella. What's the world coming to? Why don't we ever learn? After two world wars already this century. People pointing nuclear-tipped rockets at each other who twenty years ago were fighting the same enemy. I'm going to write a book. Journalism just isn't big enough. My father was right. Why are older people so often right? He says you can't change people. You never could and never will. It's built into us to fight with each other. Despite all the mouthing platitudes. I hate growing up. Being young was much more fun. You didn't have to be responsible. For anything. You still had hope for a better world."

"Wow. You have become cynical."

"When you've conducted as many interviews as me, and listened to all the tripe, you're inclined to become sceptical, if not downright cynical. Most of my interviews are with politicians. Half the time you can't believe they're talking about the same country. Another year and I'm coming home before I want to jump off the highest building."

"Just don't let me drink too much and have a hangover tomorrow."

"I'll try not to… Anyway, tell me about yourself. What have you been up to?"

"Why do people lie to each other?"

"To get something. To make themselves look better. To kid themselves."

"Would I be allowed back into Rhodesia by the Smith government?"

"I wouldn't try it. To the whites you are a traitor. Much worse than Josiah. You've taken sides against your own people. Your own kith and kin. Did you know your father is going to stand for parliament? For the Rhodesian Front."

"Come and sit down. I'm exhausted. Everything I ever believed in is flying out the window. I was taught people were inherently good."

"But they're not. We, and I include myself, are all selfish. 'Me' always comes first. Whatever we say. Selfishness and self-preservation are the fundamental building blocks of the human condition. We show empathy for others when we want to make ourselves feel better. That's the quirk of 'doing good'. It makes us feel better. Once again all the way back to ourselves. Mutual help and self-preservation is another thing. Preservation of the herd. Safety in numbers. Binding together to face a common enemy. The same self-preservation. Which is what's happening to the whites in Rhodesia. The same 'we're all in it together' syndrome during the last war in Britain. But when the danger's over, society breaks up. You throw out Prime Minister Churchill because you don't need him anymore. The danger has gone. The promises of the Labour Party and socialism now appeal to the majority. There's something in it for them. Past heroes are quickly and conveniently forgotten. And we do it time and time again. Throughout history. Until the day when we blow ourselves to pieces. When we self-destruct. I don't agree with what Smith says he is going to do in Rhodesia but it's opened my eyes. I think he's morally wrong to oppress the black people. But when they all end up hungry they may not think Smith and Welensky were so bad after all. They say Churchill went into deep depression after the war. After the British people rejected him. Don't tell me by then those who voted him out were thinking of Churchill. They only thought of him when the bombs were coming down. But on a more practical note in Rhodesia I don't see how two hundred and fifty thousand renegade Englishmen can defy the world and get away with it. The British don't need them anymore. The colonies are a liability. Especially with the Americans putting on pressure, wanting the British out so their own multi-nationals can go in and do business. Tap the raw materials. This time oil and strategic materials rather than Cecil Rhodes and the British who were after gold and diamonds, precipitating the Boer War... Sorry. This must be boring you, Petronella. I get so upset when there's nothing I can do but report what I see. Stand on the sidelines. See a whole country heading for disaster."

"You've never talked so much about politics."

"I had other things on my mind... You mind if I pour my own? I will bring you a case of whisky, I promise. And that's another thing in Rhodesia. No one wants to face the truth so we all drink too much. Poor Bergit. I just hope she realises what she's getting into. Livy Johnston of the paintings over there had it right. Why she wouldn't marry Jeremy before or after his marriage to Carmen. In the World's View farmhouse there's a Livy Johnston portrait of Carmen in the lounge. Her eyes follow you. She haunts the place. I hope Jeremy took down that painting before he left the farm."

"Help yourself. There's another bottle. I'm making money so who cares?"

"Are you pleased to see me?"

"Of course I am."

Much later when they went to bed they were both drunk. Petronella didn't care anymore about her business appointments in the morning. The lamb chops had been burned and eaten, neither of them noticing the food. On her back with Harry on top of her she looked up into his eyes. Neither of them wanted to turn off the lights.

"Love me, Harry. Just love me."

In each other's arms they slept through the rest of the night , nobody waking them. In the morning Petronella phoned her assistant and cancelled her appointments. Harry had hired a car, delivered to the door. They drove to Ashford slowly, still feeling the warmth of their night. They parked at the back of the estate, under the same wall Harry had climbed over on his first visit to Woodlands Court with Sidney, when he was looking to interview Petronella and met the old man. Harry helped Petronella shin up the tree and was about to follow her.

"What do you think you are doing!"

"Climbing over the wall, madam."

"That's private property you know."

"The estate belongs to the lady's grandfather. She's lost the key."

"I don't believe you. You're a burglar. I'm going across to my house and phoning the police."

"Tell them to tell her grandfather, Petronella is here for a visit."

"Well, I never!"

"No, madam. You probably didn't."

By the time they dropped down behind the rhododendron bushes they both had the giggles.

"Do you think she'll phone the police?"

"Now that will break the ice... I can see the horses. When you see your grandfather don't say a word. Just give him a hug."

"Are you sure? I'm so nervous. He told me never to come back."

Harry, not sure at all, worked his way through the bushes.

"Harry! What are you doing here? I thought you were still in Rhodesia."

"I've brought you a friend."

"Petronella!... Oh, it's so good to see you."

Grandfather and granddaughter were crying. Harry worked his way back through the bushes. Climbed back up the tree and dropped down into the street.

"I'm going to call the police!"

"Not necessary. They're hugging each other. What a lovely day."

Back in the car, Harry drove back to London feeling good. She would catch the train back to London when she was ready. They were going to Café Monet for her birthday on Thursday. To the wedding on Saturday. The world didn't look so bad for Harry after all.

*B*ack in his parents' house Harry went up to his old room. His mother was working in the downstairs room she used for her practice. Another patient was waiting in reception, a young man with an appalling stutter when Harry said good morning. The receptionist was new to Harry. In his years growing up, there had been quite a few of them. The income from his mother's speech therapy practice coupled with his father's salary from the *Daily Mail* had made the family comparatively wealthy, making it possible for himself and Bergit to receive a private education. Neither of them had boarded. Harry at Dulwich College and Bergit at St Paul's. Before going home Harry had returned the car to the car rental company, money well spent.

After a hot bath and a shave, dressed casually, he went downstairs to the kitchen. After the spur of the moment decision to drive to Woodlands Court, neither of them had eaten. Harry was hungry. Hangovers gave him the munchies. Both patients had gone, his mother waiting for him in the family kitchen.

"Where were you last night, Harry? I lay awake half the night worrying about you."

"Mum, I'm twenty-eight, no longer a kid."

"Doesn't stop me worrying about you children. I like Jeremy very much even if he is too old for Bergit but can't we persuade him to come back and live in England? He's got money here. Owns part of a block of flats round the corner with Livy Johnston or whatever she calls herself these days. Rhodesia is so far away. Your father says the country is unstable. You agreed with your father."

"That boy had a terrible stutter."

"I've just started with him. Now, where were you? Were you with that damn woman? You should get married to Ruthy and settle down. You said you were going to visit her last night."

"Petronella has changed. You wouldn't recognise her. She's now a publicist for musicians at Downtown Music."

"So you were with her?"

"Yes, Mother, I love her. It's no longer an obsession. I love her."

"Poor Ruthy. She was so looking forward to you coming back for your sister's wedding."

"Ruthy and I are friends. We've never been anything else."

"You're a fool, Harry. She's been in love with you since you were children."

"But I'm not in love with her. That's the difference."

"Is Petronella in love with you?"

"I don't know, Mother."

"She's promiscuous. You'll never be sure of her. Always wondering what she's up to and thinking she's with some other man."

"She's changed so much since I last saw her."

"Leopards never change their spots. Now, have you eaten? I suppose that's why you are in the kitchen. She didn't even feed you."

"We had lamb chops last night, I think it was. I just drove her down to her grandfather's house. They'd had a falling out. He'd cut off her allowance. I left her this morning with her grandfather at Woodlands Court. Being with her broke the ice."

"What about?"

"It's a long story."

"So she used you to get back her allowance."

"She doesn't need it now. It was my idea to hire a car and drive down to Ashford."

"And the money?"

"It wasn't about money."

"Get the bacon out of the fridge. I'll cook breakfast for you. You make the toast."

"I was thinking of a juicy steak for lunch."

"You're not in Rhodesia. This is England. She'll do you no good, that one. Flighty. So she fell out with her grandfather as well as her parents. You be careful with that one, Harry. She'll do you no good. Mark my words."

"Where's Bergit?"

"With Jeremy. Shopping with the boys, poor little mites growing up without a mother. I've never heard anything so terrible. Eaten by wild animals. They should be brought back to England and sent to good schools."

"World's View is Jeremy's life."

"I hope Bergit will now be his life. Why couldn't she have found a nice young man her own age that lives in England and doesn't want to go traipsing round the world? I'm never going to see my daughter. Or my grandchildren. He's ten years older than Bergit. When she's sixty, he'll be seventy. She'll be left on her own. My children never listen to me. Half the time I think I'm wasting my breath... Do you want sausages?"

"Please, Mum."

"How many? There are four of them in the packet."

"Cook the lot. I'm starving. I drank too much last night."

"So she got you drunk last night and seduced you. Men! You are all so stupid."

"She's coming to the wedding."

"Oh, my God!"

"She knew Jeremy when she was thirteen. When he worked for her father."

"Poor Ruthy. You'll break that girl's heart bringing that woman to her best friend's wedding."

"Just because you and Dad are her parents' best friends it doesn't mean I have to marry her."

"It would be nice having the same grandchildren as William and Betty. That way we would be related. There should be a word like grandmother-in-law to define that kind of relationship."

"Yes, Mother."

"So what's on the agenda for the rest of the week? Are you going to the office?"

"Sidney and I are going for drinks."

"You young people all drink too much. The caterers are coming to the house on Friday afternoon. The bottom and second floors will be used for the reception."

"Do you want a band? I'm sure Petronella could arrange a band. Bergit and her friends would be awestruck by Mango Boys. It was Petronella that put them on the map."

"Sit down and eat your food. The less I hear about that woman the better. Poor Ruthy."

THEY HAD FIRST GONE to a show. One of those frilly little musicals that put the audience in a good mood. Sweet entertainment that appealed to almost everyone. Harry had wanted to be careful in choosing the right show. After the theatre, a taxi dropped them outside the Café Monet.

"How was your grandfather?"

They had gone to the theatre in a taxi from Petronella's flat in South Kensington not saying anything about her visit to Woodlands Court. At the door, Harry had wished her a happy birthday.

"I would have stayed with him longer but I had to get back to work."

"Did you talk about it?"

"No, Harry. He would have been terribly uncomfortable. We both pretended it hadn't happened. Everything he wanted to say was in his eyes. We discussed nothing but trivia. How nice the weather. That sort of thing. We had made up, that was all that mattered. Thank you, Harry. I owe you a favour."

"That's good because I want one. When I told my sister Bergit you managed the publicity for Mango Boys she was overwhelmed. Said I'd try and get them for Saturday if they don't want too much of a fortune."

"So you told your parents you had invited me? In exchange for putting Ruthy's nose out you suggested Mango Boys. If they come as an act your parents will never afford them. I'll ask Dylan to come to the wedding. He owes me one. More than one. He also fancies me."

"Will you ask him?"

"If I can use the wedding for publicity. His songs are all about black liberation."

"Can't they sing something else? Does it have to be business?"

"In this day and age I'm afraid it does. No one does anything for nothing. The left-wing papers will gobble up Mango Boys singing at a white Rhodesian tobacco farmer's wedding. Roland Cartwright will be delighted. You can write a piece yourself. Before they come you'd best ask Jeremy."

"Jeremy's politics are pretty much middle of the road. He doesn't agree with declaring unilateral independence for Rhodesia. He thinks there should be a compromise. That everyone with a certain standard of education or wealth should have the vote. That thinking people won't want confrontation. They'll see the benefits for everyone, black and white, getting on with each other."

"I'll ask them. What do you think of the restaurant?"

"Are those original Monet paintings?"

"Prints, I should think. If the owner of the restaurant had so many original paintings he wouldn't be running a restaurant. He'd be on the beach in the South of France."

"What did you think of the show?"

"Pleasant. I didn't have to think. Sometimes it's good not to think of problems. Let the mind run blank."

"Did he give you back your allowance?"

"I told you. We didn't discuss it. Anyway, that doesn't matter anymore. I rather like earning my own living. Gives me a feeling of satisfaction. I can rely on myself, not on other people. When you rely on people like Livingstone Sithole with their own personal agenda, you're inclined to come up short."

"What about Mango Boys?"

"They rely on me more than I rely on them. Bands come and go. Producers like Richard Maguire and publicists with the right contracts like myself stay around. When I'm ready, I'm going to move my business out of the offices of Downtown Music. Make me more independent. Business is fun. I had no idea how much fun."

"They didn't teach you that in the communist party."

"Communism, politics, are just another form of business. It's all about controlling people, Harry... How do I look?"

"Ravishing. That dress must have cost a fortune."

"It did."

"There's a famous actress coming to the wedding. Another link in the Harry Brigandshaw chain. Genevieve. Have you heard of her?"

"In Rhodesia as a kid I saw her in Robin Hood. Three or four times. What's her connection?"

"She's married to Tinus Oosthuizen, Harry Brigandshaw's nephew. They live in America most of the time. The kids went to school in England. Hayley still does. Commutes across the pond on her school holidays. The boy, Barend, is at university in New York."

"There was a scandal about Genevieve. Isn't she the illegitimate daughter of Baron St Clair of Purbeck? He died recently. It was in all the papers. More to do with Genevieve than her father, Merlin. The brother inherited the very old title. He's a novelist. Titles don't mean much in England anymore... Does Genevieve want a publicist?"

"Why don't you ask her? Every now and again she does a play on the West End stage. Hasn't done a movie in years."

"Why did she get an invitation to your sister's wedding?"

"Jeremy's brother Paul is married to Beth. Beth was Harry's daughter. Tinus Oosthuizen's first cousin. The Oosthuizens are in England on holiday visiting their daughter whilst she's still at school. There's more old family friends over from America. The Madgwicks. Ralph Madgwick managed Elephant Walk for Harry Brigandshaw before his wife Rebecca inherited a slice of the Rosenzweig bank from her father and the family went to live in America. They are old friends of Jeremy. Klaus von Lieberman saved my father's life when Dad was abducted by the Nazis before the war. The American branch of the Rosenzweig bank had loaned von Lieberman money for his farming estate in Germany just before Hitler rose to power. There's a story there about the Nazis exchanging the mortgage for the lives of prominent German Jews. Bergit is named after von Lieberman's wife. Many of those Jews did well in America."

"Why do you remember all of this?"

"Good material for a book when I've had enough of the newspaper. You could be my publicist."

"You need something more topical for a subject. Like a factual book on Rhodesia."

"I want to write novels. They last longer. History often proves what's politically correct today is a disaster tomorrow. That all the self-righteous pandering to current opinion was wrong... What are you going to eat?"

"I want a cheese soufflé. A nice piece of turbot in their white garlic sauce. Did the Rosenzweig bank ever get their money back from von Lieberman after the war?"

"I don't know. Maybe Rebecca will know. I'll ask her at the wedding."

"This is so nice having you back, Harry."

Petronella stretched her hand out on the table invitingly.

"Put your hands in mine, Harry. Do you want us to be more than lovers?"

THE BELLS HAD RUNG out across Chelsea. St Giles, the small Church of England church not far from the homes of the Smythes and Wakefields and the block of flats owned by Jeremy Crookshank and Livy Johnston as she still preferred to call herself, was full of people. Bergit, Harry thought, looked beautiful, Jeremy somewhat out of place in a morning suit. The outfitters from whom he'd hired the suit had added a hat to his head. A tall, grey top hat, not the bush hat with the wide brim to keep off the African sun Harry remembered from the farm. Petronella was sitting next to him. Ruthy was in the aisle to the right, watching him. It was the first time Harry had seen her since coming back to England. She looked pretty, confident, a young man sitting next to her. Harry was jealous; why, he didn't know. As he watched, Ruthy, smiling, slowly shook her head. For some reason Ruthy was no longer Bergit's bridesmaid. Instead of bridesmaids, Phillip and Randall were pageboys. Jeremy's children were enjoying themselves making faces at their father. Next to their father at the altar stood their uncle Paul. In front of them the vicar. Harry's mother was crying, Harry's father trying not to look at her. Harry watched the ceremony through, thinking it much like the weddings of three of his friends. Sidney Cross's wedding to Caroline, the receptionist at the *Daily Mirror*, had sounded and looked much the same. At the wedding, Harry had been the best man.

When the ceremony was over they all went back to the house, filling the bottom two floors. Mango Boys had not been at the ceremony. When they arrived, Harry was introduced to Dylan Flower by Petronella. Ruthy, being sweet in front of Petronella, said they were her favourite band. Bergit was radiant, Jeremy bewildered, his two boys running rampant among the guests. Jeremy had said he wished he had brought the boy's nanny, Primrose, from the farm to keep the boys under control. Jeremy, his bride and the two boys were flying back to the farm the following Monday, where the boys would be left with Primrose while the bride and groom went on honeymoon to Lake Kariba where Jeremy had hired a houseboat complete with a crew.

"When are you coming to see me, Harry?" Ruthy said. "This is George. George is a banker in the City. Merchant bank. International exchange. That sort of thing. How've you been?"

"You haven't met Petronella. She brought the band."

"Heard a lot about you, Petronella. A whole lot about you. But who hasn't? Famous activist. Aren't you a communist? Supporter of the black struggle in Rhodesia? Surprised you're here."

"Don't be, Ruthy. I've known the groom from when I was a thirteen-year-old. He worked for my father. Heard a lot about you too. Weren't you once sweet on Harry?"

"Still am. Aren't I, Harry?"

"What about George? You look like a couple."

"We go out when we both need a partner. Business functions. Weddings."

"How convenient."

"Very. Harry, please come and see me. We've got so much to talk about. So, you're Petronella. You're much older than I thought you were. Well, you've been through a lot. Didn't you recently fall out with your family? Your old friend Josiah Makoni is now in jail in Rhodesia. You must have found it lonely. So lucky Harry came back for his sister's wedding. Mango Boys! I can't wait to hear them play. Got all their records. Have a nice time at my best friend's wedding. Those boys of Jeremy's are running riot. My poor friend. Instant family. Lucky she loves the boys. Can you imagine losing your mother so young? Africa is wild."

For a moment, Harry thought the two girls were going to scratch out each other's eyes. The man called George gave Harry a look of sympathy. People were milling around, greeting old friends, brought together again by the marriage of a mutual acquaintance. Tinus Oosthuizen, the cousin of Beth Crookshank, now had an American accent. So did his wife, the film star Genevieve. She was still beautiful but different. Not the young girl Harry remembered playing Maid Marian in *Robin Hood and his Merry Men*. The strange part of the woman was her mismatched eyes. One was blue and the other a dark brown, the pupil almost black. She caught him staring at her and smiled, making Harry blush. Standing with Tinus and his famous wife was a couple of a similar age. He guessed it was Ralph and Rebecca Madgwick, the connection of Elephant Walk where Tinus had grown up bringing them together. Petronella had seen Genevieve and stopped being nasty with Ruthy. The actress with the one name Genevieve was walking towards him with her group. She was smiling.

"I'm so sorry to stare at you."

"I'm used to it by now."

"No, it wasn't your fame. The different colours of your eyes. It's so unusual."

"Since I was born. My father who died recently had the same blue and brown eyes. Been in the St Clair family for centuries. Where do you fit in the family?"

"I'm Harry Wakefield, Bergit's brother."

"Weren't you named after my husband's uncle? Do you know our friends from New York? Rebecca and Ralph. Ralph managed Elephant Walk until Rebecca's father died and they all came to live in America."

"I know exactly who you are, Mrs Madgwick. Did the von Liebermans ever pay back your father's bank? Without the help of Harry Brigandshaw and Klaus von Lieberman I likely would never have been born."

"I know the story. And, yes, he did, the last payment of the capital sum from his estate. He died last year. Your father's saviour was not a Nazi. The Nazi was his uncle. In the end that piece of terrible history turned out well. My father's cancelling of the von Lieberman mortgage saved many Jewish lives. I have met many of the families since going to live in America. Your sister can be proud of her name. Of being named after Mrs von Lieberman. The majority of Germans hated the Nazis as much as my people feared them... What a lovely wedding. It's so wonderful to be back in England. I grew up in London. How's Rhodesia, Harry? We still miss the farm. The bush. The wild animals. We miss Africa. They say once you have lived in Africa for any length of time you always want to go back. Do you ever hear from the von Liebermans?"

"Bergit does at Christmas. What a lovely end to a terrible part of history. So they paid back the bank."

"Every penny of it... Isn't that the Mango Boys? Just wait 'til I tell my kids. That band is big in America after just one tour. Mango Boys! My goodness."

The conversation moved on, leaving Harry standing alone. The last part of the wartime story of the von Liebermans had made him feel good.

"Why didn't you introduce me, Harry? I want to be her publicist."

"She caught me staring at her mismatched eyes."

"Who was the woman talking to you?"

"Rebecca Madgwick, the daughter of Jacob Rosenzweig. The von Liebermans paid back their debt. Every penny of it."

"How nice. Never pays to give people money. Here come the bride and groom. Hello, Jeremy. Surprise, surprise. Do you remember what you told me when I was thirteen? 'Take it easy greasy, you've got a long way to slide.' I just did a bit of sliding but now I'm fine."

"You've got a good memory, Petronella. I knew you were coming. The band! My goodness. Never heard of them in the bush. How are your parents?"

"We don't speak to each other."

"Politics?"

"More personal. Congratulations. It was a beautiful ceremony. I loved the church bells. So English."

"How are you, Harry?"

"I'm just fine. We're both just fine."

"When are you flying back to Rhodesia?"

"I'm not quite sure. I still have to talk to my newspaper. To Roland Cartwright."

"I'm out of politics for the moment, Jeremy. Promoting bands."

"I'm glad. I hate politics. So often in the end nobody wins in a political argument. Got to move on. Enjoy the reception. Where the hell are my kids?"

Harry watched his mother help lay out the food. Caterers with trays at shoulder height carried round the drinks. There was Pimm's in tall glasses with slices of cucumber and fruit, Harry with no doubt whose idea that was, the memory of drinking Pimm's on World's View with

Jeremy still fresh in his mind. Other, smaller glasses held punch. The smallest glasses held tots of whisky. Jugs of water and siphons of soda were out on the tables. The noise rose with the consumption of drinks. Mango Boys played and Mango sang. Ever since arriving with his band, Dylan Flower had had his eye on Petronella, making Harry sure the two of them were having an affair. It was the way he looked at her, a proprietary, knowing look of more to come. For the first time since he met Petronella Harry didn't mind. Ever since she had asked him to take their affair further his physical jealousy for the girl had abated. He was confident, no longer besotted with his mind in a panic. Ruthy had gone to the other side of the room leaving George on his own. She was doing her rounds. Bergit still looked radiant dressed in her wedding gown, the biggest day of her life. Harry kept up with snatches of conversation with different people as he made his own rounds. Petronella was surrounded by men, all of them smiling. As he moved in her direction, Ruthy moved away. The second tall glass of Pimm's was stronger than the first. It was his habit at other people's weddings to drink too much. Tonight he had been told to stay in the house with his mother and father. His father had said his mother was going to cry with Bergit gone out of the house at the start of a journey that would take her down Africa, so far away. The bride and groom were staying the night in a local hotel which to Harry was silly. They could have stayed in the family house until their plane left for Rhodesia. With his sister flying the nest it was better for his mother that he stayed. Petronella would go home to her Kensington flat in a taxi. Or one of the men with a car would take her back. Everyone seemed to be enjoying themselves. From behind Harry was a big burst of laughter. The band had stopped playing. Most of Bergit's friends were in the room with the band, dancing. Harry hated dancing and the noise of loud music. To others it was a way not to have to make conversation with a girl or a boy. When chatting up girls Harry had always preferred to use words. He looked around for Petronella. She was still surrounded by men.

"Are you looking for someone?"

"I thought you were avoiding me, Ruthy?"

"I'd never avoid you, Harry. Just remember that whatever happens I'm right behind you. Doesn't she look lovely? There's something about a girl on her wedding day."

"Petronella wants to take our relationship further."

"Don't you believe it. Have you seen how Mango looks at her? Don't those glasses of Pimm's they're taking round remind you of sitting round Jeremy's swimming pool? Do you remember kissing me, Harry? Now off you go and see if you can rescue her from all those men. That is, if she wants to be rescued. When are you coming to live back in England? How long's your assignment in Rhodesia?"

"I'm not sure."

"Do you want to come back?"

"I'm not sure."

"Better do it soon before you become a colonial."

"It's an easy life. Cheap booze and sunshine. What else can a man want?"

"A nice girl. You be careful, Harry. Nice talking to you again. And don't forget. Wherever you are Ruthy is right behind you."

"You look good, Ruthy."

"I'm so glad. I'm going to dance. The band has started up again. George loves dancing."

For a moment they both looked deep into each other's eyes. Harry watched her go with mixed feelings, wondering what would have happened if, long before Petronella, he and Ruthy had had an affair. They were too much old friends. That was the problem.

"Come along, Harry. You and I are going to dance. The rooms in this house are far too small for a band like Mango Boys. They need a stadium and thousands of people. Come along. You do dance, don't you, Harry?"

"It's too loud in there, Petronella."

"That's the whole idea. You don't have to think. Just you and the music and the girl in your arms."

"They're rocking and rolling. They don't even touch."

"I'll get Dylan to sing us a solo. You didn't know he did love songs. It was how he started. Dylan will love to sing me a love song."

"Who were all those men?"

"I have no idea. Just men. I seem to attract them."

4

When the food had been eaten and most of the guests were getting tiddly, Bergit went upstairs to change from her wedding dress. Jeremy watched his wife so happily. The boys had run up after her. They had a new mother. They were happy. Bergit was happy. He was happy. The nightmare part of his life was over.

"You love her, don't you? Those boys are lucky. They deserve it after all they went through with losing their mother."

"Hello, Petronella. You know, Primrose became their surrogate mother. She's been so good to my boys. The boys and her children get on well together."

"Be careful. You live in Africa. I remember the kids in the compound. We all played with each other not knowing the difference. Then we grew up and mother told me not to talk to them anymore. My friends were taken away from me. Probably why I fell for Josiah. Trying to get my friends back again."

"We won't let that happen."

"It's so important for the races to mix together. We all live in the same country. We all love Africa. Racism and snobbery are so stupid. Why do we do it?"

"Man's always segregated himself. Into clans, into classes. Into countries. Most likely for mutual protection. How do you see Africa unfolding?"

"Badly. And for reasons that have nothing to do with your kids and the kids of Primrose. It's world politics at play. Not just local Rhodesian problems. If that was what it was we wouldn't be heading for the mess we all are heading for in Africa. Race division is just part of the excuse. The real fights are capitalism against communism. America wanting the end of the British Empire so their multi-nationals can move into the British markets without Commonwealth preference that makes their own products too expensive. In the old days of the empire when Britannia ruled the waves, if you wanted to sell goods to a British colony or buy raw materials from them you had to use a British ship to transport the goods. It was a form of tax. A way for the British to always be in control. If they didn't want competition for their own goods, or the raw materials were in short supply, they refused to ship for the foreigners putting the foreigners out of business."

"Who will win? America or Russia?"

"I've always thought equal distribution of wealth would sort out man's problems. Now at twenty-seven, I'm not so sure. Whatever system you use, man will manipulate the system to his personal benefit. Maybe the Tsars and what they have in Russia now aren't much different. What started as a perfect idea has been corrupted. Running out of money concentrates the mind. I've just been through it. You find you have to rely on yourself and not other people."

"Smith's going to declare UDI eventually."

"Everyone in the world other than South Africa will apply sanctions. You'll get away with a few more years of good old colonial lifestyle. And then you'll have a bush war on your hands. And believe me, I know what I'm talking about. On your own, without British military and financial protection, there aren't enough of you whites to survive."

"So I should get out?"

"But you're not going to. I'm more of an African than you, Jeremy. I was born there. But you've been there a long time. Gets hold of you. England's suburban and boring. Just making money for the sake of showing off wealth eventually becomes boring. You want the bush. The wild space of it. You want Africa. It's a virus that gets into your bloodstream whatever the colour of your skin."

"So what should I do?"

"Enjoy what you have for as long as you have it. And hope. Who really knows what will happen to us? If that German hadn't helped Harry's father before the war you wouldn't have got married today. Bergit wouldn't have been born. Neither would Harry. Let the gods decide, Jeremy. What else can we do in life? Everything's chance. Someone said to me once that if one of his ancestors way back when in a cave had said 'not tonight thank you, darling' he wouldn't have been alive. Enjoy your life wherever you are and hope for the best. Right now I feel sorry for Josiah stuck in jail in some bush camp in the middle of nowhere without any women. Now he can't be happy. And when he breaks out, as he will, he's going to want his revenge on the people that took away some of the best years of his life. He'll be thinking of the likes of you, Jeremy. And my parents. Probably me as well. He'll be full of hate."

"Don't tell all this to Bergit."

"I'm not a fool. Some of my family think I'm a fool. That was when the greasy slide began."

"What did you do to them?"

"Got caught in bed with a woman."

"Blimey. Who caught you?"

"My mother. You remember my mother when she didn't want you to have a bonus that first year? The only year you worked for us. She wants to be in control. Always."

"So what happened?"

"I got disinherited. Why I'm now working for a living. And loving it... Jeremy, why are you laughing?"

"Life's so damn funny. I'd give away the farm to have seen your mother's face. Who was the poor girl?"

"I loved her. We were at university together. Women can love women in every sense of the word. Some of us are different. We're not all made the same. And when another person is different, like the colour of their skin or their sexual orientation, we seem to shy away from them. Everyone likes the familiar. What they understand. Now stop laughing."

"But it's still damn funny. Your mother of all people. So what's going to happen? You're still her daughter. She's still your mother. That part of you that made you love a woman came from her or your father if you say it's built into you."

"We go our separate ways... Have a lovely marriage. Give my love to Africa when you get home."

"Thank you for coming to my wedding. And bringing the band."

"Always a pleasure for an old friend. Good luck."

"Have a good life, Petronella."

"I'll try."

"Your father paid my bonus by the way. Out of the farm cash he had in the safe. Without telling your mother."

"I know he did."

"He's a good man."

"Thank you. I should appreciate him more. He's always been in Mother's shadow."

"What about Harry? You know he's in love with you?"

"He'll learn. We all learn in the end, Jeremy."

He watched her go, holding back from the rest of the wedding party, amazed at how people changed: from a prim miss at the age of thirteen, the daughter of a rich tobacco farmer with her nose in the air. He wondered if Harry knew. There was so much more to other people that wasn't on view. Sipping his second drink of the day, he worried about the farm. The seed beds had gone in before he left for England with Harry. There were so many friends of the bride in England, it made sense for him to fly over for a wedding. At the end of the month, just before the planting season, there was going to be a post-wedding party in the club with all the speeches. Why there had been no speeches at the reception other than short ones from himself and his brother Paul. Jeremy hated wedding speeches. They were all so false. In the club, among all his friends and neighbours, it would somehow be different. Clay Barry had a reputation for hilarious speeches.

The band was still pumping out the music, making Jeremy feel old. The music he remembered was the jazz clarinet and classical piano of his brother, Paul. Except when the man known as Mango sang on his own, the rest was just noise. Bergit liked it. There had to be something in pounding noise. Who on earth dreamed up names like Mango Boys? The world that was England had altered so much.

"Has she gone to change? Quite a wedding."

"What do I call you now, Mr Wakefield? Is it Dad?"

"Horatio will be fine."

"Were you named after Nelson?"

"In a roundabout way. My father was in the merchant navy. Somewhere back in the family there was a connection to the Battle of Trafalgar. Time warps the truth. So I became Horatio. Got used to the name in the end... Did she tell you anything? My wife dislikes the woman, of course. She and Betty Smythe want our son to marry Ruthy. Nature doesn't work that way. One day we may have the time to get to know each other, you and I. Look after her for us, Jeremy. She's very precious. If it should get dangerous you will bring her home. Promise me that. The news from Africa that comes to us at the *Daily Mail* doesn't augur too well for Britain's last colony in Africa. The rest are all now independent."

"You work hard for something in life and then they want to take it away from you. You can't blame people who don't want to try in life. They don't have much in life but they don't feel the pain of losing. The farm, with my family, is my life. You will come and visit us?"

"When I retire. If you are still on the farm. That block of flats you part-own was a great investment."

"Yes it was. But money isn't everything."

"But it helps."

"The farm is so much more than a job. It's a way of life. Bergit loves the farm."

"So she tells me. Just look after my daughter. She's now in your trust. Good luck, Jeremy."

Seeing his glass was empty, Jeremy looked around for a full one. He was drinking whisky. The first time for years he had drunk whisky without ice. They were all worried about the future of Rhodesia. It made him feel nervous. Was he being a fool with his head in the sand? He hoped not.

"There you are, darling. That was a quick change."

"Are you ready to go? The boys will be fine for the night with your mother. She will love having them."

"Do we make a fanfare?"

"No. We slip out the back door. The band was awesome. What did Dad have to say?"

"The usual. To look after you. Come along, Mrs Crookshank."

"I like that so much. Mrs Crookshank. I'm married. The rest of my life has just begun."

"It's not going to be that easy to slip away. Here comes Sidney Cross with the camera. Have a drink. This is my third. Hello, Sidney."

"Got to photograph the bride in her going away outfit."

"You go ahead. I'll get her a drink."

"The party's just warming up. Now, Mrs Bergit Crookshank. Please smile for the camera."

Bergit had fallen in love twice. First with Africa and second with Jeremy Crookshank. She wanted excitement in her life, more than being a suburban housewife in England talking tittle-tattle to her friends. Suburbia was boring. Africa and the farm her husband had called World's View was exciting. And now she was part of it. In Bergit's view of life you had to marry a lifestyle as much as a person. She wanted four children as quickly as possible. Three girls and a boy. They would then have three girls and three boys which would be perfect. Servants. Wonderful servants to look after all the kids. Clean the big house. None of that vacuuming for Bergit. None of that stuck in a kitchen. There was the club. Tennis at the club. Farmers' wives visiting. Visits to Lake Kariba, fishing for Jeremy, enjoying the boat and the lake with her children. All those wonderful wild animals viewed from the safety of a houseboat. A houseboat with servants. For Bergit, she had chosen the perfect way of life whatever the doomsayers said about the future of Africa. In 1935, how did anyone foresee the war? The Nazis. Her father's abduction. They had all lived their lives. If a person permanently worried about the future problems of life they would never enjoy themselves. Life was for living. She was married. She was young. She was going to enjoy herself. A girl had to get on with her life or the good things would pass her by. Bergit's life was all about now.

"You like my going away outfit, Sidney?"

"Just turn your head a little to the right. If I don't get these photographs just right your brother will never let me forget it at work. Now I want shots with you and Jeremy. You with your parents. You all with the boys. It's your wedding day. In fifty years' time you want to look at my photographs and remember the happiest day of your life."

Ruthy's parents had come across, looking as if they wanted to be in the photographs.

"And Uncle William and Aunty Betty. Come and join the photographs. Stand either side of me. Jeremy, this is the most famous newspaper man in our family. I call him Uncle William. We have all lived in the same street since I was born."

"I listened to your BBC interview of Josiah Makoni on my farm in Rhodesia, Mr Smythe. I have a shortwave radio set up with a tall mast. I was a radio officer in the Royal Navy just after the war. Come and join us for the photographs. Boys! Come here. We want you in the photographs."

"I won't be interviewing him for a while."

"Probably never. Petronella knows him well. You should interview Petronella on your programme. She's here with Harry. Over there. Surrounded by men."

"We hoped Harry would be here with our daughter, Ruthy."

"Sorry. Have I put my foot in it?... Boys! Come over here. Now! And where's my mother?... Oh, there you are, Mum."

Bergit watched her mother go to the boys and bend down to talk to them whilst Jeremy's mother walked away towards her other son, Paul. Her mother patiently took one boy in each hand and brought them back into the photograph. Sidney's flashlight went off three times. In the other room, the big room her mother used for her speech therapy practice, the band began playing again. Her friends had been so impressed: a big-name band at her wedding. Poor Ruthy. There was always a price to pay for everything. Bergit caught her brother's eye and beckoned him to join them. With Petronella surrounded by men, Bergit hoped she would not want to join the family photographs.

"Ruthy! Over here. We want you in the photographs."

Ruthy looked from Harry joining the family and back to Bergit. Then she smiled and walked over.

"The bitch is hemmed in by men," Bergit whispered to Ruthy. "Harry, stand next to Ruthy. Doesn't she look gorgeous? Mother, put the boys in the front. Everyone in the photograph together. One big family photograph for our album."

"I can't hear you, Bergit. The band is too loud."

"Mrs Crookshank, can you help my mother with the boys? Boys, please do what your new grandmother tells you."

"Have I got a new grandmother?"

"Yes, Phillip. My mother. I'm your new mother and my mother is your new grandmother."

"My mother is dead."

"I know, Randall. We have to pretend. Tomorrow, your new grandmother is taking you and your grandmother Crookshank to the theatre. To see *Peter Pan*. And on Monday we fly back to the farm."

"Are my grandmothers flying back to the farm?"

"No. They live in England."

"Who's Peter Pan?"

"A small boy about your age, Phillip. Who never gets old. He's always a boy. He can fly through the air. It's all going to be magic for you tomorrow while your daddy and I have a little holiday on our own… Paul and Beth. Bring over those children of yours. Family photographs. Boys, stand in front of everyone with your two cousins. Randall, stop pulling faces at your cousin Deborah."

RUTHY WATCHED her best friend order everyone around. Since childhood, Bergit had been good at bossing people around. She was the strong one, always in control.

"Can we hold hands for the photograph, Harry?"

"I don't see why not."

"She can't see us surrounded by all those men. Your mother tells me you're staying at home tonight after the wedding and Petronella is going home. Maybe I should stay and help your mother clean up some of the mess. We can catch up on old times. It's been nearly a year since my holiday with you in Rhodesia. Your mother could do with some help. The place is going to look like a pigsty. And all this came out of a three-week holiday. When Bergit makes up her mind, she makes up her mind. I think she's very brave to take on those two boys. They're wild."

"What they need is a mother."

"She wants four more children. Three girls and a boy. Sort of balance things off."

"My goodness."

"Do you want kids, Harry?"

"Eventually."

"So do I but I don't want to have to wait too long. Does Petronella want to have children?"

"The subject has never come up."

Sidney was putting his camera back in the case.

"That's it for the photographs, Harry. Come and let's dance."

"You know I hate dancing, Ruthy."

"There's always a first time. He's doing one of his solo songs. Lovely voice. Excuse us, Bergit. I'm taking your brother for a dance. How many drinks have you had, Harry?"

"Too many. It's a bad habit in Rhodesia, drinking too much. Booze is so cheap. Do you think she'll be happy with Jeremy? I worry she jumped into it all so fast. That if anything goes wrong it'll be my fault for introducing them. Taking Bergit out to the farm."

"What can possibly go wrong? For goodness sake, she did visit Jeremy again for a couple of months. She adores him. She needs an older man she can't dominate. He's good-looking. Has a lovely farm. Got some money in England. What could possibly go wrong? They need each other. That's the best foundation for a marriage."

"And if there's a race war in Rhodesia?"

"They come back to good old England. You worry too much, Harry. We all worry too much. We should relax. Enjoy ourselves. Have a fling."

"Have you been drinking, Ruthy?"

"What else do you do at a wedding? Has a girl ever seduced you, Harry? I mean really seduced you when it wasn't expected?"

"There was a girl called Elsie Gilmore. She seduces people."

"Was it nice?"

"I was still half drunk in the morning. Don't remember much. I woke up in her bed when the sun came up. For a moment I didn't know where I was. She had the biggest bottom I have ever seen. A large, very sexy bottom."

"Sounds exciting."

On the dance floor, a small square in the centre of Mrs Wakefield's consulting room, Ruthy took hold of Harry. She had had just enough to drink to know what she was doing and enough to free her of her inhibitions. She looked up into his eyes and ran her tongue, just the tip of her tongue, through her lips. Her lips were full and painted a deep red. Harry looked down at her and saw what she was doing. Ruthy pushed her crotch into his and began to slowly rub, never taking her eyes off Harry. It was a love song, sweet and a little erotic. Harry's response was immediate, his manhood taking control. Right through to the end of the song she worked on Harry and never once did he pull away. His eyes had first opened in surprise. Now she saw in them what she wanted. For the first time she saw lust in his eyes. Lust for her. Lust for Ruthy. That look she had wanted from Harry for so many years.

"That was nice, Harry. Now I'd better take you back to Petronella if you can fight your way through the men. I'll see you later, alligator. We can help your mother and have a few drinks together. Relax nicely. Get to know each other properly again. That dance wasn't so bad was it, Harry?"

"It was lovely."

Inwardly, Ruthy smiled. His voice was husky. Men were all the same. You just had to try. I'll beat you yet, you bitch. Beat you at your own game. Then she smiled again up at Harry, licked her lips for the last time and let go of his hand.

"See you later. Don't forget." Her voice was low, just the right tone.

To be certain, as he walked away, she patted his bottom. Fighting a war, you pulled out all the guns. Feeling pleased with herself, Ruthy walked over to the drinks table and picked up a drink, not caring what it was.

"Cheers, Ruthy. First round to me."

Then she giggled, drank and spluttered.

"Blimey. That was neat Scotch."

5

*P*etronella went off with a group who were going out to a restaurant and then to a club. They were all happily inebriated. Petronella only tried once to persuade Harry to go with them. The crowd went off surrounded by their own noise. For them the fun had just begun. Weddings did that to people, Harry thought, making strangers part of a crowd. All friends together. Harry saw Petronella to the taxis. There were two taxis taking what was left of the wedding party to the restaurant. They were raucous down in the street. They poured head-first into the taxi cabs. Petronella did not look back, leaving Harry on the kerb feeling flat. His sister had gone off and now his girlfriend. The house was empty except for his mother and father, both looking lost. And Ruthy was going to help. Harry wanted a drink.

"It's not that bad, Mother."

"Rhodesia's so far away."

"Have a drink."

"I want to clean up the place first. Just look at all this leftover food. Such a waste. During the war we never wasted food. The new generation don't care. They live for the moment. Ruthy has stayed to help me clear up the mess. She's such a dear. At least Ruthy hasn't run off to Rhodesia. Bergit will have her work cut out with those two boys. I'm exhausted. The boys are spending tonight with their Uncle Paul and their grandmother. Poor woman. She lives all alone in the Isle of Wight. Her husband went down in a sailing boat off Dunkirk. His boat was full of soldiers off the beach when the Germans strafed it. She doesn't like the idea of her new daughter-in-law being named after a German. I tried to tell her the story of Klaus von Lieberman but she wouldn't listen. Said she was close to her husband. He was a friend of Harry Brigandshaw. Sit down and talk to your father while Ruthy and I..."

"We're all going to help. What a mess."

"Where's Petronella?"

"Gone off with a crowd of them to eat at a restaurant and go on to a nightclub. They were all on a roll. Where do we start? You don't mind if I drink while I work? If there's one thing I hate, it's stop-start drinking."

"Get the cat off the table. It's found a nice piece of fish. Oh, Harry, I hope Bergit will be all right in Rhodesia. It's so far away."

"You want a drink, Ruthy?"

"You bet I do. Workers have to be paid. Come here, Ginger. Off the table. I'll put that fish in your bowl in the kitchen."

"Where's Father, Mum?"

"In his study. Writing some article. He never stops working. He and that Petronella had a long conversation about Rhodesia. I suppose he's writing it down... What a wedding. I'm exhausted. Weren't the church bells lovely?"

"Mum, go up to bed. If we don't finish this tonight we'll finish it in the morning. Tomorrow is Sunday. You don't have patients on a Sunday."

"Yes, you go up to bed, Aunty Janet."

"Are you sure, Ruthy? Those boys were up so early this morning."

"Sweet dreams. I'll bring you up a cup of tea."

"You are such a dear."

"Now off you go."

They both watched her go. Ginger, the cat, had finished the fish.

"Now, where's that drink, Harry? We'll clear up the mess tomorrow. Can we light the fire and sit on the couch? It's only just winter but I do like a fire. Come here, Harry, there's something I want to do to you."

Gently, slowly, she kissed him on the mouth then led him to the couch where they sat down. Harry lit the fire, the wood catching quickly.

"Better close the door."

"And the tea?"

"Your mother will be asleep before her head hits the pillow."

"And Dad?"

"I'll put a chair in front of the door."

In the end for Ruthy it was all so simple. They made love. Beautiful, beautiful love in the light of the flickering fire.

"I love you, Harry."

"I know you do."

WHEN HARRY'S father came down from his study and pushed open the door they were both fast asleep in each other's arms curled up on the couch. Moving the chair away from the door where it had fallen over, he looked at his son and his best friend's daughter in the bright light of the fire. They were both fast asleep and smiling.

Upstairs, Horatio woke up his wife.

"What's the matter, Horatio?"

"It's Harry and Ruthy. Downstairs on the couch. Wrapped around each other."

"They're just old friends."

"Not this time, Janet. Tonight they were more than just friends. Our son's trousers were tossed on the floor. And he wasn't wearing his underpants. You think he seduced her?"

"If I know Ruthy it was Ruthy who did the seducing. Now come to bed and turn out the light. Now I'm really going to sleep. In peace. My prayers answered. That Petronella went off with a crowd of men right in front of him."

"Things have changed since our day."

"Not really. They just do it differently. Did you see the way William was looking at Genevieve? All those years and two children and he still hasn't got over her. He loves Betty but he still remembers his affair with Genevieve in New York when Betty was just his secretary. With luck, that's how it will end with Harry and Petronella."

"I'd forgotten William and Genevieve."

"He hadn't."

"Poor Betty."

"Not at all. She knew all about it before she went after William. She's happy. She got what she wanted. She got William and two children. And he's happy. Ends don't get better than that. What were you writing about, Horatio?"

"Josiah Makoni. The inside story. You know they were lovers?"

"Who?"

"Josiah and Petronella. She's worried about him. Wants the press to keep his name in front of the public."

"Poor Harry."

"Not anymore. Now go back to sleep. What a mess downstairs. I'm going to miss her terribly."

"So am I. Bergit is so much of my life. Seven thousand miles. I can't bear the thought of it. Please hold me, Horatio. We've lost our daughter."

"They'll be back in England sooner than you know. If the blacks don't get 'one man one vote' they are going to war. Petronella just told me. Right from the horse's mouth... When are those boys coming back again?"

"Tomorrow. I'm taking them to see *Peter Pan*. Poor kids. She was eaten by lions. Unimaginable."

"So were the Nazis. It's life. We all have to go through life. Whatever it brings us. The good and the bad."

"Goodnight, Horatio."

"Goodnight, Janet."

"They're still on the couch?"

"On the couch."

"When the fire dies down he'll have a cold bottom."

"Cold bottom warm heart."

"Go to sleep."

HARRY WOKE cold and alone in the middle of the night. The fire had gone out and the room was pitch dark. He groped for his pants and trousers on the floor and found them. Not remembering where his mother had moved the standard lamp for the party, he stumbled alone in the dark. Getting to the far wall he groped to the door and found the overhead light switch. The bright light seared his eyes. His head was throbbing from the drink. Ruthy must have walked home just up the street. The chair she had put against the door was back where it belonged. Harry went upstairs to his room as quietly as possible. He was smiling, the surprise of the seduction having satiated his body, the surprise as much in the performance as the seduction. It must have been the drink for both of them.

In the light of morning Harry woke surprisingly fresh. The first thing he thought of was Ruthy. The previous evening played back in his mind. Later he got up and went downstairs. His mother was in the kitchen.

"Ruthy and I had had too much to drink so I walked her home. Sorry about leaving you the mess. I put the cat out. Why are you smiling, Mother?"

"Oh, nothing. What a lovely wedding. It was so thoughtful of you staying with us last night. I'm going to miss Bergit so much. I'm going over to Beth and Paul to collect the boys later."

"Where's Dad?"

"In his study. You want some breakfast? Didn't take me long to clear up. Much better you looked after Ruthy. I see you lit the fire. There's a pair of socks tucked into the couch. Underneath the cushion. Well, they look like your socks. Didn't pull them out."

"Must be mine."

"More like a girl's."

"Oh, yes. Ruthy took off her shoes. They were new shoes for the wedding. They were pinching her feet. She must have left her socks off to walk home."

Ten minutes later the doorbell rang. Harry answered it. Standing with a smile on her face was Ruthy. On tiptoe she spoke into his ear.

"When I left someone had moved the chair."

"You mean someone came into the room!"

"Yes. The chair was back where I found it."

"I woke up bare-arsed and freezing. You were gone."

"My parents would have asked where I'd been for the night. You know Dad. He'd have killed you. I've come to clean up the mess."

"Who's there, Harry?"

"Ruthy, Mum. She's come to clean up."

"Both of you come and have some breakfast. Good morning, Ruthy. Did you sleep well?"

"Sorry we didn't clean up last night."

"I'm sure you both had more important things on your minds.

Harry's spending the day with us Ruthy. Why don't you stay? I have to go out but that doesn't matter. Tea or coffee?"

"Maybe coffee. I drank too much at the wedding."

"I'm sure no harm came of it. It's not every day your best friend gets married. It's so lovely to see you two together. Harry, do you want to take a cup of coffee up to your father? He's got something to tell you."

"Is he mad at me or something?"

"Quite the contrary. Now, run along to your father. Ruthy and I can have a little chat. When you come back I'll make us breakfast. It's a lovely day outside. The sun's shining. You two should go for a walk along the river when you've eaten. You haven't had breakfast have you, Ruthy?"

"No. My parents and Patrick are still asleep. They all like to sleep in on Sundays."

"Well, there we have it. Yes, what a lovely day. Run along, Harry."

Before going up to his father, Harry ducked into the room where he had slept the first part of the night. Under the cushion on the couch was a pair of pink panties. With his free hand, the other holding his father's coffee, Harry stuffed the panties in his pocket. Then he went upstairs to his father's study.

"Look, Dad, before you say anything, I'm sorry. We had both been drinking. You know weddings."

"What are you talking about, son?"

"Mum says you want to talk to me."

"Yes, I do. I want to persuade you to come back to England. To ask Roland Cartwright for a new assignment. I can always get you a job at the *Mail*. It's your mother. She's going to need you, Harry, now Bergit has flown the nest."

"I'll ask him. Yes, I'll ask him if I can come home. You're right. Poor Mum. It's almost a year. Before the colonial bug bites too deep. It's rather a nice way of life in Salisbury."

"Depending how long it lasts. Now, what were you just saying?"

"Oh, it's nothing. We left the mess. Didn't clear up. Mother had to do it this morning."

"She likes keeping the house in order."

"Yes, I suppose she does."

As Harry put the cup of coffee on his father's writing desk he was sure his father was smiling, his face turned away.

"Who was that at the door, Harry?"

"Ruthy."

"So she's back. You run along downstairs. Don't forget to ask Roland."

Feeling like a small boy caught in the act, Harry walked from the room, closing the door quietly as he left. Inside his pocket he felt Ruthy's panties. The touch of the silk on his fingers immediately aroused him. Getting downstairs he walked up behind Ruthy. His mother had her back to them standing at the kitchen stove. Ruthy was wearing jeans. Gently, Harry slipped the panties into her pocket.

"What are you doing, Harry?" whispered Ruthy.

"You left your panties behind last night."

"Couldn't find them in the dark."

"Mum found them."

"Oh, my God!"

"Said they were socks."

His mother turned round from the stove. She was smiling at them.

"What are you two whispering about?"

"Nothing, Mum. Kids' talk."

"You're not kids anymore. You should realise that. Among grownups it's rude to whisper. Now sit down at the breakfast table. Both of you. And eat your breakfasts."

"Yes, Mother."

"Thank you, Aunty Janet."

"Always a pleasure to see you Ruthy. Now Harry's home we hope to see lots of you."

"Are you staying in England, Harry?"

"Dad wants me to. I'm going to ask Roland for a transfer back to the London office."

"Oh, goodie. This breakfast looks good, Aunty Janet. I'm hungry."

"Eggs. Bacon. Sausage. Tomatoes. Should fill up your tummies."

"Next Sunday all of you must come to us for Sunday lunch. Just like old times."

"We'd love to."

"Mum and Dad will be thrilled."

Without another word Harry and Ruthy ate their breakfast. It was just like old times. Except the little girl he had known all those years was now grown up. She was a woman. A beautiful woman. And the two of them were now lovers.

Only when Ruthy left later in the day did Harry wonder what he was going to do. At seven o'clock, soon after his mother came back with Jeremy Crookshank's two boys from the theatre, the phone rang. Harry picked up the phone.

"It's me. Did you miss me last night?"

"Of course I did," lied Harry.

"When are you coming over? I thought we could go out for supper. Make a night of it. Those people were so boring."

"Where did you go?"

"The Trocadero. Very expensive. I missed you, Harry."

"I'll be right over."

Harry put the phone down, not sure which way to run.

"Who was it, Harry?"

"Petronella, Mum. She wants me to go over."

"Are you going?"

"Said I would. Do you mind?"

"It's your life, Harry. Nothing I can do. What about Ruthy?"

"What about Ruthy, Mum?"

"The way you two were behaving this morning at breakfast I thought she was going to be your new girlfriend."

"I'll try not to be late."

"I'll bet you will."

"What do you mean?"

"You heard me. It's your life. That woman will be no good to you."

"Why are you crying?"

"Because you are such a damn fool. Why can't you see what's right under your nose?"

PART VIII

JANUARY 1965

APPEARANCES CAN BE DECEPTIVE

1

For Harry Wakefield, Christmas had been a game of cat and mouse. Petronella had invited him to spend the holiday at Woodlands Court with her grandfather. Her parents had stayed in Rhodesia on the farm. Her father had phoned, having got her home phone number from the new girl, Grace, now running the ZANU office. Grace was a Shona like Livingstone Sithole, another political refugee with the right to live in England. Father and daughter had spoken for six minutes before the exchange cut them off. With the shortage of phone lines, overseas calls from Rhodesia were at a premium. Both Harry's mother and father had put their foot down, insisting he stay with the family for Christmas. The Smythes had joined them. When the phone call came in from Bergit on Christmas Day his mother was ecstatic.

"I'm going to be a grandmother. Isn't that exciting? Oh, I wish she was here. All those baby clothes. I loved shopping for baby clothes."

With the news Ruthy had said she wasn't feeling well and had gone home. They had just finished Christmas lunch. Patrick, her brother, offered to take her home.

"What's the matter, Ruthy?"

"I feel sick, Aunty Janet. Too much Christmas lunch. I'll be fine with a lie-down. You won't mind? We had a Christmas party in the Temple last night. Everyone in the law firm. I drank too much. George took me home."

"Are you still seeing George, Ruthy?"

Harry had watched her go. Part of him wanted to be with her. Soon after Ruthy walked home with her brother the senior Smythes had left. After that, Christmas went flat. Harry's mother had shaken her head. For Harry and Ruthy it had just been the one night. The one night on the couch in front of the fire. Ever since that night after Bergit's wedding Petronella had not let him out of her sight. Once Roland Cartwright had given him a job in London he had taken a room in South Kensington not far from Petronella's flat. Petronella had found him the room. The few things he had left in Salisbury were shipped back to him sea freight.

After they had all taken an afternoon nap, a Sunday and Christmas tradition with the Wakefields, Harry prepared to go home to his room.

"Stay the night, Harry. What's the hurry? You aren't working on Boxing Day. Why don't you walk over and see if Ruthy is all right? She looked so unhappy today. Please. For me. The Smythes have been such good friends to us."

"Maybe I will. You think there might have been something in your cooking, Mum?"

"I hope not or we'd all feel sick."

Ruthy came to the door.

"They've all gone out. They wanted to drive into Regent Street to see the Christmas lights."

"I came to see you."

"That was big of you."

"You knew I had a girlfriend."

"Then why did you sleep with me?"

"Are you feeling all right?"

"No I'm not. I'm sick as a dog every morning if you really want to know."

"What's wrong with you, Ruthy?"

"I'm pregnant, you idiot. Three months pregnant."

"Who's the father?"

"Oh, Harry."

"What are you going to do?"

"Have it, of course. Even if I wanted, abortions are illegal in England."

"Who is the father, Ruthy?"

"You're such an idiot. You are of course."

"What about George?"

"After our night on the couch I haven't slept with anyone. I've been hoping you would take me out."

"Do your parents know?" Harry's whole stomach had tightened into a knot.

"Of course they don't."

"What are we going to do?"

"You tell me, Harry. This one belongs to both of us. How's the bitch?"

"Spending Christmas with her grandfather and uncles. We're almost living together. What a mess."

"It wouldn't be if you dumped the bitch. Are you coming in? They won't be back for an hour. What a coincidence. My best friend is also three months pregnant."

"Stop crying, Ruthy."

"What the hell else can I do? I'm going to have an illegitimate child. No one will want to know me. My mother and father are going to have a fit. And if I tell them who the father is, so are your parents."

"So what are we going to do?"

"You could always marry me, Harry. I'd be such a good wife to you."

"Petronella would never stand for it."

"What kind of hold has she got over you? She's not the one who's pregnant."

"Did you know that night you were in the middle of your cycle?"

"What if I did?"

"Weren't you taking precautions?"

"Of course I was! But it's not one hundred per cent foolproof. And stop walking up and down."

"I don't know what to do."

"Why don't you go home and think about it? I've had a couple of months to think. It's not all bad. We've known each other all our lives. I love you, Harry. You'll grow to love your Ruthy."

"I couldn't face your parents right now."

"Then go home. You know where I live. I'm not running away. While you're thinking, Harry, don't just think of yourself. Or of me. Think of the child."

. . .

PETRONELLA HAD SENSED she had competition straight after the wedding. Harry had changed. He was no longer under her thumb. Sometimes his mind went off somewhere to a place that did not include her. She was twenty-seven. In her twenty-eighth year. Even Richard Maguire didn't look at her the same way anymore. Getting Harry into a room close by her flat had brought back a semblance of control. But still he drifted off. To that other place. More than once Harry casually mentioned the girl called Ruthy. His childhood friend. So it had to be her.

When Petronella returned to South Kensington after a week with her grandfather, trying to get back into his good books and his will, Harry had avoided her.

"What's the matter, Harry? You haven't wanted to bed me since I got back. What's going on?"

"Ruthy is pregnant and I'm the father. That night you went with the wedding party to the Trocadero."

"The bitch seduced you when my back was turned."

"It takes two to tango, Petronella. It's not as if I'm your only boyfriend. While we've been sleeping together there's been a whole string of them."

"Not since you moved into your room. Don't you want to marry me, Harry? I'm sure Grandfather is going to put me back in the will. You love Woodlands Court. You said you want to write a book one day. We could sell Woodlands Court for a fortune and move into the country."

"You said the house was entailed. You couldn't sell it."

"A good solicitor would fix that. You've always wanted me, Harry."

"Well, this changes things. I can't just do nothing."

"Pay for an abortion."

"It's against the law. Hell, Petronella, it's my child too. I'd be killing a part of myself. Myself, really. My future. My reincarnation. The only real future we know about after we are dead is through our children."

"We can have children."

"You don't want children."

"I want you, Harry."

"Do you really? You chop and change. How's Elsie Gilmore?"

"You slept with her as well. Oh, go to hell. There are plenty of fish in the sea. Go and marry your mousy little Ruthy and see how much fun that is after a couple of years. She'll saddle you with three kids and a mortgage. You'll go through the rest of your life in boredom. No excitement. A daily routine. You'll never write a book."

"I've got to think."

"Go and think. Make up your mind. A girl with money who fucks like a tigress. You don't get that chance twice."

"Would you really marry me, Petronella? Most of the time you've been using me."

"We all use each other, Harry. You know, I'm tired. I'm going to bed. On my own. Three big meetings tomorrow. Business is booming. The publicity game. The public are so gullible. Tell them enough times from enough directions what they want to hear and they all follow like lemmings. Why are they like that? Half my bands sing a whole lot of rubbish. When you read the words without all the shouting and noise they don't even make sense. But it makes money. Wonderful money."

"I thought you were a communist."

"A girl changes, Harry. People still think I'm a socialist. All my bands scream about equality. Image, Harry. That's what counts. If anyone suggested I run my business for the money I'd laugh in their face. Point out how much I give to ZANU and the cause of racial equality. What I do with the rest of the money is between me, my stockbroker, and my very close friends. I've worked out the system. You always got to work out the system. What people are really up to. And why wasn't the little girl being careful, Harry? She was after you. The 'I'm pregnant' is the oldest trick in the book. Especially when it's intentional. How many times did you sleep with her?"

"Once."

"And she fell pregnant! Be careful, Harry. Don't be so naïve. Nice, sweet little girls are not what they seem to be."

NOT KNOWING which way to turn the next day in his old Fleet Street office, watching Sidney Cross through the glass window in the door of his office, Harry tried to concentrate on what he was going to write. He was doing a piece on Harold Wilson, the British Labour Prime Minister, and his mind kept drifting. The problem wasn't ever going to go away: she was pregnant; he was the father, of that much he was certain. When

Harry's mind returned to the present Roland Cartwright, the sub-editor of the *Daily Mirror*, was pushing open the door to his office. Never once since Harry worked for him had Roland ever knocked.

"Come back to us, Harry. You look miles away. An old friend of yours has come to see you. The Reverend Harvey Pemberton. All the way from the Good Faith Mission in Rhodesia. He's forgiven us for suggesting he supported the armed struggle back in 1962."

"What's he want? What's he doing in England?"

"What's the matter, Harry? You can always come to Roland Cartwright with your problems. Part of the job. Business doesn't usually make you that irritated."

"You're right. This one's a personal problem."

"What, you've got some girl pregnant?"

"Don't laugh, Roland. It's not funny."

"Just don't bring your personal problems to work with you. Leave them at home. I'll have Macey bring him in."

Roland was smiling, shaking his head.

Harry got up from his desk as Macey, the new receptionist, brought in the reverend. Macey left, closing the door. Harry and the reverend shook hands.

"Please sit down. What can I do for you?"

"How are you, Harry?"

"Not so good if you really want to know. A personal problem."

"You can always talk to a priest."

"Let's leave it for the moment. What's on your mind?"

"Our old mutual friend. Josiah Makoni. I'm in Britain to launch a campaign for his release. Rhodesia may be a self-governing colony but the final say is with the British parliament. The British government. Unless the new Rhodesian Front government do something stupid like declaring unilateral independence."

"I'm writing a piece on Wilson."

"That's who must pressure Smith. If the Rhodesian government don't talk to the likes of Josiah we are never going to solve our problems. It doesn't make sense locking him up. Any more than it makes sense for the South Africans to lock up Nelson Mandela. We have to talk to each other. I want your help, Harry. Have you seen Petronella Maple?"

"Not this morning. Last night we had a row."

"Are you two dating? I didn't know."

"Part of my problem I was talking about."

"We want a march through the centre of London. As many people as possible."

"Petronella has gone into business."

"But she still believes in her principles?"

"Probably. I hope so. Why don't you ask her? She has her office at Downtown Music. She was going to move out but hasn't got round to it. She's a publicist. For Mango Boys among others. She's the one behind Mango Boys' songs that put Josiah on the map. The song 'Josiah' made him something of an international hero with the anti-colonial lobby."

"Can we go and have lunch? Over lunch we can tell each other our problems. It's always difficult talking personally in an office."

"How long are you here for?"

"That depends. Last time we talked you were staying in Rhodesia. Your sister was marrying a farmer."

"She married him. Having a child. My mother wanted me to stay in England. There were only the two of us kids. You do know Josiah was helping to build a guerrilla army in Tanzania? The Rhodesian government consider him a terrorist which gives them every right to lock him up. He wants to kill people."

"In the end they'll have to talk to him. Why not now? Before they all start tearing at each other's throats. And no, I have never supported an armed struggle. I'm a priest. A man of God. Thou shalt not kill... It's good to see you, Harry."

"Funny how people always say that when they want something."

"Don't you want to help?"

"Of course I do. You didn't do much good when you led the march on Buckingham Palace with Josiah and Petronella to free Mandela."

"We can only try to do our best in life. To do what's right."

"What's right, Reverend?"

"If you don't know the difference between right and wrong you will have a problem in life."

"Sometimes there are two rights. Just depends which side of the fence you are looking from. Like Protestants fighting Catholics for instance. Was the Spanish Inquisition right, Harvey?"

"No, of course it wasn't. There are better ways of dealing with heretics. We excommunicate them."

"But the Catholic church thought it was right at the time to torture and kill."

"You're a good journalist. You look at both sides of the story."

"That's my job. There have been religious wars throughout history. Can the *Daily Mirror* buy the church their lunch?"

"I don't see why not."

"And whoever said there wasn't such a thing as a free lunch?"

"Are we going to be friends, Harry?"

"As I said, I'm not in the best of moods this morning. A girl I know is pregnant and I'm the father."

"Petronella?"

"An old childhood friend."

"Thank goodness a Roman Catholic priest has to be celibate. Stops a lot of life's problems. You'll marry her, of course. A child has to have two parents bringing him up. Does Petronella know?"

"Yes, she knows."

"Do you love Petronella?"

"I don't know. I thought I did. Petronella is complex. She's changed. From being a rabid socialist she's now running a business for profit. What does Josiah have to say about Petronella? I presume you've seen him?"

"The prison camp is remote. They won't allow visitors. Certainly not me."

"Did he ever love her?"

"Josiah is inclined to use people for the cause."

"So he was using her."

"Not for me to say. For Josiah Makoni the struggle is more important than anything else. It's his life. As God is my life."

"You know what they say, Harvey. The moment you join politics and religion you have a problem. Be careful."

"What's her name?"

"Ruthy Smythe. William Smythe's daughter. My father's best friend. He interviewed Josiah on the BBC. We've lived in the same street all our lives. Petronella thinks she did it on purpose to get me away from Petronella."

"Not the best foundation for a marriage. So you seduced your neighbour's daughter."

"It was pretty mutual. Come on. Let's get lunch. Enough about me. When are you having the first rally?"

"You'll cover it?"

"Of course we will. It's news. I'm a newspaper reporter. Out of interest, why have so many of your students at the Good Faith Mission become radicals? What were you teaching them, Harvey? A little more than the three 'Rs' and the Catholic religion?"

"We teach people the difference between right and wrong."

"Oh there we go again. Sometimes the most difficult part of life is being able to work out what's right. It's never black and white. Never has been."

"You're rationalising, Harry."

"Probably. A pub lunch suit you?"

"Suits me fine. Priests are allowed to drink."

"Thank God for small mercies."

"You don't go to church do you, Harry?"

"Not anymore. As a journalist I've become just a little cynical."

"I'm sad for you. You'll find God again. If you don't there's no point to life."

"That's the problem. Sometimes I wonder if there is a point to life other than procreation."

"You should join the Catholic Church."

The man was smiling at him.

"Are you a good man, Harvey?"

"I hope so. I try to be. I try to live by the word of God. I believe in liberation theology. That all men and women should be free. Which is why we need to stage a rally in the heart of the capital. Rhodesia must be free for all its people. Don't you agree, Harry?"

"I'm a journalist. My personal opinion doesn't come into it. My job is to report the facts. To let people make up their own minds."

"So you are not coming back to Rhodesia?"

"Only for visits. To see my sister. Bergit married a tobacco farmer friend of mine."

"You have to believe in something."

"Sometimes what you believe in doesn't turn out quite right. Like communism. Great idea, lousy in practice. Do you really want Rhodesia to go communist under the control of Moscow? They want world domination. They don't give a damn about the people. Josiah needs them to gain power for his party. You mark my words, if the likes of Josiah do gain control it won't be to the long-term benefit of the ordinary people. Quite the contrary. A few greedy people will grab it all. Moscow won't care. So long as the puppet government of a so-called independent Rhodesia does what they want by selling them strategic minerals and toeing the communist line. It will become another form of colonialism. Only a lot more brutal. Now Josiah claims to be doing it in the name of the people. Sounds good. Sounds popular, all those promises. Reality will be something very different. And you'll be right in the middle of the mess, Harvey. You won't be the liberation hero. They'll blame you and your friends for the mess."

Not sure whether he liked priests who dabbled in politics, Harry put on his heavy overcoat. If there was one thing in England he did not enjoy it was the weather. Outside in the street it was bitterly cold but fortunately not raining.

"A brisk walk, Harvey. Do us good."

"Lead the way."

In the Duck and Drake it was crowded. Full of Fleet Street journalists trading stories, making sure the other papers didn't get one up on them. At a table in a crowd sat William Smythe and Harry's father, bringing back to him his problem with Ruthy in one fell swoop.

"What's the matter, Harry?"

"That's William Smythe over there with my father."

"The future grandfathers."

"Again you are smiling, Reverend Pemberton."

"He interviewed me back in '62. For some American newspaper, I forget which one. We want to link the Civil Rights Movement in America with our struggle in Southern Africa. Rhodesia is our first target for liberation and then comes South Africa."

"What will you have to drink?"

"A pint. A good old-fashioned pint of English draught bitter. If there is one thing I miss in Rhodesia it's a good old pint. And you're wrong, Harry. I didn't radicalise Josiah. Hopefully I taught him how to think. Fort Hare University in South Africa was where they all became radicalised. Robert Mugabe attended Fort Hare along with most of the South African leaders of the African National Congress."

"The Catholics claim that given a child by the age of seven the child will always be a Catholic. Some people a little less sensitive than myself would call it brainwashing. That's when Josiah started in your classroom at the age of seven... They do a very good steak and kidney pie. Didn't you maybe brainwash Josiah just a little against British colonialism to proselyte your religion?"

"Are you interviewing me, Harry?"

"You came to me. I'm always interviewing, Harvey. Seeking the truth. You didn't want your religion to be tar brushed by the oppression you saw in colonialism."

"Colonialism is one step away from slavery."

"May I quote you?"

"Certainly. You will anyway."

"So all those roads, railways and the rest of the whole bang shoot of modernisation, including your education, was no damn good to them. That they'd all be better off if the white man with his industry had never come anywhere near them."

"Don't swear, Harry."

"Seventy years ago there were under half a million in Rhodesia when the white man first appeared. Only two out of ten children survived. Now there are over two million and all of them fed and nine out of ten children have a life. Do you agree with an armed struggle as part of your liberation theology, Harvey? Answer me truthfully."

"Yes, I suppose I do."

"Then you're happy with Josiah killing people to further his political ends. Tell me, Reverend, is that right or is that wrong? Are you happy with what through history the church has liked to call a just war? Is there ever a just war? What about 'Thou shalt not kill'? Do you believe in the methods of terrorism? That killing white people will be justified because they oppress the black people and have stolen their land? Do you believe in killing people, Reverend?"

"Of course I don't."

"Thank you... Just doing my job... Felix, I'll have the steak and kidney."

"I'll have it too."

"And two pints of your best bitter."

"They're looking at you."

"I know they are. What I don't know is whether Ruthy has told them."

"And leaving a child without his father, is that right?"

"I'm not a priest, Harvey. I don't claim the moral high ground. And another question I would like to put to you. Is it right for the church to interfere in politics?"

"We're not interfering. We're doing what's right."

"By supporting a guerrilla army in training?"

"Are you taking notes? And of course we don't support the guerrilla army materially."

"Of course I am. I'd hate to be accused of misreporting your words."

"Do you think it right for a white minority, a small, white minority, to dictate to a black majority, Harry?"

"I'm a newspaper reporter. I don't have an opinion. My only opinion is that of the person I am interviewing... My word, the place is full today."

"Will your newspaper support our rally to free Josiah?"

"Of course it will. We support our readers' opinion. And our average reader doesn't like rich Rhodesian tobacco farmers living in luxury with swimming pools and servants like feudal barons on someone else's land. We'll be happy to support you, Harvey, to support our circulation. Are you going to see Petronella?"

"Right after my free lunch, Harry. Cheers. To happy times."

"To happy times."

"To your baby. What are you going to call your child? When's it due?"

"In six months."

"Plenty of time to get married. But if you want to do it before those two men who are now coming over find out, you'd best do it quickly. Sorry, Harry. Just doing my job... Mr William Smythe. How nice to see you again. And Mr Horatio Wakefield. We met briefly, Mr Wakefield, at the time of the Mandela march. Come and join us. Steak and kidney pie. Your son was just giving me a grilling on the church's policy of liberation theology. Colonialism is a scourge don't you think? The British people have seen the light. Now it's up to the British people who call themselves Rhodesian to also see the light. Come and sit down, William."

"I always enjoy a good discussion, Harvey. Horatio's daughter has just married one of your Rhodesians. So what do you think? Should Jeremy sell his farm and come back to England? Leave behind what he's spent the most productive years of his life building?"

"As an old friend of yours? Or as a priest?"

"As a man, Harvey."

"I'd tell him to sell his farm as soon as possible and start all over again in England."

"With all the bad politics he won't get much for his farm," said Horatio. "They may not let him take the money out of the country."

"Then leave it behind."

"My daughter just announced she's pregnant."

"Even more reason for looking at reality."

"What are you doing in England?"

"Organising a rally to free Josiah Makoni."

"Right from the horse's mouth. I'll tell Jeremy... That steak and kidney pie looks good. Bring me one, Felix."

"And I'll have the same," said William. "And bring me and Horatio each a large whisky. So, Harry, what's going on?"

"What do you mean, Uncle William?"

"Your job. Staying in England. Ruthy is all bright again now you're back. You should come round more often. She loves to see you. I hope you'll come on my BBC programme while you're in England, Harvey. We can talk about Josiah. About Rhodesia. About your march. Are you taking this one to Buckingham Palace?"

"The Houses of Parliament. We want the British government to exercise parliament's final authority over the Rhodesian government and stop all this nonsense. Tell them if they try and declare unilateral independence from Britain the government will send in the British Army."

"Brit killing Brit, Harvey. I don't think so. So many of those Rhodesians fought in the war. Were given Crown Land farms after the war by a grateful British government. Can't turn the army on your own people. I don't think the army would have it."

"You think they'd disobey a lawful command?"

"Probably. Doubt if the likes of Harold Wilson would wish to find out. The politicians would never want to chase a confrontation with the armed services so soon after the war. They won't chance their luck by sending in the army. Good to see you, Harvey. You're looking well. How's the Good Faith Mission?"

"Our school is flourishing. We are looking for money to put a new roof on our church."

"How much do you want?"

"As much as possible. My word, this food is good. And whoever said there wasn't such a thing as a free lunch? Thank you, Harry. I've been enjoying our little conversation. Apart from the weather it's always a pleasure to come back to England."

2

_____

A week after Harry Wakefield bought the Reverend Harvey Pemberton his free lunch, Arnold Sheckland-Hall died leaving his house and one third of Sheckland-Hall Limited to Petronella. Two days after the funeral Petronella sub-let her South Kensington flat to a co-worker at Downtown Music and moved all her goods and chattels to Woodlands Court without saying a word to Harry left behind in his one room down the road. When he phoned Woodlands Court, Elsie Gilmore answered the phone.

"Hello, Harry... Didn't she tell you? We're back together again."

"Why isn't she working anymore at Downtown Music?"

"She doesn't need the money. We don't need the money. I've given up my job at Sainsbury's."

"Why wasn't I told the time and place of the old man's funeral?"

"Things change, Harry. Petronella thought it better to cut you off completely."

"So, we're over?"

"Yes, Harry."

"Charming. One minute she was wanting to marry me and now it's over."

"Well, you know how it is. You shouldn't go around impregnating other girls."

"She was the one who said Ruthy did it deliberately. That it probably wasn't my child."

"I don't know about that."

"So she doesn't want to talk to me?"

"No, Harry. Petronella doesn't want to see you anymore."

"And the rally to free Josiah?"

"She won't be going. She has other obligations. To this wonderful old family house and the business. She's going on the board. Her first board meeting is tomorrow."

"So she's not going to sell her shares and give the proceeds to charity?"

"Of course not. It's quite one thing to give away other people's money but quite another to give away your own."

"What about her allowance, most of which she gave to ZANU?"

"The allowance was at the whim of her grandfather. She never felt the money was hers."

"Are either of you having any more to do with ZANU?"

"She doesn't like Livingstone Sithole. When she wanted his help he as good as told Petronella to go to hell."

"Does her mother know the money has gone to Petronella?"

"Yes she does."

"Was the mother at her father's funeral?"

"No. Not surprising, don't you think, after she was disinherited for the second time. How is Ruthy?"

"I haven't seen her."

"Then you'd better. Soon. Never run away from your obligations."

"Did Petronella see Harvey Pemberton?"

"I believe she did."

"Thank you, Elsie. Have a nice life."

"You too, Harry. It was nice knowing you. Even if it was just a one-night stand."

The girl was laughing down the phone, enjoying herself. That old saying had been right, Harry thought as he put down the phone in his office: hell hath no fury like a woman scorned.

"So that's it."

"What is, Harry? You want me to bring my camera on the march this Saturday?"

"She's dumped me, Sidney! Petronella has dumped me for a woman... Ten o'clock here on Saturday. We'll take it from there."

When Sidney left, Harry sat staring in front of him. Maybe it wasn't so clever telling the reverend he was holier-than-thou. He had forgotten Petronella and her family were Catholics.

"I wonder what he'd think of her having sex with a woman? They'll rationalise that lot one day when it suits them. What a world. What a lovely bloody world we live in."

Looking at his watch, Harry saw it was time to go home. He felt lonely. Didn't want to go home to his room and four blank walls. Outside in the main office, Sidney was ready to leave.

"You want to go to the pub, Sidney?"

"Don't be ridiculous. I'm a married man. Caroline would skin me alive if I came home plastered. See you tomorrow."

"Goodnight, Sidney."

Dragging his feet, not knowing what he wanted to do with himself, Harry walked to the Tube station. There was a light flurry of snow, leaving small white flakes on his overcoat. At the bottom of the steps in the comparative warmth of the London Underground, the rush hour traffic pushing everyone along, he changed his mind about going to his room. It was too near Petronella's abandoned flat.

Half an hour later when Harry rang the front door bell of the Smythes' Chelsea home, Ruthy answered the door.

"Hello, stranger. Come in. Quickly. It's cold with the door open."

"How are you, Ruthy?"

"Much the same. Mum and Dad are out. I have no idea what's happened to Patrick. Eighteen years old. They come and go. Mother says he uses the place as a hotel. You want a drink? Dad won't mind this once if we raid his cocktail cabinet."

"I could do with a drink. Petronella's dumped me."

"Did she know about our child?"

"I told her."

"Maybe she's not such a bitch after all. How do you feel?"

"You want to go out?"

"Let's sit round the fire. With the baby I've given up drink. A bit boring."

"Do they know?"

"Mother suspects something."

"We'll have to get married."

"Probably. First have a drink." She was smiling at him, a soft smile full of contentment.

"Make it a stiff one."

"Is that for the dumping or the thought of getting married?"

"So you won't have an abortion?"

"Absolutely not."

"Good. I don't think I could handle an abortion. What a mess we're in."

"Not really. These things happen for the best. Let me take your coat. You want something to eat? I'm a good cook, Harry. Kids like mothers who are good cooks. Now sit down. Make yourself comfortable. I'll pour you your Scotch. Dad's at the BBC doing an interview with that missionary from Rhodesia. All about some rally on Saturday. Now, how does that look? Right up to the pretty. No ice and no water. How the Scots drink their whisky."

"In Rhodesia they fill the glass up with ice."

"I'm sure they do. But we aren't in Rhodesia. Now, tell me, why are you here, Harry? Or shouldn't I ask?"

"Are you still being sick in the morning?"

"Not anymore."

"Have you seen a doctor?"

"Dr Prendergast. He says..."

"Good God, Ruthy. That's our family's doctor. He delivered me. He must have told our parents."

"There's something about doctor and patient confidentiality. Anyway, as I was trying to say, our baby is fine. Everything looks perfect. Dr Prendergast gave me some vitamins to take."

"Why did you go to him?"

"Because he knows our family medical history."

"So you told Dr Prendergast I'm the father!"

"Of course I did, Harry. They want to know both families' medical history. He was rather pleased as a matter of fact. He delivered me too, you know. And Patrick. And Bergit. It's going to be so much fun for our children. My child and my best friend's child are going to be first cousins of exactly the same age... Is there something wrong with that whisky? I can find you some ice. Let me put some more wood on the fire. So where are we going to live, Harry?"

"I have absolutely no idea. You're taking it all so calmly I can't believe it."

"I'm happy. Very, very happy. I'm going to have the baby of the only man I have ever loved in my life. What more could a girl want, Harry? That's better. Now, do you want another one? For the next six months you're going to have to drink for both of us... And how was your day at the newspaper? With all the trouble in the world you must have so much to write about... And here comes Mother."

"Are you sure she doesn't know?"

"Mothers know everything about their children. It's part of their inherent instinct. Mr Witherspoon has a very interesting case he's working on. All about a patent another firm has stolen. We're suing them for half a million. Don't understand it myself. But Mr Witherspoon does. Which is all that matters... Hello, Mum. Look who's come for a visit. I hope Dad won't mind but I poured Harry a glass of Dad's whisky. Two in fact. Has he finished the interview?"

"Hasn't started yet."

"Hello, Aunty Betty."

"Nice to see you, Harry. We were expecting you. Can I have one of those whiskies? What a day at the office. Everyone wants to know about the Makoni rally. It's going to be big. Please sit down, Harry. Make yourself comfortable. There's nothing more pleasant than coming home in winter to a roaring log fire. Where's Patrick, Ruthy?"

"I have no idea."

"He's turned my home into a hotel."

"I was telling Harry. Come and sit next to me. How does that glass look?"

"You're not having one, Ruthy?"

"No, I'm not."

Harry, not sure what the hell was going on, looked from mother to daughter. Then he sipped his second whisky. What was done was done. There was nothing he could do about it. And she was right. A whisky in front of the family hearth was indeed pleasant. The first stiff one had mellowed him. He smiled at Ruthy. Ruthy smiled back at him. He smiled at Betty. Betty smiled back at him. Everyone, surprisingly, was perfectly comfortable.

"So how was your day, Harry?"

"A few ups and downs."

"That's life. You need a few ups and downs to make life interesting."

Harry had drunk four glasses of William Smythe's whisky by the time the man himself came home. The almost empty whisky bottle was on top of the cocktail cabinet. Harry watched Mr Smythe look at the bottle and then at Harry. There was no sign of annoyance in the man's face. Before with Ruthy, when they sneaked booze from the cocktail cabinet, they were both given a lecture on using their own money to pay for their drinks. Now the man just smiled at Harry. He knew. They were all waiting. Harry squirmed in his seat. He had no money for all intents and purposes. Everything he earned he spent. Not two hundred pounds in his bank account. With Petronella money had never been an issue. Especially when she was extolling the virtues of communism. Now she was so rich Harry's mind boggled. For Harry, up to the present, money had been a come and go convenience. If he had a bit more he spent a bit more. Never in his life had he found the need to be financially responsible. In Rhodesia with cheap food and cheap booze, it had been even better but always the money was spent. Now he was facing the double responsibility of a wife and a child. As a shorthand typist Ruthy made very little. She lived at home. Drank her father's whisky when he offered it. Now it was all up to Harry. The thought of all that responsibility, when he played it through his mind, positively frightened the shit out of him. They needed a house or a flat. Baby clothes. Prams. Cots. Later there was schooling. Three mouths to feed and all Ruthy was doing from across the room was smiling at him. She was pregnant. With his child. When it came down to finances it was all going to be his responsibility. And Harry hated responsibility. Always had done. Why he had become a reporter. A free and easy life provided he stayed on top of the job.

"Of course you'll stay and have supper," said the man Harry now looked at through very different eyes. Sitting on the couch full of the man's whisky the man looked just like Harry's old headmaster. And Harry had always been intimidated by his old headmaster. Even feared him.

"I'm afraid Mother is waiting for me. Since Bergit married she likes me at home."

"But you have a room in Kensington. Did you go home to see your mother first?"

"No, I didn't."

"Then she won't be expecting you."

"I suppose she won't."

"We can drink a bottle of wine together over supper."

"What did you think of the reverend?" Harry wanted to change the subject, to find a way out of the house and away from his dilemma.

"He's deep in water he doesn't understand. If you ask me he's being manipulated by people supported by the Russians, which shouldn't make sense to a priest. The Russian communists are atheist. The man's a do-gooder when it comes to his mission but he can't see the wood for the trees. Democracy in a country where most of the people can't read or write will end in a tyranny. They'll all vote the way they're told. All part of evolution, I suppose. All that 'wind of change' of Harold Macmillan's. We British want out of the colonies. As cheaply as possible. All those Rhodesian farmers will be tossed on the scrapheap. Britain is going to look nearer to home. To Europe. All those African colonies have become a liability in the modern world dominated by America and Russia. We've lost our power. So we lose what's left of the empire. I asked Harvey in the interview when the missionaries were coming home. Suggested preaching to the masses that the Christian religion had become something of an anachronism for the average member of the British public. He got quite upset with me. The interview was recorded. I do that so I can edit. Airs on Wednesday at nine o'clock. You should listen to it, Harry. So you're staying for supper... Where's Patrick?"

"Gallivanting somewhere with his friends, Dad."

"The young generation. No sense of responsibility. They expect everything to be given to them. As if it was their right."

"Are you editing out the bit about Roman Catholicism being something of an anachronism in today's Africa?"

"Probably. Have the Catholic church on top of me if I don't."

"So what did he say?"

"That God would always be relevant. That when people looked to materialism instead of God they would create for themselves a living hell on earth."

"You should leave that bit in."

"And criticise the god of consumerism? No one would listen to my weekly programme. Have another Scotch."

"Better wait for the wine."

"Well, Ruthy, isn't this fun?"

Then they all smiled at each other. He was caught. No doubt about it. The dance continued into supper, floating around them. Harry was convinced her parents knew. They just didn't want to bring up the subject directly. Everything was friendly innuendo. They were waiting for him to speak. All of them waiting politely. Ahead of him, stretching far ahead of him, lay domestic bliss.

To get home to his room, Harry ordered a taxi. He was drunk. Terrified. Cornered. In the taxi, all he wanted was to have a pee. There was a pub on the side of the road in front of the traffic lights next to where the taxi stopped at the red light.

"This'll do. Changed my mind. It's an hour before closing."

"Suit yourself. Just don't blame me."

"Am I that drunk?"

"You tripped over getting in, mate. Don't trip getting out. Pavements are hard."

"Keep the change."

"What's the problem?"

"My girlfriend's pregnant."

"Blimey. No wonder you're drunk. Them girls should either take precautions or keep their legs crossed. Good luck to you, guv. Bloody hell. You look too young to have kids. Does she want to marry you?"

"Oh, yes."

"Heard that one before. Good luck to you."

The cab driver was laughing to himself as Harry stumbled out of the taxi. He pulled himself up straight. Took a deep, cold breath and walked into the freedom of the pub. It was hot, noisy and felt like home. For the first time that day Harry found sanctuary from his problems.

3

While Harry was hunched over his drink at the bar, not sure exactly where the taxi had dropped him, Woodlands Court was a blaze of lights. Petronella and Elsie were having a party. All the old crowd and some of the new, most of whom said they were staying the night. Mrs Weatherby the housekeeper and Janice the old maid were visibly exhausted. Dylan Flower, alias Mango, despite losing his publicist, was having the time of his life with Harry out of the way, having no idea what was going on between Petronella and Elsie. Petronella was doing her best on a Thursday night to have fun. She had thought she had Harry Wakefield under her thumb only to find out he was sleeping with the mousy little Ruthy behind her back. In a fit of temper she had cut him out of her life and phoned up Elsie. And Elsie had come running, Petronella not sure if it was her or all the money. In one flash of reality she had seen through the whole damn lot of them – Communism with all its false promise of equality, Livingstone Sithole, who used his hatred and jealousy of whites to feather his own nest, having no concern whatsoever for the downtrodden blacks in Rhodesia. On the adage that if you can't beat them join them, she had taken for herself all the power of her grandfather's money. Everyone loved a rich woman. Not surprisingly, the Reverend Harvey Pemberton had wanted some of her money for his mission after lecturing her, telling her a good

Catholic would allow Harry to marry the young girl he had unwittingly impregnated. On both counts she had delighted in telling him to go to hell. The reverend had given her one of his pained expressions that gave the impression he knew so much more than her, and departed. So now it didn't matter: the struggle, communism, her mother, or Harry. She was rich. Mind-bogglingly rich. With all that money they would all do what they were told. The idea of playing off Uncle Horace against Uncle Winfred with her one third of the voting equity of Sheckland-Hall Limited was appealing. At twenty-seven she was a director of a public company. And she knew what she was doing. When it came to publicity and advertising, oh yes, she knew what she was doing. Selling packets of sugar or some sugar-free sweetener was no different to selling concert tickets or records. It was all business. All about making money. And family politics was right up her street. So look out Aunty May and Aunty Barbara and any other bitch who got in her way. By the time she was finished she'd have control of the company. Petronella liked the feeling of power. Making others do what she wanted. So to hell with Harry Wakefield and his pregnant little missy and to hell with Rhodesia and Josiah Makoni. They were all in the past. Tonight was the future. When she'd had enough of Elsie Gilmore she'd kick her out, which made a lesbian relationship so much more convenient. There were no children involved and no legal obligation. Elsie was convenient for now. Elsie with the big bottom and the big round eyes boggling at the prospect of living in luxury for the rest of her life.

"This is so much fun, Petronella."

"Yes it is, Elsie."

"Are you happy?"

"I'm ecstatic."

"So am I. Just look at all these people. Where did they all come from?"

"There's always an army of people waiting to go to a free party."

"But they're all so enjoying themselves."

"Of course they are, darling."

"Do you love me, Petronella?"

"With all my heart... We'll have to get rid of Mrs Weatherby and Janice."

"Why? They've lived here most of their lives."

"They're too old."

"Where will they go?"

"That's their problem. They worked for my grandfather. Not for me."

"You'll give them a nice fat pension?"

"I'll think about it... What's wrong with Dylan Flower? He keeps giving me the eye. So does Richard Maguire."

"Have I got competition?"

"Of course not. I told you. From now on I'm strictly a lesbian. I'm sick of men."

"Will he marry her?"

"Good luck to him. By the time Harry's fifty he'll be bald and hen-pecked, bored out of his mind and thinking of me... Mrs Weatherby, you and Janice had better go to bed. This is too much for you. These kind of people pour their own booze. Leave it all out on the table."

"Thank you, Miss Petronella."

"And call me Miss Maple. I'm not a child anymore."

"Yes, Miss Maple. Goodnight, Miss Maple."

They watched the old woman go.

"You're not going to fire her?"

"She's not much good to us. Looking after Grandfather was one thing. Now she'd have to work. We all get put out to grass in the end."

"She'll be lost and lonely on her own."

"Stop worrying about other people. They never worry about you. Unless it suits them."

"You've changed, Petronella."

"Grown up more likely. We all start off trying to look like altruists when we want other people to give us things. Part of human nature. When the house is finally transferred into my name we'll have a proper housewarming party. Why does probate take so long? My uncles think I'm going to be a pussy. Easy to manipulate, unlike their sister my mother. No wonder they wanted Grandfather to leave me his shares. Oh dear, oh dear. How wrong can you be? Can't wait to throw my weight around... Have another drink, Elsie. Put some wood on the fire. We're throwing a party. One big, bloody party... So what do you think of my house, Richard?" The man had come up behind her.

"We're going to miss you at Downtown Music. What are you going to do with your publicity business?"

"Bring it into Sheckland-Hall Limited and employ someone to run it. We'll have the real clout of money behind our publicity campaigns. Bigger fees, better results."

"Aren't they a sugar company?"

"I'm going to turn the old family business on its head. Make it a conglomerate. You want to sell Downtown Music, Richard? You have to diversify the risk in this modern age of business. Learnt that doing economics at Manchester University. Politics, philosophy and economics. My degree, Richard. I started with politics and philosophy. Now it's the turn of economics. Are you staying the night?"

"If you'll let me."

"I'm with Elsie tonight. I mean really with Elsie. Didn't you know?"

"No, I didn't."

"There are lots of spare bedrooms in the old family house. Did you know we started the family fortune growing sugar cane in the West Indies? Using slaves. Kind of ironic don't you think?"

"You've changed, Petronella."

"So everyone is telling me. Enjoy your evening. And don't forget. You ever want to sell the record company you come to me."

When her old boss and one-time lover left half an hour later, Petronella wasn't surprised. Men were like that when they couldn't get what they wanted. Richard Maguire and Dylan left together, Petronella thinking they must have talked about her lesbian lover. For the first time since Harry told her he had made another girl pregnant, she was enjoying herself. If there was one thing Petronella had learnt in her twenty-seven years of life, a girl had to look after herself. All those nice-talking people were only interested in themselves.

Surprisingly, at the end of the evening most of the guests had gone home. A few, more drunk than the rest, had taken up Petronella's offer of a room. In the morning they too had gone. People were like that in the cold light of dawn; sober, hungover and wanting to get the hell out of the way... They had not made love, Petronella restlessly sleeping through the night. There was something wrong. She had all the money and with it the power but something was wrong. In the small hours of the pitch-dark night it came to her. Despite the way she had trivialised her relationship with Harry, only saying she was serious when it suited her, she really loved the damn man. She was jealous of pregnant Ruthy.

Jealous of an ordinary life with an ordinary family in an ordinary house in the suburbs. In the middle of the night, with Elsie's big bare bottom pressed into her, she wanted to be like everyone else. When the light finally stole into the room, pushing its wintry way through the window, she was still wide awake.

"What's the time?"

"Go back to sleep, Elsie."

"You're not really going to fire Mrs Weatherby and Janice?"

"Of course I'm not. They're family."

"Give me a cuddle."

Petronella was still thinking what she wanted to do with the rest of her life when Elsie went back to sleep. The next thing Petronella remembered was Janice bringing in the morning tea.

"Good morning, Miss Maple."

"What's all this Miss Maple? I'm plain Petronella, Janice."

"Good morning, Petronella. I've brought you both a cup of tea."

"Do we still have any guests left?"

"They've all gone. The last one left the front door open."

"How nice of them. Downstairs must be freezing."

"The sun's shining outside."

"So it is."

On the bare elm trees outside Petronella could see a pale, wintry sunlight. A pigeon was calling, answered by its friend. There was the sound of traffic far away.

"It's Friday. The rest of them had to work. What's for breakfast, Janice?"

"Whatever you both want."

"Are you happy, Janice?"

"Of course I am. Just sad the old gentleman died. We're both going to miss him, Mrs Weatherby and me. Miss him terribly. Your grandfather was the perfect gentleman. Never forgot he didn't, my Barney who was killed in the Great War. Came through it himself without a scratch did the old gentleman. All those years in the trenches and he never got a scratch. Said it taught him humanity, whatever that means. He was a good man, your grandfather. I'll be in the kitchen when you want your breakfast. My word, how the world has changed. My Barney was only twenty-one. Well, no point looking back. What's done was done. What I don't understand is why people fight wars in the first place. What was it all about? Now it doesn't matter. Except I never had my life with Barney."

The old woman was crying when she went out of the room. So was Petronella. As much for herself as Janice. After blowing her nose and putting on a smile, Petronella got up. It was another day. Maybe one day she would work out what she was really up to. The pigeon was still calling from the world outside. 'Damn Harry,' she thought. She couldn't get him out of her mind.

THE REVEREND HARVEY PEMBERTON at forty-eight was feeling old. He was tired, exhausted, not sure anymore. Maintaining the Good Faith Mission was a permanent uphill battle. The church provided some of the funding but the rest was up to him: school books, pens, paper, a reference library, maintaining the school buildings, paying the teachers, feeding the kids lunch most often their only meal of the day, the half pint of milk he bought from the local subsistence farmers to give them some cash income. It never stopped. The Catholic church had paid for the school buildings that surrounded their church. Paid his own pittance of a salary enough to pay for his food. And now she had all that money and didn't want to give him any. He was always the one doing the giving and now he was tired. All day he had gone round London asking for donations, asking for support for the rally to free Josiah Makoni. It was like getting blood out of a stone. They all mouthed platitudes but when it came to putting their hands in their pockets it mostly came down to promises or a small donation to satisfy their consciences. In the early days it had all seemed so much more fun. More worthwhile. More satisfying. Now he wasn't so sure whether good deeds and politics went hand in hand. It seemed to Harvey that he and Livingstone Sithole were coming from different directions.

"Can't you give some of this huge amount of money you have raised for the struggle to my kids?"

"Whatever for? When the struggle is won they'll be free. What more could they want? Every penny we get goes to fighting the oppressors."

"Your fellow white men, Reverend. You should go and ask all those rich white farmers for money. Not us. We need buses to bring our supporters to tomorrow's rally. And buses cost money. You need a lot of money to fight a revolution. Why are you asking me for money? What about all your friends in England? It should be me asking you for money, not the other way round. Now, tomorrow, I want you in the front. Near the television cameras. Mango is helping to lead the march. A pop icon and a priest will look good next to me in the morning papers. Don't worry about your mission. It's the rally that counts. The struggle for freedom. We're on the same side, Reverend. Think what will happen to Rhodesia when we win. Look to your children's future in the new Zimbabwe. Support the struggle. With every pound you can raise. The cause. It's the cause that will save your children."

"Is she going to give the money to the cause?"

"For some reason Petronella and I no longer see eye to eye. She's become a stinking capitalist like the rest of them. Forget the woman. She's sold out to the enemy. Money corrupts them. Now off you go and get ready for tomorrow. We're massing at Trafalgar Square before marching on the Houses of Parliament. It's going to be a great day for the cause. Pressure on the British government for one man one vote in Rhodesia. Then we'll have them. Without having to bring an army. Think of that, Reverend. Tell your friends. If they don't want a war they must force the Smith government in Salisbury to back down now. To give us all the vote."

"But you'll kill people if you bring in your freedom fighters from the camps."

"Someone always gets hurt in a struggle. Tomorrow, Reverend. Ten o'clock. Tell your friends. We want liberation. And bring some money."

The man was laughing at him.

At nine o'clock on the Saturday morning Harvey walked out into the street. It was bitterly cold, an east wind biting through his clothes to the very marrow of his bones. He had rented the cheapest room he could find to give himself freedom of movement. Staying with friends was always nice but had obligations. He had three more days in England before flying home for the start of the school term. At the mission he was more a teacher than a priest, the school taking up most of his time. The three meetings with the London Missionary Society had gone as well as expected despite there being no forthcoming of funds. Money. He was always looking for funds. Supporting his kids past and present. Thinking of Josiah incarcerated in a government bush camp for potential terrorists made him sad. Josiah made him sad. From the young excited boy thirsty for knowledge, he had come back from Fort Hare a bitter young man. At Fort Hare his fellow students had twisted his mind. Instead of Jesus Christ, Socrates and the love of man it was all about politics and the power to be found in 'promising the world' to the masses. Harvey had tried to explain it wasn't that easy. That society was complex. That everyone needed each other, the blacks needing the whites as much as the whites needed the blacks. That one created the jobs and one provided the labour. With the bottom of his cassock flowing around his feet as he strode against the wind, he tried to think of the warmth of his small house on the mission but the cold just wouldn't go away. There was no point in praying to God about the weather: He had far better things to do with the world of man in such a turmoil. His wide brimmed black hat kept off the first drops of icy cold rain, the rain making him physically miserable. His black cape would lose the battle against wind and rain. And he had not even had himself a proper breakfast. Tea and toast in the little bedsitter. What Harvey missed most as a Catholic priest was a wife. Someone to give him backup. Someone to listen to his moans. Most of the time, surrounded by all the children, he was lonely. And God was not always good company, constantly admonishing, telling him what he had done wrong. A wife would have given him the comfort of home. The companionship. Some children of his own. Sometimes, like now, his life was bleak.

Walking faster, fighting the cold and rain, it took Harvey twenty minutes to walk to Trafalgar Square. There were people milling around Nelson's Column, some standing on the steps. Many had placards demanding the release of Josiah, others demanding 'one man one vote'. They all looked excited. Most of them were young. On the top step, right underneath the towering statue of Lord Nelson on his plinth, stood Livingstone Sithole surrounded by people, some Harvey recognised as members of the Anti-Apartheid movement who were supporting the rally. Harvey acknowledged the man's wave. The rain had stopped briefly thank goodness. Far more than Livingstone, the press were interested in the man called Mango who sang the songs of freedom. There were men and women with cameras all round Mango, flash lights constantly popping. Harvey stood back, people making room for a priest. He stood on his own. No one took any notice of him. He wished he was back on the mission, sitting in his garden under the shade of a msasa tree looking at the riot of colour among the tropical flowers, the birds singing, peace on his patch of earth, Robson bringing him a pot of tea, his cat on his lap, his dogs at his feet. He was tired. He was old. He was cold. He was hungry. Where he was, God and the world had deserted him.

"Morning, Reverend Pemberton. You look freezing cold. Don't the church supply their priests with thick overcoats? That cape is far too flimsy for an English winter."

"Hello, Harry. Nice to see a familiar face."

"Did you see Petronella and tell her to keep away from me? She's dumped me."

"Please, Harry. I can't face any more acrimony today."

"There's a Lyons Corner House not far away. Let me buy you a hot cup of coffee. Nothing's going to happen for a while. I saw you wave at Livingstone. If you ask me, everyone is more interested in Mango of Mango Boys fame than they are in politics and Josiah Makoni. Do you know Sidney Cross? He's our photographer. Old friend of mine. When I first met Petronella I was with Sidney. How is she?... Come on. Have you had your breakfast? You should look after yourself. You'll catch a cold or pneumonia. You're shivering, Harvey. You'd better take my overcoat."

"What about you?"

"I'm young and haven't lived most of my life in the tropics. Just look at him, Sidney. He's blue in the face. Josiah's better off than you. He may be locked up by Smith but he'll be well fed and sitting in the shade of a tree reading a good book. I heard that camp has a library. That they are letting the inmates further their studies by correspondence. Hoping they'll learn something of value to temper their rabid politics... Now, isn't that better. Lead the way, Sidney. This man needs a cup of coffee and a bun."

"I haven't got any money."

"Didn't she give you some of her grandfather's fortune?"

"Not a penny."

"Oh, well. Whoever said there wasn't such a thing as a free breakfast?"

"Are you going to marry the girl?"

"Please, Harvey. You yourself said you can't face any more problems this morning. Let's say we're talking. We've been friends all our lives. Best friends. If it wasn't for Petronella embedded under my skin there wouldn't be a problem. For the more pragmatic giving advice, they say friendship is more lasting than love. That love is another word for lust, which, once satiated, leaves forever, while friendship stays. You're a priest. What's your advice, Harvey? What did you tell Petronella?"

"She gets off on controlling people."

"I didn't know priests knew such words."

"I'm just as human as you. Same instincts. I took a vow of chastity but it doesn't mean I'm not tempted by the devil. Or a girl with the oozing sex appeal of Petronella."

"Just one look at her grabs my hormones. Sidney's a married man so he doesn't see these things anymore. Do you Sidney?"

"Don't you believe it. Find me a man who says he isn't still looking and you'll find a liar. Whatever age we get to. Built into us. Right from puberty. Oh, she's sexy, all right. Something in the eyes. In the movement of her body. It's likely subconscious but everything she does is suggestive. Sexually suggestive. It's just the odd one like Petronella who carries so much attraction for men. In men it's mostly money that turns on women. In women it's the promise for men of sexual satisfaction. All-consuming, final satisfaction... Here we are. Priests before plebs, Reverend. Oh, isn't that nice? It's so warm inside. The smell of coffee. Bacon and eggs. What more could a man want on a cold Saturday morning?... There's a table empty over there."

"Lead on, Sidney."

Harvey took off his overcoat and gave it back to Harry. He was still shivering. Inside his heart was warm from the gesture out in the street. He was coming down with something, no doubt about it. The small table for four sat them comfortably. In the centre was a wooden stand with the usual condiments and a bottle of tomato sauce. The girl who waited on them wore a short dress. She saw him shivering. He took his black hat off his head and put it on the table.

"Are you all right? Are you a priest or something?"

"Roman Catholic. It's cold outside. I live in Africa."

"Do you now?... So what will it be?"

Harvey watched Harry order them the full breakfast with coffee. When the coffee came the smell was delicious. He was feeling better, warm except for his feet. The shivering had stopped.

"You're not going on that rally, Harvey. Forget it. I'm ordering you a taxi after breakfast and sending you home."

"Livingstone doesn't need me. He wants money. Why is it always money, Sidney?"

"In women it's basic instinct. Money means home and food for her children. After wanting to find a man for herself the strongest instinct underneath everything else in a woman is wanting to have children. According to my wife. She only told me that after she married me. Before that it was all about love... What a filthy day outside. I've got shots of Mango. Should be enough. You don't really think a rally like this will do any good for Josiah? It's all about upping the protesters' profile. And we in the press fall for it every time."

"People like to read about other people's problems," said Harry. "Makes their own problems just that little bit better. Someone else suffering. Makes them feel good. We don't feel so miserable with our own little lives... Miss, can you bring us some more toast? Harvey, when did you last have a proper meal?"

"Not since I left Rhodesia. Sorry, my mouth's full. Food is like a blood transfusion. I'll be all right for the rally. Just this little human kindness has been as good for me, Harry, as the food and coffee. Thank you. It's lonely on your own."

"God is with you, Harvey."

"I hope so. I really hope so. Sometimes I'm not so sure. Tell me about Ruthy."

"You remember her name?"

"Of course I do."

"You worry too much about other people."

"That's my job. Why didn't you ever visit me on the mission after that first interview?"

"Didn't think you wanted the company. There were people everywhere."

"Yes, I suppose there were."

"You can keep my coat for the rally."

"Wouldn't look right with the hat... Thank you. Both of you. When you are married, Harry, and visiting your sister in Rhodesia, you must bring your family to visit me on the mission. We have our own beautiful church. Very quiet and peaceful. We can all pray together...

So, now we march to the Houses of Parliament and try to make a difference."

"Does it really make any difference?"

"To ourselves if nothing else. It gives us hope."

Soon after, the girl with the short dress and the apron brought them the bill. Harvey watched Harry pay the waitress.

"That was a very generous tip, Harry."

"It's what she works for. Tips. All she really has to look forward to during the day. We'll be rejoining the rest of our friends in the press corps. You're on your own, Reverend."

4

————

While the Reverend Harvey Pemberton was building up his courage to overcome the cold, Livingstone Sithole on the other side of the square was marshalling the troops in preparation for the start of the march to the Houses of Parliament. Parliament wasn't sitting on the Saturday but the image on television was what mattered. What the people saw in their homes. Mango holding a placard demanding the release of Josiah Makoni with a backdrop of the British Houses of Parliament. What the politicians did was of less concern to Livingstone. In the end he was sure ZANU would have to fight for their liberation. After a well-publicised rally the public's conscience would be pricked and donations rolled into the party coffers. Everywhere he turned they were screaming for more money: the people in the training camp in Tanzania were constantly on his back, money all they ever asked him for; back home, the party needed funds to go about their business and pay the staff. All the Russians ever gave were arms and a few personnel to train the guerrilla army. And to add to his problem Petronella, saying her grandfather had cut off her allowance, had wanted to be paid. And when the old man died leaving her a fortune she did nothing for the cause, making Livingstone wonder why she joined the party in the first place with all the good talk about helping his people. What had been her motive? A person who went against their own people was always suspect to Livingstone. And that included any whites in Rhodesia including Reverend Pemberton now walking towards him. What were they after? What were they doing? To Livingstone, all of them were sell-outs to be treated with suspicion.

"Ah, Reverend. You look cold."

"Us Africans, Livingstone. Not used to this dreadful climate. Are we marching? Have you got a placard for me?"

"You're shivering."

"All in a good cause. Once we're on the move I'll warm up again."

"Mango on my right. You, Reverend, on my left... Everyone! Are you all ready? Let's go and deliver our message... Freedom! Freedom! Freedom to the people."

Like a tired old snake with a hissing head the Josiah Makoni rally got on its way. The tall black man with a face full of determination flanked by a flamboyant pop singer and a black-capped, black-caped priest, flash bulbs popping all round them from the circling members of the popular press, television cameras on shoulders, policemen on horses and people, thousands of people gawping at the spectacle, many of whom couldn't have found Rhodesia on the map if their lives depended on it. One of the horses shied when someone from the crowd tossed a firecracker in front of the march almost at Livingstone's feet. In solidarity for the cameras, the front three joined arms and continued the chant 'Freedom! Freedom!' as the snake made its way down the street. For a moment Livingstone wished it were all over. The struggle, the arguments, the permanent fight for money. All he wanted was a thatched hut on the Ruia River, a cooking pot over the fire, the sun warm on his skin, the three family cows grazing in the distance, a bird of prey calling high up in the blueness of the sky, calling for the sheer joy of flying, the smell of woodsmoke and peace, glorious, perfect peace with only his friends and family anywhere near him. Instead, he gripped the arms of two white men whose people had shattered his world, his face wet and cold from the dripping rain, telling himself it was all for the cause and all would be over soon.

"Are you all right, Livingstone? You're hurting my arm."

"Sorry, Reverend. I was thinking. That one day this will all be over."

"It's never over until the day we die and go up to heaven. There's always something else. Always a next hurdle. God testing us. Seeing if one day we will be worthy to sit at his side. Think of your friend Josiah without his freedom. That should concentrate your mind."

"You're shivering, Reverend. Is there something wrong with you?"

"A cold. A touch of flu. God testing me. I believe in God so I'll be fine. Don't you worry about me. It's Josiah we worry about today. Your arm is giving me warmth, Livingstone. Just not so tight. And never forget. Tomorrow the sun will be shining. Or the next day. Or the one after that. Lift up your heart and soul. God is guiding both of us. We are marching for the elevation of our fellow man. For a better world where we all love each other and live in harmony right across the globe."

"You're preaching, Reverend."

"Probably. Takes my mind off the cold."

Livingstone could feel Harvey Pemberton shiver as they marched, the shiver going right through the man's body. The reverend was suffering. And for what? Did he truly believe in the cause or was his God giving him the chance to make penance and the courage to go on?

"You should be in bed."

"Probably. I came over to raise awareness of Josiah's plight and now is the day. Let's hope it does some good. Sensible people sit down and talk a way through their differences. Let's hope we're all sensible, Livingstone. Or we'll all destroy the country we love. You, me, Josiah, and every one of us in the country we call Rhodesia."

"We call it Zimbabwe."

"It's the same country. Same people... Do you ever pray?"

"Not very often. We believe in the ancestors giving us a path to the god that made us. Sometimes I talk to my ancestors. The people who made my own life possible. Through them I have life. Once I met one of the ancestors on a rainy night when the Ruia River was flooding. I tried to cross the river when I should have stayed where I was. Halfway into the river with the water up to my knees a surge of water came at me out of the dark of the night and swept me off my feet. I was drowning, pushed over by the flood of the river against the opposite bank, unable to get a grip on a rock or a tree. A hand came out of the driving rain and pulled me out of the river up onto the bank. It was a very old man. How he had the strength to pull me out of the raging water was a miracle. I lay flat on my face shaking with fear. When I recovered and stood up on my feet to thank the old man he was gone. No one was there. I called but no one answered, the rain still lashing my face. I was so happy to be alive. A young man with his life ahead of him. When I got home and told my father he said I had been saved from the river by one of the ancestors. That I had done something good.

'*What have you done that is so good that brought the ancestor to help you?*' he asked me.

'*I've brought you a gift, Father. I've passed five O Levels in my school examinations. From Oxford and Cambridge in England. They set our exam papers. They are very difficult. All your saving to send me to school has been worth it. I have in my pocket the results. For you, Father. The paper is wet but you can still see what it says. I'll read it to you. The first O Level was for mathematics.*'

'*You made your ancestor proud of you. Why he saved you from the river.*'

'*When I tried to thank him nobody was there.*'

'*You are a lucky man to be visited by an ancestor.*'

"My father was so proud of me all those years ago."

"So was the ancestor, the messenger of God. My church would call him an angel. Be good with your life, Livingstone. You have been given two lives on this earth. Don't waste them. Give the last one to the people who share your ancestor."

"You think he was the messenger of God?"

"Of course he was. Our lives may have evolved separately but we are all the same. All the children of God, in whom we have faith... Now I feel better. I've stopped shivering. Your story has restored my faith in God. God has stopped my shivering."

At the Houses of Parliament Livingstone Sithole gave a speech into a microphone, his voice ringing out over the crowds of people. Mango sang his song about saving Josiah. The reverend blessed the crowd for supporting the downtrodden blacks in Rhodesia, people without a say, people without a vote. A petition was handed to a policeman at the Houses of Parliament, the wind and rain buffeting the three sheets of paper that Livingstone had had typed in the ZANU office the previous day. Then the police on horseback told them all to move on. The rally was over.

"Do you have anything to say to the *Daily Mirror*?" asked Harry Wakefield. Harry was surrounded by fellow reporters from the newspapers and television. His hands and feet were cold. Surprisingly to

Harry, Harvey Pemberton looked quite normal. Without Harry's overcoat. Harry knew without his thick overcoat he himself would not have survived in the wind and rain. The priest smiled at him, Harry smiling back. Livingstone Sithole had ignored his question.

"Where's the rest of the band, Mango?" someone else called. It was the music critic of the *Daily Mail* where Harry's father had worked most of his life. The man had visited the Wakefield family home in Chelsea on more than one occasion. He had a cynical expression on his face.

"Got more sense than to come out in this."

"Want a drink in the pub, Mango?... Give us an interview?"

"Why not? Don't forget, it's not about me but Josiah Makoni."

"Heard that one before," said someone Harry couldn't see.

"True as bob. Done this for Josiah."

"Good for you, Mango."

Harry watched Mango, who Harry knew better as Dylan Flower, go off with the man from the *Mail*.

"You want to follow them, Harry?" said Sidney Cross. "I'm done taking pictures for today. He looks quite normal after what he looked like in the Lyons Corner House."

"He just might be one of those rarities, Sidney. A good man. Maybe there is a God. God looks after his own. This weather is enough to freeze the balls off a brass monkey."

"Do you believe in God, Harry?"

"I'm an agnostic. I don't know. But he believes. Look at him. Wet through in the freezing rain and he's smiling. Almost serene."

"A truly good man? That one I don't believe in."

"You're a cynic, Sidney."

"A realist, Harry. They all try to look good. What's our Livingstone really up to? Mango's easy. All this press and television sells records. Fills the stadium when he sings."

"That was Petronella promoting him. It's just the reverend I'm not sure about. What's in it for him personally? Let's go and find our own pub, Sidney, and get drunk by a nice big warm fire."

"The wife will kill me."

"Got to have fun sometimes."

"Just this once."

"That's more like the old Sidney."

"Why wasn't Petronella here?"

"Given up good deeds. Now she's stinking rich she doesn't have to pretend anymore."

"Do you want her still?"

"She doesn't want me. Anyway, I'm getting married to Ruthy."

"Whatever for?"

"She's pregnant."

"You old fox. No wonder Petronella dumped you. Did she find out?"

"I told her. Did you see Harvey go?"

"Livingstone put him into a taxi. I saw Livingstone pay the driver."

"Miracles never cease."

"I'm going to drink neat whisky."

"So am I."

"Warms the cockles of your heart... Why is the English weather always so bloody awful?"

"Wouldn't have had an empire without the lousy weather. All those people who went to India, Australia and Africa would have stayed at home."

"Never looked at it that way."

"Also had something to do with the merchant navy."

"There's a pub over there."

"Let's run for it. It's starting to rain cats and dogs."

"So what are we all going to do without an empire, Harry?"

"Stay at home. Find a warm pub. Get drunk."

"Sounds good to me."

PETRONELLA WATCHED Harry and his friend go into the Chancellor's Arms across the road with mixed feelings, the rain dripping from the rim of the hat she had pulled down as much to disguise herself as keep out the rain. She was wearing a plastic raincoat over her warmest overcoat with a plastic cover over the wide-brimmed hat. She was cold, her feet and hands numb. Rhodesia at that moment among the ancient buildings of Westminster was a nostalgic memory of sunshine and warmth. No one had noticed her as she watched her old friends with their placards chant for freedom. She no longer belonged. It was a sad feeling. All the wealth in the world could not make a girl belong as she had in the communist and Zimbabwe African National Union movement her old compatriots referred to as ZANU. From being the centre of ZANU's London chapter she was standing alone, cold and desolate on the pavement watching her old lover disappear into the warmth of a three-hundred-year-old English public house. The idea of a stiff drink was less appealing than the thought of all that company. Enthusiastic company with all the passion and excitement of wanting to change a depressing world, a world that wasn't as nice as people liked to make out. She was lonely standing on the pavement. Elsie was at home in the place Petronella still thought of as her grandfather's, making herself quite the woman of the house. She was the wife in the relationship, the homemaker, quite content to sit inside on a cold winter's day and let Janice and Mrs Weatherby run around after her bringing whatever took her fancy from moment to moment. The once communist ZANU activist was now more comfortable sitting beside the fire. Elsie never so much as mentioned working at Sainsbury's. That was all in her past. Now she was lady of the manor with her feet up in front of the fire, her future taken care of, not a worry in the world. For a brief moment Petronella thought of running across the road, going into the pub and throwing her arms around Harry and telling her former lover it was him that she wanted. But underneath she wasn't sure. She wasn't sure about anything except she wanted to belong. To Harry, to ZANU, to anything. With Elsie it was the other way round. Elsie was quite content being belonged, the passive, accepting part of the relationship with all the important decisions left to Petronella. It was no good running across into the pub. The mousy girl was pregnant. The mousy girl belonged. The mousy girl was going to belong to her own family for the rest of her life at the centre of attention without an outside care in the world.

Petronella sighed and looked around. Three old buses were picking up the supporters who were dumping their 'free Josiah' placards in the luggage compartments in the vehicles' sides. Despite the rain the marchers all looked excited. They had been to a rally. They had done something good. The buses would drop them off in groups at the main London railway stations where the trains would take them home in groups, all of them belonging. In the old days she would have been part of them. Instead she had two alternatives. She could go straight home to Woodlands Court on the train and take a taxi from the station, or she could visit her Uncle Horace in his Piccadilly townhouse overlooking rain-soaked Green Park and talk business. Neither idea was attractive. Longingly, she looked across at the Chancellor's Arms. Then she laughed. One thing was certain. Living with Elsie as her partner, she was never going to fall pregnant.

Trying to remember which was the nearest Tube station, Petronella walked away. The buses had gone. So had most of the crowd. She was alone. Totally, absolutely alone.

PART IX

FEBRUARY 1965

FUNERAL PYRE FOR A LION

1
————

*J*eremy Crookshank received his invitation to Harry Wakefield's wedding at the height of the reaping season. The rains had been good through January and the first two weeks of February. There had been no rain for two days. The curing barns were full of Virginia tobacco, each barn taking nine days to cure before steam was pumped in to give moisture to the dry leaves so they wouldn't break when the hands of tobacco were taken from the barns to the bulks where they would stay in piles awaiting grading in the grading sheds. With all his barns full, Jeremy had driven in the truck to the post office in the small village of Centenary. Each farmer had a post box where he collected his mail. The boys were at school and Bergit at home. At three and a half months into her pregnancy, Bergit preferred to avoid the jolts and bumps of the dirt road.

"Well, I'll be buggered. What brought that on so suddenly?"

The invitation was for the third week in March just five weeks away. Jeremy smiled. 'She's pregnant. Ruthy is pregnant. What the hell happened to Petronella?' he thought, sitting in the truck where he had opened the envelope. The rest of the mail looked like bills. During the growing season the bills built up, most of them only to be paid when the auction floors opened in April and the money came in. Growing a crop of tobacco cost a large amount of money. Jeremy, like the rest of the farmers, left the bills on his office desk, putting off the paperwork for as long as possible. All of them hated paperwork. They were farmers not office workers. With the Centenary sports club close to the post office, Jeremy decided the wedding invitation called for a drink. He liked Harry. They were going to be brothers-in-law. Related for the rest of their lives. 'Well, there's a thing. Our kids will be first cousins.'

Jeremy turned the truck off the small section of tarred road that led through the village of Centenary and drove up past the cricket field to the club. There were four cars parked in the driveway. The bar was always open. Four women in white dresses were playing tennis behind the parked cars. Jeremy waved to them as he stepped out of the truck. One of the women called 'forty-love' as she waved back at Jeremy. It was Mary Barry, wife of the member-in-charge, the most senior policeman in the block. Inside the club, Clay Barry was sitting up at the bar.

"Aren't you working today, Clay?"

"What brings you to the club in the reaping season? What are you having?"

"All the barns are full. If any more of the tobacco ripens I'm in the shit. I'll have a Castle. Cold as you've got, Noah. I don't mind heat at this time of year, it's the humidity that gets me. You remember that chap Harry Wakefield who worked for the newspaper? He's Bergit's brother. He's getting married in England next month to Bergit's best friend. Didn't you meet Ruthy?"

"I rather think I did. Pretty girl. Are you going over for the wedding?"

"We'll have to. Bobby can look after World's View for a couple of weeks. It's his fifth tobacco season. Primrose is quite capable of looking after the boys at the weekends when they come home from Umvukwes. Bobby will pick them up from school. I'll go down to the Isle of Wight and visit my mother. She gets lonely on her own. My brother Paul is so busy these days running the Brigandshaw business he never gets a chance to go down for a visit. We'll fly Central African Airways direct to London. Stops in Nairobi... Thanks, Clay. Cheers. Here's to the happy couple."

"You'll freeze in England."

"Probably."

"How's the crop?"

"I need more curing barns. Always the same at the peak periods. So, what are you doing here at lunchtime on Tuesday?"

"Same as you. Drinking a beer. The station is quiet. For once everyone is behaving themselves."

"Mary's playing tennis."

"My excuse for a beer. Lunch in the club with my wife."

"Bergit's looking after the baby. She's so excited."

"It isn't born!"

"Doesn't matter to Bergit. She sits with both hands holding her stomach and smiles. Never seen a woman so happy."

"Wait till it keeps her up all night."

"She'll cross that bridge when she gets to it... This beer does taste good. The first one doesn't touch the sides."

"So when are you going?"

"Next month. Shotgun wedding if you ask me. Ruthy always did fancy Harry. Now she's got him. Friends since they were kids."

"It'll work. Those kinds of marriages work. When the bloom wears off they'll still be friends... George here tells me a lion is killing his *mombes*. Rubbish if you ask me."

"I tell you it's a lion," George Stacy growled from his corner.

"Have you seen it?"

"I can show you the spoor, Clay. It's a bloody lion. What else could kill a full-grown cow?"

"You got a point there. Just after the war they shot out the game to get rid of the tsetse fly and make this area fit for human habitation and farming. Wild animals don't fall sick from the tsetse like domestic cattle and ourselves. Sleeping sickness is a terrible way to go. Saw a chap with sleeping sickness in the Zambezi Valley when I first came out to Rhodesia. Poor fellow was in a hell of a state. Died a week later. You don't want to get sleeping sickness. Still no cure. Why we haven't seen lions in the block before. Are you sure it is a lion and not one of our federated brethren making it look like a lion so he can have beef for supper?"

"I'm telling you it's a lion. I know a lion kill when I see one. No offence to you, Jeremy, bringing back bad memories."

"My wife wasn't in the Centenary when she was killed by lions, George. She had driven as far as the Zambezi escarpment. Carmen was drunk. Lost."

"Your poor boys."

"So what are you going to do about your lion, George?" Clay was enjoying himself. It wasn't the first time George Stacy had got the police out on a wild-goose chase.

"I've set the bugger a trap. An old sheep died. Don't like eating sheep when they die of natural causes. Put the bloody sheep in the shed that houses the pump down by the dam. Series of rope and string to my double-barrelled shotgun's triggers. So when our lion grabs the sheep he'll set off the gun and shoot himself in the back of the head."

"Have another drink, George. When you show me a dead lion, I'll believe you."

"True as bob, Clay, it's a lion."

"How many cows has it killed?"

"Just the one. She was my best breeder. Every bloody year that old cow produced a calf. Looked after them. Always bulls."

"A bit like your bullshit, George."

"You'll see when we shoot the lion."

"Careful you don't shoot yourself, that's more likely. Sounds real Heath Robinson, your gun trap. Why don't you sit up at night with a flashlight? Hear a noise near your old sheep and turn on the light. Bang. Bang. Dead lion."

"I've tried that."

"You shot at the bugger?"

"Stop taking the piss out of me, Clay. No, I sat up last night but the bugger didn't come. I have to work during the day. Can't sit up every night waiting for the lion. It's the reaping season. I'll phone you when my gun trap goes off."

"You do that... Now. What are you having, George?"

"Make mine a Castle, Clay. So you're going back to England, Jeremy? Haven't been home for twenty years. Parents are dead. Had no brothers and sisters. Can't see the point. By now I'll have nothing in common with the chaps from school... Make it the coldest you've got, Noah."

"How's this year's crop, George?"

"Not bad, Jeremy. See what it looks like after grading. Just hope we get last year's prices. Do you think Smith will declare UDI?"

"No politics in the bar."

"Just a question. How the hell are we going to make a living if the British apply sanctions and won't buy our tobacco?"

"There are always ways round sanctions."

"What do you know about exporting tobacco? You're a policeman."

"Let's say I've heard the government have a plan."

"I bloody well hope so. What a mess. Hate to see all my hard work in Africa over the years come to nothing. Have to go back to England with my tail between my legs. That would be terrible."

"We'll survive, even with sanctions."

"Are you behind Smith, Clay?"

"No politics in the bar, George. Anyway, I'm a civil servant. Do what I'm told to do. It's the politicians who make the decisions."

"Hope they make the right one. It's all a bit of a mess. I hear they're letting that Josiah Makoni out of jail. Pressure from London. Now there's a bloody terrorist if ever I saw one. He'll flee the country the moment they let him out of that camp and start stirring more of his shit. I heard he was training terrorists in a bush camp in Zambia before they locked him up. Or was it Tanzania? Once a *terr*, always a *terr*. What you say, Clay? Why the hell did they let him out?"

Jeremy watched them while he drank his beer. Clay had gone quiet. The lion had been forgotten. All three of them were thinking of the bigger predator. A well-trained guerrilla army. Trained by the Russians. Jeremy swallowed the last of his beer. He shuddered. It was as if someone had walked over his grave.

"Give us another round, Noah. For everyone in the bar. The conversation just got depressing. Didn't know he was out. Petronella will be pleased."

"You know Josiah Makoni?"

"Not exactly, George. He was educated by a friend of my father's. The same man that suggested after the war I come to Rhodesia. Harry Brigandshaw. I wonder what Harry would think of UDI and terrorism were he alive? I hope your trap gets your old lion. Did you set the trap properly?"

"Perfectly, Jeremy. The old bugger will get a blast right in the back of his head. Then I'll skin him with his head still attached and put him on the floor in the lounge."

"You can't do that exactly, George. Not if he blows his head off."

"You're right. Hadn't thought of that. It'll just be the skin on the floor. Teach the bugger to kill my cows."

"He only killed one."

"So far. Once lions kill domestic animals and find it easy, they don't hunt in the bush. My old cow couldn't do ten miles an hour."

The lion was kept in the conversation as they drank the next round. There wasn't a great deal to tell each other except talk about tobacco. Anything new in the club conversation was welcomed. They had known each other for years. They had all heard each other's stories a dozen times. Jeremy smiled to himself. Sitting at the bar in the club talking about a phantom lion made for a pleasant afternoon. It was their main form of entertainment. No one wanted to talk about Josiah Makoni and what was going to happen in the future. They all wanted to live in the present. The right now. Jeremy had been looking at Noah when George said Josiah Makoni was being let out of jail. The barman's eyes had lit up with excitement. When he saw Jeremy looking at him he had picked up one of the wet glasses standing washed on a cloth on the bar and began to polish furiously. Jeremey kept watching him until he looked up again. Their eyes met. Behind the black man's eyes was hatred. The jovial man behind the bar had gone, the disguise shattered in one brief moment. For the first time Jeremy realised they were enemies. Underneath all the smiles as he served the white man year after year, Noah had had enough of being subservient. Jeremy would have liked to talk to him but that was impossible. Not the thing to be anything but superficial with the club barman. Jeremy wondered how many in his own gang hated him. Hated being ordered around from one year to the next, never seeing the chance of a change, of moving up in the world. He wondered, looking away from Noah, what Primrose thought of him. What she really thought of his children. What her children, Moley and Happiness, would think of the way of things when they grew up. Could they all still be friends as grown-ups? That had been Petronella's gripe growing up with the piccanins. Being told to stop being friends with the black children when they grew up. In England they said the class system was beginning to break down. In Africa the race system was as strong as ever, the British keeping socially completely to themselves. Master and servant. Employer and employee. That's all it was. No one had ever really talked to each other.

Jeremy tried to bring his mind back to the conversation in the bar. Life was never easy. You could provide people with jobs, create wealth out of nothing, but it was never enough. Now they could see the comparison between themselves and the life of an Englishman. There had to be jealousy. It was the nature of man. Before, without the comparison, they were happy to live in a mud hut and struggle for a living against the elements. Now they saw comfort. Cars, electric light, running water from taps, the water drinkable, warmth in the winter at night. A place to live where a storm did not rip off the thatch. And they wanted it. They wanted the comfort, the easy way of life. Sitting in bars. Playing cricket. Watching their wives play a game of tennis. Their children getting educated. Making money. Accumulating wealth so they could put their feet up at the end of a life like the white man. His mother had had a saying: 'What the eye doesn't see, the heart doesn't grieve about!' She was talking about man's infidelity but it applied equally to material wealth. They could now see and they wanted. Josiah and his friends were the way to the white man's riches. A life of comfort. Just human nature. Nothing wrong.

Beyond the window on the cricket field a black man was sitting on a tractor pulling a grass cutter behind. Cutting perfect straight lines in the grass that was watered from the club dam if it didn't rain. The sight screen showed the extremity of the field. Next to the big white screen a scoreboard from last year's cricket: one hundred and thirty for nine. The cricket season would start again at the end of the reaping season which came with the end of the rains. The scoreboard was between the sight screen and the clubhouse with its long veranda. In the room behind the veranda was the long bar where Jeremy sat trying not to think of that look of hatred in Noah's eyes. When he went back to England for Harry's wedding he would look at the block of flats in Chelsea he part-owned with his old girlfriend Livy. Thinking of Livy made him smile. She had been right about the future of Rhodesia. Why they had never married, Livy not wishing to commit her daughter by her brief marriage to Frank St Clair to the vagaries of African politics. She had been right to make him invest some of his money in England rather than extending the farm. He wondered what his new wife Bergit would have to say about the possibility of going back to England. She wouldn't like it. Bergit liked the comfort and luxury of Africa. Not to mention the sunshine. Thinking of his pregnant wife made him happy. The bad taste in his mouth went away. Outside, where the grass was being cut so perfectly, the sun was still shining. It would all be fine in the end. They needed each other, black and white.

The girls came onto the veranda still in their white tennis dresses and sat round one of the low tables. Noah went out to serve them. He was all smiles. Their tennis rackets were put on the table. The girls were laughing. Not a care in the world. A beautiful place in the sun with everything they wanted. Tennis on a weekday. Drinks at lunchtime on a weekday. What more could they want? The doves singing from the trees to each other. Not a storm cloud in the sky. A perfect day in Africa.

"Maybe the lion will eat your sheep, George, without killing itself."

"Right through the back of its head. Both barrels. You'll see... Now, who wants another drink?... Noah, when you've finished giving Mrs Barry her drinks please give us another round."

The rhythm of colonial life went on, no one other than Jeremy realising it had been interrupted. Jeremy didn't look at Noah again.

"I'd better be on my way back home. Bergit will wonder what's happened to me."

"Nonsense, Jeremy. We're enjoying ourselves. Why don't you join Mary and the girls for lunch? The cook is making his French salad with fresh herbs and garlic. George brought him a box of herbs and vegetables from his kitchen garden. There's some rather nice cold pork and an apple sauce. Give Bergit a ring on the party line. We're only ten minutes from World's View. Didn't you come in the truck? Your wife can drive over in the Chevrolet. Good to give it a run. If you drink too much she can drive you home. We'll make it a party."

"Haven't you work to do at the police station, Clay?"

"Place is quiet as a mouse. Has been for weeks. Everyone's too busy reaping the tobacco to get up to mischief. They know where I am. A man has to relax every now and again."

"I'll give her a ring."

"That's the idea. Cheers, Jeremy. You're a good chap. Now tell me. How did a nice English girl like your wife get a German name like Bergit for God's sake?"

"It's a long story."

"We like long stories. We're all staying for lunch."

"I'm sure I've told you."

"Then tell us again. Anything to stop George going on about his bloody lion."

"It's Bergit's story really... During the First World War, after his brother was killed in the trenches, Harry Brigandshaw left Elephant Walk and went to fight for the British, one of the first Rhodesian pilots in the Royal Flying Corps. He became one of the RFC's most successful fighter pilots. The war in the air was a war fought with chivalry, something that doesn't happen anymore. One of the German pilots went down in a field. Crash-landed and began to burn after Harry's Vickers machine gun shot him down. Harry circled the wreckage in his biplane and saw the pilot was still alive but trapped in the wreckage of his triplane. Harry landed in the field. The back of the plane was burning up towards the cockpit. The German observer was dead. Harry pulled out the pilot. His name was Klaus von Lieberman, a German aristocrat with an estate close to the border of Switzerland. Bergit tells the story better than me. The two young pilots became friends after von Lieberman was captured. He had been taken away by a platoon of British soldiers. He had crash-landed behind the British lines. After the war they kept in touch. Klaus in Bavaria, Harry back in Rhodesia. When Klaus married he brought his new wife to Rhodesia for their honeymoon. Her name was Bergit. Just before the Second World War Bergit's father was in Berlin with Ruthy's father William. You remember Ruthy? She's the one marrying my brother-in-law Harry next month. Horatio Wakefield and William Smythe were doing an investigation on the Nazi party for the newspapers back in England. The Gestapo grabbed Bergit's father. For all intents and purposes Horatio had disappeared. Harry Brigandshaw and Bergit's father Horatio were friends. When Harry found out about Horatio's disappearance he contacted Klaus von Lieberman and asked for his help. Klaus von Lieberman's uncle was a powerful man in the Nazi Party. Horatio got safely back to England. It was before Bergit was born. Without the help of Harry Brigandshaw and Klaus von Lieberman neither Bergit nor her brother Harry Wakefield would have been born. Bergit was named after von Lieberman's wife, her brother Harry after Harry Brigandshaw. How I came to have an English wife with a German Christian name. Harry Brigandshaw always said his close friendship with Klaus von Lieberman was an example of the insanity of war. Two good friends who one time in their lives had been trying to kill each other. Harry hated war and politicians. Said the politicians created the wars and sat back from a safe distance watching others kill each other."

Deliberately, Jeremy had been watching Noah as he told the old story. Again their eyes met in understanding. This time the look was different. Still defiant but not so certain.

"Got to call my wife. Back in a minute. The party line at times like this makes life easy. Two long rings and one short on the handle and Bergit will pick up our phone."

As Jeremy walked into the small office behind the bar to make his phone call no one in the room knew why he had gone to such lengths to tell his wife's story. To them it was just a story to pass the time. On the way through he touched Noah briefly on the shoulder. He hoped Noah had understood the point of his story. That they should be friends and not enemies. That ending up trying to kill each other wouldn't help anyone other than the politicians. Even if Clay Barry had seen the gesture, Jeremy didn't care.

Bergit picked up the phone at the other end almost immediately.

"I'm at the club, darling. Your brother is marrying Ruthy. Invitation was in our mail box. Called in for a beer to celebrate. Clay and Mary are here. Want us to join them for lunch. Clay says if I got too pissed we can leave the truck at the club and you can drive us back in the Chev."

"And if we both get pissed?"

"Then I'll drive the truck."

"Give me half an hour. Got to put on a dress and make-up. Harry marrying Ruthy. What happened to Petronella?"

"Doesn't say on the wedding invitation." He was smiling. It was nice hearing the sound of his wife's voice.

"Are we going over?"

"Your brother marrying your best friend? Of course we are. You realise the kids will be cousins?"

"You think Ruthy's pregnant?"

"The wedding's next month. Out of the blue."

"The naughty girl. How wonderful. We'll have so much to talk about. Don't drink too much before I get there."

"What about the baby?"

"This is a family celebration. How exciting. Harry marrying Ruthy.

Our parents will be over the moon. Don't worry. I'll drive you home. Just one gin to celebrate shouldn't hurt the baby. I'm so thrilled. How long are we going for?"

"A couple of weeks. Bobby can look after the farm. As you said, it's a family celebration. And I want to check on that block of flats."

"Doesn't the agent handle it?"

"Just like to keep my hands on things."

"You're not thinking of Livy?"

"Of course not. She's happily married to Claud Gainsborough. We're all happily married."

"Then why look at the flats? They can't have flown away."

"Get dressed quickly. I miss you."

"Quick as I can. I told Primrose her kids could swim in the pool."

"Of course they can."

"The house is a bit empty without the sound of children."

"The boys will be back at the weekend."

"Of course they will."

"How's our baby?"

"Our baby is fine."

Jeremy put down the phone, cranked the handle once to tell the others on the party line the line was free, and went back into the bar. Noah was taking another round of drinks to Mary and her tennis friends on the veranda. The tractor with the grass cutter was still going up and down the cricket field. Jeremy went outside to look at the weather. Far away, behind the distant range of mountains, clouds were building up. Rain was coming. It was good. A few days' rain would stop the tobacco ripening. Give him time to cure some of the tobacco in his barns and make room for the next reaping. There was a lot of luck in growing tobacco. It all depended upon the weather.

Back in the bar the men were talking about tobacco, Clay Barry beginning to look bored. Clay liked to be the centre of attention controlling the conversation. When they went on to the vagaries of growing tobacco he had nothing to say. He was idly looking out of the window at his wife in animated conversation on the veranda. The swagger stick he always carried had come off the bar and was tapping the leather leggings that went with his boots, the leggings and boots always perfectly shined.

"It's going to rain tomorrow, chaps. Give us time to cure what's in the barns."

"Thank goodness." The answer was a chorus from all the tobacco growers.

"Is your wife coming to lunch?"

"Be here in half an hour, Clay."

"Why do they always talk about tobacco? It's so boring."

"That's what we do. Not so exciting as being a policeman. Not as much action."

"Place is as dead as a doornail."

"Don't worry. If Smith declares UDI there'll be plenty of action."

"I can't wait."

"Be careful what you wish for, Clay."

"The last problem we had was Herman Scanlan who drove his car into the bloody river. Pissed as a newt, of course. Said he hadn't had a drink all day. The insurance company paid him out. We had to cut him out of the wreck. Been sitting half in the water for an hour before Bobby Preston found him and went to us for help. The whole side of the car was pinning his leg under the water. Herman said it was nice to have a swim in the river."

"Bobby told me. He's my manager. You know, he gets five per cent of the gross this year as a manager. Should be enough with the last four bonuses to let him get a farm. They want five years' apprenticeship and twenty-five per cent of the first year's growing costs before they'll allocate him a Crown Land farm. He'll start right from scratch. Stumping, ploughing the cleared lands, roads, barns, a grading shed. Says he's going to live in a tent the first year until he has enough money to build a house. Farm buildings first and then a small cottage. Much later he's going to build himself a proper house. The boy's so excited. He was eighteen when he first came to World's View."

"I'd forgotten he was your assistant."

"You never forget anything, Clay."

"Have another drink. Your wife's driving. What would we do without our wives?"

"Drive into the river like Herman Scanlan."

"My new constable, Bill Packman, said Herman was singing when they were cutting him out. Had a bottle of whisky in the cubbyhole for emergencies."

"Sensible chap. I always have booze in the car," said George.

"You drink too much, George."

"No I don't. Anyway, what else can a bachelor do with his spare time? Cheers."

"Cheers, George."

"You'll see. I'll show you the bugger when he shoots himself through the back of his head."

"Seeing's believing."

"I'm telling you, Clay. It's a lion."

"How long have you had this new constable?"

"A few months. Been out from England just over a year. Trained him in Salisbury at the police barracks and sent him out to me. Wet behind the ears. They all are straight from England."

"Silly bugger should have stayed in England. Joining a colonial police force at this point in British history is madness."

"He was going to join the Hong Kong police and changed his mind. Told Fred Rankin Africa sounded more exotic."

"They're romantics at that age. Whatever happens he'll find Rhodesia an experience he won't forget. Better than getting a job in the bank and pushing a pen for the rest of his life, getting bored out of his mind. Won't find lions eating cows in England. Biggest excitement in England is a fox getting among the chickens. Only got one life. Might as well do something with it. Before you know, it's too late. Better to look back and regret what you have done than regret what you haven't done when it's too late. When you're too old."

"Quite the philosopher today, George."

"It's the drink. I always get sentimental when I drink."

"Which is every day, George."

"Some men get fighting drunk. Want to have an argument. I just wax sentimental."

"What have you regretted looking back, George?"

"Not much. A wife and kids I suppose. Then I see what happens to some families and I'm not so sure. Maybe I'm better off on my own. No one to tell me to stop drinking. No one to spend my money. You know that saying the women always bring up about dying a lonely old man.

Prefer that than the constant moans of some of the wives, the constant nagging."

"Tell me about it, George. And all the kids ever seem to want is more money. They always want something. Never satisfied."

"My kids aren't like that."

"You're lucky with your kids, Jeremy. Circumstances made you three so close together. How's your new wife coping with the boys?"

"Seems all right at the moment. Primrose has been so good to my boys. Without the nanny I don't know what I would have done."

The conversation kept on going round, everyone at the bar listening. Everyone chipping in except Noah. Noah just listened and served up the drinks. When Bergit arrived, George Stacy, after God knew how many drinks, still wasn't drunk. Never once in all the years had Jeremy seen George blind drunk. Never sober but never drunk.

"Come and join us at the bar, darling. George here has been telling us a lion has killed one of his cows. George has set a gun trap. Clay doesn't believe it was a cow that killed George's *mombe*."

"Right through the back of his head."

"Noah, can you bring my wife a gin and tonic?... Cold pork and salads for lunch, darling."

"How many drinks have you all had?" Bergit was smiling at everyone, comfortable among the men in the club.

"We never count."

Jeremy gave Bergit the invitation to read while Noah poured her drink.

"Doesn't say where they're having the reception, Jeremy. You're right. This wedding has been put together in a hurry. Cheers, everyone."

"Cheers to you and your baby, Bergit."

"Thank you, George. You always were the gentleman. Now tell me all about this lion that's killing your cows."

Jeremy squeezed his wife's hand. She always said the right thing. She liked everyone in the Centenary. While George went about retelling his old lion story, Jeremy watched his wife instead of Noah. It was going to be a wasted day on the farm but it didn't matter. He was happy. Bergit was happy. His life was back on the rails.

Halfway through the story, Clay put on his peaked hat and picked up his drink. Jeremy had seen it coming. The man was bored, having nothing more to say. With the drink in one hand and his swagger stick in the other the policeman went out of the bar to join his wife and the girls on the veranda. Noah had just brought the girls another round of drinks. Clay had his problems in the club on a day like today. All the men in the bar owned their own farms. None of them were farm managers or assistants. In Rhodesian society the farm owners were the top, rich and often envied with their big houses and swimming pools and cars like his Chev Impala out in the back next to the tennis courts, the roof down, the coachwork shining from all the garden boy's washing and polishing. Jeremy suspected Clay felt out of it. A policeman on a policeman's salary. Plenty of power but not much money. And when he retired or lost his job through the looming change in the politics he would have nothing but a small pension. He didn't own a farm he could sell. Places like the Centenary Club would be out of his reach. One of the founding rules of the club had been to give free membership of the club to the local member-in-charge of the Centenary police. Whoever wrote the first rules had made good politics. Whoever you were it was best to stay on the right side of the authorities. Henry Scanlan had been a perfect example. If he had been charged with drunken driving his insurance wouldn't have paid out for his smashed-up car. Clay was not as secure as he wanted to be, which made him try and dominate the conversation. Policemen were different, it was as simple as that. Which was why when they all talked about their problems in farming, Clay felt out of it.

"Excuse me, darling."

"Where are you going?"

"To talk to Clay. Time we went in to lunch. Aren't you hungry?"

"Starving. Feeding for two don't forget. You really think it's a shotgun wedding and Ruthy's pregnant?"

"Find out when we get there."

"It's going to be freezing in England."

"Nothing's perfect."

2

They both drove home after lunch, Jeremy having stopped drinking. Clay had not ordered wine. George and the rest of the farmers had stayed in the bar, their voices getting louder as they drank. The three girls playing tennis with Mary had gone home before lunch. Most of the wives were responsible driving back to their farms through the bush. It was all right for the men to get drunk and drive into the river but not for the women. Some kind of unwritten code broken by Carmen, the mother of Jeremy's two boys. Carmen had got herself drunk, blind drunk, and driven. She had taken the wrong dirt road in her confusion and run out of petrol. The lions had attacked her as she tried to walk back. It had been a warning to some of the women. Get drunk in the club and have hubby drive back or get drunk in the safety of home. Jeremy guessed all three of Mary's tennis partners would pour themselves a drink when they got home. They had all started drinking. For many people once started it was difficult to stop. They all said the same thing. In the African bush what else did a girl do? They all had servants and nothing much to occupy themselves. Time went faster with a drink in your hand.

The road home from the club was well fenced, keeping the cattle from straying onto the road. The farmers regularly checked their fences. Hitting a big cow at full throttle made a mess of a car. And the occupant.

Henry Scanlan had been lucky driving into the river. Carmen had not been so lucky. Always, on the road back from the club, Jeremy thought of Carmen. He blamed himself for not paying her more attention. With Bergit he was not going to make the same mistake. The idea of being a rich tobacco farmer's wife sounded glamorous but it was lonely, hours alone in the house with only the servants, most of whom couldn't speak more than a few words of English. Jeremy was glad Bergit had fallen pregnant so quickly. The baby would give her something to do when he was out working in the lands. The trip back to England would unfortunately be in the middle of the growing season but over lunch with Clay and Mary, Bergit had been excited, telling them how she had grown up with her brother's fiancée Ruthy in the same neighbourhood. Clay had been happy listening to a pretty girl talk, eating his cold pork and salads. Bergit was driving the big Chev five hundred yards in front of him, giving most of the dust kicked up by the car time to blow away from the road. It was better to follow in case something went wrong. They would have a swim in the pool before Jeremy went down to the barns to check on the curing. The trick in curing tobacco was increasing the barn temperature at the right moment so the moisture in the leaves was driven out but not so quickly as to damage them. Good curing increased the price of tobacco on the auction floors by as much as thirty per cent. Farming was all in the detail if you wanted to make a profit. Detail. It was all in the detail.

Bergit had put the Chev in the garage. Jeremy got out of the truck in their driveway as she walked towards him.

"Do you want me to book the flight?"

"Of course, darling. I'm going to have a swim to get rid of the dust and go down to the barns. I'm impressed you only had one gin."

"So am I. You have no idea how much I wanted another one. There's nothing worse than being the only sober person at a lunch party."

"Mary was sober."

"You can see when a girl's been drinking. She'd had a few. Thanks for inviting me to lunch, Jeremy."

"I was naughty to call in for a drink."

"You think it's going to rain?"

"I hope so. With the curing barns full, cloud and rain stops the tobacco ripening."

"Can I put a call through to Ruthy to tell her we're coming?"

"Of course you can. They'll probably only give you six minutes calling England. Take a few hours to come through the exchange. Make it person to person."

"I'm so excited. Harry and Ruthy getting married."

"I might have thought you'd phone your brother."

"I want to find out what happened. Harry won't tell me. Men are like that. Wouldn't it be nice if they came to Rhodesia for their honeymoon? They could go up to the lake. Come here for a while. I can't wait to get a good talk with Ruthy. She's my best friend. Always has been."

"Just don't ask her what happened to Petronella... You know, those dogs of ours are quite mad. When there are people at the pool they chase round the trees barking."

"I love it. I love everything about Rhodesia. I'm so lucky. Are you sure the boys will be happy alone with Primrose in the weekends we're away?"

"They won't mind. They're pretty independent together."

"Everything is so exciting. You think it really was a lion?"

"Time will tell. Old George is good at telling stories. Part of his charm in the bar. Everyone loves George."

The day went back to normal, Jeremy glad he had stopped drinking when they went in to lunch. Clay too had stopped drinking. Never once had Jeremy seen Clay drunk. The man was always on duty. Ready to be called if something went wrong in his jurisdiction. As a policeman, Jeremy considered him one of the best.

Jeremy was looking carefully inside a barn of curing tobacco, the heat from the furnace that fed the flues overpowering, when Bobby Preston caught up with him. Jeremy had just read the temperature of the thermometer that hung from the bottom tier of tobacco, the hands of tobacco on long sticks across the tiers rising high up in the barns, only the bottom leaves visible.

"I checked that one half an hour ago, boss."

"Looks fine. The stems are still green with moisture. Another day at that temperature should do the trick. Tobacco looks good this season. Your five per cent should put you over the top. The kids will miss you, Bobby."

"And I'll miss the kids. Had a phone call this morning when I went back to the cottage for breakfast from my friend at the Ministry of

Agriculture in Salisbury. He says there is a problem with my application for farm land."

"There can't be. You'll have done your five years with me at the end of this season and with this year's bonus have enough money to get your loan from the Land Bank to cover the rest of your growing costs."

"They say I'm too young. Even at twenty-three they think I'll still be too young to have all the responsibility of my own farm. They want me to wait until I'm twenty-five."

"You're welcome here for a couple more years. Suits me just fine. Stay as long as you like. It was you I was thinking of."

"That's the snag. They think I should have a couple more years with another grower to get a second perspective. There's a chap in Glendale looking for a new manager. He was grower of the year two years ago. Frankly, what I've learnt from you, boss, is more than enough. The rest is experience."

"What are you going to do?"

"What I'm told. Can't argue with the banker."

"You know what? That's a damn good idea if you have to wait a couple more years. I'll be sad to lose you. Thought you'd go at the end of the season anyway. Running the finances of a farm puts on a lot of pressure. You sometimes wake up in the middle of the night worrying your guts out. Especially when you're working on an overdraft."

"Vince can take over from me. He'll enjoy having the cottage to himself. He's sick of my music."

"Where is Vince?"

"Down by the bottom land with a gang fixing the road buggered up by that heavy rain. It's going to rain tonight. Stop the leaves over-ripening in the lands."

"I said you were ready. Can you manage the place next month for a couple of weeks? The boys in particular. Harry Wakefield is marrying Ruthy. You remember Ruthy when she stayed with us on her visit with Harry and Bergit?"

"Do I remember Ruthy!"

"Of course. You were sweet on her. With the extra bonus money you will get in Glendale you should take a holiday in England for three months in the off season. Look for a wife. A chap on his own farming needs a wife or he ends up drinking too much like George Stacy. Had a beer in the club after picking up the mail. George was sitting on his usual barstool. There are half a dozen letters for you."

"Any from England?"

"Didn't look. Come up to the house and I'll give them to you. Poor old George thinks a lion killed one of his *mombes*. He's set up a gun trap over the carcase of an old sheep that died of natural causes. Clay Barry thinks he's talking bullshit."

"A lion inside the Centenary. Hasn't been any of the big five here for years. The occasional elephant up from the valley in the dry season but never a lion. Do you mind my going at the end of the season?"

"Of course not if it's for your own good. But go to England now you have an opportunity. Harry Wakefield can introduce you to girls. He's a newspaperman. They know all the girls and the places. Go in the middle of April. Vince and I can do the grading. The chap at Glendale won't need you before the start of the season when the seedbeds go in at the end of September. Give you lots of time to check out the talent and see your family. Your parents must miss you."

"I might just do that."

"That's the idea. And if Smith declares UDI you might want to stay where you are. They've let Josiah Makoni out of the prison camp. Must have been pressure from the British government. He's going to be trouble if Smith takes the route to UDI. Frankly, I think he'd do us more harm than good. Without British government backing we'll be stuck on our own. Out on a limb. No backup."

"South Africa will help."

"So they keep saying. But South Africa has its own problems. The Anti-Apartheid movement is gaining ground in England and America. In America they're in cahoots with the Civil Rights movement and those chaps are powerful."

"You can't spend your life worrying about politics."

"You're young, Bobby. And ambitious."

"And what would I do in England?"

"Join the club. What I've been saying to everybody for years. Come up to the house for your mail."

Thinking how much Bobby Preston had changed since he came out from England five years before, direct from school, Jeremy checked the temperature in twenty-four more barns, all of the barns the height of a three-storey house. The temperatures were correct. The boy had learnt how to grow tobacco, the most difficult crop of them all. Maize and cattle had their problems but squeezing the right amount of profit out of tobacco was an art, the buyers so finicky when it came to putting in their bids on the auction floor. A ten per cent increase in weight, a ten per cent increase in quality from careful curing and grading made a huge difference. The other way round a farmer could be out of business. Bobby Preston was going to be a successful tobacco farmer if he got his opportunity. And if he brought himself back a wife. In the bush alone a man needed a wife. Like Bergit. Whistling happily to himself, Jeremy went home to his new wife. The four Alsatians greeted him at the gate of the homestead. He had trained them only to follow him from the house when he called to them. They were big dogs. Lovable dogs. When you were on the right side of them.

"Get down, Shumba. We'll go for a walk with the gun later. See if we can find ourselves a guinea fowl."

Bergit was still at the pool.

"How's our tobacco?"

"Just fine. Bobby's leaving us in April. England for a holiday. Then he's joining some farmer in Glendale for the extra experience before they'll let him have a Crown Land farm. They say he's still too young to go out on his own."

She was sitting back in a deck chair, both hands on her stomach and the baby inside. She looked so content. Jeremy gave her a kiss on the brow and sat down next to her. Without being asked, ten minutes later, Silas brought them a tray of tea, the silver tray with the silver teapot and a plate of sandwiches. It was a tradition at World's View every afternoon whenever Jeremy had the time to sit down by the pool with his wife. Tea and sandwiches. Most always with cucumber. Like in the old days on the lawn in summer at the Crookshank family home in the Isle of Wight. Before the war. Before his father was killed by German aircraft in his yacht off Dunkirk. Before the British Empire began to crumble.

"Did you get through to Ruthy?"

"Call's still coming through."

"Telephone calls not on the party line take a while in Rhodesia. Part of the charm of the place."

Bergit poured the tea. They were comfortable. Far away behind the range of mountains shimmering in the heat haze the clouds were building up. Big black clouds boiling at the centre. The heat and humidity was oppressive under the shade of the tree.

"You really want sandwiches, Jeremy?"

"Can't break the rules. What's left over Silas will take home to his wife. Or eat them himself. Tradition. Never does to break with tradition."

They heard the two long rings and the short coming out to them across the lawn from the house. With the storm building up the birds had gone quiet. Everything was still. Not a breath of wind.

"That's my call."

Without getting up Jeremy watched his wife run from the pool across the lawn. The four dogs watched her. It was too hot for the dogs, their tongues hanging out of their mouths to perspire. Far, far away came the faint sound of thunder. Jeremy picked up one of the sandwiches without thinking and began to eat. He was thinking of Bobby. He would miss him. Vince was good but vague. Vince Ranger was a dreamer, his dreams never practical like Bobby's. There would be less tea and cucumber sandwiches without Bobby. More work. More checking up. All four dogs were lying on their sides round his deck chair, all of them panting. Pulling off his clothes, Jeremy dived into the water. When Bergit came back from taking her phone call he was still in the pool. The water was tepid but pleasant.

"She's pregnant! Same as me. Four months. Seduced Harry after our wedding. Big wedding. Lots of media. All Harry's friends. Mango's going to be at the wedding. Our parents are over the moon. Ruthy can't wait to see me. She's getting married in white. St Giles, Chelsea. Where we were married. She'd love to come here for her honeymoon. She's going to give up her job when the baby is born. At least for a year. Getting a flat. Not sure where."

"All that in six months!"

"It was breath-taking talking to Ruthy. I miss her so much. She's going to be here. Right here in just over a month. Can we book them a houseboat on Kariba?"

"It'll not be too hot on the lake at the end of March. I was thinking of buying a houseboat. Going to surprise you."

"We could all go together."

"On their honeymoon?"

"She's pregnant. Not the virgin bride. I'm so happy for her."

"I can only presume Petronella won't be at the wedding. Just kidding. Take your clothes off and jump in the pool. No one's watching."

"What about the gardener?"

"Who cares about the gardener?"

"It's all so exciting. We can stay with my parents. They'll love to have us... Here we go."

In the water they splashed each other, both of them laughing.

"I'm so lucky, Jeremy. I'm so lucky."

"Give me a kiss."

"The gardener!"

As Jeremy bent to kiss his wife the thunder rolled. The storm was closer. It was going to rain and the tobacco in the lands was not going to over-ripen. It was always the same in the season. Whatever else was happening, the crop and what was happening to the crop was always in the back of his mind. Worrying. It never stopped. Every season the same. Looking up at the sky. Worrying about the weather. Worrying about covering the huge amount of growing costs and making a profit.

When the rain finally came they were sitting down to dinner, the temperature outside beginning to drop. The first few drops were so big they sounded like hail, sending Jeremy onto the lawn in a panic. Hail on a land of tobacco was devastating, shredding the leaves, making them worthless. Looking up at the pitch-black sky with the light from the veranda still showing his face Jeremy let the rain soak him to the skin. It was just water. Beautiful, wonderful water. Above the sound of pounding rain on the new tin roof of the house he could hear the thump of the generator from the workshop next to the barns. Bobby had turned on the generator after collecting his mail from the house. The rain was so cool on his skin, Jeremy forgot about the mosquitoes.

"What are you doing out there, darling?"

"Enjoying the rain. Since I put on the new roof big drops of rain can sound like hail, frightening the shit out of me with tobacco in the lands. Why don't you come and get wet?"

"Don't be silly."

"The dogs are loving it."

"I can't hear you properly with the pounding rain."

"It was better with the thatch. If it wasn't for a bush fire that nearly took out the house I'd have left it alone."

"The mosquitoes are biting me."

Bergit had come out on the steps to look down at him standing on the lawn.

"Did you take your malaria pills?"

"Of course I did. Please come in, Jeremy. It's a thunderstorm. Lightning. I'm frightened."

"Don't be frightened. There are lightning conductors on both ends of the house."

A clap of thunder drowned out his voice. Turning from the storm and dripping wet, Jeremy went back into the house.

"Wouldn't it be better for the boys to stay at home when we're in England?"

She was looking at him worried, fear in the back of her eyes. Jeremy folded her in his arms. She was always worrying about his children.

"Probably. But they'll hate it. Yes, maybe we'll leave them at school."

"You're soaking wet."

"Of course I am, Bergit. I've been standing in the rain."

"You're impossible."

"Thank God we're insured against hail. If that had been hail instead of large drops of rain banging on a tin roof it would have wiped out all the tobacco in the lands. Farming was never easy. You can never relax. One year we had caterpillars eating the leaves. Sprayed with DDT. All the caterpillars did was sit up, lick their chops and go back to eating my tobacco. Can't insure against caterpillars. Cost me a fortune those bloody caterpillars. They were huge."

"You worry too much."

"You just have to think ahead."

"Are you going to change your clothes?"

"First time I've been really cool all day."

"You can't sit down like that. What would Silas think?"

"Probably wish he could do the same thing... It really can rain in Africa. Just listen to it."

"It frightens me."

"Never be frightened of rain. Without rain we couldn't farm. Why I want to build dams right across the farm to irrigate every land and stop having to worry about rain. That's thinking ahead. If the politicians don't screw it up we'll turn the whole of Rhodesia into a wonderland. A land of plenty. The granary of Africa. No one will ever go hungry."

"She's been looking at me."

"Who?"

"Carmen. All that talk about George Stacy's lion."

"We can't take down her portrait. It's the first thing the boys go to look at when they come home from school."

"Of course. The eyes follow me."

"Livy Johnston is becoming one of England's great painters. Why her portraits are so alive. I'll take it down if it worries you."

"No, leave it. I know how much it means to the boys. Just go and change your clothes for me. Please, Jeremy. You're dripping wet."

"Your wish is my command, my lady. What's for pudding?"

"I have no idea."

"Do you want one big wet kiss before I change?"

"No, I don't."

"Then stop giggling."

"Go and change."

"Back in a flash."

Feeling guilty he had not explained his long affair with Livy Johnston before he married Carmen, Jeremy went to the bedroom to change his clothes. Bergit had not been a virgin when he met her and she had told him nothing of her sexual past. On the way back through the lounge to the veranda where they were eating dinner, Jeremy smiled at the portrait of Carmen. There were some things better left unsaid. Past affairs were one of them.

"You're right. That feels better. So what is for pudding?"

"Silas made an apple tart. Try it. Sprinkled with sugar. Is it going to rain all night?"

"Probably. The rivers will be flowing all the way to the Zambezi."

"Who turns off the generator tonight?"

"Vince. That's his job today. Nine o'clock on the dot. Reminds me of 'lights out' at boarding school. Nine o'clock. Farmers and schoolboys have to get their sleep."

*I*t rained for two days and two nights, the rivers flowing down the *spruits* cutting off the farm from the outside world, hundreds of small rivers raging on their way to the Ruia which flowed into the much bigger Zambezi. By Friday afternoon, when Jeremy and Bergit drove the truck to Umvukwes to pick up the children, the rivers were again passable. The small rivers that cut the road came up fast and went down fast. From raging torrents to almost nothing in less than twenty-four hours. When Jeremy told Phillip and Randall about going to England. the excitement of getting out of school evaporated.

"Why can't we go?" they whined in unison.

"Because you have to go to school. Without a proper education you'll amount to nothing in life. It's only two weekends you'll have to stay at school. If you ask Bobby nicely he'll drive over and take you out each Sunday."

Bergit was smiling, the boys placated, happy smiles back on their faces. When Jeremy told them Harry and Ruthy would be coming for a holiday the moment of gloom had been forgotten.

With six more barns of tobacco on the bulks in the bulk shed the gang had reaped all day to fill the empty barns. Despite the rain and lack of sun many of the bottom leaves on the plants were ready for reaping. By Saturday night the barns were again full. On Monday, Sunday being the day of rest unless there was a dire emergency, four more barns were emptied of cured tobacco and filled with freshly reaped leaves. The cycle was a constant fight to get as much tobacco as possible through the barns, all part of good management.

"What you've got to do on your own, Bobby. You got to think and manage the farm properly. Can't afford to over-capitalise with too many barns. You got to milk maximum profit out of what you've got. You too, Vince. One day you'll have your own farm. In farming, like any business, you always got to think."

On Tuesday morning, a week after Jeremy's lunch with Clay and Mary Barry, he received a phone call as he was getting out of bed to start the day. The dawn was just breaking. Outside, far behind the distant range of mountains, the night sky was paling. Irritated by an interruption to his morning schedule, Jeremy picked up the phone from the wall bracket in the lounge. He could barely see. Carmen's eyes were just becoming visible.

"Hello. Jeremy Crookshank."

"Are you always so grouchy in the morning?"

"Who's this?"

"George Stacy. I'm phoning everyone. You got to come to my farm. Shot himself right through the back of the head. Mangy old lion. On his last legs by the look of him. Why he killed my *mombe*. Easy prey."

"You know what time it is?"

"Of course I do."

"Have you been drinking, George?"

"Last night, of course. This morning my head is as clear as a bell. Right through the back of the head. No one believed me so everyone is coming over. I'll be serving you all breakfast. Clay's on his way. Said he'd only believe me when he saw the poor bugger with his own eyes. You can bring Bergit. Girls just out from England don't see dead lions every day."

"I don't think she'd want to see it."

"Are you coming over?"

"Of course I am. Seeing is believing."

"That's my boy. You're a good neighbour, Jeremy. After breakfast we'll all go to the club."

"Have to see about that one."

"Wait till you see my lion. It'll be a wake for the old fellow. My gun trap took him out of his misery. Old age is a bugger when you live too long. Sorry to wake you."

"I was up. Work to do."

"Leave it to Bobby and Vince for today. Right through the back of his head."

On his way out of the lounge to the bedroom Jeremy smiled at Carmen, the light strong enough now to see her eyes. If the old lion was that old it was possible the poor old bugger had been one of the pride to have killed his wife. In the thought there was no satisfaction. To a hungry lion a cow or a person was simply food. Jeremy grew tobacco to buy his food. The old lion just killed and ate whatever was available.

"I'm driving over to George. That lion has shot himself. Right in the back of the head. He's asked half the block to come over and have a look."

"I'm coming with you."

"George is serving breakfast. You really want to see a dead lion?"

"Of course I do. It's exciting."

"Afterwards he wants to celebrate in the club."

"Then I'm definitely coming. Are you reaping today?"

"One barn. Maybe two."

"Leave it to Bobby. You won't have him next year. Enjoy your freedom while you've got him. I've never seen a lion before."

"Not even in the zoo?"

"That's different... The light comes up so quickly. I'm wide awake. We'll have our tea and drive straight over. How exciting. Right through the back of the head?"

"As the man said."

Early mornings were the best part of the day, all the birds singing with joy. It was cool in the truck with both windows open, Bergit's hair flowing back as the air swept through the car. She looked so happy with both her hands on her stomach. Jeremy kept glancing at his wife as he drove down the dirt road, dust streaming out behind. Where the sun was rising behind the mountains the sky was blood-red, the sun half up over the mountains, big and red. The mountains were blue. All round the bush was green from the plentiful rains. Jeremy had never felt so alive. Never felt so happy. Intermittently on both sides of the road were lands of tobacco and maize. All the crops looked good. At the turn to George

Stacy's farm they were met by two cars from the other direction. One was a police van with Clay Barry driving. Everyone honked their horns. In front of George's big house were five more vehicles. Everyone was up on the veranda. As Jeremy and Bergit got out of their truck, smiling at Clay and Mary, another truck came up the driveway.

"Where's the bloody lion, George?" called Clay.

"We're going to wait for everyone to arrive. Good morning, Clay. Good morning, Mary. You want a cup of tea before we all go down to the dam? My chaps are making a funeral pyre from last year's stumping to give the poor old chap a good send off. At the moment he's still where he shot himself right through the back of the head. Good morning, Jeremy and Bergit. Breakfast will be served on the veranda after the funeral. Then we all go to the club for the wake."

When fifteen cars and trucks were in the driveway they took four of the cars to the dam. To all get in as few cars as possible and keep up the fun, Bergit sat on Jeremy's lap in the back of George Stacy's Mercedes which George had specially taken out of his garage for the occasion. On the bonnet, hooked to the Mercedes star, was a small wreath of flowers.

"I thought you were going to skin the poor old fellow and put him on the floor of your lounge?"

"Too mangy. You'll see."

On the far side of the earth dam wall was a shed next to the pump that sent water to a holding reservoir close to George Stacy's house. George led the way to the small shed. The door had been left open, the top of the opening newly closed by three boards of wood. Through the opening Jeremy could see the back of the lion. Everyone got out of the cars and followed George. One by one they bent down and looked into the shed. Inside was a dead lion with the back of its head blown open by the blast from two barrels of a twelve-bore shotgun rigged by wire from the ceiling. The lion had had to bend down to get at the sheep carcase at the back of the shed, pushing its head through a loop that was attached to the triggers of the gun and pulling it tight. By some miracle of bad luck for the lion he had pulled both triggers, shooting himself in the back of the head as he bent down to feed off the carcase of the dead sheep.

"Heath Robinson would be proud of you, George."

"It worked, Clay."

"Seeing is believing. Without seeing that with my own eyes I'd have thought you a liar for the rest of my life. Policemen are like that. Disbelieving. The oldest lion I ever saw. Half his fur has come out. He's just skin and bones. It's a black-headed lion. Up from the valley I'd expect. Well I'll be buggered."

Standing outside the shed were five of George's black workers who had piled branches of dead trees into a mound of wood with a platform of tree trunks on top.

"Put the *shumba* on top of the pile, Custin."

Over the years, George had taught his bossboy to speak English. Without further ceremony the carcase of the lion was taken from the shed by the workers and heaved up onto the platform. With a backdrop of water from the dam that went back half a kilometre into the trees, and in the first glorious light of morning, the old lion once more looked magnificent.

"You do the honours, Clay. I want to stand for a moment in silence for the old chap."

"Quite a funeral," said Clay, taking George's cigarette lighter and going over to the pile of dry wood. At the bottom, newspaper had been stuffed under the brushwood. Clay lit the pyre and stood back. George lifted his right hand in salute. The fire spread from the paper to the wood sending up a cloud of smoke that quickly turned to fire engulfing the carcase. Last year's wood, despite the rainy season, was tinder dry from two days of hot African sun.

The farmers, two with their wives, climbed back into the cars. Jeremy looked behind through the back window of the car. A plume of smoke was rising high into the sky, going straight up in the still of the morning. As befitted a funeral, George, driving the Mercedes, looked sad. All through breakfast on the veranda George Stacy looked sad. Only when they got to the club to pull Noah out of his house at the back of the clubhouse did George begin to perk up. As the drinks flowed George began to smile. Soon he was laughing. They were all laughing. When later Jeremy went out on the veranda of the club he could see the plume of smoke from the funeral pyre. The smoke was still going straight up from the bottom. Only high up was the smoke dispersing.

"Must be twenty miles away. Didn't realise you could see so far."

"Come back to the party, Jeremy. It's just warming up."

"Seems wrong drinking after breakfast on a workday, George."

"Enjoy yourself. Think of the old lion. It's a wake."

Far away beyond the plume of smoke high in the sky, behind the range of mountains, was where Jeremy had buried what the lions had left of Carmen. Jeremy had placed a wooden cross over the grave. On the cross he had burned the words 'Go well, my darling'. It was still there. Every year on his first wife's birthday he took the boys to see the grave of their mother so they would never forget. They took a picnic which they ate by the grave that looked over the Zambezi escarpment, the small river close by running out over the edge vertically down into the valley like the white lace veil of a bride.

"What's the matter, Jeremy?"

Bergit had come out and found him staring into the distance.

"I was thinking... You're right. Let's have a drink."

"You were thinking of her weren't you?"

"It's the lion."

"I'm sorry. I'll leave you for a moment with your memories. It must have been hard."

"Thank you, Bergit."

"Come back to the bar when you're ready."

It was the plume of smoke rising all the way up to heaven that had got him. Brought the lump to his throat. After five minutes he turned his back on the funeral pyre of the old lion.

"My poor boys," he said out loud as he walked back to join the party at the bar.

George was now enjoying himself. More people had arrived who had not been at the breakfast on his farm. It was going to be an all-day party. One big party. In the middle of the African bush it didn't take much to have an excuse for a party. The word had quickly spread.

"Give me a double Scotch, Noah."

"Coming up, Mr Jeremy."

Working on the principle of 'if you can't beat them, join them', Jeremy joined in with the party. His day was going to be wasted. By his fourth double Scotch he didn't care it was a working day on the farm. Much later, when he went back out onto the veranda, the smoke had dispersed. A thin whiff of grey was still just visible, the last memory of the old lion.

"To you, old boy," said Jeremy, lifting his glass. "I'm sure lions are welcome in heaven."

"You shouldn't talk to yourself, old chap."

"Sorry, George. Quite a party."

"Right through the back of the head."

Soon after, a police motorcycle arrived and Clay Barry left. His wife stayed. She was enjoying herself.

"What was all that about?" asked Jeremy as he and George walked back into the party.

"Whatever it was Clay sobered up in a second. Looked as mad as hell. Hate to get on the bad side of Clay Barry. Saved my neck from the insurance company when I drove into the river. Clay's a good chap. Poor fellow, having to leave a good party. Someone said that work was the curse of the drinking classes."

"Any idea what it was, Henry?"

"Heard a bit of it. One of Clay's informers reported a man not from the block recruiting young men to train as terrorists."

"Clay told them in Salisbury they shouldn't have let that bastard Josiah Makoni out of jail. He's a troublemaker. Should have thrown away the key. Let him rot in the bush with his friends. You know the Russians are backing him."

Jeremy turned his head from one person to the next as they spoke.

"I think it's the Chinese, old chap."

"They're all bloody communists."

"Part of the cold war. America and Russia fighting for hegemony whatever that bloody word really means. Always best to get someone else to fight your wars. The cold war's about power and money if you ask me."

While the rest of the farmers went on about communism, completely oblivious of Noah standing right in front of them, Jeremy watched from where he was standing at the back of the crowd. All the barstools were taken up by the women, the men standing in front. Jeremy didn't think Noah could see him watching. The black man's eyes had narrowed. He was listening, remembering every word. A man's pride was at stake. Jeremy thought pride in himself and his people had more to do with Noah's look of concentration than communism, Russian or Chinese. When Noah looked up over the crowd and saw Jeremy watching him

their eyes met. Jeremy smiled. Noah looked away quickly and picked up
a wet glass from the cloth where it was drying on the counter just below
the top of the bar. Noah concentrated on polishing the beer glass. When
he looked up Jeremy was still watching him. This time he smiled,
shrugged his shoulders and began preparing a round of drinks.
Whatever they said to each other would be no good. They were on
different sides and always would be. Black and white. English and
Shona. Both fighting over the same country. For Jeremy it was a
revelation... He either stayed in Rhodesia and cast in his lot with the rest
of his fellow farmers or got the hell out of the way. Far away. From the
brewing trouble that one day would crash over all of them. There were
always wars. It was the nature of man. As Jeremy turned away another
Scotch was put in his hand. Jeremy was grateful. He was too old to
change. Mentally throwing in his lot with the rest of them, for better or
worse, he joined in the fun. This time he tried not to look at Noah.

"That's more than one gin, Bergit," he said to his wife up on her
barstool.

"After the second I thought 'What the hell'. The baby is going to
drink anyway. Might as well learn from his mother. Isn't it smoking that
is meant to hurt the baby? No one really knows. Harry says all the scare
about smoking and lung cancer is to let the British government put up
the tax on tobacco. Hell, we're tobacco farmers. It's our livelihood. I won't
drink at home. Only at parties. There's nothing worse than being the
only sober one in the room. Poor Noah must get bored stiff listening to us
when we've all been drinking."

"I don't think he's bored." She was tight. No doubt about it.

"He's such a good barman. Cheers, darling. To George's lion. Quite a
funeral. Are you all right now?"

"Of course I am."

"What a party."

Thinking of Carmen, who had drunk like a fish through both of her
pregnancies without any apparent harm to the boys, Jeremy smiled at his
wife. When they both drank together it was better. If they both talked a
bit of rubbish it didn't matter. It was when one partner was drunk and
the other stone cold sober the trouble began. She was being too
protective of her baby. A little relaxation did no one any harm. Mother or
child. Whichever one was more sober would drive the car and try not to

go into the river like Henry Scanlan who was well on his way talking tobacco to Eddy Harrington.

"So how's the crop, Jeremy?"

"Bloody marvellous, Eddy. Just hope the buyers give us the right price at auction."

"Or Smith doesn't declare UDI before we get the crop to auction. That would bugger it up. They say we'd lose the whole British market. If it isn't too little rain it's too much rain. The type of tobacco is wrong. Or the world market is flooded with tobacco. Who the hell would want to be a tobacco farmer? I have enough problems making the farm pay without worrying about politics. Let the politicians argue. I'm a farmer."

"So was Smith before he went into politics."

"Good luck to him."

"Good old Smithy," said an inebriated George Stacy. "It's those Labour buggers in England I worry about. Why is it socialists are so good at giving away other people's money? Or telling other countries how to run their lives? They never make any money themselves. Never create any wealth. All those promises are to get themselves into power so they can give away other people's hard-earned money and live off their fat salaries."

"You're right, George. Some of those politicians in Westminster should come out here and try and run my farm for a couple of years. All they do is talk. We grow the tobacco that makes them big tax money. Chap told me in Salisbury the tax on cigarettes in England pays for the National Health Service. They should be kissing our bottoms for growing their damn tobacco, not threatening us with sanctions if Smith takes a parting of the ways."

"Damn right."

"Bugger the politicians in London."

"Who wants another round?... Noah. Set 'em up. Drinks all round."

To Jeremy, George and Eddy and the rest of them had missed the point. It wasn't the people in London they should be worried about but the likes of Noah standing right in front of them. For all they all knew, their own labour force was right now being recruited for Josiah Makoni's guerrilla army. Right under their noses. While they drank in the bar. Jeremy put his empty whisky glass down. He had had enough. 'Let's go' he mouthed to Bergit. She looked at him, puzzled. Jeremy leaned forward.

"Let's get out of here before I drive us both into the river. Go to the loo. I'll meet you outside by the truck. Please, darling. I can't afford to lose another day's work tomorrow with a hangover."

Jeremy turned to the jug of water on the bar counter, leaned over to pick a wet glass off Noah's cloth and poured water into the glass to the top. He drank it down. And another. A third pint of water he had to force down his throat. It always worked. Far better than the stuff from the chemist. It flushed him out. Without looking at anyone, Jeremy left the party.

Outside by the truck, Bergit was waiting.

"When they're drunk they don't talk a whole lot of sense. That party in there is going to go on all day. I don't know where George and Henry put it all."

"Did you drink your three pints of water?"

"I did. Let's go. If I have to stop for a slash by the side of the road it doesn't matter. Try to say goodbye and they won't let you go. Why do we all drink so much? It's self-destructive. Makes you feel good for a while and lousy the next day. I hope I caught my water trick just in time. The trouble is, you can't socialise if you don't drink. You have to stay with their level of drinking if you want to make sense. How many drinks did you have?"

"I didn't count."

"Then I'll drive. Just have to concentrate."

There was no sign of the funeral pyre as they drove, Jeremy trying not to think of Noah. He drove slowly just in case he had had too much to drink. When they reached World's View it was well past lunchtime. Jeremy drove through the farm buildings not stopping to check the temperatures of his barns. A tractor and trailer, the trailer stacked with hands of green tobacco tied to long wooden sticks, was standing outside the open door of an empty barn. Vince Ranger was supervising the unloading, his bush hat shading his young eyes from the sun. Jeremy waved. He didn't like his farm staff to see he had been drinking in the middle of the day while they were working.

At the house Silas was waiting to serve lunch.

"Put it on the veranda, Silas. Then you can go back to the compound.

Won't be needing supper tonight with such a late lunch. Bit of a party at the club."

They ate the cold lunch mostly in silence before going to bed for a snooze, their habit when it was a Sunday afternoon. Jeremy felt guilty not pulling his weight on the farm. When he woke it was pitch dark. He could feel the hangover from the day's drinking despite his three pints of water. The next time he woke it was morning. The birds were singing. He felt better. The pints of water and the long sleep had worked. Next to him Bergit was still fast asleep. Jeremy got out of bed and pulled on his short khaki trousers. Pulled on his khaki shirt. Put the bush hat with its wide brim on his head and went outside. The dawn was beautiful. The *simby*, an old plough disc with a length of metal for a gong, was ringing out in the clear morning air, calling the gang in the compound to work. The tractor and trailer would be waiting to take them to the lands. They were going to be reaping the last of the bottom lands, the virgin soil down by the river, Jeremy's best tobacco of the season. He smiled at the beautiful morning. His day had begun.

As he got in the truck to drive round his farm, Silas brought him a wicker basket with a flask of hot tea and his breakfast.

"Thanks, Silas. What a beautiful day."

"Going to rain tomorrow, boss."

"You think so?"

"My grandmother says it's going to rain tomorrow afternoon."

"She knows. Take my wife tea when she calls for it. Let her sleep. When the boys are home she can't sleep in the morning with all the noise."

The first job was checking every one of the barns. The temperatures in two of the barns was too high.

"Did Boss Bobby check the barn temperatures in the night?" he asked the barn boy who stayed at the barns feeding the furnaces with wood all night."

"Boss Vince last night."

They were speaking Fanagalo to each other.

"Don't put any more wood in barns fifteen and sixteen until I tell you. They're too hot."

Jeremy got back into the truck and drove down to the bottom lands by the river. Vince was supervising the reaping.

"Where's Bobby?"

"Told him I'd take care of last night and this morning."

"Some of that tobacco you've reaped is too green. And fifteen and sixteen are too hot."

"I'm not sure every time what to do. Bobby gave me the temperatures."

"Takes years of experience to get the best cure. Don't reap more than you have to. It's going to rain again tomorrow."

"I heard that lion at Stacy's farm shot itself."

"Right through the back of the head."

"Well I'll be buggered."

"You got some tea?"

"Brought it with me. Saw the smoke from the funeral pyre."

"Word does spread quickly."

"The drums. The gang told me. I'm learning Shona instead of the bastard Fanagalo."

"Good for you, Vince. Never learnt Shona myself."

"Bobby's leaving us at the end of the season."

"You'll be taking over as assistant manager. Two per cent of the crop. You'll have to learn how to cure the tobacco better, Vince."

"Two per cent is one hell of an incentive."

"I hope so."

"Bobby's going to England to find a wife."

"I hope so... Look. That chap's got green tobacco. Go and help him. Show him what to pick. Green tobacco doesn't cure properly."

Feeling confident back on the job, Jeremy went into the rows of tobacco and followed each member of the gang. You had to watch everything. It was all in the detail. He was glad he had left the club when he had. Glad he had drunk the three pints of water. It was a beautiful day.

When the trailer was piled high with tobacco the gang sat on the edge at the back. The driver got up on the tractor. The tractor started first time, Jeremy listening carefully to the sound of the engine.

"That engine's got a knock in it, Bowlegs. Take it to the workshop when you've unhooked the trailer next to the barn. Take the spare petrol Ferguson. Tell Bobby to listen to that engine."

Again he was speaking Fanagalo to the tractor driver. Preventing mechanical breakdown before it happened saved Jeremy money. The tractor went off back to the barns, the gang swinging their legs over the back of the trailer. Vince Ranger got on his two-stroke motorcycle, kick-started the small putt-putt engine into life and followed the tractor and trailer. Jeremy walked to his truck and took out the wicker basket with his breakfast and began walking through the tobacco to the river. The tobacco was up to the top of his shoulders, some of the plants higher than himself. He was checking whether any leaves of ripe tobacco had stayed on the plants.

"Not bad, Vince."

At the small river he sat down under a tree and took the flask of tea out of the basket. All round him the birds were singing. A frog with a red head jumped into the water in front of him. Jeremy could see the frog had long skinny legs as it dived in the river away from him. He unscrewed the top and poured a hot cup of tea into the plastic cup. It was his first cup of tea of the morning. He could still taste the previous day's booze in his mouth. The tea tasted delicious, better than any of the whisky. Only then did he see the kudu across the river. The big male was standing quietly under a mukwa tree, the big horns high above its head. The morning sun was dappling through the leaves of the tree, matching the dapples on the brown skin of the buck. The buck was watching him. Slowly, Jeremy made out the rest of the animal hidden in the bush. The other side of the river was virgin country, not yet stumped out of trees to plant a crop. Then he saw them. One by one. The mother without the horns. The three small calves. He was going to eat his breakfast in the company of a family of kudu buck. Feeling deep pleasure and contentment Jeremy ate his breakfast and drank his tea. It was a beautiful place that he lived in. When he got up to walk back down the row of tobacco the family of buck were still standing in the trees. None of them had moved. They were at peace with each other, man and beast.

For two hours Jeremy walked up the river in the shade of the riverine trees. He was looking for a place to weir the river and extend his irrigation system that when he finished in the years ahead would span the whole of World's View, giving him water on command on every inch of his land. It was expensive. Requiring capital. Moving carefully through the thick bush, avoiding the buffalo grass whose seed on a man's skin causes itching to a point close to insanity and difficult to get off,

Jeremy looked for his spot. He had left the breakfast basket back in the truck. The further he got into the thickets the more he wished he had brought a gun. Along that part of the river both banks of the small river were mud. He was looking for rock on both sides to anchor his weir. He gave up and slowly returned to the truck. The gang was back reaping. In the place of the diesel Nuffield stood the petrol Ferguson.

"Boss Bobby looking at it, boss." Bowlegs was grinning.

Jeremy couldn't see Vince, only his motorcycle. Somewhere deep in the lush green tobacco, his assistant was checking the gang reaping the tobacco, making sure they didn't leave ripe tobacco or take off leaves too green to properly cure. It was a constant battle to get the most value out of the crop of tobacco. Jeremy drove off. His next job was in the workshop. With Bobby. Seeing what was wrong with the diesel engine of the Nuffield, hoping they could fix it themselves and not have to bring the mechanic out from Salisbury. He was thinking of Bergit. Glad she had gone with him to the club. It was boring for a young girl to sit alone on the farm all day by herself. Which had been the problem with Carmen. Why she had taken to drink. The drink that in the end, with the help of the lions, had killed her. This time Jeremy was not making the same mistake. Girls needed entertaining. He was happy they were going to England, lucky this time round in his marriages to have enough money. When later he drove up to the house, Bergit was down at the pool.

"How are you feeling, Bergit?"

"Lousy. Wish I'd drunk your three pints of water. You don't think I've hurt our child?"

"I'm sure you haven't. The Nuffield is buggered."

"What's wrong with it?"

"We don't know. Bobby's stripping the engine."

"Your hands are covered in grease."

"Jack of all trades. You have to be able to turn your hand to anything on a farm a hundred and twenty miles and over two hours' drive from civilisation."

"I've booked our air tickets. We'll get to London three days before the wedding."

"Sounds perfect."

"Coming for a swim?"

"Too much work to do. I was thinking of you. Popped in to say hello."

"Hello, Jeremy."

"Hello, Bergit."

They both laughed. Jeremy bent down and kissed his wife, careful to keep his greasy hands out of the way. She was smiling. She was happy, despite her hangover from their previous day's drinking. Jeremy walked to the truck and drove back to the workshop.

"It's a gasket."

"Thank God for that. We need this tractor working."

"She all right?"

"She's fine. When you get yourself a wife, Bobby, don't make the mistake of leaving them alone. They get bored."

"I'll remember."

"We're going over second week in March. The tobacco will be out of the barns. You'll be grading."

"Don't sweat. In two weeks nothing can go wrong. And if it does I'll fix it."

"Just watch Vince. His mind wanders. He needs a woman."

"Don't we all? Women and children. A family. That's what life is about."

"I'll talk to Harry for you. Have a mob of women lined up."

"I only need one." Bobby was grinning at him with hopeful expectation.

The day went on. One job to another. It was always the same. Watching everything. Making sure nothing went wrong. As Jeremy walked round his curing barns he was smiling. It was a good life on an African farm. Not everyone had a chance to breakfast with a family of kudu.

PART X

MARCH 1965

THE BELLS OF ST GILES

1

The four propellers of the BOAC Viscount were going round when the three policemen, mildly polite, escorted Josiah Makoni to the foot of the steps of the London-bound aircraft. When he was seated, looking out of the window, he could still see them standing on the tarmac. They were glad to see the back of him. The agreement between the Rhodesian and British governments had included his free flight to England. He was on his way. Out of prison. Excited, thinking of Petronella. Fourteen months in prison, with only men to look at, had sent his hormones to the pitch of high screaming. Of all the things he wanted now he was out of captivity the most important was a woman. As the aircraft began to move, turning onto the runway, he watched the control tower and terminal buildings of Salisbury airport, wondering when he would see them again. That he would see them again he was certain. They were going to win their independence from Britain. By letting him out of the bush camp, the Rhodesian Front government had shown their susceptibility to international pressure. With luck they had seen sense and going to war would no longer be necessary.

Looking around the half-empty aircraft Josiah could not see another black man. He smiled. That would change. He would see to it. Make certain. He and his friends were going to be the next Rhodesian government. The first Zimbabwean government.

"Would you like anything, Mr Makoni?"

"A girl called Petronella."

"That I can't help you with. A drink, maybe? Compliments of the captain and British Overseas Airways."

The air hostess was smiling at him. He was smiling at the girl. She was pretty in her blue uniform.

"A whisky and soda."

"I'll bring it to you when we are airborne. Have a good flight, Mr Makoni."

"Thank you, Miss Taggert. What's your first name? What does the J stand for? Or is it Mrs Taggert?"

"All our air hostesses are unmarried. Jean. My name is Jean."

"Thank you, Jean. You're the first person to be genuinely polite to me since my father's funeral. My return flight to London was delayed for fourteen months."

"Have a good flight with us. Buckle your seat belt. The red light is on."

Josiah watched the girl's tight bottom move away down the aisle. He began to relax. The ordeal was over. Petronella came back into his mind, the girl's bottom having accelerated the scream from his hormones. Seventeen hours to London. After a few drinks he was going to sleep. It was nice to be free. To live again like a civilised man. The pitch of the propellers increased as the plane increased speed down the runway. They took off. It felt to Josiah as if he was floating. They climbed up into the African sky. As the plane banked to get its course for Nairobi, Josiah looked down on the ground. There were a few houses, some with blue swimming pools. One day, one of those houses would belong to him. The aircraft settled to a steady drone. Josiah lowered the small table from the back of the seat in front of him. A small bottle of whisky, the size of the palm of his hand, with a can of soda was put in front of him.

"Thank you, Jean."

"You're welcome."

He poured his own drink. The alcohol tasted good. He had not had a drink for a long fourteen months.

'Cheers,' he said to himself. 'You needed this one. A few good drinks now and a few good drinks with Petronella will make my life perfect.'

After the third dinky bottle of whisky, Josiah fell asleep. He was tired, mentally and physically. When he woke they were coming in to land.

"You must fasten your seatbelt again, Mr Makoni. You had a good long sleep."

"Where are we?"

"Almost at Nairobi. After that it's London. You haven't had any food. I didn't want to wake you. Supper will be served when we take off from Nairobi."

"Thank you, Jean."

"It's my pleasure."

He watched the tight bottom walk away from him, thinking of Petronella and what he was going to do to her. Life was good again. He was back in control. The worst part of jail was not being able to make his own decisions. The total lack of freedom. Captivity was the worst of experiences.

The supper when it came was delicious. Roast beef in nice thin slices. Unlike the chunks of stewed meat in prison where you didn't know what animal it came from. He didn't drink alcohol with his meal. After the cheese and crackers he drank a cup of coffee. He wanted a clear mind when he got to London. Fourteen months was a long time in politics. ZANU politics. The kind of infighting he had seen in prison. Relaxed and replete, Josiah fell into sleep. He dozed on and off for the rest of the flight, not sure whether some of his thoughts were dreams or real. All the way through the sleep, upright in the seat, he was being chased. He was running away. Once, he spoke to the spirit of his father, Tembo smiling at him. When he woke from half sleep he was happy.

An hour out of Heathrow, Josiah washed and shaved, cramped in the small men's toilet at the back of the aeroplane. When he came out carrying his sponge bag, Jean was waiting.

"I'm sorry for your troubles, Mr Makoni." She had known who he was. What they had done to him.

"So am I, Jean. Thank you for looking after me so well."

"It was my pleasure."

They were all so polite it was almost a joke. Trying to work out when people were being genuine had never been Josiah's strong suit. He hoped she was. She had a nice tight bottom.

Back in his seat the tension in his mind and body began to mount. He had no idea if anyone was meeting him. He had no money and nowhere to live. The only item of value he hoped was still in his possession was the portrait of Princess, his mother, by Livy Johnston, from their brief meeting at his mentor Harry Brigandshaw's funeral. There had been small items in his Holland Park digs. Most likely the landlady had thrown them out. They had given him back his Rhodesian passport, a British colonial passport with his right to live in Britain. In his pocket were five Rhodesian pounds they had given him for the work he did in the prison garden. He would look for a bank at the airport and try to exchange them for English pounds. He wasn't even sure if Livingstone Sithole, or anyone else, knew he was on his way back to England. All he had was a small canvas bag in the luggage compartment above his head.

When the aircraft landed he was a bundle of nerves. He took a deep breath, walked down the steps and into the transit bus, carrying his bag. At immigration they stamped his passport, the man behind the counter barely looking up at him. He went through customs presenting his bag. There was a noise of shouting coming from the other side of the plate glass window with its automatic exit. Absorbed with his own feeling of insecurity he had not looked up. When he did he could see them. People with placards, all of them shouting with their mouths open. At the front of the crowd stood Livingstone Sithole, his face close to the big plate glass barrier. He was smiling his big teeth smile. Everyone in the crowd outside was looking at him. He waved at them. Ran his eyes up and down the crowd looking for Petronella. There were plenty of girls but none of them Petronella. Through the door as it opened in all the hullabaloo he could hear what they were shouting. They were shouting his name. Shouting 'Josiah'. Every one of the placards had the same word, 'freedom'. As he came among them they all wanted to shake his hand, the flashlights of the press cameras exploding in his face. Another much younger crowd began screaming the name of a man they called Mango. This Mango was apparently famous. Livingstone shook Josiah's hand.

"Welcome home, brother. That's the famous singer, Mango of Mango Boys. Helped to get you out of prison."

"Where's Petronella?"

"She doesn't work with us anymore."

"Why not, Livingstone?" The excitement was rapidly draining out of his body.

"It's a long story."

"Tell me. I've heard nothing in fourteen months."

"Her grandfather cut off her allowance and she wanted us to pay her."

"Didn't you pay her?"

"Of course we didn't. Her father's one of the farmers who stole our land."

"You get paid by the party, don't you?"

"Of course I do. I don't have rich parents."

"So what happened?"

"She went into business as a publicist. Mango over there being mobbed by all those girls was her first client. When the old man died he had changed his mind and left her a fortune. Big estate with a mansion. She switched sides. She's a capitalist. On the board of directors of the family company. A big public company quoted on the London Stock Exchange. You would hardly recognise her."

"So where does she live?"

"Look, Josiah, this is a big reception for you. The press want interviews. That man Harry Wakefield has been onto me ever since it was announced Smith was letting you out of the camp and sending you back to Britain."

"Where does she live, Livingstone?"

"At the old man's country house in Ashford."

"How far is it?"

"Not far."

"Get me the phone number."

"Hey. I'm the boss of ZANU in London."

"No, you are not, I am. From this moment." Leaning forward, Josiah spoke quietly into Livingstone's ear in Shona. "You're going back to Tanzania to coordinate the recruitment for the liberation army."

"Who said so?"

"I did. And all the other top ZANU officials in the camp."

"You're lying, Josiah."

"Then prove it."

"How do I prove it?"

"By going back to Rhodesia and getting yourself arrested."

"What's the matter with you, Josiah?"

"You should have helped her when she needed it."

"She's a white girl playing games with us."

"She was dedicated to the struggle... Good morning, Harry," Josiah said, breaking back into English. "My, what a reception."

"Quite the hero's welcome. Harry Brigandshaw would be proud of you."

"Would he? Where's Petronella?"

"You'd best forget Petronella, Josiah. I've forgotten her. I'm getting married to my childhood sweetheart, Ruthy, in two weeks' time. You going to give the *Daily Mirror* an exclusive interview?"

"Of course. Do you know where I'm staying?"

"Back in your old digs. They kept everything for you. Petronella took care of Livy's painting of your mother. Welcome back to London. Welcome to freedom. You know you and I have a lot more in common than politics. We have Petronella. She got under the skin of both of us. Take my advice and forget her. You remember Elsie Gilmore who worked part-time in your office? She was at Manchester University with Petronella. They are lovers. Living together at Woodlands Court now she's lady of the manor."

"I don't believe you."

"You must have known she was bisexual?"

"That was to turn on the men. The idea of your girlfriend having it off with a woman drives a man crazy. It was one of her ways of controlling men."

"Well, now she's a lesbian through and through. Where do you want to do the interview?"

"If you take me back to my old digs and the landlady welcomes me I'll feel less vulnerable. Prison does things to your self-esteem... Livingstone, I'm going with Harry. Be in the office tomorrow. Make sure your desk is cleared out."

Josiah pushed through the crowd followed by Harry Wakefield. Livingstone's big teeth smile had gone. It was best to let the man stew. All part of politics. They would clash again tomorrow when Josiah's mind was settled.

"Have you got a car, Harry?"

"Grab a taxi. The other journos are pissed off I've collared you. In some ways journalism is like politics. It's a jungle. So what's going to happen now in Rhodesia, Josiah?"

"We are going to win. One way or another."

"My grapevine says Ian Smith is going to declare UDI. They think all the hot air from London about economic sanctions will be a three-day wonder once the British are faced with a *fait accompli*."

"And what do you think, Harry?"

"My father-in-law to be, who interviewed you on the BBC, thinks the Rhodesian government are wrong. Very wrong. William Smythe says Smith is living with his head in the sand and can't see the days of the Raj are over."

"Will the British send troops?"

"Probably not."

"Sanctions will take years."

"At least the world, and particularly America with its Civil Rights movement, won't be able to point fingers. The British are going to wash their hands of the Rhodesians."

"Then we will go to war."

"Can I quote you?"

"Certainly. Also announce in the paper tomorrow I am taking over ZANU in London from Livingstone Sithole. And send the ZANU office a copy of your paper first thing in the morning. Will I be headlines?"

"Depends on the editor. Probably... Taxi!... In you go. Let's get out of here. What about your friend Livingstone?"

"I'll see him tomorrow. In the office."

"You want me to do your dirty work."

"You wanted an exclusive interview."

They both laughed and climbed into the taxi.

"Holland Park, driver. What I would really like to know is what you were saying when you spoke in Shona to Livingstone."

"Who organised my old digs for me?"

"Your office. I asked Livingstone before your plane landed. He was going to take you himself. Then I heard you two arguing."

"Sometimes you journalists hear more than you should."

"It's our job. Is that all the luggage you've got?"

"All my worldly goods are in this bag."

"Aren't you cold without an overcoat?"

"Haven't had time to think of it."

"You want some money?"

"Is the *Daily Mirror* bribing me?"

"Don't be silly. We don't pay for stories. We're a bit like two ex-husbands who had the same wife. There should be a name for such a relationship."

"Did you love her, Harry?"

"I think so."

"She had so much sexual power over men."

"And over women. Here's fifty quid. In case your office haven't paid your landlady's rent."

For the rest of the journey to Holland Park they were silent. Josiah was thinking of Petronella. He suspected Harry, with his faraway look out of the taxi window, was doing the same. Josiah was sad, suddenly deflated. Maybe, like Harry, he had loved her himself.

"Here we are, Josiah."

"Yes. I rather think we are. I'll pay you back the fifty quid."

"You do that."

When Harry left an hour later to go to his paper to write his article, Josiah sat in his old chair and stared at the wall. Harry had put a shilling in the gas meter to give them some heat, the gas fire hissing at him. In the background outside the one window that was closed against the cold he could hear the London traffic. It was a tired old room let by the landlady together with a few bits of old furniture. Like the landlady, the furniture had seen better days. She had been pleased to see him and collect her two months' rental. He would get the second month back when he left. It was home. As near to home as anything he could remember after leaving his father and mother's hut on Elephant Walk, the farm the Brigandshaw family had sold to Anglo-US Incorporated after Harry Brigandshaw's death. Harry, his mother and Harry's first wife were buried on Elephant Walk so far as Josiah could remember. With the hissing sound from the gas fire intruding, his mind began to wander. They were good times growing up on the white man's farm. Just before the shilling in the gas meter ran out his mind came full circle. He was thinking of Petronella. Of how it was in life that when you couldn't have something you wanted it so much more. Instead of his mistress, to be used when he liked, she was now a rich lesbian, her money taking her far from his reach. They had had communism and the struggle in common and now that was gone. All he had left was his sexual wanting. The more he thought, the more he wanted her. The gas fire went out. Josiah did not move. The old landlady had made up his bed. Standing up feeling lonely, Josiah took off his clothes. Then he climbed into bed. In his pocket were Harry's fifty pounds in notes. No coins for the meter. Tomorrow he would face Livingstone to secure his own position in the party. It was always the same. You had to fight for what you wanted. The thick eiderdown on top of the blankets soon made him feel warm. He was still thinking of Petronella as he fell into a troubled sleep.

Harry Wakefield had stood at the end of the road for ten minutes before successfully hailing a taxi. The invitations to the wedding had all gone out. He had done the right thing. Whether he would be marrying Ruthy were she not pregnant he was not so sure. In the days when people stayed virgins until the day of their marriage life was a lot more simple. He had his headline: 'They'll fight for their freedom – Josiah Makoni' firmly in his head. He wrote most of his articles in his head before going to his typewriter. When he typed he was almost word perfect. His mind strayed back to the wedding. At his father's request they had sent out invitations to the entire Brigandshaw family.

"Harry Brigandshaw was so important in my life and William's, Harry. You and Ruthy owe him so much. And Beth Crookshank is your own sister's sister-in-law. Your kids will be cousins. I've got Dorian and Kim Brigandshaw's addresses from their sister. We're lucky Kim will be in England. He drifts around the world. Dorian's new book is a bestseller. Never does a journalist any harm to rub shoulders with a bestselling novelist. One day you'll try to write a novel. We all do. It's said most journalists are frustrated novelists. Frank, who changed his name by deed poll to St Clair when he finally found out Barnaby St Clair was his natural father and not Harry Brigandshaw, should also be invited. You know his natural parents got married. It's the Honourable Barnaby St Clair's only marriage. They too were sweethearts as children, though in those days it was the class system that stopped them from marrying. Her father was a railway porter. His father a Lord. You're doing the right thing, Harry. You and Ruthy have been friends since childhood. Your mother thinks it's lucky she got herself pregnant. You're going to make both our families proud. After the passion wears off friendship is more important in a marriage. Getting on with each other. Liking each other. The same things in common. If you are lucky the passion for each other will last a couple of years... What's the matter, son? You're not still thinking of Petronella? Put her out of your mind. You and Ruthy have your whole lives ahead of you. You are going to be happy. With Petronella you would never have been happy. Much too flighty. You would never have known where you stood. What she was up to behind your back. And with all that money her grandfather left her she'll be able to do just what she wants. You'd be playing second fiddle for the rest of your life. With Ruthy you'll be partners. Like me and your mother."

"Is the Chelsea church hall going to be big enough for the reception?"

"William thinks so. And he's paying the bill. Bergit will be here three days before the wedding. Your mother and I can't wait to see her and Jeremy. I just wish they'd come and live in England. The whole of Africa is going to be a mess without the colonial powers keeping the peace. All those different tribes are going to be at each other's throats. What I'm hearing at the *Mail*. Look at the Congo since the Belgians got out. What are you hearing at the *Mirror*?"

"Much the same... Ruthy can't wait to have a good chat with Bergit. I don't think Jeremy will come back to England. Loves that farm of his too much. So Tina Brigandshaw and Barnaby St Clair finally got married? Frank will be happy. That's a love story. Dorian will likely turn it into a book. His editor likes them 'light and fluffy'. Dorian's words when I spoke to him once. Met him a couple of times. The light and fluffy novels make money. All those frustrated housewives."

Back in Fleet Street, Harry went straight to his office and closed the door. At his typewriter the words flowed easily. When he'd finished he took the two sheets of typed paper to Roland Cartwright, standing while the sub-editor read the article.

"It's an exclusive. Whisked him out of the airport before the other papers could get hold of him."

"He's threatening the Rhodesian government with a war if they don't agree to a 'one man one vote' election. Do we want to get involved with this kind of thing?"

"He's using us to negotiate. I think it's good. Somewhere down the line there has to be a compromise, Roland. I want to send a copy of the exclusive to a friend of mine at the *Rhodesia Herald* in Salisbury, hoping his editor will publish it. It's what the fourth estate does best, bringing up problems before they get out of hand. Before people start killing each other... Did you get your wedding invitation?"

"Thank you, I did."

"Are you coming?"

"Mr and Mrs Cartwright will be delighted to attend. How could I ever turn down William Smythe when he requests the pleasure of my company?... Do Josiah and his friends have a big enough army to make a dent in the Rhodesian armed forces? Smith was a fighter pilot in the last war but I don't suppose he'll be leading a squadron of Hurricanes this time."

"They won't fight a conventional war. It'll be a guerrilla war aimed at the farmers. The farmers are vulnerable, stuck out in the bush on their own. Josiah and his friends will be able to terrorise the farmers. They won't have to mount attacks very often to keep everyone on edge. Terrorist wars get on people's nerves. Wear them down. Just the threat of an attack in the middle of the night will ruin the farmers' lives. A terrorist war can go on for years, wearing down any government. Costs far more to prevent than perpetrate. According to my reading on the subject, no one in history has ever defeated a guerrilla army. The Russians and Chinese are going to arm and train the blacks and sit back and watch. Much better to get someone else to fight your wars and stay back in the shadows. Rhodesia is just a small part of the plan for a communist takeover of the world."

"So you don't think Smith could win?"

"Not in the long run. Why this article of ours placed in the *Rhodesia Herald* might frighten some sense into a quarter of a million whites who want to play King Canute and hold back the tide of black nationalism."

"Will a black government be better for them?"

"Likely be worse for everyone. Once the whites get out the place will fall apart according to the people I met in Salisbury. You need skills to run a modern infrastructure, let alone the economy. Peasant farming is one thing, modern commercial farming quite another."

"You haven't put that in your article."

"Of course not. Poor old Jeremy. He's going to be pissed off with me when he reads this article. Josiah wants me to send a copy of the paper to the ZANU office first thing in the morning. Before he gets to the office. He's having a turf war with Livingstone Sithole. Life never changes whatever your background."

"We'll run it."

"Thank you, Roland."

"What a bloody mess the world's in."

"Always has been. Nothing changes... Jeremy and Bergit want us to go to Rhodesia for our honeymoon."

"Are you going?"

"It'll be the perfect honeymoon. Before the shit hits the fan. We're hiring a houseboat on Lake Kariba. They say you can see all the animals on shore from the boat. Sail right past them. Elephant, buffalo, rhinoceros, giraffe and every kind of buck imaginable. Before they all go. Once a war starts the animals will suffer. Food for the guerrilla fighters who'll be living off the land. Oh, we're going all right. Before it's all gone. Ruthy and Bergit grew up together. They can both talk until their tongues fall out. Both of them are pregnant."

Roland gave him a smile.

"You youngsters, Harry. Did William point a shotgun at you?"

"Not quite."

The next job was Moss Bros in Regent Street. Ruthy wanted a white wedding which Harry thought smacked ever so slightly of irony. Brides in white were supposed to be virgins, not pregnant. He took the Tube. Taxis, like the ones he had taken with Josiah, were for expense accounts. The Tube was cheap. The man at Moss Bros had a long tape measure hung round his neck. He was the shop assistant in the hiring department. The man measured Harry and brought him a morning suit. Harry put it on and looked in the mirror, smiling at himself looking ridiculous.

"You need a dove grey tie. Looks better with a shirt and tie. Do you have black shoes?"

"Tradition. What we do for tradition."

Harry gave the man the date of the wedding.

"Three-day hire, sir. You pick it up the day before and return it the day after."

"How many men have worn this suit?"

"I couldn't say."

Outside in Regent Street he turned up the road to the offices of British Overseas Airways. He had told the receptionist at the *Mirror* he would be out for lunch with a man he was interviewing. Which was a lie which she smiled at. So much of life was telling white lies... They were going to fly to Rhodesia two days after the wedding, a week before his sister went back to Rhodesia with Jeremy. Jeremy was booking the houseboat on the lake. They would go to World's View and let the two girls talk each other to a standstill. The airfare made Harry go cold. He gave the booking clerk a cheque. She was young and in some kind of blue uniform. Hopefully, you only married once, he told himself. Girls wanted a honeymoon to remember. Something to talk about afterwards. For years. When they were old. To remind themselves of who they had been. The white wedding and the honeymoon. That was important for Ruthy. With a nice white dress over her stomach the baby wouldn't show. Not that it mattered. Everyone knew. Trying to feel excited with the plane ticket in his pocket, Harry took the Tube back to the office, buying himself a sandwich on the way out of the Tube station... It was no good. He was still thinking of Petronella. Once they were married and the baby was born he would get over it. Or so he told himself. Poor Ruthy. Everyone else in the families was happy for him. It was all so close. Soon it would all be over. No more life-changing decisions.

2

The morning paper, like the milk, was delivered to Woodlands Court every morning. The *Times* of London had been put through the letter box in the front door for over a hundred years, according to Mrs Weatherby. The milk was left outside the door in exchange for the empty milk bottles. No one had ever stolen the milk. Bored, Petronella had gone to fetch the morning paper. On page three she read of Josiah's arrival in England. She didn't want to say anything to Elsie. Better not to bring up Josiah. Like all couples who lived together they deemed it better not to start a conversation that would lead to a fight. Feeling mind-bogglingly bored with nothing to do she took the paper back to their bedroom. Elsie, lying on her back, was still fast asleep. There wasn't much in the article. She lay back on the bed thinking about everyone in the ZANU office and all the excitement. Which brought her full circle back to Harry. Harry who was getting married in two weeks' time at St Giles Church, Chelsea. A mutual friend had told her the time and place of the wedding. She had not received an invitation. Not that she had expected one. There was a board meeting at Sheckland-Hall Limited at the end of the month. All she had to look forward to. Being stinking rich, living in a mansion, wasn't all it was cracked up to be. Petronella was bored to distraction.

.   .   .

Six days before the wedding Frank St Clair walked into Harry Wakefield's Fleet Street office.

"Frank! Nice to see you. You don't have to answer the wedding invitation in person. With Harry Brigandshaw having such an influence on both our lives, Ruthy and I thought it right to ask the Brigandshaw family to our wedding. I still think of you as Frank Brigandshaw. So glad to hear your mother and father married. Must make you feel very satisfied with all you went through."

"Finding out my mother had slept with another man other than Harry wasn't the best part of my growing up. They're old now. Being married makes it easier on their social lives." Frank sat down in the high-backed chair in front of Harry's desk. "And my secretary accepted your invitation formally to William Smythe."

"So what can I do for you, Frank?"

"We want you to come to Hastings Court tomorrow. Two-thirty in the afternoon to be precise. We are asking your father and William Smythe. Your wedding invitations brought Harry Brigandshaw's children together for the first time in a while. We all phoned each other and arranged a reunion. Dorian got out of his foxhole in Cornwall. Kim was in London from South America. Dorian just finished a new book. You know Kim's brief career in the theatre came to nothing?"

"You want some coffee?" Harry waved to the receptionist outside in the general office, mouthing the word 'coffee'.

"Thank you, Harry... Dorian brought up the subject. He wrote a bestselling book on Sebastian Brigandshaw, Harry Brigandshaw's father. He's more concerned with the family history than the rest of us. We're bringing Harry Brigandshaw, his mother Emily and his first wife back to his mother's ancestral home to rest forever. The Mandervilles have lived at Hastings Court since the time of William the Conqueror. All of them buried at Hastings Court. My half-brother, Anthony Brigandshaw, has a memorial in among the cedar and yew trees. He was shot down during the war over Berlin. Some of the graves are so ancient only the top of the headstones are above the ground, the rest sunk into the earth. With all the turmoil in Rhodesia we thought it best to bring their remains back to England for reburial."

"Seeing Harry wasn't your father, why are you involved?"

"My father owns Hastings Court. When Harry died my mother

wanted to live in London. There wasn't much money in Harry's estate after death duty. The main asset was Hastings Court. That was before Tinus Oosthuizen, Harry Brigandshaw's nephew, went to Rhodesia and recovered the fifty-nine carat diamond Harry had hidden in full view embedded in the mantelpiece in the lounge of the main house on Elephant Walk. Mother wanted to live in style in Mayfair with Chin-Chin, her Pekinese dog and a companion. Mother was feeling sorry for herself after Harry died. She also wanted to be nearer my father's townhouse in Piccadilly. Dad wanted a place in the country he could visit over the weekends. Surrey is a lot closer than Dorset and the St Clair ancestral home. Anyway, as the youngest son, Dad was never going to inherit Purbeck Manor. Dad wants his own dynasty. With Hastings Court the old place will go to me when he dies... Will you come to the burial?"

"Of course. We'll all drive down together. Who brought back the remains?"

"Kim. He flew out and brought back the exhumed coffins. You see, Harry Brigandshaw's first wife Lucinda, who was murdered soon after their wedding, is my aunt. Why Dad and I are so happy to be involved... Thank you, kind lady. That coffee smells good."

"Her name is Macey."

"Thank you, Macey... So tomorrow half past two. If it's raining bring an umbrella."

"We'll be there. All of us."

They were silent for a while as both of them thought of Harry Brigandshaw's remains coming back to England. Frank sipped at his hot coffee.

"How's business, Frank?" Harry said finally.

"Not bad at all. Picked up the account of Mango Boys since your old girlfriend got out of business. PR is all about knowing people, isn't it, Harry? Well, I'll be going along."

Harry sat thinking for a long while after the door to his office closed behind Frank St Clair. He was glad they had invited the Brigandshaws to the wedding. That the man he was named after was coming home where he could rest forever under the cedar trees with his ancestors undisturbed through the centuries.

. . .

IT TOOK them three quarters of an hour to drive to Mickleham. William Smythe drove with Harry in the backseat behind his father. When they drove up to the old house with the crenellated battlements the sun was shining, the first sweet breath of spring. They followed some old people through the cedar trees to the burial site of the Mandervilles. Someone called one of the old women Mrs Ding-a-ling. She was crying. Harry suspected they were friends of Harry Brigandshaw. There were three open graves. Three new headstones. Three old, weathered caskets that had been flown from Rhodesia. They stood at the back behind the family. Harry read the headstones. 'Emily Brigandshaw, née Manderville.' Next to her looming grave was the headstone of Sir Henry Manderville Bart, Emily Brigandshaw's father. In the middle was Harry Brigandshaw. On the other side 'Lucinda Brigandshaw née St Clair and unborn child.' In front of Harry Brigandshaw was the memorial to his eldest son, 'Flight Lieutenant Anthony Brigandshaw DFC, died fighting for his country three days before his twenty-first birthday.' A priest in long robes read from the Holy Bible. The weathered caskets were lowered into the ground by Kim and Dorian Brigandshaw on one side of the coffins, Frank St Clair and Paul Crookshank on the other. Everyone prayed for the souls of the departed. A pigeon was calling from the trees behind the cedar trees towards Mickleham common. When it was over, they left to drive back to London, Harry, his father and William Smythe having paid their respects. All the old people and the family had gone into the ancestral home of the Mandervilles. Halfway up to London it began to rain.

"He was a good man," said Harry's father. "One of the few truly good men I ever met."

To Harry's surprise his father was crying. Harry looked away. They would see the family at his wedding. It was better they hadn't stayed. Family and Harry Brigandshaw's personal friends. It was how it should have been. It was right for them not to have stayed.

"Who was Mrs Ding-a-ling?"

"Ding-a-ling Bell's wife. Ding-a-ling was Harry Brigandshaw's adjutant in the Royal Flying Corps during the First World War. Some called him Ding-Dong Bell. Never did find out his Christian name. Where you want to be dropped off, Harry?"

"At the office."

"You work too hard."

"Tell that to Roland Cartwright."

"See you at the wedding."

William Smythe turned round and smiled. Harry got out of the car.

"Where are you two going?"

"To the pub."

Slowly, mostly looking down at his feet, Harry walked up to his office. It was six o'clock, just in time for the night shift.

WHEN JEREMY and Bergit Crookshank came out of customs pushing a trolley with their luggage on the Thursday morning, three days before the wedding, Harry Wakefield was relaxed and resigned to his fate. His mother had driven them to the airport in his father's car, Harry still not owning his own vehicle. After they came back from their honeymoon he and Ruthy were going to buy their first car, a white Ford Prefect they had ordered from the Ford agent. Together they had scraped up enough money for the deposit, Harry now on a budget controlled by Ruthy. With the baby due in less than five months it was essential not to waste money. A married man has responsibilities. He had only to look at Sidney. His days of spending every penny of his monthly salary were over.

With a rueful smile and recognition of what was to come, Harry watched his sister and fiancée gush and perform. His mother was equally excited. Neither girl seemed to listen as the words gushed out of them, all about babies and marriage. Jeremy gave him a shrug and a smile. With the two best girlfriends arm in arm, Bergit having first hugged her mother, tears pouring down their faces, Harry and Jeremy followed behind, Harry now pushing the trolley.

"How's the crop, Jeremy?"

"Pretty good. Still has to be sold. Depends on the buyers on the auction floors. How are you?"

"Nervous. Resigned. Trying to be relaxed. Marriage is a life-changing experience."

"Don't tell me. You'll be all right. She's a good girl. You picked the right one... Where's the car?"

"Third floor, row D. Dad's car. Welcome home."

"Rhodesia is my home."

"Yes, I suppose it is."

"When you get to Salisbury airport on your honeymoon there's a hire car booked for you at the Hertz kiosk. At Cutty Sark Hotel they'll give you the keys and directions to the houseboat. The marina is close to the hotel. Ten days sailing the lake."

"It has sails!"

"Manner of speaking. You sail round the world on an ocean liner. Anyway... Two ten-horse outboards on the back. A chap who will run the boat for you. Cook the food... You know which road to take for Kariba. When you get back to Salisbury from the lake we'll be back. I've timed the hire to give you time to drive back the day we fly into Salisbury from London. We'll drive up to World's View together."

"You've thought of everything. I'm going to enjoy being your brother-in-law. Those two can really talk. My poor mother can't get a word in edgeways. Pity you're not going to be living in England."

"Yes, I suppose it is for the girls."

"Time will tell. I interviewed Josiah."

"I know you did. Read your article in the *Rhodesia Herald*. Nothing I can do but get on with my life, I'm afraid."

"What did you do with the boys?"

"Left them in boarding school."

"Your brother and sister-in-law are coming to dinner at my mother's tomorrow night. We all thought it best to give the girls a day of their own to talk."

"We're all driving down to the Isle of Wight to see my mother after your wedding. Don't know about Paul's kids. Go across on the ferry if the weather's not rough. Sometimes you have to wait. Good to see you, Harry."

"Good to see you, Jeremy. That Christmas when I brought the girls up to World's View sorted us both out."

"Suppose it did. I'm happy. Your sister is easy to live with. She's so looking forward to her kid."

"So is Ruthy. First cousins. Whoever would have thought it that first day on the farm?"

"That's life. Never know what's going to happen next. Where do we leave the trolley?"

"In the garage. Who do I pay for the houseboat?"

"You don't. The boat and the car hire are your sister's and my wedding present. It's not exactly the *Queen Mary*. More a raft than a boat. Eight forty-four gallon drums tied together with a deck and a thatch roofed cabin built on top. The whole of Africa runs on forty-four gallon oil drums. They clean the oil ones up and give them a coat of paint. More an anti-rust. Then they clamp on the two outboards and there you have it. A Rhodesian houseboat. If the wind comes up you chug into shore. Best holiday anyone can imagine. Just the two of you and the one chap who's sort of in charge of the boat and the cooking. Won't notice him. At night you anchor in-shore."

"It's our honeymoon!"

"Oh, he'll sleep on shore. Has a tent. All organised."

"Thanks Jeremy."

"My pleasure... You think they'll ever stop talking?"

"Probably not. That's Dad's car. I'm driving. There's a bit of a reception for you at your brother's flat in Hammersmith... Mum, you get in the back with the girls... You know Paul has a grand piano?"

"Plays classical piano and jazz on a clarinet. My brother is a frustrated artist. Unless you are lucky, art, creative or performing, doesn't make any money."

"How are you, Jeremy?"

"I'm good, Mrs Wakefield."

"Call me Janet. I told you that at the wedding."

"I could always call you Mum."

"Better not. You're a bit too old to be one of my children. So, you're about to make me a grandmother. Now that makes me feel old."

"You don't look old enough to be Harry or Bergit's mother."

"You old flatterer."

"I mean it, Janet."

They all laughed as Harry drove from the garage and out onto the road.

3

*A*t eleven o'clock on the Saturday morning the bells of St Giles began to peal over Chelsea calling the wedding guests to the church. The pews began to fill up, most of the men in suits, the women and girls wearing hats. Harry could hear the bells from the front room of his mother's house, the room she used during the week for her speech therapy practice. Sidney Cross, his best man, was with him, Sidney more nervous than Harry.

"Stop fiddling with your speech, Sidney."

"I'm a photographer, not a speech writer."

"If you start to stutter look at my mother and remember, it's from the tip of the tongue that you speak."

"I don't stutter, Harry. It's just the thought of all those people. We'd better go. Don't want to arrive after the bride."

"Ruthy will be late. She likes being late. Highly organised except when it comes to timing... Those bells sound so beautiful. There's something so very English about church bells. Reminds me of old Norman churches and small English villages that have nestled in the country for centuries undisturbed."

"Let's go, Harry."

"How do I look?"

"In that morning suit? Bloody ridiculous."

Outside, Sidney's car was waiting. They were the last to leave the house. The drive took them three minutes.

"We should have walked."

"Wouldn't have looked right. Now get out of the car. You can't run away. She's pregnant. The bells have stopped pealing, the sign for the bride to arrive. Get out of the bloody car... Harry. What's the matter? You've gone white as a sheet."

"She's over there. Across the road from the church."

"Shit! It's Petronella. Don't look at her."

"She just waved."

Harry got out of the front passenger seat and stood outside the car holding onto the roof. She was thirty yards away. Every instinct in Harry made him want to run to her. They stood staring at each other, neither smiling. Then she turned and slowly walked away up the street in the direction of the river. He felt Sidney take his arm in a firm grip.

"Come on, old friend. You're getting married to Ruthy."

Tears were trickling down Harry's face. Sidney gave him the handkerchief that had been decorating the top of his breast pocket. Harry kept watching the back of Petronella walking away. At the end of the road from the church she turned and gave him a forlorn wave. Then she disappeared round the corner of the street. Harry wiped his eyes, gave Sidney back his handkerchief and walked into the church. Five minutes later his bride arrived. The wedding ceremony began. By half past twelve it was over. He was married to Ruthy. The bells were ringing out again. With her arm in his, Harry walked from the church to William Smythe's car that was waiting outside to take them to the reception. The same car with the white ribbons on the bonnet that had brought Ruthy to the church. He looked up the street. The corner was empty of people.

"What's the matter, Harry?"

"Nothing, Ruthy. Oh, I'm sorry. Nothing, Mrs Wakefield."

He was smiling. It was over.

"I've wanted to be called that all my life. I'm so happy, Harry."

"So am I."

"That's better. Now you're smiling."

. . .

HARRY DRANK TOO MUCH at his own wedding. Sidney drank with him, not letting Harry out of his sight. Their speeches from the top of the table were a mess but everyone laughed. Grooms and best men were expected to be nervous. The caterers had put trestle tables, all fitting together, down the centre of the church hall. Like some medieval banquet, it seemed to Harry, as he sat down after his disjointed speech. Everyone in the big room looked happy. His new father-in-law had hired a band with the help of Paul Crookshank. Soon after the speeches Paul took his clarinet out of its case and went to play in the band. It was odd to Harry seeing a man of stature in the world of business playing in a band. When he played, Paul was better than Harry had expected. Now they were all related. Like Jeremy Crookshank and Bergit they were spending their first night in a hotel, their bags packed for Rhodesia.

"You'd better stop drinking, Harry."

So he stopped. Cold. In his tracks. There were people other than himself to be considered. Ruthy threw her bouquet and went off to her parents' house down the road to change, Harry going round the guests accepting their congratulations. The hotel they were staying in was not far from the Chelsea block of flats owned by Jeremy Crookshank and Livy Johnston. Harry had heard that if Jeremy had given up the farm and gone back to England he would now have been married to Livy and not Harry's sister Bergit. And Jeremy and Bergit were happy. So who knew in the strange ways of life? Hopefully in the end he would look back on Petronella and thank heaven he had married the less complicated Ruthy.

They made love in the hotel, quietly. Ruthy was so content. He put his hand on her stomach, imagining what the person inside would one day become. A new life was growing, the process about to start all over again. They slept in each other's arms right through the night.

A taxi took them to the airport in the morning. They had wanted to be on their own. They were early to board the plane and went into the coffee shop in the airport concourse. Harry had bought two bottles of whisky in the duty free shop next door.

When the plane took off everything was left behind. All of his past. What he now had was all in the future. With a girl he had liked and laughed with all of his life. They were airborne. The three of them going places. He, Ruthy and their unborn child, the twists and turns of life indeed strange. A few brief moments on the couch and here he was.

"Hey, I'm a married man."

"Does it feel different, darling?"

"That's the first time you've called me darling."

"We're married, Harry. Going to have a family. I've never been more happy in my life. Are you happy, Harry?"

"Of course I am. Africa. Sunshine. A boat on a lake even if it is a load of petrol drums tied together underneath an African thatched hut. Ten days all to ourselves. Would you mind if we left the boatman on shore and did the cooking ourselves? The lake isn't that big. You can see both shores at the same time, one shore in Zambia the other in Rhodesia. I've been out on the lake before. Know all about the winds. The beginning of April is the best time of the year. The main rains will be over. Not much wind. Not as hot as midsummer. We can be on our own. You know, in all the years we've grown up together we've never really been on our own. There was always someone in the family around. A few hours, maybe, by the River Thames but never days on our own."

"It's going to be so wonderful."

"In five months we'll have a baby and never again have the chance of really being on our own."

"Oh, Harry. You're so romantic."

"When we're old together we'll be able to look back on our ten days alone... Look, they're serving breakfast. I'm starving."

"So am I."

"Sidney has lent me one of his cameras with a telephoto lens. I'm going to make a photo album of our honeymoon with the lake and all the animals, of Jeremy's farm. So Rhodesia will keep forever in case the politicians destroy the place. It will always be fresh. As it was. As it is now. You and I young. Our whole lives to look forward to."

"Do you know how to use it?"

She was smiling with a faraway look as the stewardess handed her a tray of food.

"I listened carefully to Sidney. He's one of the best photographers in London... What have we got?"

"Scrambled eggs, sausage and bacon."

"How English."

"We are English, Harry. The aircraft is British. I like being British. All that wonderful history."

"So is Rhodesia British for the moment. I'm so glad we're going. It's the last true British colony in Africa. Almost the last in the world after Hong Kong. It's the end of empire. Our kid won't even understand there was once a British Empire that spanned the entire globe. That when his father was born the Union Jack flew over one fifth of the world's surface and one in four people were subjects of the King Emperor. Now that's all over. We're going to spend our honeymoon in the last outpost of empire."

"Does it matter it's gone? The empire. Aren't people better off governing themselves?"

"Of course it doesn't matter. Empires come and go. Ask the Greeks and the Romans. I just hope we leave behind a legacy as strong as the Greeks and the Romans."

"Don't eat so fast, Harry."

"I'm hungry. And you've got to feed the both of you."

"What are we going to call him?"

"You're sure it's a boy?"

"You want a boy, don't you?"

"If the baby is healthy it doesn't matter whether it's a boy or a girl. We'll love whatever we're given. I'll tell you one thing. British Overseas Airways can't make tea."

"Not much good at scrambled eggs."

When the trays were taken away and the small tables locked back in place into the back of the seats in front of them they sat holding hands. The seat next to Ruthy was empty. They were on their own. Out of the corner of his eye, Harry looked at Ruthy. She was dreaming. Far away. She looked so happy, giving Harry a surge of wellbeing. He was content. Everything was going to work out all right for everybody. All those years of friendship between the Wakefields and Smythes and now they were truly united, their blood mingled in the child in Ruthy's belly. It made him happy. Happy for everyone.

EVERYTHING JEREMY HAD TOLD him was laid on. At Hertz he showed them his British driving licence and took the keys to the car. The car was just outside the door to the airport, an airport minuscule in size compared to Heathrow. It was hot outside the airport building.

"The car's got air conditioning. Good old Jeremy."

"Do you know the way, Harry?"

"There aren't too many roads out of Salisbury. You go northwest to Kariba. South to South Africa. Southwest to Bulawayo. East to Umtali and Mozambique. Pretty simple. The road to the Kariba Dam is good. From the dam wall the lake goes west to Victoria Falls stopping short at about fifty miles from the falls. Took years for the lake to be full. Well over a hundred miles long, twenty, thirty miles wide where the lake follows the rivers. Full of fish. Mostly Kariba bream. Best fresh water eating fish in the world."

"You're not too tired to drive?"

"Three hours. Maybe four. Lunch at the Cutty Sark Hotel for my bride and then we go on the boat. First night we'll stay in the bay down from the hotel. First light I'll show you the lake in all its morning glory."

"When we get our own car at home I'm going to take driving lessons. Dad says it's bad for a husband to try and teach his wife to drive."

"Your father is always full of good advice."

"They're so happy we're married."

"Didn't he get mad at you for getting pregnant?"

"Not with you, Harry. Provided you married me."

Ruthy had put his hand on her knee. Half an hour later, having driven through the centre of Salisbury, Harry found the great north road. An hour before lunchtime, Harry stopped the car at the Makuti Hotel perched on top of the Zambezi escarpment. In silent awe they both stood in the car park of the hotel and looked down into the valley shimmering far below in the heat of the day, everything so silent, everything bush, not a sign of man except for the dirt road trailing down into the valley.

"I can't see the Zambezi River or Lake Kariba."

"Heat haze, Ruthy. Come on. Let's go down."

"It's so beautiful. Oh, Harry. Just look at it."

"Don't you fall in love with Africa like Jeremy and my sister. They say it's a bug. A bug you never recover from. Bush fever. You drink the water of the Zambezi River and never want to leave again."

"I'll have to be careful not to drink the river water. They are so lucky, Bergit and Jeremy. What a beautiful life on an African farm among all this. Pity it won't last."

"Nothing ever lasts, Ruthy. Life itself. The trick is to enjoy whatever you have at the time. Come on. We'll have a cold Castle lager at the hotel. Then we'll have an African lunch. Their beef steaks are an inch thick and cover the plate."

"I'm going to remember our honeymoon for the rest of my life."

"I hope so. Let the safari begin."

Dense bush on both sides of the dirt road prevented them from seeing wild animals until they wound down onto the floor of the valley, Harry driving slowly. A giraffe, its small knob horns on top of its head like antenna, browsed the top of a tree, watching them pass, a shoot of the tree motionless in its mouth. Two elephant, back from the road, took no notice of them. On a rise in the road they saw the lake, a great sheet of water. It was still far away. To the right, up on a hill, stood the village of Kariba. The village overlooked the dam that spanned the Zambezi built by the Italians. The buildings on the hill looked out of place. They followed the road away from the village to the shores of the lake. The Cutty Sark Hotel was close to the lake, high on a ridge above the water. Harry parked the car. At reception he was told where to find the houseboat at the marina. Harry looked around. Lunch was being served outside next to a thatch-roofed bar. They both drank down a Castle lager to settle the dust from the road. They ate lunch at a table under an umbrella, the steaks the size of the dinner plates, the view out over the lake spectacular.

At the marina they found the boat. Harry paid off the boatman the same money he would have earned had he gone with them. The man seemed pleased. Harry suspected he would be paid again by the marina from the money given them by Jeremy. It didn't matter. They wanted to be alone. The boatman showed Harry how everything worked. The outboard motors started first pull of the ropes. Slowly, sitting on a wooden bench between the two outboards holding the handles, Harry sailed them through the neck of the bay out onto the lake. They had decided not to stay one night in the hotel and go out at first light in the morning. Harry kept to the shore.

Further down they saw a campsite with a few tents. There was no one around. Next to the campsite up to their knees in water was a herd of buffalo. They had food and drink on board for ten days. Most of the food in tins. There were fishing rods and a bucket full of wet earth crawling in worms they would use for bait. Five minutes past the buffalo. Harry steered the houseboat into a bay. Sticks of wood, old trees killed by the waters of the rising lake, protected the shore. Harry anchored in between two old trees, tying the boat to them. Within a minute of dropping their lines into the water, the earth worms wriggling, they both caught fish. There were weighing scales in the galley of the boat. Harry's fish weighed two pounds, Ruthy's three ounces more. The bay was teeming with fish. The sun had begun to go down, slashing the horizon in red. There was ice in a coolbox that would last three days. Harry gutted their fish and opened the bar. They sat next to each other on canvas chairs and watched the African sun go down, sipping their gin and tonics. Birds, big birds of prey, circling high in the sky, were calling. All round them they could hear the echoing sounds of wild animals splashing. There were grunts and strange noises. All of the noises content. They felt safe high above the water on their deck.

Later, Harry fried both of the fish in the galley before the light was gone. They each ate a fish with a glass of white wine. Harry had put the bottle in the coolbox. A small hurricane lamp burned inside the cabin. When the mosquitoes began to bite they went inside. There was netting over the windows which let in the soft breeze from the lake but kept out the bugs. The sounds of the animals around them grew louder as night settled over the shore by the lake. Soon all they could see were the two sticks of trees they were anchored to.

They went outside on the deck to look at the stars. Three layers of stars spread high in the heavens, twinkling at them. The moon had not yet come up. They held hands for a moment and went back inside before the insects found them. On the one double bed they made love, Ruthy's cries mingling with the night cries of Africa. Soon after, they fell asleep. Both replete. Both happy.

The wild geese woke them, calling up the dawn. Naked, they walked out on deck. A soft cool breeze came across the lake brushing their skin. Silently they stood not wishing to break the moment. Their fingers were touching as they stood side by side. The sun rimmed over the hills, blushing the lake red. The wild geese were chasing each other across the water, calling as they went. It was the mating season, the male chasing the female, the female playing hard to get, wanting the strongest male.

Harry went back into the thatched cabin and put on the kettle. He started the outboard engines, let loose the ropes on the trees and chugged out into the deep of the lake where there were no crocodiles or hippopotamus. Harry anchored the boat. They dived over the side into the cool of the water, washing away yesterday's dust from the road. They swam around smiling at each other, the surface of the lake perfectly still. Ruthy had made the tea, letting it stand to draw out the flavour. When they came on board they sat on the canvas chairs, looking out on the dawn, drinking tea. They were both still naked. Still neither of them spoke, absorbed with the dawning day.

After tea they sailed down the lake. There were many small islands made by the rising water. On all the islands were animals. Day by day, inch by inch, the islands were growing smaller giving the wild animals less to eat. Man had cast his ways on the Zambezi River. Harry had heard there was a Noah's Ark operation being mounted to save the animals, to take them back to the mainland shore where they could roam once again deep into the bush. Some people called it progress giving Rhodesia hydro-electricity. Harry was not so sure. There were always winners and losers. The second cup of tea when they drank it was good, the cosy keeping the teapot warm. So were the bacon and eggs cooked by Ruthy over the small gas stove in the galley.

After breakfast they lay on a mattress on the deck in the warmth of the early morning sun. They made love. The day had fully dawned and along with it something else for Harry. For the first time in his life he knew the meaning of true happiness. He loved her. He loved his Ruthy.

For ten days in a world of their own they sailed up and down the lake looking at the birds and wild animals, never for a moment bored. When they sailed back into the marina near the Cutty Sark it was the day of Jeremy's return from England. The Hertz car was waiting. In three hours they were back at Salisbury airport as Jeremy and Bergit came off the plane. With the Hertz car back with its owner, they drove in the Chev Impala back to World's View, Jeremy's car having been parked in the airport garage while the Crookshanks were in England. It was strange to be back in the world of people. In the backseat with the roof down Harry and Ruthy were silent. Enthusiastically, Bergit and Jeremy talked of their trip to England. Neither Harry nor Ruthy wanted to share their experiences on the lake with anyone. It was private. It belonged to them.

"I've never known you so quiet, Ruthy."

"You've never known me so happy."

"Thanks for the houseboat, Jeremy."

"That good, was it?"

"It was perfect."

PART XI

NOVEMBER 1965

THE COMFORT OF HOME

*I*n November, when London was shrouded in fog and Harry Wakefield's daughter was sixteen weeks old, he received a phone call in his Fleet Street office from Josiah Makoni telling him Ian Smith, the Rhodesian Prime Minister, was about to declare UDI in defiance of the British government.

"Why are you telling me, Josiah?"

"You have been good to me, Harry, when ZANU needed publicity. The real struggle is about to begin."

"Who told you?"

"Why don't you go out to Rhodesia and find out? Be on the spot. Good for your career. Congratulations on a baby girl."

"Have you seen Petronella?"

"Not a word."

"Thanks for the tip-off."

In Roland Cartwright's office Harry told the sub-editor of the *Daily Mirror* what he had just heard.

"Pack your bags, Harry. Since you left we don't have our own man in Salisbury."

"How long, Roland?"

"As long as it takes. A unilateral declaration of independence by the Rhodesian government will stir up all kinds of shit. Go and stay with your sister in the heart of white man's country and give us a first-hand report about how the events affect the people. Our readers are more interested in the people than the politics."

"Should I take Ruthy?"

"Better not. Let her stay with her mother. It could get rough."

"You think the government will send in the army?"

"Who knows? You'll be on a full expense account. Just don't drink too much booze and put it on our account. Didn't your sister have a baby?"

"A boy. Craig Crookshank. The name's a bit crunchy. Judy Wakefield sounds a lot better."

"Keeping you awake?"

"Ruthy gets up. The problem is getting back to sleep. Especially when you have something running through your mind."

"You'll enjoy the break... He won't tell you his source?"

"They never do. My friend Josiah is a canny politician. He had Livingstone Sithole back in Africa three days after he flew in from Salisbury after Smith let him out of jail."

"How far do you think Josiah will go?"

"All the way if someone doesn't take him out. These liberation movements have a bad habit of fighting among themselves. It's all about power. Absolute power."

"Could he run a country?"

"For whose benefit?"

"The people they purport to liberate."

"Probably not. The leaders are more interested in looking after themselves than the ordinary people."

"Do I detect a little vitriol, Harry? Josiah and you were in competition for Petronella."

"Petronella is right out of my life."

"I'm so glad to hear it. Keep it like that. Off you go. Smith might declare independence any moment... Shit, UDI. That'll put the cat among the proverbial pigeons."

"Do I get my own byline?"

"Yes you do, Harry."

"A man has to look after himself."

"A bit like the politicians."

.   .   .

HARRY REACHED Salisbury late the following evening, booking himself into Meikles Hotel. None of the locals seemed to have any idea of what was about to happen. The bar in the hotel was the same old colonial mix of khaki shorts and shirts and wide-brimmed bush hats. The same old tall stories of life in Africa. Harry looked at them sadly, knowing it was all about to end.

After two drinks he went upstairs. From his hotel room he put a call through to his sister.

"What are you doing in Rhodesia, Harry?"

"Can I come and stay?"

"Of course you can. Are Ruthy and the baby with you?"

"I'm on assignment for my paper."

"What's the matter?"

"Tell you tomorrow. Why's it so hot?"

"The rains haven't broken. October was just as bad. You know they call October suicide month in Rhodesia."

"How's my nephew?"

"A fine bouncing boy."

"See you tomorrow. I may go via the club. Get some local colour for the newspaper. Will they let me go in on my own?"

"I'm sure they will. If the chairman of the club wants to throw you out you can write it up in your paper. Those bad old colonial farmers. To become a member you need five sponsors. Keep out the wrong types. Bit like the rubbish in some London clubs."

The next day was Armistice Day in England. The day the nation remembered their war dead from the two world wars. At eleven o'clock Queen Elizabeth would lay a wreath at the Cenotaph.

In the morning at breakfast the place was a buzz. Harry had rented a car and after breakfast was going to drive up to the farm. The four farmers at the next table were laughing and joking. More like they would have been at dinner after a bottle of wine.

"Excuse me. I've just got in from England. Can you tell me what's going on?"

"Smith's addressing the nation on radio at one-fifteen this afternoon. In the lunch hour. Rumour has it this is it."

"What's 'it'?" Harry was fishing.

"Do you live here?" The man who asked was looking suspicious.

"My sister does. I'm about to drive up to the farm. One-fifteen, you say? Thanks."

"Good old Smithy." The suspicion on the man's face had turned to a smile.

"Yes...of course. Good old Smithy."

Harry finished his breakfast, the tension mounting inside of himself. Up in his room he sent London a cable and packed his bag. Like their new car in England the hire car was a Ford Prefect, Harry thinking it lucky the rains had yet to break. There would be no water in the rivers crossing the dirt road up to World's View. With steady driving, watching out for animals on the road, he would get to the club by midday. If the buzz at breakfast was the same in the Centenary, the farmers would congregate in the club to listen to the speech of their prime minister.

With the window of the small car open to cool the humid heat inside, Harry took to the road. As with a few other good stories for the *Daily Mirror*, Harry found himself in the right place at the right time. On the way out of Salisbury everything looked the same. Harry wondered if it would all look the same when he drove back.

The inside of the car was covered in dust when Harry drove up the tree-lined driveway towards the Centenary Club. The cricket field to the left was empty of people. There were many cars parked next to the tennis courts, surprising for a Thursday. Four women in white dresses were playing tennis.

As Harry got out of the car one of the girls called 'thirty-love', her voice strangely echoing out into the beyond. Behind the clay courts was the bush and the distant hills. The hills were the colour of lavender. To Harry the bush and the hills seemed to be brooding.

There were people on the veranda at the low tables having drinks. Inside, the bar was full. At one end, holding court, was Clay Barry, the member-in-charge for Centenary, and the man Harry had argued with in the same club on his Christmas visit two years earlier. The Christmas that had changed his own life and Bergit's. Noah, the barman, was looking agitated.

"News does travel fast. Look who's here. The man from the London *Daily Mirror*. Hello, Harry. Where's Jeremy? He's late."

"I'm on my way to the farm, Clay. Got here from London yesterday."

"Better stay here. We're all waiting for the PM's speech. So it must be

UDI if the British press are here. What are you going to drink? It's going to be quite a celebration."

"You think UDI will work?"

"I'm just a policeman, Harry. Do what I'm told. How's your friend, Josiah Makoni?"

"He was fine when I spoke to him the day before yesterday."

"So they know?"

"Probably."

"Not that it makes any difference. It'll be all over in a couple of days. The British will get used to it. Once it's done, what can they do?"

"Send in the British Army."

"Don't be ridiculous. They'd have a mutiny on their hands. We British don't shoot at each other. They'll be glad to get us out of the way. Wash their hands of the problem. They want us to be independent under Smith or the country will disintegrate. They know that. Just can't shout it from the rooftops... Noah. Give the man what he wants. Better still, put up a round for everyone. This is going to be quite a day. A day to go down in history. Good old Smithy."

"You said you avoided politics, Clay."

"Slip of the tongue. My goodness, you do look pale. You should get in the sun. Didn't I hear from Jeremy you're a married man with a daughter?"

"When's it going to rain?"

"When it's ready. The clouds are building up more and more every day. Then the heavens will open. So what did our friend Josiah have to say?"

"Not much."

"Is your trip a coincidence?"

"Not really."

"We are talkative, today. After a few drinks you'll be singing like a bird... Here he comes. Jeremy, look who just flew in from England. Just in time for the fun. What are you drinking, my friend?"

"Hello, Harry. Your call last night was a surprise. Is this a coincidence?"

"Not really. Where's Bergit and my nephew?"

"At home. She doesn't want to listen to the speech. So, how long are you staying with us? George, how are you? I see Mary is playing tennis, Clay. I think she and her partner are winning."

"How's the crop, Jeremy?"

"Be fine if we get some rain. Shit, it's hot. How's our niece, Harry?" Jeremy was looking from one to the other. To Harry, he looked agitated among all the bravado.

"Yells at night. Shits in her pants. Honks over Ruthy. She's fine. We've never been happier in our lives. And you two?"

"Just the same. The boys are fascinated by Craig. Just goes to show. So, is he going to do it, gentlemen?" With a fixed smile on his face Jeremy looked round the bar.

"We'll have to wait and see what Smithy says in an hour's time. We've rigged the radio up behind the bar. Good old Smithy."

All round Harry, the farmers lifted their glasses to Smithy, chorusing the words of George Stacy. Harry watched them carefully. Under all the show of bravado he detected a feeling of uncertainty. The barman brought them their new round of drinks. Harry withdrew from the conversation, wanting to listen to what they were all saying, a piece milling in the back of his mind. In their eyes he saw fear as well as joviality. Harry was glad the problem wasn't his. At least Jeremy owned part of a block of flats in London if the bottom fell out of this world.

When it came. no one was sure right up to the end. When the speech finished everyone in the bar was silent. Harry could hear the conversation of the girls through the open window out onto the veranda. The girls were talking about the tribulations of servants. One of the servants had broken a prized dish on the kitchen floor, smashing it to pieces.

"Did he do it?" asked George Stacy into the silence.

"Oh, yes," said Clay Barry. "That's it all right. From now on we are completely independent from Britain."

"Will they apply sanctions?"

"South Africa won't apply sanctions. Neither will the Portuguese with their colonies in Angola and Mozambique. Even if the British and the rest of the world apply economic sanctions, it won't matter to us. Friend of mine in Salisbury says getting round sanctions will be easy."

"What about them buying our tobacco?"

"You make out a certified invoice saying the tobacco was grown in

Malawi or Zambia. Get full Commonwealth preference, according to the chap in Salisbury. You falsify the shipping documents. Simple as that. He says if sanctions come, his company will set up an office in Johannesburg to issue the false documents."

"Won't South Africa object?"

"Of course not. They want us as a buffer. All those hordes of blacks to the north. Relax. It's going to be fine. Noah, give us all a drink. This round is on me."

"What if they send in the British Army?"

"We'll shoot the shit out of them. Like we did the last time. I'm an Afrikaner. The old British lion's roar is worse than its bite. They're a has-been. It's the Russians we got to worry about. The Russians and the Chinese. All those bloody communists. The Americans won't want the commies to run all over us. Too many strategic minerals in Africa. Smithy got the nod from Pretoria, you can bet on it. Now we can get on with our lives. Don't have to put up with the British government telling us how to run our country."

"Marius is right, all those threats were just threats. We'll be all right."

"I hope so."

"So do I."

"All right for you, you're a British citizen. Born in the UK. I'm fourth generation Rhodesian. Pioneer stock on both sides of the family."

"Everyone lift their glasses. To Smithy. To good old Smithy."

Soon after, the party broke up. People wanted to get home. To think about it on their own. Harry itched to take notes. Not to forget anything. His mind alert. He followed Jeremy Crookshank out of the bar.

"How long are you staying with us?"

"Not long. This is one hell of a story. Better I write it in London. Roland Cartwright wants our readers to see the face of the people."

"Will they apply sanctions?"

"Oh, yes."

"Will they hurt?"

"Won't do any good. No more British investment. The Rhodesian government will have to freeze your money in the country. Bring in strict exchange control."

"So if I wanted to sell the farm now it wouldn't do me any good?"

"Something like that."

"The price of tobacco will drop on the auction floors. Britain is our biggest customer. You can't falsify the origin of the entire Rhodesian crop even if the overseas buyers are in collusion. The combined tobacco crops of Malawi and Zambia don't add up to five per cent of our crop. The British customs would quickly see what we were doing... Where's your car, Harry?"

"The white Ford Prefect. Hired it at the airport. Expense account."

"How was the road?"

"Took it slowly. Just hope the rains don't break until I get back. I'd better drive back tomorrow. Saw and heard just what I wanted for a good story in the club."

"Don't run us down, Harry. It was Hobson's choice. We either got out or stood up on our own."

"You think it will work?"

"Who knows? Sanctions take years to have the desired effect. More like steady attrition. Bit like a terrorist war. That's what I fear most. Your old friend Josiah Makoni. Harry Brigandshaw would turn in his grave."

"You know the family brought his bones back to England just before my wedding?"

"I didn't... So even Harry's gone. We're going to be lonely on our own. Our only friend South Africa. And who's to know how long the Afrikaners can last in South Africa? Livy Johnston was right. So was my brother Paul. I should have sold up and gone back to England while I still had the opportunity to get my money out. We never listen to advice when it isn't what we want to hear."

"You still have the flats."

"But they are not my life."

"You have family in England. Your lives will go on. You'll find something else to do."

"But it won't be the same."

"Nothing ever stays the same."

"All those years of work for nothing."

"I'm sorry, Jeremy."

"So am I. Your sister so loves Rhodesia. So do the boys."

"You'll still have your memories."

"I don't think I'll want to look back on World's View stuck in a flat in

London. In that miserable climate. You know it's the sunshine that makes you smile. All that rain and drizzle in England makes me depressed."

"You can go to the theatre."

"Not every day. That's escapism. Here the sun shines every day. You're not hemmed in by people. You can see the horizon. Watch the sun come up and go down. Hear the birds. Smell the flowers. Feel alive. England in winter is so damn depressing."

"Maybe it'll be a three or four day wonder? By the end of next week everything could be back to normal."

"You don't really believe that, Harry. You're saying it to lift my spirits."

"You never know in life. Look, I enjoy my life in England. So does Ruthy. And I lived for a while in Rhodesia."

"You have a career in London, I'll have nothing. I'll end up the janitor of my own block of flats listening to the tenants' complaints."

"It won't be as bad as that. You and I will still be able to go down to the pub and get drunk together. The cousins will grow up knowing each other. Think of Judy and Craig becoming best friends. Sometimes the worst things in life turn out the best."

"What would happen to the people on the farm that depend on me for a livelihood?"

"Someone else would run the farm."

"And if they don't know how to run it properly? Growing tobacco on a large scale isn't easy. I don't think the locals could do it, however hard they tried. My bossboy would be lost without my direction. I have to watch every last little detail on the farm to stop things going wrong. It's taken me years of experience, going all the way back to my National Service commission in the Royal Navy and learning how to treat the men. How to get the best out of them. How to manage people. There are so many aspects to running a big business. When it's up and running people think it looks easy. But it isn't. It's damn hard work and you have to think on your feet all the time. You have to concentrate on what you're doing. Doesn't happen by wishful thinking. Any more than you writing your article for the *Daily Mirror*. If we pull out of farming, this country will become a mess. Put that in your article... See you back on the farm."

"Is it going to rain tonight?"

"Not for a couple of days. We can have a swim. Sit round the pool.

Farm's quiet just after the dry planting season. I'm glad you're here, Harry. So is Bergit."

"All I can give is my moral support."

"That's all we need. In times like these it's nice to know you have a friend. Nice to have a family... What would we do without our families, Harry?"

"I really don't know."

2

'The Last Days of Empire', his article for the *Daily Mirror*, began to write itself in his head. In the car he took his Dictaphone out of the glove compartment and talked out most of what was in his head. That Afrikaner still hated the British for the Boer War. Clay Barry had had a smirk on his face right from the start, as if he knew what was going to happen. Or was it a grave face? Like Jeremy, Clay Barry had nowhere else to go. Certainly not now working for a police force that many in the British government would consider to have mutinied. The poor sods were out on a limb. History had caught up with them. As the tide of empire went out, the white Rhodesians were being left high and dry on the shore. The ten-minute drive was enough to talk his story onto the machine. He would type it out in his office in England and edit the piece carefully. By then they would know if the British government had applied sanctions.

His sister, oblivious of the drama that had played itself out in the club, was pleased to see him. So were the dogs. The four Alsatians had to be patted before they ran off barking round the trees that dotted the well-cut lawn, running through the flowerbeds ravaging the flowers.

"Dogs! Get out of the flowerbeds... This is a surprise, Harry. So what happened, Jeremy? I didn't want to listen on my own. Harry, come and see your nephew. For once he isn't howling his lungs out.

Don't know what I'd do without Primrose. The boys come back from weekly boarding school tomorrow. How long are you staying? Have some tea. Give your sister a hug. How are Mum and Dad?" The words tumbled out of his sister she was so nervous. Harry gave her a long hug before walking over to look at the baby in the pram under the shade of a tree.

"Just look at him. You know, before I became a father I never looked at babies. Look at that, he's grabbed my fingers. Knows I'm his uncle."

"So what happened, Jeremy?"

"He did it. For better or worse. We're on our own."

"Is that good or bad, Harry? You probably know more what's going on than we do."

"Only time will tell. I'm flying back on the eleven o'clock flight tomorrow."

"Harry, you've only just arrived."

"The story needs to be written in London. I don't want to try and send it over the phone. This is the first time a British colony has unilaterally declared itself independent from England since the American declaration of independence and that one led to a war."

"But the British lost it."

"The Americans were united. They didn't have a majority in the country who didn't agree with the government. Wait and see. What politicians say they're going to do and what they actually do are two different things. Most of it's bluff. The British want your tobacco which they pay for in sterling as much as you want to sell it to them. Saves them dollars. In ten days' time my paper will have another story to sell to the public. People have short attention spans... How about that cup of tea and a swim in the pool? Those flowering trees are sending out the sweetest perfume. Just look at those faraway mountains. I'd forgotten just how beautiful it all looks. I think you called those trees that dot your lawn ringed by flowerbeds msasa trees: the ones that flatten out at the top giving perfect shade from the sun."

"Come and sit down and tell me all about Ruthy and the baby. How's she liking being a mother?"

"She's so content. I've never seen another human being look so content."

Jeremy began to walk away.

"Better go and check on Vince, Harry. He's now the assistant manager of the farm. Make yourself comfortable."

"What happened to Bobby Preston?"

"Went down to Glendale to work for Callum McFay to further his experience and qualify for a Crown Land farm. You have to know what you're doing before the Rhodesian government allocate you land. Then the costs start. Putting in roads. Stumping out the trees. Building curing barns. Forget about a house. It never stops. You two have a good natter while I check out the farm. If it doesn't rain in three or four days we'll have to replant the lands with tobacco seedlings. When we dry plant we slop water into the hole. Soon dries up in the heat. Nice to see you again, Harry. We'll have a few drinks together on the veranda before supper. Quite a day. Never thought Rhodesia would come to this. Falling out with the home government won't do anyone any good. Blacks, whites or the British. Why can't people compromise? So much more simple. Everything changes. You got to change with the times. I hope we'll all be saying 'good old Smithy' in a few years' time. Anyway, glad I don't have his job. Damned if you do and damned if you don't. Better being a simple farmer. Right now I'll bet he wishes he never left his farm in Selukwe I think it was. Someone said it was never his intention to go into politics. Anyway, we're on our own so we'd better get behind him. Nothing's ever certain in life. We just try and do our best. Will you be gone before I pick up the boys from school tomorrow?"

"I'm afraid so."

"Pity. They like you. They'll be disappointed they missed you. So you're booked on tomorrow's flight."

"Booked the return flight in London. My editor doesn't like wasting company money on expenses. Told me to go and get the story from the Rhodesian perspective and bring it home."

"Don't be too hard on us, Harry. It's easy to criticise when your way of life isn't at stake. Smith thinks we whites can do a better job of running this country until the blacks are better educated. Only time will tell... Ah, Silas. Put the tea tray on the table. Look at that. Cucumber sandwiches. Anyone would think we are English."

Harry watched the servant in his shorts and white shirt walk up the lawn towards the house. Behind the house was the tall mast for Jeremy's shortwave radio. Silas was barefoot and didn't wear shoes.

"Why doesn't he wear shoes?"

"He doesn't like them. The soles of his feet are as hard as nails. Says shoes make his feet so uncomfortable."

Harry sat back in the deck chair, his teacup on his lap, and picked up one of the small triangular sandwiches. The sandwiches were made from fresh bread. Silas had placed the perfectly cut quarters of bread round the edge of his saucer. It was all so civilised. All so British. A cat was watching him from under a tree where it sat on its front paws not moving, not taking its green eyes off Harry. The dogs were still having fun chasing each other round the lawn. There was no sound from the baby in the pram. Harry wondered what kind of a future would come to his nephew, Craig. Whether, when he grew up, they would still be taking tea and eating cucumber sandwiches round the pool in the shade of the msasa trees. There was more than one scent coming from the flowers. The perfume was exotic and tropical. The lavender-coloured mountains in the distance were starkly exaggerated by the cumulus clouds rising high behind them. There was a feel of menace from the distant clouds. At the bottom they were black. It was going to rain sometime soon. The real reason Harry was in a hurry to drive back to Salisbury. Even if he didn't get on the plane straight away. He knew the rivers came up quickly and blocked the road for days. He had a big piece to write and didn't wish to waste the opportunity of so important a report with his name on it going wrong. With a wife and kid he needed promotion. More money. Two rooms in Chelsea close to both their families would soon be too small. The baby would be crawling. Standing up on her feet. Wanting a garden to play in... With one eye on the cat and one eye on the weather Harry tried to relax. It wasn't so easy. The speech at lunchtime had changed everything on World's View. It didn't take too many brains to realise life in Rhodesia would never be the same.

For an hour before Jeremy arrived back in the truck, they talked about everything except what was hanging over them; it wasn't the stiff upper lip but rather the fear of not knowing that stopped them bringing up the subject. They talked of their childhood together. Of their parents. Of Bergit's lifelong friendship with Ruthy. The baby, the cat and the dogs were quiet, the dogs tired in the heat from their manic chasing... They had both been for a swim. Silas in his bare feet had collected the tea tray, only half the sandwiches eaten. Jeremy strode down the lawn to them.

"I can pick up the BBC if you want to listen to the news. Do you remember, Harry, how as kids we listened to the six o'clock news during the war? I remember so many of the ends to the bulletins. Mum listened for the end, not where the RAF had raided over Germany that night. 'Three of our planes failed to return.' Then she would cry, thinking of Dad, lost when the *Seagull* went down off the beaches of Dunkirk. She never got over losing Dad. None of us did."

"Why are you talking of war, Jeremy?" asked Bergit. "You think the British government is going to send in the troops? I don't want to hear the news. You two go up to the house."

"Better to know than worry. Always face a problem. Why don't you come up to the house, Harry? The BBC overseas programme do a broadcast every hour on the hour. Afterwards, once we've heard the bit about Rhodesia, we can have a drink on the veranda and watch the last of the sun go down. Silas is doing a leg of lamb for supper. Mint sauce. All the trimmings. I've taken the cork out of a bottle of South African red wine. If they apply sanctions at least we'll be able to get our wine from South Africa."

The dogs got up and followed them. They were just in time for the six o'clock broadcast. The light was fading fast. The shortwave reception was not the best but Harry could hear what the man was saying. Rhodesia had declared UDI. There was no immediate reaction from the British government. Five minutes into the news, with Harry and Jeremy about to get up from their chairs where they were sitting in Jeremy's study, the news cast was interrupted by a special report. The British government had imposed comprehensive economic sanctions against Rhodesia. There would be no trading between the two countries. No banking. All Rhodesian assets in London were frozen. Then the bulletin reverted to Israel... They looked at each other, Jeremy transfixed in his chair.

"That was the bad news," said Jeremy. "At least they're not sending in the army by the sound of it. Now we'll have to see who follows them with sanctions. You know Smith moved our foreign reserves from London to Switzerland? The Swiss won't apply sanctions. They traded with Nazi Germany throughout the war. Let's go and get a drink. We'll be all right, Harry."

"I hope so."

. . .

THE NEXT DAY AT DAWN, Harry drove away from World's View with the sad feeling he was abandoning a sinking ship. The rain had held off during the night. Distant thunder had kept Harry awake most of the night worrying. About getting to Salisbury across the rivers. About his sister and her family. Over supper they had not told Bergit about sanctions. They had all tried to enjoy themselves. By half past eight they were in bed. Farmers got up early in the morning. By eight o'clock Jeremy had been yawning, Friday being a working day. The same as all working days according to Jeremy. Farming would go on. Life would go on. It just wouldn't be quite the same.

By the time Harry reached Heathrow Airport he was thoroughly sick of aeroplanes. From the cold and fog to the heat of Africa and back to the streets of London, all in three days. Harry thought if Bergit and her family had to come back to England they would find the English weather the worst of their tribulations.

Harry took a taxi from the airport direct to Fleet Street and his office. Two hours later he gave his written piece on Rhodesia to Roland Cartwright, sitting quietly in his sub-editor's office while Roland read the two pages he had written so carefully making sure not one word was wasted.

"Poor sods. This is good, Harry. You've perfectly captured the atmosphere in that club. Just what we wanted. Did anyone tell you you can write? You should try a book, Harry. Make yourself famous. 'Last Outpost of the Empire.'"

They both laughed.

"We'll print. Just as it is. How's Ruthy?"

"Haven't been home yet."

"Go home, Harry. Take the rest of the day off. You're yawning in my face."

"Didn't sleep much on the farm. There was a thunderstorm brewing. Never could sleep on aeroplanes."

"You've got to the heart of the white Rhodesians. Tomorrow you go see Josiah Makoni. Write his side of the story."

"I'm glad it isn't my problem."

"So am I. The trick of being a good newspaper reporter is not getting too involved with your subject. Report what you see and get out of the way."

"I'll remember that, Roland."

"You do that, Harry."

Back in his office Harry made up his mind not to go home just yet.

Outside, the earlier sleet had turned to rain. Harry pulled up the collar of his old raincoat that had been hanging in his office. He had an old hat on his head with a wide enough brim to keep the rain out of his eyes. He walked down the street to the Tube station. Ten minutes later he got out of Paddington Station and walked to 125 Sutherland Avenue, and the ZANU office. He had deliberately not made an appointment with Josiah Makoni. Harry smiled to himself on entering the office. Everything had changed since the days of Petronella, Livingstone Sithole having made himself comfortable. The reception room was full of people. Unlike the tension in the Centenary Club, the excitement in the Zimbabwe African National Union office was palpable. Harry had taken off his hat on entering the building. Rain was still dripping from his raincoat. The room was pleasantly warm. No one took any notice of him as he stood letting the warmth of the room seep into his body. There were as many whites in the room as blacks. Everyone seemed to be talking. Not sure who to approach, Harry stood and listened. A big black man Harry had not seen before was the centre of attention. The man's head was shaven, the black dome of his head shining in the electric light. He was the biggest black man Harry had ever seen. He was speaking in heavily accented English.

"Just where we want them. Smith's done us a favour. Don't have to worry about the British. Now it's us and them. Now it's an armed struggle backed by our communist friends and the British won't do a damn thing about it. We've got them. In a few years we'll kick every white man out of the country."

"Who'll run the economy?"

"Who cares? Zimbabwe will be ours."

The man moved away, dropping his voice as he saw Harry standing inside the door. Then he came across.

"Who are you?" he asked belligerently.

"Harry Wakefield of the *Daily Mirror* to see Josiah Makoni."

"He's not here."

"Will he be back soon?"

The door to a connecting office opened.

"Hello, Harry. Come into my office. I was rather expecting you."

Harry followed him into his office. Josiah closed the door.

"They're all a bit over-excited."

"Who was the big chap?"

"His real name or his *nom de guerre*?"

"Either will do."

"They call him Hitler in Tanzania. He's a senior commander in the army. I helped train him."

"He didn't want me to see you."

"Probably not. How was Rhodesia?"

"You knew I went?"

"It's our business to know what is going on in our country."

"The man gave me the shivers."

"Yes, he probably did. Comrade Hitler is a dedicated member of the party."

"Why's he in London?"

"Oh, Harry. Please... Now, what do you want to hear?"

"You're opinion of UDI."

"Here's our statement. The same one we give to all the papers. Put simply, Smith has done us a favour."

"Don't you owe me more than that?"

"Maybe later. For now that's all we are saying."

"Why do they call him Hitler?"

"He doesn't like the colonial British. I'll show you out. Thank you for calling, Harry."

"Are you staying in England?"

"No, I'm not."

"Look after yourself, Josiah. Have you heard from Petronella?"

"In a roundabout way. Sheckland-Hall Limited, of which she is now an executive director, has bought out Downtown Music, Mango Boys' label. Dylan Flower told me. She's now quite the capitalist. How people change. I won't ask you about Rhodesia. I'm sure I'll read it in the paper."

"What are you going to be doing?"

"Winning the struggle, Harry. How's the new family?"

"Mother and daughter are fine."

"That's the stuff. I think that's the way you British say it."

"They brought Harry Brigandshaw's remains back to England."

"Did they now? Wise people."

Harry put the hat back on his head and walked from the room.

"I like the hat," came the voice of Josiah Makoni from behind him. The man was laughing at him. Like Rhodesia, everything in the ZANU office had changed. Without looking at the big man with the shaven head, Harry walked out of the reception room into the corridor. When someone closed the door behind him a shudder ran through his body, as if someone had walked over his grave.

Out in the street it was still raining, the sky low when he looked up. First he went back to his office and wrote a small piece on Josiah Makoni and the man called Hitler. Then he went home.

"Darling! You're so wet. You're shivering. Are you all right? How was the trip?... I've been talking to Mother and Father. Now the baby is four months old I'm getting a job. With our two salaries together we can get a mortgage so we can buy a house in the suburbs. We'll have to commute up to London, of course. A little garden in the front with climbing roses. A garden in the back with a swing for Judy. We'll be so happy. Our own home, Harry. Give me a kiss. It'll be bliss. Mother's going to help me look for our own little house. We'll still be able to come up once a month for Sunday lunch with the Smythes and the Wakefields. You look tired, darling. Let me take your coat. Judy is asleep in the cot. You can look but don't wake her up."

Harry kissed his wife and stood back, looking round the room with all its familiar bits and pieces.

"So what's for supper?"

"I'm doing a macaroni cheese. Your favourite. Did anyone meet you at the airport? We'll find a crèche for Judy during the day. I'm so excited. When we've got it all organised, in a couple of years we'll have another baby. Now, come and sit down after you've looked at your daughter. Tell me all about Bergit."

"Macaroni cheese, you say?"

"Your favourite."

With his wet raincoat taken away for him, he went over and looked in the cot at his daughter. It was always the best time when she was sleeping. She looked like an angel. He moved away from the cot and sat down in his favourite chair. The gas heater was burning. The room was warm. He was home. Comfortable. Ruthy was smiling at him. What more could a man want, Harry asked himself.

FULL CIRCLE (BOOK TEN)

CONTINUE YOUR JOURNEY WITH THE BRIGANDSHAWS

If you hope well in life, everything turns out fine. But hope for Rhodesia is fading...

Granted a Crown Land farm, all Bobby Preston wants is a life of happiness. With a woman by his side. His estate to flourish. A family. With that, he proposes marriage. To a girl, he barely knows...

Full of optimism and excitement, Katie accepts and begins her voyage to Africa. Spending her first night under the African stars, it all seems perfect. But then doubts begin to set in. Tensions are rising with stirrings of a vicious conflict on the horizon. Black nationalism continues to grow, and the future is looking very bleak. For some...

The best of times are over and for Britain, its domination in Africa is beginning to crumble. Peter Rimmer's tenth outing, *Full Circle*, in the massive Brigandshaw Chronicles, will leave you with so many questions and a deep yearning for all it once was.

PRINCIPAL CHARACTERS

~

The Crookshanks
Beth — Paul's wife and daughter of Harry and Tina Brigandshaw
Carmen — Jeremy's late wife
Henry and *Deborah* — Paul and Beth's children
Jeremy — Paul's younger brother and tobacco farmer in Rhodesia
Paul —Works for Brigandshaw Limited
Philip and *Randall* — Jeremy and Carmen's sons

The Makonis
Goodson — Tembo's elder son by his first wife
Josiah — Son of Tembo and Princess and an African revolutionary
Princess — Tembo's fourth wife
Tembo — Harry Brigandshaw's boyhood friend and bossboy on Elephant
Walk

The Maples
Florence (Flossy) — Petronella's overbearing mother
Bertie Maple — Flossy's downtrodden husband and Rhodesian tobacco
farmer

Petronella Maple — Communist activist and daughter of Bertie and Flossy

The Sheckland-Halls
Arnold — Petronella's grandfather and wealthy retired businessman
Barbara — Horace's wife
Conrad and *Damian* — Winfred and May's sons
Horace — Arnold's eldest son
Winfred — Arnold's youngest son and Managing Director of Sheckland-Hall Limited
May — Winfred's wife
Tinkerbell and *Hyacinth* — Horace and Barbara's daughters

The Smythes
Betty — William's wife and secretary
Patrick — William and Betty's son
Ruthy — William and Betty's daughter
William — Foreign Correspondent and friend of Horatio Wakefield

The Wakefields
Bergit — Harry's sister
Harry — Journalist at the *Daily Mirror* and principal character of *The Best of Times*
Horatio — Harry and Bergit's father, also a newspaper reporter
Janet — Harry and Bergit's mother, a speech therapist

Other Principal Characters
Bobby Preston — Learner Assistant on World's End Farm
Bonner — The Woodlands Court head gardener
Caroline — Receptionist at the *Daily Mirror*
Clay Barry — Rhodesian policeman and known as the Scorpion by the Africans in Centenary
Dylan Flower — Lead singer of Mango Boys
Eddy Harrington — A Rhodesian tobacco farmer in the Centenary
Elsie Gilmore — Petronella's girlfriend
Evan Trollip — Bertie Maple's farm assistant
Fred Rankin — Clay Barry's second-in-command police officer
George Stacy — A Rhodesian tobacco farmer in the Centenary

Harvey Pemberton — Catholic missionary and activist

Janice — The old maid at Woodlands Court

Joyce Rankin — Fred Rankin's wife

Livingstone Sithole — Josiah's revolutionary comrade

Mary Barry — Clay Barry's wife

Max — Articled Solicitor who works with Ruthy

Mrs Wade — Landlady in Salisbury, Rhodesia

Mrs Weatherby — The cook at Woodlands Court

Noah — The barman at the Centenary Club

Pamela Crumpshaw — Roger Crumpshaw's English wife

Primrose — Nursemaid to Jeremy's children

Richard Maguire — A record producer and friend of Petronella's

Roger Crumpshaw — A farmer from Marendallas

Roland Cartwright — Sub-editor of the *Daily Mirror*

Sidney Cross — The *Daily Mirror*'s photographer and Harry's friend

Silas — Jeremy's African house servant

Vince Ranger — Jeremy's farm assistant

GLOSSARY

∼

Baas — Afrikaans word for boss

Braai — Afrikaans word for barbeque

Bwana — Swahili word for boss

Maître d'hôtel — The head waiter of a restaurant

Memsahib — In India a married white or upper-class woman

Mombe — Shona word for cow

Nom de guerre — An assumed name in warfare

Piccanin — A word used to describe an African child

Rongwa — Small fortification

Shumba — Shona word for lion

Simby — An old plough disc with a length of metal for a gong

Spruit — Afrikaans word for a spring

Stoep — Afrikaans word for veranda

Terr — A black insurgent in the Rhodesian Bush War

Tokolosh — In Zulu and Xhosa mythology, Tokolosh is a malevolent evil spirt

DEAR READER

~

Reviews are the most powerful tools in our kitty when it comes to getting attention for Peter's books. This is where you can come in, as by providing an honest review you will help bring them to the attention of other readers.

If you enjoyed reading *The Best of Times,* and have five minutes to spare, we would really appreciate a review (it can be as short as you like). Your help in spreading the word and keeping Peter's work alive is gratefully received.

Please post your review on the retailer site where you purchased this book.

Thank you so much.
Heather Stretch (Peter's daughter)

PS. We look forward to you joining Peter's growing band of avid readers.

ACKNOWLEDGEMENTS

~

With grateful thanks to our *VIP First Readers* for reading *The Best of Times* prior to its official launch date. They have been fabulous in picking up errors and typos helping us to ensure that your own reading experience of *The Best of Times* has been the best possible. Their time and commitment is particularly appreciated.

Hilary Jenkins (South Africa)

Thank you.

Kamba Publishing

Printed in Great Britain
by Amazon